Henry, Himself

Also by Stewart O'Nan

FICTION

City of Secrets
West of Sunset
The Odds
Emily, Alone
Songs for the Missing
Last Night at the Lobster
The Good Wife
The Night Country
Wish You Were Here
Everyday People
A Prayer for the Dying
A World Away
The Speed Queen
The Names of the Dead
Snow Angels
In the Walled City

NONFICTION

Faithful (with Stephen King)
The Circus Fire
The Vietnam Reader (editor)
On Writers and Writing by John Gardner (editor)

SCREENPLAY

Poe

Henry, Himself

STEWART O'NAN

VIKING

VIKING
An imprint of Penguin Random House LLC
penguinrandomhouse.com

Library of Congress Cataloging-in-Publication Data

Names: O'Nan, Stewart, 1961– author.
Title: Henry, himself / Stewart O'Nan.
Description: New York, New York : Viking, 2019. |
Identifiers: LCCN 2018031783 (print) | LCCN 2018032378 (ebook) |
ISBN 9780735223066 (ebook) | ISBN 9780735223042 (hardcover) |
ISBN 9781984877635 (international edition)
Subjects: LCSH: Domestic fiction. | GSAFD: Mystery fiction.
Classification: LCC PS3565.N316 (ebook) | LCC PS3565.N316 H46 2019 (print) |
DDC 813/.54–dc23
LC record available at https://lccn.loc.gov/2018031783

Printed in the United States of America
1   3   5   7   9   10   8   6   4   2

Set in Fournier MT Std

DESIGNED BY MEIGHAN CAVANAUGH

For my father

and his father before him

The autumn wind
on its way
sets a scarecrow dancing

BUSON

Henry, Himself

In Memoriam

HIS MOTHER NAMED HIM HENRY, AFTER HER OLDER BROTHER, a chaplain killed in the Great War, as if he might take his place. In family lore the dead Henry had been a softhearted boy, a rescuer of stranded earthworms and fallen sparrows, presaging his vocation as a saver of souls. Salutatorian of his seminary class, he volunteered for duty overseas, sending home poems and charcoal sketches of life in the trenches. At church the stained-glass window that showed a barefoot Christ carrying a wayward lamb draped about his neck like a stole was dedicated in loving memory of the Rt. Rev. Henry Leland Chase, 1893–1917, the mock-Gothic inscription so elaborate it verged on illegibility, and each Sunday as they made their way to their pew up front, his mother would bow her head as they passed, as if to point out, once more, his uncle's saintliness. When he was little, Henry believed he was buried there, that beneath the cold stone floor of Calvary Episcopal, as below the medieval cathedrals of Europe, the noble dead moldered in cobwebbed catacombs, and that one day he would be there too.

When Henry was eight, his mother enrolled him as an altar boy, a vocation for which he betrayed no calling, picking at his nails inside his billowy sleeves through the weighted silences and turgid hymns, afraid he'd miss his cue. He had nightmares of arriving late for the processional in his baseball uniform, his cleats clicking as the holy conclave paraded down the aisle. The cross was heavy, and he needed to stretch on tiptoe with the brass taper to light the massive Alpha-Omega candle. Funerals were the worst, held Saturday afternoons when all of his friends would be at their secret clubhouse deep in the park. The grieving family huddled beside the casket, praying with Father McNulty for the repose of their loved one's soul, but once the service was done and the candles snuffed, the funeral director took charge, bossing around the pallbearers like hired porters as they lugged the box down the front steps and slid it into the hearse. Invariably Henry pictured his uncle, his nose inches from the closed lid, on a train crossing bomb-pocked French farmland, or in the dark hold of a ship, cold water gliding by outside the thin steel skin of the hull. He had so many friends and well-wishers, the story went, that the visitation—in their grandparents' front parlor, where his sister Arlene taught Henry to play "Heart and Soul" on their Baldwin—lasted three days and nights.

Arlene was named after Arlene Connelly, his mother's favorite singer, which Henry thought unfair.

To avoid confusion, among company his mother called him Henry Maxwell and his uncle Henry Chase, a nicety her side of the family dispensed with, christening him Little Henry.

Henry—though not one to make a fuss—would have preferred a nickname of his own choosing, something rough and masculine like Hank or Huck. He thought Little Henry was bad luck, and in private moments, rooting through his father's workbench in the cellar for a spool of kite string, or on a rainy day, hiding from Arlene in the lumber room beneath the eaves, or after midnight, climbing the boxed back stairwell with a filched sticky bun, he felt watched over by a ghost neither kindly nor malevolent, merely a silent presence noting his every move like a judge. His mother never said precisely how his uncle had died, leaving Henry, with a child's dire imagination, to picture, in a flash, a German shell catapulting a rag doll of a doughboy through the air, scattering his limbs over a cratered no-man's-land, one arm caught in a coil of barbed wire, the hand still clutching a small gold cross.

On his mother's dresser, in a silver frame that captured fingerprints, surrounded by other, less interesting relatives from before Henry was born, stood a bleached Kodak of her brother on the dock at Chautauqua, proudly holding up a glistening muskie. Each time Henry snuck into his parents' bedroom to puzzle over this snapshot as if it were a clue to his future, he remarked that the fish, like his uncle, was long dead, while the dock and cottage were still there at the water's edge, awaiting them every summer like a stage set, but exactly how these facts were related he couldn't say, only that he felt vaguely guilty looking at the young and happy not-yet-reverend Henry Chase, as if he'd stolen something from him.

Pedigree

The Pittsburgh Maxwells—no relation to the auto-makers or coffee company—came from the moors of North Yorkshire, with the main concentration around Skelton. Originally sheepherders and tenant farmers, after the signing of the Magna Carta their descendants filtered into the village proper and became at first guildsmen and then merchants, one, John Lee Maxwell, ultimately serving as a tax collector and deacon in the Church of England. Generations later, an intrepid or maybe disgraced scion of that line, John White Maxwell, sailed on the *Godspeed* for the Virginia Colony at Jamestown, there taking as his wife the fourteen-year-old Susanna Goode. This according to a genealogy compiled by a retired pharmacist from Olathe, Kansas, named Arthur Maxwell, a pair of which Emily, whose AOL address had been included in a mass email the week of Thanksgiving, purchased sight unseen as Christmas presents for their two grown children, Margaret and Kenny. Rather than gilt-edged, leather-bound keepsake editions, what arrived by regular mail in a crushed Amazon box several days after the children had packed up the grandchildren and as many leftovers as Emily could foist on them and fled were two overstuffed three-ring binders of cockeyed photocopies riddled with errors both typographical and factual, including the incorrect year of his uncle's death.

Henry made the mistake of laughing.

"I'm glad you find it amusing," Emily said. "I paid good money for these."

"How much were they?"

"It doesn't matter. I'm getting it back."

He doubted that was possible but nodded thoughtfully. "It's fascinating stuff if it's true. It says here we were horse thieves."

"I'm not happy. It was supposed to be a big gift. It's too late now anyway. At this point I'm thinking I should just send them back."

They'd been married nearly fifty years, and still he had to smother the masculine urge to counsel her on how the world worked. At the same time, agreeing with her too readily would be seen as appeasement, a worse offense, and so, as he often did on matters of little import, he chose the safest response, silence.

"Nothing?" she asked. "You have no opinion whatsoever."

He'd forgotten: He wasn't allowed to be neutral.

"I think it's interesting. Let's keep one for ourselves at least."

"Honestly," she said, backhanding the page she was reading, "*I* could do this. I'm going to send him an email."

The holidays were hard on her. It didn't have to be the genealogy, it could be Rufus throwing up on the carpet, or some passing comment of Arlene's about the mashed potatoes. Lately the smallest things set her off, and though in her looser moments she freely admitted that she'd always been a terror, an only child used to getting her way, as her husband he feared her impatience hinted at some deeper frustration with life and, by extension, their marriage. In this case his hope was that she would cool off and eventually relent, that the bother of repacking the binders and running them over to the post office would outweigh her anger. Her moods were fleeting, and the man had obviously done a lot of work. As if tabling the issue, she set the box out of the way, upstairs, on the cedar chest in Kenny's old room, where it stayed well into the new year (1998, incredibly), until one day at lunch she asked if they had any packing tape.

"Did you get your refund?"

"Only after I bugged him a million times. He said we could keep them, but I'm not going to. He's got to understand he can't do this to people."

"Right." So, his copy too. A traitor, he'd enjoyed finding out more about his Kentucky cousins, and General Roland Pawling Maxwell, the hero of Yorktown.

"I didn't want to tell you, they were sixty dollars apiece. For sixty dollars they should be nice, and they're not."

"I agree," he said, honestly shocked at the price. For all their differences, they were both thrifty.

"It's a shame, because there were other ones I could have ordered."

"It was a nice idea."

"If you want to try, have at it. I'm not doing that again."

"At least you got your money back."

Again, he was missing the point. She'd wanted to do something special for the children and it had turned into a debacle.

He would never understand why she took these defeats to heart. There was nothing you could do about them.

"I'm sorry," he said.

"Why? It's not your fault. Just let me be angry. I'm allowed to be angry."

He had to run out later and grab some new wiper blades for the Olds. The post office was right on his way.

"That would be helpful," she said. "If you don't mind."

He didn't mind, though, alone in the Olds, cruising down Highland with the defroster going, he glanced over at the box on the seat beside him and frowned as if she'd tricked him.

Near Miss

HE'D LIVED IN HIGHLAND PARK HIS ENTIRE LIFE, SO HE COULD be excused if he thought of the stop sign at Bryant—installed over a decade ago—as new, but in truth, that afternoon he never registered it. He was still picking at the knot of Emily's unhappiness when he realized a school bus was pulling out in front of him, tall as a boxcar, and that he'd ram it broadside if he didn't stop. Too late, the driver saw him and honked, and at the last second Henry jammed on the brakes. The tires screeched and the nose of the Olds dove. The box flew off the seat, smacked the dash and bounced around the floor.

He was short by a couple of feet. He was lucky the road was dry.

"Damn it," he said, because he was at fault. The sign was behind him. He hadn't even seen it.

The driver threw up his hands and glared.

"Sorry," Henry said, and held up his own as if he meant no harm. Above him, children who might have been first graders peered down from the windows, pointing and making faces, bouncing on their seats like trampolines. He was the excitement. It was on the local news every night, the old fart who hit the gas instead of the brake and ended up inside the dry cleaners.

Henry expected the driver to jump out and yell at him, but the bus eased forward, clearing the intersection, and kept going. The car behind it waited for Henry to take his turn.

He nodded. "Thank you."

He wanted to protest that he was a careful driver, not like Emily, who couldn't see at night and four-wheeled over curbs, and the rest of the way to the post office and then coming home he concentrated, lips pinched, eyes darting to cars peeking from side streets. It was one slip, but all it took was one, and he worried that it might have happened before, he just hadn't noticed. Near the tail end of his life, his father couldn't see well. When they visited him, all four corners of his bumpers were smudged with different-colored paint. He refused to give up his license, even after being stopped repeatedly by the police for driving too slowly. After he died, Henry rolled up the garage door of his condo and discovered the whole front of his Cutlass was pushed in, as if he'd hit a wall.

His father had taught him to drive in the park, on the winding road that circled the reservoir. "The more room between you and the other fellow the better," his father said. "You don't know what he'll do. All you can do is stay as far away from him as possible." Henry had tried to pass along this wisdom to his own children, but they thought they knew everything from taking driver's ed. As a teenager, Kenny totaled their station wagon on black ice one New Year's Eve, breaking Tim Pickering's leg, while Margaret, coming home late from a party, took down a section of the Prentices' fence that Henry made her pay for. He'd hoped their accidents might teach them a lesson. He wasn't sure they had.

This time at Bryant he stopped at the sign. When he got home, he three-pointed the Olds at the end of the drive and backed it into the garage perfectly straight, waiting for the rear tires to kiss the two-by-four he'd rigged.

Emily was at the kitchen sink, peeling carrots.

"How was the post office?" she asked.

"Uneventful."

It was only as he was hanging up his keys that he remembered the wipers.

Hide-and-Seek

WHILE HENRY NEVER CONSIDERED HIS FAMILY RICH, THEIR house on Mellon Street, like many built in Highland Park around the turn of the century, had stained-glass windows on the stair landings and servants' quarters tucked beneath the eaves. By the time he was born, the servants were gone and the third floor given over to storage, the gas and water capped so that in winter frost rimed the inside of the panes. Here, among the dusty bassinets and rolled rugs, the banished lampshades and cast-off fashions from the Roaring Twenties, he and Arlene played house, making pretend meals in the kitchen, taking pretend baths in the tub. Queen Arlene ruled by divine right of being firstborn. According to her whim, they were mother and baby, or teacher and student, or husband and wife (this involved hugging and talking seriously across an imaginary dinner table), and sometimes they played a game in which she was the maid and he the butler, innocently replacing the rooms' former occupants. Eventually, no matter what the scenario, Henry lost interest, and Arlene would have to assuage him by agreeing to play his favorite game, hide-and-seek.

He liked hiding because he was good at it. When she was at school and there was nothing to do, he practiced on his own, fitting himself into steamer trunks and wicker hampers, crouching in the musty dark, listening to his heart and the skittering of mice. He could even squeeze himself into the oven if he took out the rack.

"I give up," Arlene called from the hallway. "Come out, come out, wherever you are. C'mon, Henry. I said I quit."

He waited until she went downstairs before reappearing. He knew better than to give away his best places.

As prey, Arlene was obvious, too impatient. She hid behind doors or in closets, waiting till the last second to leap out, shouting. He crept along, holding his breath, his fingers curled into claws before him, braced for attack, and still he shrieked.

The house was still there. His parents had held on to it too long, well into the seventies, selling only after his father had been mugged and their car stolen. The new owner chopped it into apartments and paved the backyard for parking. Since then the porch had rotted off, replaced by precast concrete steps that gave it a barefaced look. The stained glass was gone, and the slate roof, the ornate gables now clad with vinyl siding. A few years back it was offered as a sheriff's sale in the paper for eight thousand, tempting him, but there were crack houses on the block, and summer nights, sleeping with the windows open, they heard scattered clumps of gunshots from the far side of Highland, like the rapping of a hammer. Day or night, he avoided Mellon Street, and while Grafton was holding its value, he feared that eventually he and Emily would face the same dilemma.

"Or you will. I'll be dead by then."

"That's not funny," she said.

At seventy-four he was five years older than her, and overweight, his cholesterol a problem. There was no question he would go first. When they were younger it had been a joke, what she would do with the insurance money. Now she scolded him.

"I'm just trying to prepare you."

"Don't," she said. "You're not dying any time soon."

"You don't know," he said, "I could go at any minute," but she'd turned away, her face averted, hurt.

"Please stop."

He apologized, massaging her shoulders, wrapping his arms around her, a cue for Rufus to push between their legs like a referee breaking up a clinch.

"Someone's jealous," he said.

Emily clutched at him. "You know I hate that."

"I know."

"I worry about you and all you do is make fun of me."

"I don't mean to."

"I don't think you have the slightest clue what it does to me when you say things like that. If you did you wouldn't say them."

He could see her side, and promised to be more considerate, though part of him maintained his innocence. Wasn't it better to laugh at death?

It was almost dark out. She had to get dinner started, and released him. He retreated to his workbench in the cellar—just like his father, he thought—where he was prepping the mailbox for Chautauqua that Kenny and Lisa had given them for Christmas. The old one (who knew how old) had rusted through, eaten away by the seasons, and as Henry clipped the stencils and taped them to the smooth new metal, he was aware that this one, like the cottage, would outlive him. His father had died alone in his condo in Fox Chapel, stubbornly independent to the end, though they'd offered him Kenny's room. Cleaning out his apartment, Henry found a fat biography of Teddy Roosevelt on his nightstand he'd almost gotten through. As if in tribute, instead of adding it to the library sale pile, Henry took it home with the idea of reading it. It was upstairs somewhere, the bookmark still holding his father's place.

Overhead, Emily crossed and recrossed the kitchen. You don't have a clue, she accused him, but he knew. He wasn't sure why he did it. He wasn't trying to be cruel. At some point—he couldn't pinpoint when—the joke had become the truth, unfunny. He'd have to remember that, and after the other day he wasn't sure he could. He pried open the can of Rustoleum and mixed it with a stirrer, churning the glossy white like heavy cream, took up a clean brush and bent to his work, intent, steadying his arm against the edge of the bench, patiently filling in the numbers, giving them a thick coat so they'd last.

Spring Song

Twice a week throughout the school year, Arlene took piano lessons at the Shadyside YWCA. The other five days she practiced on the upright in the back parlor to the steady ticking of the metronome, lagging behind the tempo then rushing to catch up, tripping over tricky fingerings, making her way page by page through yet another red Thompson book. "Spinning Song." "Blind Man's Bluff." "Dreaming." The year culminated in an Easter recital they dressed for like church, at the end of which Henry, cued by their mother, approached the stage and presented Arlene with a bouquet of red roses even if she'd made a half dozen mistakes. When, one evening at dinner near the beginning of school, his mother asked Henry how he would like to take piano lessons like his sister, the question was rhetorical. She'd already signed him up.

A pleading glance at his father told him there would be no appeal. As in everything, his parents were agreed. Henry's education, like Arlene's, was his mother's purview, and any further protest would be held against him. Henry stewed over his meatloaf, defeated. How long had they been plotting this?

He did his best to keep it a secret, knowing his friends would be merciless if they found out. The YWCA, as the name stated, was for women, meaning he'd be doubly shamed. Having donned an altar boy's robes, he'd already been accused of wearing a dress, an insult which prompted a wrestling match that stopped when Chet Hubbard accidentally ripped Henry's collar. At the sound of cloth rending, the circle of club members urging them on went quiet, as if a sacred rule had been broken. As Chet tried to apologize, Henry inspected the tear—glaring, irreparable—knowing what awaited him at home. The only thing he feared more than being called a mama's boy was his mother.

Now he entered a world completely female, and strange. The teachers at the YWCA were students from the Frick Conservatory, high-strung young women who flocked from around the world to study with Madame LeClair, who'd studied with Liszt, who'd studied with Czerny, who'd studied with Beethoven himself, a lineage his mother trotted out for relatives and dinner guests alike, as if Henry or Arlene might be an undiscovered genius. To earn their room and board, Madame LeClair's students helped the daughters of Pittsburgh's rising middle class with their sight-reading and finger dexterity, bringing them along note by note, bar by bar. At the recital they rose to introduce their pupils, then sat back down in the front row to bear their inevitable flubs with serene equanimity. They stayed two years, occasionally three, before setting off for life on the concert stage, never to be heard from again.

Arlene's teacher, Miss Herrera, was returning, but Henry's was new. Miss Friedhoffer was German, a willowy strawberry blonde with a slight overbite whose ringless fingers spanned a full octave and a half. She was taller than his mother yet slender as a girl, which made her hands even more freakish. The practice room was a cell, just the piano and a chalkboard lined with staves on the opposite wall, no window. Miss Friedhoffer closed the door and took a seat beside Henry on the bench. To his confusion, she was wearing makeup, her cheeks rosy with blush. Her posture made her seem alert, a soldier at attention.

"Sit up straight," she said, gently pulling his shoulders back. "Relax your elbows. Like so."

At ten, Henry was unused to the company of young women, exotic or not. At school his teachers were his mother's age or older, the girls in his class catty and standoffish. With her accent and her lipstick, Miss Friedhoffer was like someone from a spy movie. When she reached across him to fix his wrists, she smelled warm and yeasty, like fresh bread. On her neck she had a caramel birthmark the size of a dime, like a giant freckle. Under her pale skin a blue vein jumped.

"We play the C to begin," she said, pointing a manicured nail, and Henry obeyed. "Good. So. You know the C is here, you are never lost. You know where you are, always."

She pressed the key and sang, "C, C, C, C. Now you. Sing with me. Good. Now we go up a full step to D, here."

At first when she patted the small of his back to make him sit up straight, he flinched. Soon he anticipated it, just as he looked forward to her shaping his fingers over the keys. He imagined when she was his age people made fun of her hands. Like a knight, he wanted to defend her from them. As he blundered his way through the major scale, he was aware of her humming along beside him, their legs nearly touching, and when the lesson was over and she let in the next student, he lingered at the door, his stiff new exercise book tucked under one arm, as if he'd forgotten something.

"Goodbye, Henry," she said, rewarding him with a smile. "Practice well."

"Thank you," he said. "I will."

On the trolley, he thought it was the first time he'd ever liked his name.

"How was your lesson?" his mother asked.

"All right."

Later, over dinner, his father asked the same thing.

"It was okay."

"His teacher's pretty," Arlene taunted.

"Is that right?" His father was amused.

Henry was caught off guard. He thought only he could see Miss Friedhoffer's true beauty.

"Do you like her?" his father asked.

Any answer Henry might give would be wrong. He shrugged. "I guess."

"Apparently she's also German," his mother said. She would never forgive them for killing his uncle.

"I'm sure she's fine," his father said.

"I'm sure she is."

That his secret love was also forbidden added an operatic guilt to his
yearning. To win her, he resolved to be a perfect student, except that without her there to inspire him, practice was drudgery, and despite his best intentions he quickly fell behind. Instead of looking forward to the bliss of
Miss Friedhoffer's presence, he began to dread disappointing her, and manu-
factured a series of suspiciously timed illnesses. After a meeting with Miss
Friedhoffer, his mother charged Arlene with overseeing him. Now, five
days a week, while he served his hour in the back parlor, she hectored him
from the loveseat, looking up from her book if he went silent for too long,
and day by day, page by page, miraculously, he began to improve.

"That's very good, Henry," Miss Friedhoffer said, turning to him. "You
see what happens when you practice."

When she looked into his eyes, he felt a paralyzing helplessness, as if she
could read his mind. He imagined her taking him in her arms, her warm
fragrance enveloping him, his cheek pressed against her slippery silk blouse.
Instead, she licked a fingertip and flipped to the next page, an exercise meant
to strengthen his left hand.

The truth could be hidden only so long. One gray Thursday in Novem-
ber as he and Arlene were getting off the trolley, Marcus Greer and his little
brother Shep were waiting to get on. Henry was still in the sated, dreamy
state that possessed him after a lesson, and didn't have the presence of mind
to hide his book. The red cover was a giveaway. Marcus nodded, leering, to
let him know he'd seen, and the next day, after a long and restless night,

Henry girded himself for the worst. He was early for school, the bell hadn't rung yet. His friends were waiting in their customary spot at the top of the steps, by the flagpole. Out of a sense of poetic justice, he hoped Marcus would say something to him, but before Henry could reach them, Charlie Magnuson, who'd lost his front teeth riding his bike down the steps on a dare, shouted, "Hey, Mozart!"

In the principal's office, when his mother asked him why he'd been fighting with a friend, Henry told the truth. "Because I have to take piano lessons."

"That is not an answer," his mother said.

"I know you don't like going to lessons," his father said later, the two of them alone in his office after dinner. He sat at his roll-top desk in his shirt-sleeves. Spread across the blotter were curling blueprints for the building his firm was working on downtown. There was no chair for Henry, who stood like a prisoner, arms at his sides. "We all have to do things we don't want to in life. We do them for the people we love, or for the greater good. Sometimes we do them for our own good, without knowing it at the time. Do you like going to school every day?"

Henry hesitated, unsure if he was supposed to answer. "No."

"No, but you understand it's for your own good. Your mother and I have good reasons for wanting you and Arlene to take lessons, so I suggest you make the best of it."

Henry wanted to ask if he'd ever had to take piano lessons, but there was no point extending the pantomime. He'd paid his debts to all parties, and he was getting what he wanted. "Yes, sir," he said, penitent, shook his father's hand to seal the deal, and he was free.

That winter he lived to be with Miss Friedhoffer. The keenness she brought to the sky at dusk as he and Arlene waited for the trolley, the evening star caught in the wires. For Christmas he gave her a tin of cookies he'd iced himself and a card he'd drawn of a tannenbaum with Merry Christmas written in German. *Für Fraulein Friedhoffer,* he printed. He still didn't know her first name.

For his recital piece, she chose Schumann's "Spring Song," whose loping tempo Henry struggled to control. He practiced extra after school, which pleased his mother. She wandered in from the kitchen with a dish towel and stood in the doorway, praising him each time he foundered. "It sounds wonderful," she said, but she was his mother. He knew it wasn't good enough. He needed to be perfect, and set the metronome swinging again.

Her name was Sabine. It was in the recital program, right beside his. She'd braided her hair for the occasion, and wore a sequined black gown as if she were going to perform. Backstage, in his church clothes, poring over his sheet music, he heard the murmuring of the crowd. The youngest students went first. In the past Henry had laughed at their mistakes; now he understood how cruel he'd been. One girl dropped note after note and returned in tears. Another stopped in the middle of a Chopin etude, lost, and had to be rescued by her teacher. Henry was next.

He'd never played for an audience before, and when Miss Friedhoffer finished her introduction and he walked out of the wings into the blinding lights, the applause startled him. It faded before he reached the bench, leaving just his footsteps. In the darkness someone coughed. At church he could hide behind Father McNulty and all the pomp and pageantry. Here everyone was watching him.

His score rattled as he propped it on the stand. By rote, he drew himself upright and located middle C, relaxed his elbows and wrists and arranged his hands over the opening notes. With her voice in his head, he counted himself in.

At home he'd gotten so he could make it through the whole piece with just some small wobbles, but that was with the metronome. Now he had to keep time by himself, and while he and Miss Friedhoffer had worked on this, he hadn't practiced enough. As soon as he started, he felt his left hand falling behind and began to rush. He tried to hold back, summoning her humming to slow the tempo, but his fingers seemed to move of their own accord, unconnected to him. From a remote vantage deep inside his head, he watched himself play. The notes were correct, if hurried, and rather than panic, a stunned wonder flooded him, and he left himself entirely, his thoughts looping away, out over the audience, picturing Miss Friedhoffer in her black dress, and his mother and father, the whole darkened auditorium. He was there but not there. He could hear the piano, faintly, as from another room, though it was right in front of him, his blurred reflection caught in its polished finish. His foot tapped the time. His fingers rose and fell mechanically, pressing on through the piece, the familiar hills and valleys. Come back, he told himself, as if he could will it, just as he reached the last bars. He lifted his hands and the final notes resolved into silence. For a second he thought he'd gotten lost and stopped at the wrong place, that there was another refrain, and then the crowd broke into applause. As if waking up, he turned to see Miss Friedhoffer smiling and nodding at him. He'd done it. It didn't seem possible, yet he had. In his relief he forgot to take his bow and walked straight into the wings, where Arlene awaited her turn with the older girls.

"Lucky," she said.

He didn't argue. He knew he was.

She wasn't, but their mother presented them both with roses anyway.

Afterward, in the gym, there was a reception with punch and cookies. It was here, in his daydreams, that Miss Friedhoffer rewarded him with a kiss. Instead, she gave him a certificate and a new book he was supposed to work on over the summer. On the cover, in her perfect cursive, she'd written his name. At home, weeks later, when September seemed impossibly far away, he traced the loops with a finger and remembered her hands guiding his.

Again, he vowed to practice, but once school let out, he was at the park all day. August they spent at Chautauqua, where there was no piano, and even Arlene fell behind. He was resigned to disappointing Miss Friedhoffer when, a week before school started, his mother told him he would have a new teacher.

Miss Friedhoffer had returned to Germany. They didn't know anything more than that.

He would have Miss Segeti, from Hungary, with whom, in his grief, against his will, he would also fall in love.

In high school he would have crushes he worshipped and despaired of, and real girlfriends who introduced him to guilty ecstasies, yet he never forgot Miss Friedhoffer. During the war, as his division ground through a bombed-out town in Alsace, they rolled over an old upright smashed to kindling in the middle of a street, the keys strewn like teeth across the cobblestones, and he wondered what had become of her. She would have been in her late thirties by then. She might be dead, buried under the rubble of a church like the one in Metz, the stench making them cover their noses as they passed. At night, wherever the column stopped, women infiltrated their bivouac, going from tent to tent, often with hollow-eyed children in tow. He imagined her pulling back his flap and recognizing him, and while they all knew the Army had regulations against it, he resolved to somehow find a way to save her.

After the war, when he and Emily were first dating, she played for him in her sorority's high-ceilinged front parlor, her posture and slender fingers recalling the stuffy practice room and the smell of chalk dust. He knew the tune from a dozen recitals.

"Mendelssohn," he said, taking a seat on the bench beside her.

"Do you play?"

"Not really. I used to take lessons when I was a kid."

"It's your turn."

"No, it's been years."

"Please? For me?"

He arranged his hands above the keys and tried to bring back "Spring Song." It unraveled after a few bars. He was surprised he remembered it at all.

"Don't stop," she said, and picked up where he'd left off, slowly, so he could join in. He'd never told her, so how could she know, when he kissed her neck, what she'd completed?

One morning shortly after running the stop sign, he was on his hands and knees in the kitchen, his head ducked under the sink, trying to remove the grease trap, when he recognized from the stereo in the living room the piece's familiar opening notes. He set down his wrench and used the counter to haul himself to his feet and went to tell Emily, but her chair was empty. Rufus, curled in a ball by the fireplace, raised his head for a second, then subsided.

Their piano sat in the corner, topped with his mother's old metronome from Mellon Street. Neither Margaret nor Kenny had appreciated their lessons, and eventually Emily tired of fighting them. While the grandchildren banged away on it at Christmas, the rest of the year it sat unmolested save for Betty's biweekly dusting.

How long had it been since they played together? They used to sing duets. *Button up your overcoat, when the wind is free. Take good care of yourself, you belong to me.* At their parties everyone would gather round and belt out old favorites. That was ages ago, when the children were little. The neighborhood had changed. Gene Alford was gone, and Don Miller, Doug Pickering. Of the old gang, he was the last man standing.

He lifted the hinged cover and folded it back with a clack, exposing the keyboard, pulled out the bench and drew himself upright. Rufus came over to investigate.

"Let's see what the old guy's got left."

He flexed his knitted fingers, settled and played the first phrase. Still there, after all these years. There was more, and he followed along, amazed at the reach of memory. Miss Friedhoffer would be proud.

On her way downstairs with the laundry basket, Emily stopped as if shocked, making both of them turn to her. "What in the world are you doing?"

"Practicing," he said.

Isn't It Romantic?

FOR VALENTINE'S DAY HE CHOSE AN OLD FAVORITE, THE TIN Angel. Perched atop Mount Washington, cantilevered out over the precipice, it offered a postcard view of the Point and a prix fixe menu featuring filet mignon and chocolate mousse. "Well, well," Emily said. "Elegant swellegant." They rarely went anywhere but the club anymore, and she seized on the occasion to have her hair done and air her fur. She'd need it. The wind chill was supposed to be below zero. They were running late, and she had him put Rufus out and give him his treat. Henry took the opportunity to warm up the Olds. Floodlit, the frozen snow sparkled. Sensibly, Emily wore her boots and carried her heels. A fresh dusting made the flagstones treacherous, and he gave her his arm.

Highland was lined with tire tracks, stoplights swaying in the wind. Bridges would be tricky. He'd go slow and stay off the brakes. If they were late, they were late.

As they coasted down Bigelow Boulevard, Emily said, "I wonder how Margaret's doing."

Her name was an alarm. He focused on the road.

"I need to call her. I guess Christmas didn't go so well."

His first thought—unfair—was that she was drinking again. "When did you talk to her?"

"Last Wednesday, when you were at the dentist. She and Jeff aren't getting along."

"Is this something new?"

"It's the same thing. He wants her to do a program."

"And she doesn't."

"She says she just did one in the fall."

This was news to him. "And he wants her to do another."

In the dark he couldn't see her face. It was easier to talk this way, disembodied, coolly neutral, as if logic might solve Margaret's problems.

"I don't know," Emily said. "I have a feeling I'm not getting the whole story."

"Maybe we could email Jeff."

"I don't think that would be helpful. She'd think we were taking sides. I just need to call her. I've been putting it off because I really don't want to. Isn't that awful?"

No, he wanted to say, what's awful is how she treats you, but they'd had that fight too many times. He would always lose. He was supposed to be ashamed that he couldn't forgive Margaret, as if they had wronged her all these years and not the opposite.

"I think you're very patient with her."

"I don't think so," Emily said. "But thank you. I didn't mean to ruin the mood, she's just been on my mind. I worry about her."

"I know you do."

He waited for her to go on. While he would never admit it, he loved to talk with her like this, to hear her take on family members and friends—even Margaret—as if she were divulging secrets. She knew everything about their neighbors, and everyone at the club, keeping up with their lives as if they were characters on her favorite soap opera. She knew more about what was happening at church than he did, and he was a member of the vestry. Just today he'd overheard her on the phone with Louise Pickering, speculating on whether Kay Miller was selling the house. He was a private person, yet her gossip thrilled him. It was also reassuring to know that in most cases they agreed. Over the course of their marriage he'd come to realize he was oblivious, perhaps willfully, of the struggles of others, even those closest to him, and while he sometimes accused her of not understanding the larger ways of the world, without her he knew nothing.

"She won't do it," Emily said. "She'll say no and they'll break up. That's what I'm afraid of."

"You think he's looking for an excuse?"

"I think he's got more than enough excuses, if he needs one. A lot of men wouldn't put up with what he's put up with."

"I wouldn't."

"You've got it easy. Your wife's perfect."

"Don't tell her. She'll get a big head."

"Too late. Honestly, I think he's only there for the children. I don't know whether that's good or bad."

"For her or for them?"

"Maybe he needs to leave. Maybe that's the only way things will change."

The prospect of it dumbfounded him. She would lose the children and the house and come live with them. He could see her holed up in her old room with the door closed, coming down for meals in her bathrobe.

"I'm sorry. I shouldn't have said anything."

"No," he said. "I'm glad you did."

"I promise not to mention it again." She raised her hand as if taking an oath.

"Until tomorrow."

"Until tomorrow."

With the heater whirring, they swooped through downtown and up the ramp of the Fort Pitt Bridge. The roadway was glazed.

"There's ice in the river," she said, but he was changing lanes and couldn't look.

They parked in a snowy lot at the bottom of the Incline—another surprise for her. It was an old favorite. A transplant from the boonies, she'd fallen for it the same way she'd fallen for the city, and him.

"You are a silly man," she said.

"I figured since we're over here anyway."

He tried to find a spot near the stairs.

"I don't know if I can make it that far in these shoes," she said.

"Just keep your boots on."

"I am not walking into the Tin Angel in my crummy old boots, thank you. You'll just have to carry me."

He did the next best thing, shuffling across the packed snow while she hung on his arm.

To his dismay, there was another couple in the waiting room—young, and dressed for the weather. He'd hoped he and Emily would be alone, as if, like a titan of industry, he'd arranged for a private car. He thought of waiting for the next one, but she was shivering. Finally it came—empty—and they rode up, taking one corner, gazing out over the steaming city, the bridge traffic and the lights of the skyscrapers mirrored in the dark water. Patches of ice drifted downstream, headed for Cincinnati, Cairo, St. Louis. Halfway, they passed the other car coming down. He leaned in to steal a kiss and she gave him her cheek, patting his arm like a promise.

On Grandview, restaurant row was mobbed with cars, valet parkers jogging back across the street from the lot. He'd thought of Le Pont, where they'd had their twenty-fifth anniversary, but the last time they'd been there they'd both been disappointed with the food. He was surprised to find it closed, butcher paper taped to the windows.

"When did that happen?" he asked.

"Months ago. I told you. It was on the news."

"You'd think someone would want that space."

"I'm sure they're asking a fortune."

It was warm in the Tin Angel, and boisterous. In the bar, a pianist with a snifter full of tips was romping through "Anything Goes." Their window table was waiting. Beside a guttering votive, a crystal bud vase held a single red rose. The greeter led Emily to the seat facing the city, while Henry looked down the Ohio. Snow swirled and floated in the darkness, hung suspended like sediment. He could make out the concrete doughnut of Three Rivers Stadium on the North Shore, and beside it, fainter, the skeleton of the Steelers' new home.

To start, the server brought them each a glass of champagne.

He raised his to Emily. "To us."

"To us. Mmm, that's nice. You know you didn't have to do all this."

"There's no way I was going to let you cook on Valentine's Day."

"We could have just gone to the club."

"We always go to the club."

"Well I appreciate it. I know I'm lucky."

"That makes two of us."

They touched glasses and drank, but after their talk in the car, the idea lingered. Had Margaret and Jeff just been unlucky, a bad match? It had to be more than that. Marriage was about balance, about complementing each other. He wondered what they'd be doing tonight, and, unbidden, like a visitation, pictured Arlene watching TV in her apartment. Had she been unlucky too? Was she unhappy, as he sometimes feared, or was she happier alone, and was it wrong of him to feel sorry for her?

With the prix fixe there was no need to order. Their shrimp cocktail came, arranged like spokes around the rim of a martini glass. The horseradish in the cocktail sauce would upset his stomach later, despite his Prilosec, but for now he enjoyed each sinus-clearing bite.

Halfway through his second glass of champagne, nodding along with "Night and Day," he was aware of his reflection in the window, a ghostly twin hovering above the abyss.

"It's a blizzard out there," Emily said. "Feel how cold it is."

"The wind's picked up."

"We should just sleep here."

"I wonder if they serve brunch."

Her fillet was perfect—black and blue—and again he congratulated himself on choosing the right place. All around them, other lucky couples were celebrating, toasting their good fortune. He drained his glass. The last swallow was tart, almost sour, and he thought of Margaret, how she couldn't allow herself a taste, even today.

Christmas hadn't gone well. What did that mean? He'd heard her and Jeff bicker but never fight outright. As a teenager she'd been given to messy scenes at the dinner table, starting arguments that escalated into screaming matches, then shoving back her chair and dashing upstairs, leaving Emily in tears and him and Kenny bewildered. Now, supposedly sober, she was touchy and curt over the phone, liable to go silent when questioned. From everything Emily had read, she suspected Margaret was bipolar, a diagnosis that, true or not, was little comfort. It seemed clear to Henry they'd failed. He felt sorry for Jeff, as if they should have warned him.

"I really want to finish this," Emily said, "but if I do, I won't have room for dessert."

"Lunch tomorrow," he said.

He would have liked a cognac with his chocolate mousse, but responsibly ordered coffee.

"I don't think this is on the diet," she said.

"I don't think any of it is."

"I won't tell Dr. Runco if you won't."

"Deal."

Along with the check, the server brought Emily's leftovers, wrapped, as was the custom there, in tinfoil fashioned into a swan.

"This reminds me of England," she said, because once, in London, they'd given her the same thing and in the taxi it had leaked all over her good coat.

Now she inspected it, checking the tablecloth for a stain. "You can never be too careful."

"Better safe," he said.

"Thank you, it was wonderful."

"It *was* nice, wasn't it?"

"Are you all right to drive?"

"I are."

The girl at the coat check helped Emily on with her fur and held the door for them. "Be careful, it's slippy out."

The parked cars were coated but the sidewalk was salted—all but one neglected stretch in front of Le Pont. He carried the swan while Emily clung to his arm, the wind making them duck.

"I'm sorry," she said, tottering along. "I should have brought my boots."

"It's not that far."

Inside the station it was quiet and warm. Save the clerk at the ticket window and the engineer in his raised control room, the place was deserted, but the car had just left, its roof dropping away beyond the spotlights. While Emily perused the confusion of historic photos on the walls, he watched the geared wheel paying out cable and remembered doing pulley problems in college, the opposed arrows on the diagrams. $T1 = T2 + T3$. A simple machine, the Incline had been operating since before his father was born and would be hauling tourists up Mount Washington long after he and Emily were gone. Looking out at the snow, he tried to imagine the city back then, the mills and railroad bridges, the busy switchyards at the Point. His father's firm had wired the Gulf Building, for decades the tallest in town until the U.S. Steel Building went up, well after his father retired. During his own lifetime, the skyline had grown so crowded he no longer knew what everything was, and as he waited for the other car to emerge from the darkness, once again he had to fend off the sense that he belonged to the past.

"Are we there yet?" Emily asked.

"It's coming." He pointed to the wheel as proof.

"I hope so, because I have to pee."

"There's a restroom."

"I'm not going to go here."

When the car finally arrived, it was empty. They took their corner, huddled together against the sudden chill. He was sure some other couple would come barging in at the last second, but the warning bell rang and the door slid shut. The bell rang twice, and with a lurch, as if cut free, they descended.

He closed his eyes while they kissed and felt himself falling.

She laughed. "That's why you wanted to take the Incline."

"Remember the first time I took you?"

"I remember you were a perfect gentleman."

"Maybe not perfect."

"You're going to have lipstick all over you."

"I hope so."

At the bottom he had her wait by the stairs while he went to fetch the car. The lot hadn't been plowed, and as he hurried across the packed snow, he slipped. He flung out his arms for balance, and the swan went flying. He landed hard on his rear, his glasses knocked cockeyed.

"Are you all right?" Emily called.

"I'm fine," he said, though his tailbone hurt. He might have wrenched his knee. He stood and tested it. "Nothing broken."

"Be careful."

"Thank you."

The swan's neck was bent. He fixed it and set off again, leaning forward like an ice skater, using the parked cars to make his way to the Olds. Emily was waiting on him, so he got the wipers and defroster going and pulled around before scraping his lights and the other windows. He'd definitely done something to his knee.

"Are you sure you're all right?" Emily asked. "That looked like it hurt."

"Just my pride."

"You're lucky you didn't break your hip."

It was a bugaboo of hers, ever since Audrey Swanson had died from a blood clot after a fall.

"If the Germans couldn't kill me, a little spill won't."

"I'm not worried about the God-blessed Germans," she said. "I'm worried about you."

He babied the Olds across the bridge. A plow passed them, chains ringing, the blade pushing a breaking wave of snow. Fixed to the tailgate, a spinner scattered cinders in its wake.

"How's the road?"

"Not wonderful."

On Bigelow they had to slow for an accident, a wood-paneled minivan like Margaret's hung up on the median. The police had set out flares that cast a pink glow over the scene. As they crawled past, Henry worried they wouldn't make their hill.

"Are we going to make it up the hill?" Emily asked.

"That's exactly what I was thinking."

"That's why we're married. We're both worriers."

"We are," he conceded.

"I still have to pee."

"Do you want me to stop somewhere?"

"I just want to get home."

Another accident had closed the Bloomfield Bridge. Two police cars sat nose to nose to form a roadblock, their lights wheeling.

The detour took traffic through Oakland. Emily helped navigate.

"It doesn't look too bad," she said of the bridge on Baum.

Highland was in good shape as well, but they were both paying attention now, and there was no real chance of talking. The everlasting question of Margaret would have to wait.

When they turned onto Grafton, he expected an ice rink, and was surprised to find it plowed. He almost felt let down, as if they'd missed out on a challenge. The driveway was shoveled—Jim Cole, no doubt, saving him from a heart attack. The garage door rolled up, and Henry swung the Olds in headfirst, inching forward until the front tires nudged the two-by-four.

"Well," Emily said, "that was exciting." She rewarded him, as always after an evening out, with a quick kiss.

"Aren't you going to wear your boots?"

"There's no point now."

He didn't argue. She waited as he came around to help her across the flagstones. His knee was stiff from sitting and he was glad to go slow. Inside, Rufus barked nonstop, as if they were burglars.

"Quit it," Henry said, sorting through his keys with one hand. "It's just us."

"Open the door," Emily said. "I'm going to wet my pants."

He set the swan down on the glider to let her in, Rufus bounding past him and squatting in the snow, all the while looking over his shoulder. It was too cold, even for him. Once he was done, he dashed back inside and raced up the stairs after Emily.

"Yes," Henry said, "I missed you too," and shut off the spotlight.

He stuck the swan in the fridge and hung up his coat. Now that they were home again, he felt the closeness of being out together slipping away. He wanted a scotch, and called to Emily to see if she felt like something.

"A little port would be lovely, thank you."

He thought of Margaret as he poured it at the sideboard, and the idea of luck and happiness. How much of life was accidental and how much was work, and practically, what were they supposed to do?

He set Emily's glass beside her chair and turned on the fireplace, a draft making the flames waver, then stood by the mantel warming himself. The knees of his slacks were damp, two dark spots. The knee itself was tender and slightly swollen. He might ice it later.

Rufus came down first, anticipating her every step. She'd changed back into her sweater and was carrying her book. Henry, still in his jacket and tie, smiled to hide his disappointment. He should have dimmed the lights, or turned them off entirely.

"I take it you made it."

"Barely."

She stopped by the bookshelf to dial up QED, filling the room with the ceremonial pomp of a trumpet concerto. Once she was seated, Rufus settled himself, curled on the hearth at her feet.

At Chautauqua, when they were first married, they'd come in from ice skating and make love by the fire, no preliminaries, just throw their clothes off and fall on each other. They couldn't wait to be alone. He thought it was still true, though that part of their life was over.

He raised his glass to her. "Happy Valentine's Day."

"Happy Valentine's Day. Thank you, it was very nice."

"It was."

He leaned down to give her a kiss, which she chastely returned, her lips tasting of port. He squeezed her hand, retrieved his glass from the mantel and took his place across from her, their positions fixed as the stars. The fire flickered. Rufus twitched. Inevitably she would pick up her book and he would lose her. Tonight, after all of their misadventures, he wanted more.

"So," he said, "what happened at Christmas?"

Double Coupon Days

FROM THE VERY BEGINNING OF THEIR MARRIAGE, ONCE THEY returned from their honeymoon at Niagara Falls and set up housekeeping, Henry proudly assumed his husbandly duty as dishwasher. Being the baby, always underfoot, he'd learned at his mother's elbow, later honing his skills pulling KP during basic training, and finally in college, picking up shifts at the Schenley Grill, making pocket money to take Emily on dates. He was quick and efficient, if sometimes loud, banging the pots around, with a professional's respect for knives and a high tolerance for scalding water. After Emily served dessert, she was banned from the kitchen till it was spotless again. When the children were old enough, they grudgingly took over, the chore counting toward their allowances, a brief and contentious era memorable for its lack of quality control—melted Tupperware lids and silverware chewed by the disposal. Since 1977, when Kenny left for Emerson, save for holidays, Henry had manned the post alone, and as sole proprietor was responsible for inventorying his supplies. The last few days he'd been nursing the green jug of Cascade beneath the sink, wedging it upside down between a bucket and a plastic basket of onions to get the dregs. When, late that afternoon, Emily asked him to run out to the Giant Eagle for a red pepper, he saw it as an opportunity.

He thought they had a coupon. He remembered cutting one out of a Sunday insert a few weeks back, though with dish detergent it was hard to say, they were so cyclical. He consulted Emily's miniature accordion file on the side of the fridge, and there under KITCHEN, to his great satisfaction, was a dual coupon for a dollar off, one for Cascade and one for Cascade Sparkling Rinse, both with the same expiration date, March 15. All he needed was the Cascade, so he folded it along the dotted line, first one way and then the other so he wouldn't tear the barcode, and carefully separated the two.

"Anything else?" he asked.

"No. I need it to make dinner, so allez vite, s'il vous plaît."

Meaning the East Liberty Giant Eagle. Normally they shopped at the big new Jyggle across the river in the Waterworks, where the meat and produce were better. The East Liberty store was cramped and dirty, unimproved, like the neighborhood, a holdover from the fifties. His mother had shopped there for years, switching to Edgewood only after Martin Luther King was shot. Not that it was unsafe, but he wouldn't want Emily to go there alone this time of day. Which was likely why she'd asked. It was his mission. He grabbed his jacket and his Pirates cap and headed out.

To market, to market, to buy a fat pig, his mother used to say, bundling him up for the walk to the trolley. If he was good, she'd let him pick out a treat— a box of animal crackers designed like a circus wagon, with a shoestring handle for carrying. He loved to dunk them in milk and bite their heads off, the gingery biscuit dissolving to sweet mush on his tongue. He was an easy child, a pleaser like Kenny, another reason he would never understand Margaret. Half the time he didn't get Emily.

With the snow gone, the drive took all of five minutes. It was rush hour, not quite dusk, a stream of headlights coming the other way. At the bus stop by the plaza entrance, workers from the nursing home waited in puffy coats and scrubs, breathing steam, blue plastic bags slung from their arms. Behind the shelter, abandoned at all angles, sprawled a dozen shopping carts.

The lot was busy with people picking things up on the way home, and he had to park in the farthest row. His knee was still stiff, making him wince. By the doors, a decommissioned police car blocked the crosswalk, a jitney driver helping a heavyset woman with a purple turban into the front seat. DOUBLE COUPON DAYS, said a hand-painted sign in the window, a promising development. Usually they didn't double anything above ninety-nine cents. Now he wished he'd brought the other coupon. Eventually they'd need more rinse.

There were no handbaskets in the vestibule, and the few carts all had scraps of trash in them. Inside, arms folded across his chest, a security guard built like a linebacker watched the doors with undisguised menace. Reflexively, Henry tipped his cap. The man didn't flinch.

"Grumpy," Henry muttered, well past him.

The checkout was crowded and loud, the lines backed up into the aisles. The paneled drop ceiling and dull fluorescent lighting only added to the claustrophobia. Though he would deny that he was a racist—an accusation Margaret as a teenager delighted in applying to the city in general and Highland Park in particular—he was relieved to see he wasn't the only white person there. Among those waiting, conspicuous in her matching cloche and camel-hair coat, leaning half on her cane and half on her cart, was Evvie Dunbar from church. He watched her, hoping she would look his way, but she was focused on the tabloid racks. She'd lived in one of those prewar apartment buildings over on Fifth forever. Probably shopped here out of habit, which he considered brave and maybe foolhardy at her age. He understood, though. After so many years, why change?

Despite the produce section being one quarter the size of the Waterworks', the peppers were surprisingly nice—smooth-skinned and shiny. He bagged the best and headed for the rear of the store, noting, as he passed through the shampoo aisle, that the razor blades he used were locked behind a complicated plastic display. He couldn't imagine it was a problem, yet someone had patented the contraption.

Against logic, the dish soap wasn't with the laundry detergent. He tried the next aisle, and there was the Cascade in his preferred scent, lemon.

From experience, he knew to check the fine print. Sometimes you had to buy two or a certain size to qualify. Some instructed the merchant not to double the coupon. In this case he was reasonably confident, yet when he fished the coupon from his pocket, it wasn't for regular Cascade but the Sparkle Rinse.

"What the heck."

He confirmed the impossible, biting his lower lip, then peered up the aisle as if someone might be playing a joke on him.

He must have put the other one back in the folder. Probably flipped it around when he ripped it. But why wouldn't he look to make sure? He was missing a step. He might have looked right at it—just as he'd probably looked at the stop sign—and not seen what was there. Near the end, his father repeated the same story about a rival firm testing the Grant Building's Morse code beacon for the first time. He told it so often in company that Henry dreaded it, alert for the first sentence. Over and over he and Emily listened to how, all night, the light flashed P-I-T-T-S-B-U-R-K-H to passing planes, and each time they would laugh and glance at each other helplessly. Now it was his turn.

He also had his father's brain when it came to math. With the doubled Sparkle Rinse coupon, he could get two dollars off, buy the Cascade for the regular price and technically break even. He could also come back tomorrow, he argued, but, flustered by his mistake, gave in to impatience and grabbed a jug of both.

The express line was no faster than the rest, and traffic going home was slow.

"Thank you," Emily said, taking the bag from him. "Was it a zoo?"

"You'll never guess who I saw there. Evvie Dunbar."

"Of all people."

"I want to say she's a regular."

"God bless her," Emily said. "Now shoo. I should have started this a half hour ago."

While she washed the pepper, he went to the fridge and checked the folder. There was the one he wanted, startling as the reveal at the end of a card trick.

After dinner he did the dishes and was gratified to finish the old jug—proof that he'd made the right decision. He squeezed the air out of it to save room in the recycling bin. Thursday was garbage night, the weekly purge, the wastebaskets upstairs and down freshly relined, Rufus's frozen poop scooped and double-bagged, the wheeled plastic can parked at the curb for the hydraulic-armed truck to empty while they slept, yet Henry felt as if he'd missed something. The next day, without telling Emily, he made a special trip to East Liberty to use the coupon, and while he got his two dollars off, putting him ahead of the game, now every time he filled the dishwasher and set the Cascade back under the sink with its twin, he recalled not the money he'd saved but the shock of discovering the wrong coupon, and resolved, with the indignation of the deceived, to be more vigilant.

The Inconvenience

HIS KNEE WAS STILL SWOLLEN, AND DIDN'T FEEL ANY BETTER. In the medicine cabinet there was an Ace bandage from a couple summers ago when Emily sprained her ankle playing badminton with the grandchildren. He couldn't tell if it helped. At night he strapped on her fancy ice pack, wrapping it in a hand towel, his skin numb under the covers. By morning the goop inside was warm and he was stiff. He had to be careful coming down the stairs. It hurt if he stood too long at his workbench, and he took to using a stool, shifting his position every so often. The Aleve did nothing. His yearly checkup was scheduled for next week, and rather than pay for an extra office visit, he decided to wait and ask Dr. Runco about it then, a decision Emily declared silly.

"That's why we have Medicare."

"I doubt they could get me in on this short notice."

"Not now," she said. "Maybe if you'd called when it happened."

"I didn't think it was that serious."

"You can barely walk."

There was no need to exaggerate. He wasn't the macho fool she thought, but the opposite, cautiously optimistic, hoping if he slowed down and watched it closely, the knee might heal on its own. He wasn't going to be like Hubie Frazier, having his hips and then his knees done one after the other at eighty so he could play tennis. Though in public Henry tried to hide his limp, he liked to think he was free of vanity on that scale.

The weather didn't help. When it snowed, he let Jim Cole shovel the walk again, but couldn't stop himself from spreading salt.

His knee was puffed up and spongy with fluid. At church he couldn't kneel, and balancing his rear on the hard edge of the pew, he braced himself against the bench in front, resting his forehead on his folded hands. "We confess that we have sinned against you," he recited, eyes closed, "in thought, word and deed." In the silence he had time to review his week. He'd been greedy about the coupons, and impatient with the line and the other drivers. He would always be guilty of pride. Thinking he was right. Not listening. Holding grudges. He needed to be kinder to Margaret and stop feeling sorry for himself because he was old and useless. "Amen," he said along with the congregation, though he could think of more now. Resentment. Envy. Deceit. Once you started listing your sins, there was no end to it.

Monday morning he was in the backyard with Rufus, refilling the birdfeeders, when Emily called him from the kitchen door, waving the phone. "It's Linda from the doctor's office."

He stood on the mat in his boots so he wouldn't get her floor wet. He didn't see why she couldn't just take a message.

"Mr. Maxwell," Linda said. "I'm afraid we have to reschedule your Wednesday appointment. Dr. Runco's had to take a leave of absence."

"Is everything all right?"

Emily looked at him as if it were grave news. He shrugged. It might be anything.

"It's a personal matter, but thank you. Dr. Prasad and Dr. Binstock will be taking care of his patients, but for the time being we're shorthanded. We hope you'll bear with us."

"Of course," Henry said.

"Thank you. We apologize for the inconvenience."

"No, please, I understand."

The first opening they had was in three weeks, with Dr. Prasad. Henry asked her to give Dr. Runco his best.

"What is it?" Emily asked.

"He's taking some time off."

"How much time?"

"She didn't say."

"That's not good. I wonder if Patsy knows anything."

She took the phone into the living room, already on the case, while he went back out to top off the feeders. He and Dr. Runco were both Class of '49 at Pitt. Henry had been going to him over thirty years. He was a big skier, with a place at Okemo, and three boys, the youngest Kenny's age, but beyond his vacation plans Henry knew little of his private life. Once they'd bumped into him at a Pirate game with one of his sons, and, unfairly perhaps, Henry was surprised he was drinking beer. Trim himself, he was always trying to get Henry to lose weight, an ongoing failure that bothered Henry, who saw his sweet tooth as a character flaw.

He capped the last feeder and gathered up the bags. Rufus nosed at the spilled sunflower seeds. "Come on, Tubbo. All done."

Rufus ignored him.

"Come!" Henry called, and Rufus dashed past him for the door. "Why do you have to make me say it twice?"

By dinnertime, through Emily's web of church, University Club and Friends of the Library friends, they knew Dr. Runco was in St. Margaret's cancer unit. Henry was surprised they didn't know his prognosis.

"You'd think he could arrange something on an outpatient basis," Emily said. "The hospital's the last place I'd want to be."

Henry didn't want to speculate, and chewed his chicken à la king.

"Of course at this point he may not have a choice. The chemo makes you so weak. I remember Millie, she was completely out of it. You'd have to have a nurse. He's still married, isn't he?"

"As far as I know."

"It's awful. It doesn't help you with your knee either."

"My knee will be fine."

"Who knows how it'll be in three weeks. I think you've let it go for too long as it is. Maybe we should try somewhere else."

"I'm not going to get in anywhere else in three weeks without a referral."

"What if it's an emergency?"

"It's not an emergency. I can walk on it."

"You probably shouldn't be."

"The sky is blue," Henry said.

"It's night out, so it's black, smart-ass. Fine. If you want to hobble around for the next three weeks and make it worse, go right ahead, but don't expect me to play nurse when they have to operate."

Forty-eight years, and he would never get used to how quickly she could turn. Sometimes she apologized, but he'd learned not to wait. He wanted to think she didn't mean what she said, though it was the tone that hurt the most—as if, like a willful child, he'd purposely driven her beyond the limits of her patience.

Were they really talking about his knee, or was it the fact that he and Dr. Runco were the same age? He didn't blame her for being afraid. He wasn't sure what he could do, beyond promising he wouldn't die.

The next morning he called the office to see if they could move up his appointment in case of a cancellation. He was free anytime, and they were three minutes away. His knee was causing him pain, he said, which wasn't a lie. Linda said she'd make a note in their system. He apologized and asked her, again, to give his best to Dr. Runco, but as he hung up he thought the sentiment rang false. As someone who valued his privacy, he couldn't think of anything worse than everyone knowing your business, especially when you were helpless, and all morning as he chipped away at their taxes, whenever it crossed his mind he went sullen, clenching his lips as if he were the object of his own misguided pity.

When a few days later Linda called to say there'd been a cancellation, he thought Emily would be pleased.

"It's only been what, a month? If you'd gone in when you should have, you'd be better by now."

"I'm just glad they could fit me in," he said, and let it rest there, a stalemate if not a draw.

He expected Dr. Prasad to be Indian, like so many doctors around town now, older and gnomelike, with glasses, a heavy accent and white lab coat, and was unprepared for the rangy young man in rolled shirtsleeves and a leather tie who shook his hand like a car salesman. He was American, his smile the obvious product of orthodonture, his hair gelled and sleek as a male model's. He set Henry's file aside and squatted to palpate his knee while Henry described the fall and his symptoms.

No, he had no history of knee problems. He was in relatively good health besides his cholesterol.

The doctor held Henry's shin with one hand, instructing him to push against it.

"Hard as you can."

"That's it," Henry said.

The doctor cupped his heel. "Pull. Does it hurt?"

"It feels weak."

Dr. Prasad stood. "PCL. Probably just a partial tear, but we'll do an MRI to make sure."

Posterior cruciate ligament. He could walk on it, but he should try to avoid stairs. The doctor gave him a prescription for an anti-inflammatory and a month of physical therapy. There was a good place in Oakland, and another in Squirrel Hill, if that was easier. It was a matter of doing his exercises and giving the knee the best chance to heal.

"Did Carmen take your height and weight when you came in?"

"Yes," Henry said, knowing what came next. Strangely, it was then, during the lecture, that he missed Dr. Runco the most.

Emily was right—he should have called them as soon as it happened. But he didn't tell her that. She seemed satisfied that they didn't have to operate. She was less interested in the details of his physical therapy. "So, did you hear anything?"

"No."

"Did you ask Linda?"

"No."

"You have to ask. How else are you going to find anything out? I knew I should have gone with you. I swear, you drive me crazy."

As always, he didn't understand what he'd done wrong. "I'm not trying to."

"I know you're not," she said. "That's what makes it so frustrating."

The Second Sunday
in Lent

SUNDAY IN THE MAXWELL HOUSEHOLD WAS CALL YOUR MOTHER Day, so late that afternoon when the phone rang, he paused above the overturned kitchen drawer he was regluing and glanced up at the floor joists, waiting for Emily to get it. The footsteps he expected never came. The phone rang four, five times before the machine answered, and then, instead of leaving a message, the person hung up. He'd thought she was doing her crossword by the fire, but it was possible she was taking a nap. It was a day for it, gray and rainy, the parking lot at church a lake. He leaned into the heat of his work lamp and squeezed a bead of glue along the last seam, capped the tube and gently pressed the two pieces together. While he was holding them tight, the phone rang again.

"It's like Grand Central Station," he said.

Again, no message.

The glue was a new epoxy that was supposed to work in thirty seconds. He stood there with the drawer in his hands, careful not to get epoxy on them, silently counting to sixty before he placed it on a clean sheet of newspaper and applied the clamps. It was an interesting problem. Under normal use, the drawer was more than strong enough, but in fits of culinary frustration Emily had the habit of slamming it so the overloaded silverware tray rammed the rear wall, weakening the three joints there till they failed. Without the rear wall for structure, the bottom gradually separated from the sidewalls so that weeks later, without warning, when Emily opened the drawer too quickly the entire contents fell out the back. At this point, rather than try to minimize the damage, she yanked the broken pieces free and dashed them to the floor, swearing, saying they needed all new cabinets, a threat he discounted as empty, since they couldn't afford them. His strategy, as with the Olds and the rest of 51 Grafton Street, was to keep things going while spending as little as possible, a plan that succeeded only because he was handy. When he was gone the place would fall apart, but at that point, as the joke went, she would have his insurance. Till then he played the superintendent, always on call.

According to the instructions, for maximum strength he should let the glue set for five minutes. He'd give it thirty, leaving more than enough time to put the kitchen back together before Emily started dinner. He made sure the cap was screwed on tight, hung the extra clamps on the pegboard and turned off the lamp.

Upstairs her music played, softly. She was sitting in her chair where he'd left her, doing the crossword. Beside her, resting facedown on the end table, in case the children called, lay the phone.

"I thought I heard the phone ring."

"You did. I didn't think you'd want to be bothered."

"Who was it?"

"Who always calls right around this time?"

Meaning Arlene. "The kids."

"Here's a hint: Someone who can't just leave a message."

"She doesn't call every Sunday."

"She did last Sunday."

"She needed help with her doorbell."

"Call her," Emily said. "I'm sure she's got some chore for you to do."

He would never understand this pointless jealousy, and thought it was because he was a man. What he knew about women he'd learned from his mother and Arlene, and then Emily and Margaret, all of them strong-willed and uncompromising if not always rational. How much energy they spent rehashing old grievances. Attuned to the tiniest slight, they kept score, forming new alliances doomed to explode. To Arlene's chagrin, their mother was fond of Emily, even more so after the children were born, while Arlene, like Margaret, once the favorite, became Margaret's confidante. While their mother was still alive, having the four of them together was a trial. Early on he learned from his father how to play the diplomat, sympathetic to all, but as a husband he owed Emily his final allegiance, though sometimes, as in the case of Margaret's weight, he might disagree with her methods. He could see Kenny taking the same role with Lisa as if it were inevitable, and wished he'd set a better example. Being agreeable didn't make people less difficult.

He took the phone into the kitchen, shadowed by Rufus, who was hoping he might put him out. Henry used it as an excuse to stand on the back porch and watch as he chose a spot in the patchy snow. Rain dripped from the sycamore.

"There you are," Arlene said.

"Sorry. I was doing something in the basement and couldn't get to the phone."

"I thought maybe you were at the home and garden show."

"No." They'd gone once, years ago. "So, what's up?"

It was her disposal. She was in the middle of making lemon squares for the library bake sale when it stopped working all of a sudden. Could he come take a look at it?

"Did you check the breaker?"

"That's the first thing I checked."

"Okay," he said, "I'll be over," though he had no idea what he could do.

He had Rufus stand on the mat so he could wipe his paws, kneeling on his

46

good knee. The physical therapy was helping, but he still needed to use the counter to pull himself up. "Good boy, yes, let's get a treaty-treat."

He returned the phone to the end table.

"Well?"

"Her disposal's not working."

"Say hello to her for me."

"I will," he said.

Conveniently, Arlene lived ten minutes away in Regent Square, where she rented the top half of a duplex a few blocks from Frick Park. Her apartment was crowded with their mother's furniture from Mellon Street, the same familiar pictures from childhood on the walls, the same books on the shelves, all perfectly preserved yet somehow wrong removed from their original context. The Wax Museum, Emily dubbed it, and while Henry defended Arlene's (and his mother's) taste, he dreaded his visits, as if by marrying and having a family of his own, he'd abandoned her.

Her street was red brick and slippery. There was a spot in front, and he angled for it, letting the Olds coast to a stop. He'd brought his toolbox and lugged it up the walk like a plumber.

She must have been watching. As he neared the crumbling front steps, she came out on her balcony and tossed down her key—attached, for that reason, to a white plastic parachute that did nothing to break its fall. They were neither Irish nor Catholic, yet her door sported a flashy St. Patrick's Day wreath too new to be left over from her teaching days.

She was waiting for him at the top of the stairs. "How's the knee?"

"Getting there."

"You look like you're moving better."

"How are you doing?"

"I'm ready for spring to get here."

She wore a candy-cane-patterned apron over a scarlet cardigan that hung on her like a bathrobe. Growing up, she'd been taller than him until he reached the ninth grade. Now every time he saw her she seemed hunched and shrunken, as if she were dwindling away.

"Sorry to bother you. I didn't think it could wait till tomorrow."

"It's no bother. I just hope I can do something."

The living room smelled of burnt sugar and her cigarettes. Like their father in his condo, she kept the lights off to save electricity. In the gloom, an aquarium shone from one corner, garish as a beer sign. She led him back past their old dining room table to the kitchen, where she'd laid out her meager array of tools on the counter, including a hammer.

Like a detective, he craned over the sink, aiming his flashlight down the drain.

"It was making a lot of noise before it stopped, but it always does that with lemons. It's old."

"This it?" he asked, and tried the switch by the window. Nothing.

He ran the tap to see if there was a clog. "You can use it for water at least."

"That's good to know," she said, as if he'd done something.

She'd cleaned out the cupboard beneath the sink so he could get to the disposal—old but solid state, no fuses. A corrugated hose ran from the dishwasher to the side of the drum, held firmly in place with a clamp. He ran a finger along the underside of the hose to make sure there were no leaks. He was convinced the problem was electrical, a fried motor or solenoid, beyond his skills. With parts and labor, probably not worth fixing, which was fine—her landlord would have to shell out for a new one—and yet, with her standing there watching, he couldn't quit.

At Jackass Flats, when anything went wrong, the techs said, "It's not rocket science," and invariably they were right. The reactor never failed, or the engine. Their design worked. It was always something basic like a relay or a pressure gauge that stopped them from launching. A fix could be as simple as: Is it plugged in?

It was. He unplugged it, counted five and plugged it in again.

"Try it now."

"I am."

"Okay, turn it off."

He propped the flashlight in the corner, shining straight up, rolled onto his back like a mechanic and knocked it over so it bonked him in the face. "God love you." The space was tight, and he shifted to his side, balancing awkwardly on a hip. Straining, one arm trapped beneath him, he reached around to where the waste pipe connected to the drum, PVC attached with a ribbed collar. He had his wrenches. He could pull the whole thing out, but that would take time and then she couldn't use the sink. Blindly he felt along the joint and the pipe that ran to a cutout in the wall, checking for moisture, and then, finding none, down around the bottom of the drum. The metal was warm, a sign the motor might have overheated, and as he traced the base plate, feeling open holes and raised bumps that might be the heads of screws, his fingers dipped into a beveled depression and hit a plastic nib like the plunger of a pen that gave under his touch. He pressed it in. It seemed to stay.

"Try now."

The motor whirred, the chamber rattling, spinning empty.

Off. On. It was fine.

He squirmed free and clambered to his feet, red-faced and light-headed.

"What did you do?"

"There's a reset button on the bottom. It probably just overheated. From now on throw your old lemons in the garbage."

"Thank you," she said, as if he'd saved her, and he was glad he'd come.

She wanted him to take a plate of lemon squares, but he knew Emily wouldn't appreciate them, and took just one, the gooey, still-warm middle square, wolfing it in the car as he splashed along Penn Avenue, inhaling the powdered sugar so he nearly choked, then brushing the crumbs off his front. As good as their mother's, he wanted to say, magnanimous after his victory. While it was just dumb luck, and the sugar high would burn off soon enough, for now he was inordinately proud of himself, filled, Scroogelike, with goodwill toward the whole world.

He thought he'd been quick, but when he got home, Emily had already started dinner—a lamb roast crowned with sprigs of rosemary. To make room on the counter, she'd exiled the silverware tray to the corner by the door. The sink was a jumble of mixing bowls and measuring cups.

"How is Arlene?" she asked stagily, as if it were expected of her.

"She's fine."

"Did you fix her disposal?"

"I did."

"Good. I moved your thing over there because it was in the way. Just let me get this in the oven, then you can do whatever you want."

He waited till she was peeling carrots at the sink to bring the drawer up and fit it into the track. He squirted a dash of silicone spray on the rollers, opened and closed the drawer to spread it around and replaced the silverware tray.

"Ta-da," he said.

"We'll see how long that lasts," she said, testing it. "But thank you."

The Record

EVERY NIGHT BEFORE BED THEY WATCHED THE WEATHER, YET when spring finally arrived it was a shock. One morning they woke to fog in the trees and robins on the lawn. By noon the snow was gone, the gutters glinting with runoff. The sunshine felt like a reward for surviving the winter. The crocuses beside the basement hatch poked through, and the daffodils around the birdbath. While Emily weeded in her coolie hat and kneepads, he scooped the thawed poop and bundled the fallen branches, picturing Ella and Sam hunting Easter eggs. It was too early to mulch, according to Emily, so he satisfied himself with taking down the feeders and vacuuming up the chaff, terrorizing Rufus with the hose. Though it was still cold enough that he had to wear a jacket, she opened the windows and aired out the house.

The next day was supposed to be even nicer. While the Deep South was getting hit with tornadoes, the weatherman expected the system to stay in place till the weekend, with temperatures in the seventies. Friday they had a shot at breaking the record, set in 1889.

The warmth seemed tenuous, a fluke, and still he couldn't resist pulling the Olds out and washing off the salt. He liberated the grill, which was low on propane, giving him an excuse to run over to the Home Depot, where the garden center tempted him with its bales of peat moss and sacks of grass seed. In the parking lot they'd set up a makeshift corral of dogwoods and redbuds and prefab sheds. Driving home he caught part of the Pirate game from Bradenton, another promise of summer.

Emily was defrosting steaks on the cutting board.

"You read my mind."

"I hate to tell you," she said. "It's not that hard."

The grill lit on the first try. He closed the lid and sipped his Iron City, letting the heat build till the gauge reached 500. The cooking didn't take long. They both liked theirs bloody.

They could have eaten outside if he'd brought up the porch furniture. Afterward, they took Rufus for a walk around the block, meeting a white standard poodle named Jean-Luc, a pair of yappy Pekingese Rufus wanted nothing to do with, and several new people pushing strollers. The hedges were budding and the air smelled of mud. On Sheridan some kids were playing street hockey, their sticks clashing, making him think of Kenny and his friends, and his own friends from childhood, the games they'd played at dusk, the streetlights flickering on, nighthawks swooping through the dark. They called them nighthawks, but he wasn't sure what they were. He'd never seen them since, and wondered if they were something he and his friends made up. There was no one who could tell him now. Even if there were, what would it matter? He'd seen them. He remembered them, even if he was wrong.

Emily liked the fresh air, so they slept with the windows open. At four when he got up to pee, the room was freezing. Rufus had moved to the bathroom, sprawled on the heated tiles. Henry tried to go back to sleep but the birds had already started. A car crawled along, clanked over a manhole and then stopped, idling right outside their window. A car door opened, followed by footsteps and the whap of the paper hitting the front walk, and the Coles', and the Marshes', and the Buchanans', and on down the street to Highland. Their carrier was Mary, a Nigerian woman with an unpronounceable last name who sent them a Christmas card each year with a return envelope meant for her tip. They'd never seen her, though once on his way back to bed he'd glimpsed her car, a boxy old station wagon that probably served as a jitney during the day. It seemed like overkill. He'd done his route on foot, and he was ten. He could picture each house, could walk the route block by block, his bag gradually growing lighter. He did now, recalling the doors and porches of their neighbors, chucking tomahawks, and then he was in Germany, by the canal where they'd found the drowned tank, except Duchess was there, still alive, and he knelt down and hugged her and told her she was good, she was sweet, yes, she was his sweetest bestest girl.

He woke to the cold, bundled under the covers.

"It's so much nicer with the windows open," Emily said. "How did you sleep?"

"I was a little chilly, actually."

"Do you want to switch places?"

"No."

It was a ritual, like the church rummage sale or the flower show. Without it, the season was incomplete.

Putting out Rufus, he thought of Duchess. How many years had she been gone now? One more than they'd had Rufus, so four. *Duchess, Duchess, the dog who's just so Muchess.* A snorer and a slobberer, she was his dog as sure as Rufus was Emily's. He still missed her, though he thought of her less and less, which seemed wrong after such devotion.

He parted the living room curtains to let in the day, unlocked the front door and picked the paper off the walk—not a tomahawk but folded inside a green plastic bag. He stripped off the wrapper and dropped it in the kitchen trash on his way to the breakfast nook when the headline stopped him: 5 DEAD IN HIGHLAND PARK SHOOTING.

"What is it?" She took the paper from him. "Turn on the news."

There was a commercial, and then a story on a church in McKees Rocks that was supposed to have the best fish fry. Beneath the video ran a blood-red crawl that said the police were still searching for two suspects. Later that morning the district attorney was going to visit the scene and make a statement. Not coincidentally, he was running for attorney general and the primary was coming up.

"It's so senseless," Emily said. "One of them was pregnant. Where's 1431 Euclid?"

"Up by the park, on the other side of Highland."

"That close?"

He didn't want to worry her. "It's probably drugs. There are a lot of rentals over there."

A placard introduced BREAKING NEWS.

"Here it is," she said.

"Police are calling it an ambush," began the young black reporter who usually covered broken water mains and cars that plowed into houses. He stood in a brick alley littered with yellow evidence markers, the one in the foreground numbered 33. The camera panned across a backyard where overturned lawn chairs ringed a cheap grill.

"Those are our chairs," Emily said, and they were. Everyone on their side of town shopped at the Home Depot.

"Around nine o'clock last night, detectives say someone with a forty-caliber handgun standing right about here fired shots into a neighborhood gathering behind this home on Euclid Avenue. When panicked partygoers ran for the back door, a second suspect hiding behind this fence opened fire on them with an assault rifle."

"I'm surprised we didn't hear anything," Emily said.

"Especially with the windows open."

"Nine o'clock."

"We were watching that movie."

"The one that put me to sleep."

Like them, the family at 1431 Euclid Avenue was celebrating the good weather with a cookout, friends dropping by as the evening wore on. On Grafton, they used to do the same thing. Doug Pickering would light the tiki torches to let everyone know the bar was open, and they'd all bring their lawn chairs, making a circle that grew as new people showed up, the children racing around the yard, playing freeze tag. The idea of someone ambushing them was ridiculous. Nothing like that would ever happen on this side of Highland, but thirty years ago he would have said the same of Mellon Street. Euclid was the next street in. The only real surprise was the weapon, an AK-47.

"Who would do something like that?" Emily asked.

A soldier, Henry wanted to say. Someone young, convinced he was at war. He could see the battle dozer pushing a pile of the dead like rubble as they cleared the bridge. In the shallows below, more floated facedown, as if they were trying to swim to shore. "I don't know. It's terrible."

"I hope they find them."

"I'm sure the D.A.'s got everyone working on it."

Later that morning they were pruning back the raspberry canes by the driveway when a helicopter flew over, followed closely by a second. Instead of zooming off like the LifeFlight, they loitered, droning, their rotors beating the air, as if preparing to attack. They stayed through the noon news, shooting live footage Henry and Emily watched as they ate lunch.

"What about Channel 2," asked Emily, "can't they afford one?"

From above, the house and yard were unremarkable. It made Henry think of Gettysburg, the great battlefield now empty meadows. Instead of marble obelisks and Doric-columned monuments, teddy bears and flowers mounded around a phone pole commemorated the dead. Three of them were sisters. The D.A. said a male family member still in a coma may have been the intended target, in retaliation for an earlier shooting. Community leaders were planning a march and a candlelight vigil for Friday night. There was a website where viewers could donate to a fund set up to help the victims' families.

"Think how much a funeral costs now," Emily said. "Imagine doing three at once."

He'd imagined his own many times, fretting over the mess he'd leave her. "I can't."

Both choppers returned at five o'clock, as if there might be something new to see. Inside the cordon of police tape, their chairs lay capsized. The young grandmother who'd lost her three grown daughters made a plea for peace. "Whoever did this doesn't have to answer to me. They have to answer to God." The police were offering a ten-thousand-dollar reward for information.

"You don't think they know?" Emily asked.

"The police?"

"The family. Someone knows. They're not telling us everything."

"I'm sure they can't." Though at heart he agreed, and he was just as curious as she was, it seemed wrong to speculate about the case as if it were one of her whodunits. Finally it didn't matter who'd killed them. The mystery was how the neighborhood—how the world—had come to this.

That night in bed, as she enjoyed the sleep of the innocent, he listened to the buzzing of the streetlight and the wind in the trees and the distant thrum of traffic, all the while expecting gunshots. Riding convoy during the war he'd learned how to catnap, snapping awake at the slightest noise. Once the line got moving, he dropped off, but tap the brakes and he alerted like a guard dog. On bivouac he stayed in his rack all day. Now he was lucky to string six hours together around trips to the head. Rufus kicked the dresser, running in his sleep. A train dieseled through East Liberty, its horn plaintive, sounding a warning, and he thought of the bridge outside of Freiburg, how afterward they'd laughed because it was so easy. The enemy were teenagers and old men, local farmers conscripted for this last stand, armed with their own hunting rifles. The .50 cal split them in half. He fed in belt after belt as Embree swept the barrel back and forth across the deck, kicking up chunks of tarmac. Later while they were helping graves detail police the bodies, Embree came across one that had been decapitated. "Aww," he said like Elmer Fudd, pressing a finger to the dimple in his chin, "did I do dat?" and from relief or exhaustion or sheer gratitude at being alive, they laughed. On Euclid Avenue the killers hadn't stuck around to see what they'd done. Henry thought it made all the difference. You appreciated what a job involved when you had to clean up after yourself.

As promised, Friday was the nicest day of the week. Overnight the Coles' dogwood had popped, and the Millers' magnolia, the whole city in bloom, awash in pollen. By late afternoon the temperature topped eighty. Under the circumstances, it seemed wrong that they should break the record. The weatherman celebrated with a flurry of virtual confetti as if they'd won something. "Tomorrow we're looking at rain showers, so enjoy it now." There was nothing new on the investigation, only the same sound bites from the family and the D.A. The first funeral was scheduled for tomorrow afternoon. After dinner, near sunset, as he and Emily were walking Rufus, Henry imagined the three of them crossing Highland and continuing on to Euclid Avenue, joining the march in solidarity, but feared they wouldn't be welcome.

The next morning he thought of driving by. He had to run over to the Home Depot for more lawn and leaf bags, and while Euclid was the wrong way, it would only take him five minutes. He wasn't sure what he expected to see that hadn't already been on the news, just as he didn't know why he was drawn to the murders, beyond proximity and the excitement of crime. The idea seemed ghoulish, indecent. What curiosity was he trying to satisfy? It might have been his neighborhood once, but he hadn't set foot on that block in fifty years. The only business he had was on Mellon Street, and even there he knew no one and no one knew him. At Highland he turned left for East Liberty and the Home Depot. Instead of being proud of himself for resisting, he wondered why he was tempted in the first place, and suspected that if Euclid had been on the way, he would have gone ahead and driven down the alley.

The rain came, and behind it the cold. That night they slept with the windows closed. Well into morning, he thought he heard a helicopter approaching. As it flew over, the Doppler caught up, and the whistling rotor became the roar of a jet, a harmless cargo plane headed for New York or Boston.

The coverage was relentless, inescapable. The Sunday paper had a long feature on redlining and gun violence. In church, during the Prayers for the People, the deacon read off the names of the dead, and at coffee hour Judy Reese and Martha Burgwin said they'd heard from their cleaning lady, whose aunt knew the grandmother, that the ex-boyfriend of the middle girl was a drug dealer. Henry abstained from the conversation, excusing himself to graze the cookie table. Later, when Kenny called, it was the first thing he and Emily talked about. As she parroted the rumor, Henry was surprised to find he was resentful, as if she were sharing their secrets.

"It's a circus," Henry said when she finally put him on. "I'm sure things will calm down by the time you guys get here. Someone will get shot in Homewood and all the TV crews will run over there."

He was being cynical, joking, as he often did with him on the phone. He didn't really believe what he was saying, he was just jazzing around, yet that was exactly what happened. After getting kicked out of a bar, a man returned with a gun and killed three people, including the owner, a fixture in Homewood known for coaching their Pop Warner team. Decades of his players turned out for the march. There were plans to name a field after him.

Meanwhile, the funerals for the Euclid Avenue victims straggled on, mingling with those in Homewood, the news lumping them together as if the shootings were related. When they'd first heard, Henry had meant to make a donation to the fund set up to help the families. Now he waffled, wary of his motives, afraid they might be sentimental or patronizing. They already gave at church and to the United Way, whose programs served those neighborhoods. Several times he thought of discussing the matter with Emily, or donating anonymously through the computer without her knowing, but as the days passed and the dead were laid to rest, the need seemed less pressing, and in the end he did nothing.

Spring Ahead

OF ALL PEOPLE IT WAS MARGARET WHO REMINDED HIM TO change their clocks. He'd known, vaguely, but like so many inessential things, it had gotten lost in the growing backlog of errands and chores. They'd been working in the garden every day, and by nightfall he was ready for bed.

"Is it that time already?"

"I know," she said. "I wake up too early as it is. I don't need to lose another hour of sleep. You've heard about that study that says it causes accidents."

"No."

"People fall asleep at the wheel."

"Makes sense," he agreed, but after they said goodbye, he thought it was like her to fasten on the morbid. She was a strange bird, as his mother once said. She'd seemed sober, at least, though, almost finished with his scotch, maybe he wasn't the best judge.

"What I want to know," Emily asked, "is why she's calling Thursday night. What was she doing all day Sunday?"

"You want me to guess?"

"Stop. Be nice."

They'd never know. Like all addicts, she was secretive, a practiced liar. As a girl she'd hidden candy bars in her closet. As a teenager it was cigarettes, then pot and pills. Emily regularly went through her shoeboxes. Now she'd have bottles stashed around the house—in the basement and the linen closet and in the back of cupboards. Jeff said he checked, but she was only working part-time. Most afternoons she was alone until the children came home from school.

She might be sober. There was no way to tell. He thought he should be more charitable, but after all her troubles, he'd learned to temper his hopes. Fool me once.

Before she called, he'd been thinking of having another Dewar's. Now he did on principle, remembering his Al-Anon. He would not be a hostage to her problems.

"You're going to have a headache," Emily said.

"I already have two," he said, pointing at her and Rufus, but in the morning she was right. He wanted to blame Margaret.

"You should listen to me," Emily said.

"I should."

"I don't care, we're still mulching."

"As long as we do it quietly."

Every year the job seemed more involved, the garden taking over the yard. In the garage he dug up a crusty pair of work gloves and loaded a shovel, two rakes, a pitchfork and an edger into the wheelbarrow, their handles jutting forward like a prow so he could make it through the gate. His old scissors were dull. It was quicker to tear the plastic with his bare hands. The mulch was wet and cold and stank like compost. Not halfway to the birdbath, they ran out and he had to go back to the Home Depot for more. With each bag, the rear of the Olds sagged, the springs creaking. At the end of the day they still had the whole right side left to do. His lower back hurt. For Emily, it was her fingers. They both took some Aleve and went to bed early.

Saturday the sky was low and the Home Depot was overrun. They spent all morning finishing, a misty drizzle wetting their faces, soaking their clothes. Rufus watched from the French doors, bored. It was a day to stay inside, Henry thought, but the yard looked good and he was glad to be done. After a hot shower, they had tomato soup and grilled cheese sandwiches, an old favorite of the children. Emily took a nap, leaving him free to putter in the basement. He got the Pirate game from Bradenton on his transistor, plugged in the jigsaw and started cutting pieces for a spice rack he was making for Chautauqua. He sanded and stained them on the bench, falling into a pleasant rhythm. The game went to the tenth inning, ending in an unsatisfying tie. When he checked his watch, he was shocked to find it was almost five.

As the local news signed off, the anchorman reminded viewers to spring ahead. The national news had a feature on why Ben Franklin invented daylight savings, and how several states were trying to repeal it. Henry didn't need them to tell him how arbitrary time was. For years he'd followed a rigid schedule, getting up at five-thirty so he could be at the lab by seven. Now he didn't know what day of the week it was, let alone the date. Emily was the keeper of the calendar, warning him of appointments and the grandchildren's birthdays like a secretary, but for the most part his time was his own. Like a farmer, he followed the seasons, one eye on the weather. Losing or gaining an hour didn't matter to him. Like jet lag, it was a question of simple relativity. The sun hadn't moved, only his position.

As with anything mechanical in the Maxwell household, the clocks were his responsibility. He waited until Emily was ready to head up to bed and went around the downstairs room by room. She used the stove and microwave every day, yet claimed not to know how to change the time. What was she going to do when he was gone? His computer would adjust automatically, and the atomic clock on his bookshelf. He wound the Black Forest cuckoo clock in the breakfast nook, waking the bird, inserted the key in the face of the grandfather clock and twisted, making the chimes ring as he brought the minute hand full circle. He'd locked up and turned off the lights when he saw the glow of her stereo.

"Tricky," he said, because it always got him.

Upstairs Emily had left the bathroom light on for him and was reading in bed, Rufus sacked out at her feet. Henry fixed the clock radios in the children's rooms and the banjo clock in the den before adding an hour to his father's watch and setting it on his dresser.

"We are officially in the future."

"What?" Emily lowered her book.

"We're living in the future for the next couple of hours."

"That's great," she said. "I'm reading."

The new time seemed wrong. It wasn't really that late, but he didn't feel like reading, and didn't bother turning on his light. His back ached from lifting all that mulch. He stretched, absorbing the warmth of the electric blanket. He'd forgotten to take his Aleve. Too late. He'd be up in three hours to pee anyway.

Finally Emily closed her book and rolled away from him, raised up on one elbow.

"I'm setting my alarm for eight," she warned.

"I don't think we'll need it," he said, but in the morning he was dreaming and didn't want to get up.

It was too early. His back hurt, and his eyes burned as if he'd been on the computer too long. As he was brushing his teeth, the cap of the toothpaste got away from him, bouncing along the counter. He lunged to catch it one-handed and batted it off the glass of the shower stall so it rolled into the corner behind the toilet. Stiffly, bent over, bracing himself on the closed lid, he was reaching for the cap when his back spasmed, making him grunt and straighten up. "Dammit."

The only handy tool was the plunger, which he immediately vetoed. Ultimately he used a towel, limply fishing in the corner. On his third try he managed to snag the cap, but as he was dragging it out, he knocked the toilet paper loose, the spring-loaded holder coming apart, sending the roll unfurling across the floor.

"Nothing's easy," he said, an observation his father applied to the universe when frustrated by a stripped screw or a balky engine, and deliberately, with the grim efficiency of a hired killer, Henry retrieved the roll and fit it back in place, rinsed off the cap, screwed it onto the tube and stuffed the towel in the hamper.

As every spring, the last clock he changed was the one in the Olds, a single touch of a button. After the bathroom, he was careful driving, remembering what Margaret had said. In church he prayed for her, for all those in the grip of addiction, and their loved ones. He was looking forward to talking to her, for once. He wanted to share his misadventures with the cap of the toothpaste and tell her she was right—a small point of agreement, but something. He knew she'd enjoy imagining him playing the fool, and that he'd exaggerate his bumbling to make her laugh. When she was a girl he used to make up stories for her. *Please*, she asked. *Pretty please? Okay. Once upon a time there was a brave little chicken named Margaret.* The plot had something to do with a fox and a dog and a chicken coop, he couldn't remember. Maybe she would. All afternoon he waited for her to call, but she never did.

The Fearsome Foursome

GOOD FRIDAY, KENNY AND LISA AND THE GRANDCHILDREN were scheduled to land around five, meaning Henry would have to battle rush hour traffic through the tunnel both ways. All week they braced for the invasion, getting the house ready, making beds and emptying dressers. Emily planned her menus like a general, her recipes marshaled on the dining room table. At Christmas her mashed potatoes had been salty, and though it had been Arlene who'd pointed it out, what she remembered was that Lisa had agreed too quickly.

"And she didn't have to say anything," Emily said. "That's what a polite guest would do. Arlene I expect it from. You wouldn't do that, would you?"

"No." His mother had taught him to eat everything on his plate and not complain, advice he'd followed, for better or worse, his whole life.

"No, because it's rude. I'm not making them again."

"I like your mashed potatoes."

"Tell that to her. Maybe she'll make you some."

She and Lisa had clashed from the beginning, a mismatch, yet at Penn Mac in the Strip, watching Emily choosing fancy organic cheeses for Saturday's appetizers, he sensed she was still hoping to impress her, as she'd hoped, years ago, to impress his mother. His mother had liked her for try-ing, a small-town girl so obviously out of her depth, spreading butter on her roll at the club with her fish knife. As the lady of the house, his mother's gift was making everyone feel welcome. Lisa felt no such obligation, and he wanted to tell Emily not to bother. There were some people who would never care for you no matter how hard you tried.

Thursday, in the midst of their preparations, Henry was supposed to go golfing. Fred Knapp was back from Sarasota and had gotten them a ten o'clock tee time at Buckhorn. Henry offered to cancel, but Emily said he should go. It was his first time out, and the weather was perfect. She had everything she needed to make the lasagna and planned on cooking all day. He'd just be in the way.

"Maybe we can get out next week," he said.

"Let me get through today first."

Loading his clubs into the Olds, he thought that after fifty years he still had to work at reading her. Not that he was wrong. She sounded put-upon, but if he stayed it would be worse. She honestly wanted him to go. At the same time, she needed him to appreciate the sacrifice she was making, though if anyone asked, she would say it was no sacrifice and that she loved to cook.

Golf was simpler. Their foursome had been playing together since the mid-seventies, when they were at the lab, and their games, like their person-alities, were fixed. Fred, who played all year long, was a big hitter with a terrific slice, where Cy Wallace was short and straight down the fairway. Henry's strength was his chipping, while his partner Jack Beeler lived and died by his putter. Together the Fearsome Foursome had won a dozen com-pany scrambles over the years, and if individually they now struggled to break 80, the competition for the scorecard—the ultimate prize, after a life-time of striving—was that much fiercer. Loser bought lunch.

The Parkway inbound was backed up to Churchill, and though he had nowhere to be, racing out of town past stopped traffic felt like playing hooky.

Murrysville was dully exotic, one long strip mall of stores he'd never visit. A creek wound alongside him as he burrowed into the hills, the road lined with mailboxes and raised ranches, landscapers guiding riding mowers over sprawling lawns dotted with forsythia and wishing wells. He couldn't imagine living out here, though it was actually closer to the lab, and probably cheaper. Safer, certainly. It was too late. He'd been born in the city and he would die there. He couldn't say why, but the idea filled him with pride.

Designed by Arnold Palmer, Buckhorn was supposed to be the centerpiece of an exclusive new development, an adult community of custom homes clustered around a championship links. The builders completed just the back nine before the bank foreclosed, leaving behind a maze of blank cul-de-sacs and a rusting bulldozer marooned in a sea of reeds off the second tee. The course was well tended, but its nine holes were useless for leagues, and in the middle of the week it was reliably empty. The clubhouse was the construction manager's leftover trailer with a pressure-treated deck and snack bar tacked on. Jack's Caddy was pulled up by the carts, Jack sitting on the back bumper, changing into his spikes. Besides a couple of muddy pickups at the far end of the lot, there were two huge SUVs and a Corvette parked together.

"Are they on already?" Henry asked.

"I guess. I didn't see them. How was your winter?"

"Good, how was yours?"

"Long."

"I hear you. Doesn't get better than this though."

"Here they come," Jack said of Fred and Cy, pulling in together. "Better late than never."

Cy was driving a new Acura. Next to the Olds it looked futuristic, all angles, like a stealth fighter. Emily would have said it was too young for him.

"What happened," Jack asked, "you hit the lottery?"

"It's last year's. I got a deal."

"Pretty snazzy."

Fred was unseasonably tan and wore an old Westinghouse-logo wind-breaker Henry had at home.

"How's Florida?" Henry asked.

"Like hell—hot, crowded and full of New Yorkers."

They would have all day to catch up, and dug in their bags, swapping their wallets and keys for gloves and tees and ball markers. Since the season hadn't officially started, the price for eighteen and a cart was only twenty-five dollars, a bargain. They donned their Pirates and Steelers and Nike caps, strapped in their bags and headed off. As always, Jack drove, flooring it, Henry gripping the handle built into the roof as they jolted over the rut-ted path, the wind cold on his cheeks.

The course was theirs, the threesome nowhere in sight, furthering the illusion of Buckhorn being their private club. One, like most opening holes, was a medium-sized par-four, straight, with acres of fairway. Henry stretched, taking extra practice swings to loosen up his back. Dew silvered the grass, capturing footprints, and he dried off the head of his driver with a towel. No one could remember who had honors from last year, prompting an Alzheimer's joke. Fred stepped up and hit a bomb that rose and then turned over, slicing sharply into the rough. "Fuck, a, duck."

Cy skulled his. It skimmed the women's tee, spinning up spray before dying in the wet grass.

"Ugly ugly ugly."

"At least it's straight."

Jack deferred to Henry.

He tested the wind before addressing his ball. Ideally he wanted to be on the rise just to the left of the white 150-yard marker. He had a tendency to open his front shoulder, and tucked it in. Head down, follow through. His practice swing was clean. He reset his feet and squared up the ball with the club face. He tried to take his time with his backswing. He didn't have to crush it, but he was anxious and he rushed, dipping on his back leg for more power, turning his hips early, and duck-hooked it into the rough.

"Terrible."

"It's all yours, Jack."

"No pressure."

His drive was long and straight, carrying the rise easily.

"Nice ball, Jack," Henry said.

"Somebody ate their Wheaties."

"You guys showed me the way."

"The wrong way."

The rough seemed high, but Henry made a nice recovery with his four-iron and a decent chip before leaving his putt short for a bogie.

"Hit the ball," he said, squeezing his Titleist as if to crush it.

He bogeyed two and three as well, hitting last, which he never liked. His back was fine, and his short game, he just couldn't get his driver going. Jack was the only one doing anything. Fred was all over the place. Cy lost a ball in somebody's yard and another in the pond on six. But they'd picked the right day, especially with the crazy weather they'd been having. Fred passed around sunscreen. Henry didn't need his jacket and tossed it in the basket. Waiting for Jack to hit, he stood absolutely still, arms crossed, a tee clamped in his teeth. Above the woods, hawks rode the thermals, circling, while close by a nail gun chunked. The trees were budding, bright clouds sailing through a too-blue sky, and though he knew it wasn't true, he had a sense of the world turning, and him along with it. He saw it as a promise. Winter was over, summer was coming, unstoppable as the creeks running high and cold with snowmelt.

After the turn, wading through the tall grass, searching for a stray three-wood, he came across a fresh pile of deer pellets like black beans and felt the same elemental thrill. Like the boy he'd been, a fisher for minnows and tracker of squirrels, as he approached the pond on twelve, navigating a minefield of goose poop, he listened for the plunk of frogs. A few years back a flock of wild turkeys had crossed a cart path right in front of him, and while he'd never seen them again, today, as always, he looked for them. A woodpecker rapping unseen, a chipmunk chirping, a trio of turtles sunning on a log—everything served as a reminder that he needed to get outside more.

He wasn't going to win, but he wasn't going to lose either, and relaxed, parring fifteen and sticking his second shot within inches of the pin on sixteen for a gimme birdie. He gave back the stroke on seventeen, overthinking his approach and plugging it in a bunker, and closed with another bogie. After the last putt, they shook hands like the pros.

"Good game, Henry."

"Good game."

He managed an 83, not bad for his first time out. Jack, solid all day, took the card. Cy stood lunch, thanks to the penalty strokes—sandwiches and beers on the deck. They replayed their favorite shots, bemoaning their fluffed chips and yipped putts. The sun was warm and the course was empty. The temptation was to stay and play another eighteen, but they had to get back. They sauntered to their cars and changed into their shoes.

"Any big plans for Easter?" Jack asked him.

"My son and his family are coming in from Boston."

"Nice. We're heading down to my daughter's in D.C. Seven hours in the car."

"Good luck," Henry said.

Driving home, he marveled at how fully he'd put their visit—and Lisa—out of his mind. It was why he loved golf. On the course he concentrated on the next shot and let go of his worries. Now they returned, inescapable as the fast-food drive-thrus and nurseries and discount tile outlets of Murrysville, and as he crawled from light to light, he fretted, trying to recall the awe he'd felt watching the clouds scudding over the hills, but the spell, being delicate, was broken, and he felt foolish for thinking it had meant anything.

In the garage, while Rufus barked, Henry lifted his clubs out of the trunk to make room for their luggage tomorrow. He was tired, and the bag was heavy. He'd be going out again next week, maybe with Emily, and leaned it against the stepladder.

"Yes," he told Rufus, "I'm home. It's very exciting."

Emily had the back door open, so he could hear her music. She was stirring something at the stove and looked up when Rufus pushed through the screen ahead of him.

"How was it?"

"It was beautiful. What can I do?"

She pointed past him with her free hand.

In the corner behind the door sat the silverware tray and the drawer in pieces.

"Hell," Henry said.

"Hell, indeed," Emily said.

The Designated Driver

HE HATED US AIRWAYS. THEY'D BEEN DELAYED TWICE ALREADY, thanks to the rain in Philly, and no one at the ticket counter could tell him anything. When the arrival time on the monitor slipped again, he used his cell phone to update Emily, who was busy entertaining Arlene. By now she'd had a few glasses of wine and laughed at the absurdity of it all. She'd keep dinner warm for them, though with the drive they wouldn't sit down to the table till well after nine.

"Go ahead and eat," Henry said.

"We're eating. We're having appetizers."

In the background Arlene added something, but the concourse was noisy and he could barely hear Emily. He wasn't good with the cell phone. He always felt like he was yelling.

"The children should get something," she said. "There's no reason they should go hungry."

The concession was unnecessary. Henry hadn't mentioned it, for fear of upsetting her, but they'd eaten a good hour ago. He was hungry himself. At the end of the day his energy faded. He could use a coffee, but it would keep him up later, and guiltily, aware that he was spoiling his dinner, he bought a

Clark Bar at a newsstand and gobbled it down, the chewy nougat sticking to his back teeth.

Upstairs, in the one bar outside security, the TVs were showing highlights from the Masters. He watched until a hockey game came on and then wandered the hall, scrutinizing crayon drawings by schoolchildren and reading about the Tuskegee Airmen.

Their flight had boarded and was on its way, according to the monitor.

"Hallelujah," Emily said.

He waited in an atrium between the rental car desks, watching the arriving passengers descend a pair of tall escalators that emerged like chutes from the ceiling, clusters of loved ones gathered at the bottom recognizing them and stepping forward. Was it spring break? There seemed to be a lot of college students. Each reunion reminded him of waiting with Emily, years ago, for Kenny, coming back from Emerson. At the time, Margaret had shacked up with one of her druggie boyfriends and stopped talking to them, leaving him an only child. Their holidays were quiet, Kenny going out at night with friends from high school and then sleeping late, drinking all their beer. For Henry it was enough to have him home. Emily, of course, wanted more. In the car, after they'd seen him off, she cried, and while Henry felt for her, Kenny had his own life now, as they had theirs, and that was as it should be.

At Penn Station his mother had wept when he left for basic training, knowing he was shipping off to war. His father had shaken his hand and looked him in the eye, as if this was another pact between them. He would have been embarrassed if his father had held or kissed him, and was relieved. Late in life, after his mother had died, his father cried at baptisms and funerals and sappy movies on TV, age stripping away a final protective layer. Now Henry could feel the same softening taking place inside him, a helpless grief for the past and boundless pity for the world, and that was right too. No fool like an old fool.

A flight had arrived, a few early birds with roller bags stepping down the escalator on the left ahead of the crush. Around him, people stood to get a better look, blocking his view, making him get up as well. Sometimes you could tell where passengers had come from by their clothes—Red Sox hats for Boston, shorts for Florida. He didn't see any Phillies or Villanova gear, just a Navy sweatshirt, which could mean anything. Quickly the crowd thinned and dissipated, the escalator running empty again.

The monitor said the plane was at the gate.

The escalator on the right dispensed a new batch of arrivals. Henry positioned himself opposite the bottom, hoping to spot the children before they saw him. One family held up signs welcoming home a soldier. As Henry searched the moving queue for a uniform, the other escalator released a second wave, among them a teenaged girl with Down syndrome in an oversized Flyers jersey.

He was picking his way through the mob making for baggage claim when he saw Ella waving, and there was Kenny behind her, and Lisa with a hand on Sam's shoulder as if he might fall.

Henry posted himself to one side so they wouldn't be in the way.

Ella reached him first, bright-eyed and stick-thin, shouldering a massive backpack. In his arms she was a bird, all bones.

"There's my Ella Bella."

"Hey, Grampa."

"What have you got in there, bricks?"

"Homework."

"Be careful," Lisa said, holding back Sam, who looked bleary, a purple crescent like a shiner under one eye. "He's got a sinus infection. We almost didn't come."

"I'm sorry, buddy. That's no fun." Henry squeezed his shoulder. He'd been sick at Christmas too, a stomach bug Emily suspected he'd passed on to Rufus, an accusation he thought odd.

He gave Lisa a quick peck. "How's everything else?"

"Other than spending all day in the airport," she said, "peachy."

"Good old Agony Airlines."

"Hey, Dad." Kenny embraced him—a recent development, and a welcome one, yet it still felt clumsy, like strangers learning to dance. "Thanks for coming to get us."

"I wasn't going to let you take the bus."

"Sorry we're so late."

"It wasn't your fault."

"It's been a long day."

Henry sympathized, remembering their vacations, impatience giving way to mute anger, brute will, and finally resignation. "You're here. That's what counts."

There was a backup at baggage claim, too many flights arriving at once, and by the time they got on the road it was past nine. He let Kenny tell Emily.

"They did," he said into his phone. "We just had a snack. Okay, love you too."

He closed the phone. "They're waiting dinner on us."

"I told you," Lisa said from the backseat.

"I told them to go ahead and eat," Henry said.

"It's fine," Kenny said. "Actually I'm a little hungry."

At least they didn't have to fight traffic. Except for some airport shuttles, the parkway was empty, billboards floating out of the dark. They rode in silence, Sam falling asleep against Lisa. When they emerged from the tunnel and the lights of downtown towered above them like Oz, Henry let the view pass without comment.

Emily and Arlene were waiting for them on the back porch. Behind the screen, Rufus whined, excited.

"We were afraid you weren't going to make it," Emily said, taking Ella in her arms.

She ignored Lisa's warning and kissed Sam, who shied away, hiding his face against his mother.

"He's exhausted," Lisa explained, suffering the briefest of hugs.

"I'm sure all of you are," Emily said, and passed her to Arlene. "Thank you for coming."

"Of course, Mom," Kenny said. "Thanks for having us."

"I'm going to take him up." Lisa didn't wait for Kenny to answer, just herded Sam toward the door. When she opened the screen, Rufus pushed through, jumping on Ella.

"Down!" Emily said. "Now!"

Henry dropped the bags he was carrying to help her, but Emily already had his collar.

"What are you doing?" she said. "You don't do that. Honestly. All right, let's get something to eat. I don't know about the rest of you, but I'm starving."

Henry thought Lisa might apologize, but she didn't. When he delivered their bags to Kenny's room, she and Kenny broke off their conversation as if caught.

"I don't think she did it on purpose," Henry said in the kitchen.

"She wasn't thinking," Emily said.

"What can I do?"

"Nothing. It's all done."

There was a broken wineglass in the trash. He hadn't noticed on the porch, but Arlene was bombed, slurring her words. He'd have to drive her home later, and took a pass on the Chianti, making dinner interminable. After sitting in the oven all night, the lasagna was dried out, the top layer brittle. Emily didn't finish hers, apologizing to the table. Kenny had seconds and helped Ella clear the plates.

Lisa and Ella were headed up.

"Don't you want dessert?" Emily asked. She'd had Henry make a special trip to Prantl's for their almond torte.

"I'm sure it's wonderful, but we've been up since six this morning."

"Thank you for dinner," Ella said, giving Emily a kiss on the cheek.

"Yes," Lisa said, "thank you."

"I'm sorry it wasn't better."

"It was fine." She was trying to be polite, yet Henry detected a trace of exasperation, and knew Emily would make something of it later.

Kenny stayed and had a good-sized slice. It was too late for coffee. Instead, he had a scotch, Emily a port.

Now that everyone else was settled, Henry felt safe taking Arlene home. In the car, nodding off, she muttered to herself. He had to dig her keys out of her purse and help her up the stairs. The fish drifted in the glowing tank. On their old dining room table sat a stack of magazines and one of newspapers tied with twine, ready for recycling. "You're a good brother," she kept saying as he helped her off with her shoes and into bed. He left the bathroom light on in case she needed it later, and made sure her door was locked, wondering what kind of shape she'd be in for the flower show tomorrow.

Driving down Highland, the night's final mission complete, he thought of the Dewar's waiting for him like a reward, and the promise of good talk, just the three of them like the old days, but when he got home the lights in the dining room were out and the house was quiet. Someone had done the dishes—probably Kenny, ever conscientious—the dishtowel draped over the handle of the oven. Upstairs the doors were closed, the hall a box. Emily snored, one arm flung across his pillow. He still wanted a scotch, and pictured himself sneaking down to the sideboard and drinking it in the dark like Margaret or his father at the end, alone in his condo, raving like a mad king in his boxers and socks. The idea troubled him, and rather than join that sad fraternity, he changed into his pajamas, crept past Rufus sacked at the foot of the bed and slid in beside Emily, careful not to wake her.

Tulip Fever

HE'D BEEN GOING TO THE FLOWER SHOW HIS WHOLE LIFE. From its advent during the city's gilded age, his Grandmother Chase's garden club had been responsible for the tulips framing the main entrance of Phipps Conservatory. Every spring, save the two years he was overseas, he and Arlene helped her weed the massive beds that welcomed visitors inside the grand Beaux-Arts solarium, and even then he'd asked after them in his letters home, knowing she'd appreciate it. He was no poet like his uncle, but the glass palace of Phipps seemed impossibly fantastic and fragile when everything around him had been smashed flat.

Like Easter, the flower show signaled rebirth and the resilience of life, and that first spring after the war, before he met Emily, he spent countless hours silently tending the beds, remembering the narrow roads and mountain towns of the Black Forest. There, on his knees, covered in mud, lost in irredeemable thoughts, he found Sloan, or she found him.

She was a Whitney, famously engaged to a Mellon. He knew her from childhood, from church and the garden parties at his grandmother's. She'd developed earlier than the other girls, and ran with an older crowd. At fifteen her parents had shipped her off to a Swiss convent school as if she might become a nun. She was tall and slim-hipped and gray-eyed, spoiled as a cat. She scared him. She didn't care. "You don't like it," she said, knighting him with a broken stem, "you can kiss my lily-white behind." He liked it. She had a Packard convertible she refused to let him drive. They used his rusty Hudson, a jalopy bought with combat pay, parking up by the Schenley overlook, her long bronze hair freed from her scarf. Her neck flushed when she was heated, red as a rash. He'd never seen a black bra before, and was shocked. How easily they betrayed the rest of the world. He could say she confused him, but that was just an excuse. He knew what he wanted was wrong. He'd spent his whole life trying to do right.

Because she was rich and wild he didn't take her seriously, as if she was slumming, and by the time he understood she wanted him to rescue her, it was too late. They raged at each other, making up tearily, their secret torturing and sustaining them. He gave her a key to his rented room as if it were a ring. They made love recklessly, breaking his bedframe, spilling whisky, shattering lamps. The wedding was announced, the invitations sent (his grandmother received one). "You know this is over once I'm married," she said. He knew, desperately, yet when it happened, for months he expected her to turn up at his door after midnight, and was hurt when she didn't. Only later did he read in the paper that she'd moved to New York.

He was still mourning her when he met Emily, and partly out of delicacy and partly because it reflected poorly on him, he couldn't tell her. He must have been mad, he reasoned. Both of them were, there was no other explanation. He'd loved her but he'd been mistaken. Now he had to pay. He'd thought she was saving him, restoring to him all the strength and beauty of the world. Then why, so many times with her, had he wanted to die?

Where Sloan was unstable, Emily was steady. She kept a log of every penny she spent, and when her aunt June sent a check, she didn't splurge, just offered to split dinner. She played the piano and wanted to be a schoolteacher. "Let's keep our hands to ourselves," she'd say, straightening her blouse. Sloan would have called her a virgin and a grind, but she was fresh and earnest, and she believed in him. She didn't need to know what he'd done during the war, trusting it was necessary. He was braver than she'd ever be, she said, an assumption he let stand despite dire objections. That she thought him good was flattering, after hating himself so often with Sloan, and he vowed he wouldn't propose to Emily until he could live up to her rose-colored image of him. Gradually, with her help, he became the man she thought he was, and if the urge to confess never left him, as time passed it seemed less important. He'd had a girlfriend, like anyone else. He rarely thought of her, Emily so filled his life, and then the children, and his friends, his work at the lab. Only in spring, when the tulips bloomed, did he recall Sloan's neck and the smell of her hair and how they drank in bed and fought all night, trying to save each other from their preordained fates.

Now, standing in line outside Phipps with Emily and Arlene and the whole family, watching Ella take a close-up of a tulip, their weeks together seemed a dream, as if they'd never happened. Sometimes he wished they hadn't. At others he was grateful. That was Sloan. After all these years, he still didn't know what to make of her.

"They always look so nice," Emily said.

"They almost don't look real," Lisa said, leaning in to inspect a red one.

"You know your Grampa and Aunt Arlene used to do all this."

"All of it?" Ella asked.

"It felt like it sometimes," Arlene said.

"We had help," Henry said.

"It looks like a lot of work."

"It was," he said. "But we had fun."

"He had fun," Arlene said. "I didn't. It was work."

The line was finally moving. Of course they'd come on the busiest day. Once they were inside he'd be fine. Out here he could see Sloan kneeling beside him, her fingernails packed with dirt, a streak of mud on her cheek, a bright wisp of hair sneaking from beneath her scarf.

Sloan Maxwell, she'd said. *It has a nice ring to it, don't you think?*

"Here we go," Emily said. "Get your tickets ready."

Lisa took Sam's hand, Emily took Ella's. It would be like the tropics inside, the air perfumed, the panes fogged and running with condensation. That was the miracle, he thought. Anyone could raise flowers in a hothouse. Their tulips had grown through the snow, at the mercy of the cold. Though it wasn't possible scientifically, he liked to believe some of the bulbs they'd planted still bloomed. At the doors, the line split, funneling through a bank of turnstiles. As they shuffled forward, he looked back as if he were leaving her, then turned away, letting Kenny go ahead of him so he was the last one in.

St. Henry of Assisi

THERE WAS A BIRD IN CHURCH. DURING THE OFFERING, A SPAR-row flitted across the open space of the chancel, looped around the no-longer-shrouded rood and lit on a ledge of a pillar. Sam, bored up until then, pointed. Henry shared his delight, thinking it a happy sign. The sparrow cocked its head, blinking, looking out over the congregation from its niche as if it belonged there.

The service didn't stop. The doxology blared and they all rose while the ushers processed with their collection baskets, delivering them to Father John to be blessed. As a member of the vestry and chair of the last capital campaign, Henry knew a normal take barely covered that day's operating costs, but the weather was perfect and the house was even bigger than it had been for the Christmas pageant. He imagined all they could do with the windfall. The icemaker in the parish hall kitchen had died. The fridge needed a new compressor.

The sparrow was still there. It must have come in through an open win-dow, though the only one he could think of without a screen was in the second-floor men's room, and that door would be shut. With all the wind, they'd had problems with cracked panes of old stained glass letting in the rain. Even a temporary fix was expensive, but they had no choice. Nothing was more destructive than water.

The organ roared, and there went the sparrow, Sam tracking it with a finger as it flew across the rood and over the roofed pulpit, drawn to the sunstruck windows of the transept, and then, as if sensing an invisible wall, stalled, wings fluttering, and swooped back around, retreating to its perch. It was lost, probably confused by all the noise. Once everyone left, the sexton could open the doors wide and it could find its way out, or so Henry hoped. Last fall a squirrel had gotten into their attic and built a huge nest of leaves he discovered only when he went up to bring down the Christmas decorations. He set a Havahart trap himself, but Emily didn't trust him on a ladder, so he had to pay a roofer to install new flashing around the chimney. He couldn't imagine what an exterminator would charge to catch the bird. He'd probably have to poison it, which Henry didn't want to picture.

They knelt for the Lord's Prayer. Though Sam couldn't read yet, Lisa shared her prayer book with him as if he might follow along, and Henry remembered his mother doing the same. *Give us this day our daily bread, and forgive us our trespasses, as we forgive those who trespass against us.* The weekend had gone well, no major blowups. They were already packed. After brunch at the club, he'd take them to the airport. On the way back he needed to stop at the Home Depot for propane and Drano and one other thing he'd forgotten. In the silence accompanying the breaking of the bread, he watched the sparrow and tried to recall the third item, the list revolving like a litany—propane and Drano and what, propane and Drano and what.

The music at communion was Vaughan Williams, according to the program, the bell choir and a brass quartet accompanying a hired tenor from the Pittsburgh Opera. The ladies of the Altar Guild had done their usual wonderful job. Gaudy flower arrangements worthy of Phipps Conservatory lined the stairs and choir stalls and crowded the chancel rail, where the great

Alpha-Omega candle, in storage most of the year, shone forth the good news. Bare, in Pittsburgh's gray weather, Calvary could be austere. Today, dressed up, with the congregation in their best and the clear spring light coloring the windows, the sanctuary felt warm and luxurious. Visitors would never suspect they were running a deficit.

When they came back from taking Communion, the ledge was empty. He and Sam glanced upward, scanning the vault. He found the bird first, tucked into a niche above the new speakers, and pointed it out to Sam, who smiled at their secret.

Receiving the Easter blessing, Henry remembered: grass seed. He wished he had a pen so he could make a list, but knew Emily would disapprove. He'd just have to memorize it. Propane and Drano and grass seed.

"Go forth and serve the world," Father John said, arms raised, dismissing them.

"Thanks be to God. Alleluia, alleluia."

"Is it over?" Sam asked.

"Yes," Lisa said, "you're free."

Released, the congregation seemed hesitant to leave, lingering in the pews, milling in the aisle, waiting to pay their respects to Father John. The line was long, and Henry took the opportunity to step away and collar the sexton as he was crossing the transept.

His name was Ed McWhirter, and Henry had been part of the committee that hired him. Burly and bearded like a professional wrestler, he was dressed not for church but like a mechanic, in a gray work shirt, black dungarees and heavy brogans, a key ring the size of a softball riding his hip. Henry had never seen him wear anything else.

The bird was still in its niche above the speaker.

"I don't know how it got in," Henry said, "but it can't stay."

"It won't," McWhirter said with the conviction of a hit man, and Henry believed him.

In the car, mostly for the children's benefit, Emily gushed over the lilies and the bell choir and how well the tenor sang. "I do love the Easter service, even better than Christmas. It's more of a celebration. What was your favorite part?"

"The bird," Sam said, getting a laugh, and Henry admitted it was his too.

Solutions

IT HADN'T RAINED IN WEEKS, AND THE BACKYARD WAS DOT-
ted with dead spots where Rufus had peed, burning circles in the grass,
turning it a brittle yellow, a natural, low-level chemical warfare. Emily kept
his water bowl filled, providing him with an endless supply of ammunition.
Six, eight, ten times a day he went. Henry didn't remember Duchess having
such an active bladder, or maybe, being female, her urine was milder, less of
an herbicide. All of his efforts against the grubs and voles and dandelions
and squirrels were squandered so long as Rufus used the lawn for his private
toilet. Henry couldn't walk him every time he needed to go, like his last outs
before bed, standing by like an accomplice while he inflicted more damage—
could only try to dilute the poison, uncoiling the hose and dragging it across
the spotlit yard to soak the affected area.

"What in the world are you doing?" Emily asked from the doorway.

"I'm trying to save what's left of the grass."

"I'm going up," she said. "I'll see you when you're done marking your
territory."

His idea was to cordon off the yard with string except for a corner behind
the raspberry canes, turn the dead spots and plant new grass. By the time it

came in, Rufus would be used to going in one place. Henry had bought four jugs of all-in-one seed rated for a mix of sun and shade. The key was watering often.

"I wish you luck," Emily said, never taking her eyes from her book.

"You don't think it'll work?"

"I think you're going to drive yourself and me crazy. Dogs pee. That's what they do."

"I'm not trying to stop him from peeing, I just need him to pee in one place."

"You're already driving me crazy. All I want is to read this one page."

Rufus murmured as if they were disturbing him.

"Okay, Grumpy Joe," Henry said.

"Shush."

He wasn't obsessed, as she implied, just focused on a goal and the best means of achieving it. An engineer, he had a respect for the practical that extended to every facet of living, and was happiest when he saw an opportunity to fix a problem. Not everything could be perfected, but his natural inclination—with machines or systems—was to look for design flaws and ways to eliminate them. The thrill was seeing the new iteration succeed, a victory they'd finally been denied with the Odysseus, testing it at Jackass Flats to prove it could fly yet never sending it into space. Nine years he'd worked on the project before Congress cut their funding. The prototype Henry had pictured navigating Saturn's rings now rested in a crate in some desert warehouse, already a museum piece. Since he'd retired, he missed the challenge of the impossible and brought that same dogged curiosity and inventiveness to his household tasks. In place of titanium, he worked with white pine. Instead of tweaking the reactor, he tuned the mower. There were days when he was at the Home Depot four or five times. Emily joked with the children that the clerks knew him by name. It wasn't true. No one cared who he was, just another old fogey who needed help finding the Gumout. Henry didn't mind. Interplanetary travel or cleaning a carburetor, the satisfaction was the same. At the end of the day he liked to feel he'd gotten something done. There was nothing he enjoyed more than lying in bed, making a list of all he had to do tomorrow.

In the morning, as Rufus watched, Henry sectioned off the yard, using a packet of wooden shims as stakes, stretching the string taut, forming rhomboid plots on both sides of the flagstones. The string wasn't knee-high, a single flimsy strand, yet for now, unsure what it signified, Rufus honored it like barbed wire. Turning the dead spots took longer than Henry had thought. By the time he spread and watered the seed it was midafternoon and the sun was behind the house. He surveyed his work like a farmer.

"Okay," he said, "grow."

The next morning he followed Rufus out in his slippers to check on the bare spots, as if grass might have sprouted overnight. Just mud. It was wet enough, and the weather was supposed to be warm. Rufus did his business behind the raspberries and came dashing back, ready for his breakfast.

"Good job," Henry said to reinforce the lesson.

Later, after a frustrating round of golf, he stood at the French doors and watched a fat robin hop across the yard, stop in the middle of a muddy patch and peck at the ground. He rapped a knuckle against the glass. The robin ignored him until he opened the door, then settled on the peak of the garage, waiting for him to leave.

"Go on, get!" Henry shouted, bursting out, flailing his arms, and it flew off over the Coles'.

"You are aware," Emily said, "that you look like a crazy person."

"He's eating my seeds."

"You think he's the only one?"

Sparrows, finches, pigeons, doves—all the birds that frequented their feeders were chowing down as if this were dessert. As much as he might want to, he couldn't stand guard over the plot like a scarecrow. Emily suggested hanging flattened pot pie tins, but they only made the strings sag. He thought of fixing boxes of chicken wire over the spots, except then she would be right. He needed to be reasonable. In the end, he resigned himself to what he hoped would be acceptable losses, and still, every time he saw a bird on the lawn, he knocked on the window. When knocking didn't work, he barked.

"You're worse than Rufus," Emily said.

"I'm not the one who ruined the lawn."

"Oh my God, Henry. He didn't do it on purpose. He's a dog."

Nights he set out the sprinkler, going barefoot, the cuffs of his trousers rolled, moving it from one side of the yard to the other while it was still arcing, spraying him in the face, wetting his shirt. After a full week, there was no visible growth. Had he overseeded? Overwatered? He was a patient man. All he wanted was some sign of progress.

The next morning, instead of new shoots poking through the mud, he found a paw print. When he reported it to Emily, she admitted that Rufus might have crossed the lines last night chasing a rabbit.

"You have to watch him all the time," Henry said.

"I can't stop him from chasing bunnies."

"If you see a bunny, don't let him out."

"I didn't see one. I can't see in the dark like you."

Once he got the water bill, he stopped sprinkling every night. He watched the weather, hoping the rain would save him. The scattered showers Channel 11 promised were never enough, leaving the patches blond as sawdust, and then one night it rained too much, a thunderstorm lighting up the sky, a downpour turning the mud into slurry, washing out spots. To make certain, he decided to reseed.

"So we're starting all over again," Emily asked.

"That's correct."

"How much does sod cost?"

"We can grow grass. There's nothing wrong with our grass except someone peeing on it."

While he tended to the new batch, she concentrated on Rufus. Among her many catalogs, she received one called Solutions, which featured hare-brained yet expensive household gizmos he associated with in-flight magazines. Without consulting him, she ordered a flat rock impregnated with a scent that, by some occult principle, was supposed to entice dogs to mark it. While Henry was skeptical, he appreciated the support, and by now he was desperate enough to try anything. If it didn't work, they could return it within thirty days and get their money back.

Emily placed the rock in the far corner behind the raspberries, in a mossy notch beside the downspout. At first she led Rufus to it and stood there pointing, encouraging him to go, which, after some prompting, he did—just a token squat in the grass, not on the rock at all. If Henry sometimes discounted Emily's judgment, he never doubted her determination. To prove a point, she'd make Henry himself pee on the rock. Every time she took Rufus out now, she walked him to the corner. Grateful, Henry followed suit, and eventually, through sheer repetition, Rufus grew used to it, heading directly there before they stepped off the porch.

Within a week the new seed germinated, sending forth fine, needle-like blades. Henry gave them room to grow, going creakily to one knee to pinch up wayward pebbles and flakes of old leaves and the tender sprigs of baby weeds he'd accidentally encouraged. He misted his crop with the sprayer, careful not to overwater, and every morning admired its slow progress like a proud father.

"It looks good," Emily said.

"It's a start."

Though he was hopeful, so far their gains were modest. The patches were sparse compared to the rest of the yard, which had grown thick and bushy and needed to be cut. He took down the strings and stakes and skirted the new areas with the mower, tipping it on two wheels so it didn't crush the seed-lings, clipping the scruffy fringes with Emily's garden shears, in the process tearing open a blister.

In the end the real triumph was Emily's, teaching Rufus to use the corner.

Though the rock had nothing to do with it, when Emily told the story at coffee hour, she gave it all the credit.

"Where did you find it?" Dodie Aiken asked.

"It was from a catalog. I'm drawing a blank. Henry, help me. What's the name of that catalog?"

His victory wasn't as clear-cut. When the new grass finally filled in, it was a deeper green. After he'd waited so long, now it grew too fast, bristling higher like the hair on Rufus's back when he heard the mailman approaching, and even after he removed the stakes for good and mowed everything the same height, the new patches stood out, the yard spotted as if diseased.

"I think it looks fine," Emily said. "It feels nice."

"It's better than it was," Henry said, but often, by himself, gazing out the French doors before dinner or looking down from Kenny's old room, he thought he should have just ripped it all up and started from scratch.

Mimosas

FOR MOTHER'S DAY, SINCE THE CHILDREN COULDN'T BE THERE, he took Emily to the club for brunch. Surrounded by large, lively parties decked out in their Sunday best, they shared a quiet table for two. He recognized several young families from Calvary, the boys in blue blazers and ties, the girls in pinafores and Mary Janes—perennials Kenny and Margaret had worn thirty years ago. The flocked wallpaper was the same, and the crystal chandeliers, the servers in their white jackets and gloves reaching across to refill water goblets and deliver fresh rosettes of butter. While nothing had changed in generations, the passage of time seemed pronounced here, as in a museum. As a child he'd stood in the same buffet line, holding the same heavy plate rimmed with gold, still warm from the dishwasher, looking past the gauntlet of salads and steaming chafing dishes to the dessert table. The handles of the silver were worn smooth from use, the club monogram softened. The finger bowls, the sterling salt and pepper shakers and candlesticks—everywhere he looked were relics, themselves included.

Knowing she liked mimosas, he ordered them a pair.

He raised his glass. "Happy Mother's Day."

"I'm not your mother."

"You're the mother of my children."

"That's different."

"It counts."

"I suppose."

Emily smacked her lips and frowned as if hers were sour. "I miss being a mother."

"I didn't know you could quit."

"When they're young they need you all the time. I miss being needed like that."

"They still need you."

"It's different when they're little. They're still sweet. After six or seven they don't need you as much. That's why it was so nice having Sam here."

"It *was* nice." She'd actually spent most of her time that weekend with Ella, who at twelve seemed perfectly sweet to him—as did all the grandchildren— but he knew better than to contradict her. "I need you."

"Thank you, but it's not quite the same. Though I must say you are pretty helpless."

He clinked glasses with her again. "Rufus needs you."

"That is true, he's my baby. I don't know why it makes me sad. It's stupid. It's just life."

"It's not stupid," he said.

"I don't know, lately I've been thinking about my mother, being stuck with just me. I didn't make things easy for her."

"She was very proud of you."

"I know that, that's not what I'm talking about. Imagine if we just had Margaret."

He didn't want to. "You're not at all like Margaret."

"Please, I know what I'm like. Where do you think she gets it from?"

Her temper, she meant, not the drinking or the secretiveness. Those were from his side. "And where did you get it from?"

"That's the mystery. My mother and father could never figure it out. I think it was just me."

"You turned out all right."

"That was later. For the longest time we fought over every little thing, and then I left—just like Margaret. How did things change? Because at the beginning everything was good. That's what I've been thinking about lately."

"That's a lot."

"I'm sorry. I shouldn't have told you."

"No, I need to know these things."

"Maybe a little heavy for brunch."

"Maybe." The drinks were skimpy—his glass was nearly empty. "To your mother."

"To my mother. And yours, God bless her."

"Do you want another? It is your day."

"Ow. Twist my arm."

The second seemed sweeter.

"This is nice," Emily said, taking his hand. "I suppose we should get something to eat."

"I suppose."

"It wouldn't do to be blotto for her call."

"No, it wouldn't."

One thing about the club had changed—the food had gotten better. A chef's station at the end of the buffet was offering her favorite, lobster Benedict, which lifted her mood, along with another mimosa. For dessert they had bananas Foster, made tableside, wispy blue flames licking over the bubbling butter and brown sugar.

"Definitely not on the diet," she said.

"Banana's a fruit."

She didn't mention her mother again until they were in the Olds, on their way home. Out of nowhere, as if picking up the conversation, she said, "I don't think she knew what to do with me. I wasn't a bad child, I was just stubborn. I remember her locking me in my room when I refused to listen. I'd be banging on the door and she'd be downstairs vacuuming or doing laundry. Now it sounds bizarre, but back then I didn't think it was strange. I thought that was how everybody lived."

"What about your father?"

"He'd spank me, but that was easy. He didn't want to, he just did it for her benefit. That was normal for the time. You know."

"I do," he said, though his father had never touched him. At worst, his mother might twist his ear.

"I don't know why, being locked in bothers me more. Being ignored. I don't understand what she thought it would teach me."

"To mind her."

"It didn't. It made me hate her."

Drink normally turned her maudlin and philosophical. He waited for her to qualify the remark, to say she forgave her, but she was watching the old mansions on Fifth slide by, vestiges of the city's gilded past.

"Do you think Margaret hates me?"

"No," he said. "Why do you say that?"

"I didn't treat her very well."

"She didn't treat you very well either. In any case, she can't say you ignored her."

"Maybe I should have been more like you."

It was tricky ground. While long ago he'd decided to let Margaret live her own life, Emily, out of guilt or the misplaced need to save her, still wanted to believe they could fix things, even on occasion defending her against him. Sometimes, for Emily's sake, he wished she would give up, but understood she couldn't. Just as often he doubted his own position, accusing himself of coldness, cowardice. What kind of father had so little faith in his daughter?

"It wouldn't work," he said. "That's not who you are."

"It would be easier. I get tired of it."

"She's lucky to have you for a mother."

"I don't know about that."

"I do," he said.

It must have been the right thing, because that was the end of the subject, though he expected any second for her to start again.

Kenny and Lisa and Sam and Ella were on the machine. "This is your Mother's Day song," they sang. "It isn't very long."

"Very nice," Emily said, erasing it.

Margaret didn't call till late that afternoon.

"Why, thank you, dear," Emily said, delighted, as if surprised. "Happy Mother's Day to you too."

She set aside her crossword, turned the music down and wandered into the dining room, as if for privacy, where she stood looking out the French doors. Behind the *Times*'s science section, Henry listened for any hint of discord. He couldn't hear what she was saying, only her tone, and gauged it for the smallest trace of impatience. In the car he'd reassured her that Margaret didn't hate her, as if it were an impossibility. Now he could see them screaming at each other across the table, Margaret flinging down her napkin and stalking for the stairs with Emily right behind. He and Kenny learned not to wait for her to return. They ate in silence, the cuckoo clock ticking in the breakfast nook.

Emily laughed, a false alarm, prompting a grumble from Rufus, sacked out on the hearth. She wasn't saying much, just nodding along. After a while she came back into the living room and made a yammering puppet of her hand. In her more manic phases, Margaret had a tendency to ramble.

"All right, I have to go get dinner started. No rest for the wicked. I hope you have a lovely time. Your father sends his love. Thank you. I love you too, dear."

She hung up and replaced the phone in the holder.

"How is she?"

"She sounded good."

"Good."

"The big excitement there is that Sarah's going to be the lead in *Bye Bye Birdie*. Apparently she has a major crush on Birdie. That's a quote—'major.'"

As she relayed the details, he thought he'd worried for no reason. She and Margaret battled the way he and Arlene had as children—endlessly, innocently, being natural rivals. He understood that bond, and yet as much as he wanted to, he couldn't stop replaying what she'd said in the car about her mother—the locked door and the vacuum—and wondered why she'd picked today, of all days, to unburden herself. Having always been loved, he liked to think he'd never hated anyone, especially the people closest to him. They were different, the two of them. He couldn't fault her honesty. Any other time he would have welcomed her confession, but he was unprepared for it, and while it paled in comparison to his own secrets, at heart he was shocked, and couldn't shake the feeling that it had become, already, unfairly, something he would never forget.

Root-X

THE SEWERS ON GRAFTON STREET, LIKE SO MANY IN PITTS-
burgh, were old, made of glazed terra-cotta pipe prone to cracking. Roots
snaked their way in, their blind capillary hairs curling, forming balls that
clogged the lines. Plugged solid, they gradually filled with a mix of sewage and wastewater that backed up and overflowed the drain in the basement, leaving a stinking pool Henry couldn't squeegee away until the
plumber had come.

It was the price of owning an old house, along with sagging floors and
drafty windows and coal dust in the attic. Rather than dig up the front yard
and drop fifteen thousand they didn't have to replace the line with a single
impregnable length of PVC, every spring and fall Henry flushed three cup-
fuls of bright blue copper sulfate down the powder room toilet, closing the
door so Rufus couldn't get in. The crystals were deadly, according to the
nonrecyclable container, and though Henry was no chemist, he accepted
their toxicity as a testament to their effectiveness. The first day of spring
he'd duly carried out the task marked on his calendar, so he was surprised,
the morning before they were supposed to go up to Chautauqua to open the

cottage, as he was retrieving their rusty old cooler, to discover a narrow puddle of water on the basement floor.

"You've got to be kidding."

Halfway between the dehumidifier and the drain, it might have been from either. The edges had dried, leaving a white outline, so it had been there a while. He tried to remain hopeful, though the center of the puddle was gray. The hose of the dehumidifier could have split. The water could have melted from the cake of ice stuck to its coils.

He knelt and sniffed the air, getting a dank whiff of sewage. If there was any doubt, the drain cover was dotted with bits of dried toilet tissue.

"Dammit."

He'd done everything he could, he protested. Since the last time, he'd tie-wrapped one of Emily's old stockings onto the discharge hose coming from the washer to act as a lint trap. He Dranoed the sinks religiously, and never put grease down the disposal. He'd been as careful as he could be, and it hadn't been enough. Just to have the plumber come out cost a hundred dollars.

As he knelt there, beaten, feeling sorry for himself, the pipes above him sang.

"Turn it off!" he yelled at the ceiling, more in panic than anger. He knew Emily couldn't hear him.

Without a sound, dark water welled up through the holes of the cover, quickly filling the shallow bowl, breached the lip and overflowed, a tongue streaming for the puddle. He shoved the cooler out of the way and ran for the stairs, calling her name.

She wasn't in the kitchen.

"What's wrong?" She came rushing down from the second floor as if he'd cut off a finger. Rufus bounded past her, happy, almost running him over.

"Don't use the water."

"I'm not."

"You were."

"Is it flooding again? I thought we fixed that."

How many times had they gone over this? "We did not fix it. It's not something that can be fixed."

"Don't yell at me. I didn't do anything."

"I'm not yelling at you. I'm trying to keep it from getting worse than it already is."

"How bad is it?"

"It's worse now."

"I'm sorry, I had to flush."

"It's not your fault," he said. "I don't know what happened. I thought we were all right."

Now doubt crept in. Had he forgotten to add the crystals? He could picture it, could hear them plopping into the water, but the memory might have been from the fall or last spring, the seasons overlapping.

"Sometime today I need to do laundry," Emily said. "I still have all the sheets and towels."

"We'll see how long it takes for them to get here."

The magnet with the plumber's number was on the basement fridge for this very reason. The woman who took his information seemed uninterested, and he wondered if it was an answering service. She couldn't tell him when someone would be there. They'd call to let him know they were on the way.

"We'll be here," Henry said.

The puddle was wider, covering the hose of the dehumidifier. He couldn't begin to clean it until the clog was gone. He lugged the cooler upstairs, spritzed the inside with Windex and left it on the back porch to air. Normally he'd take satisfaction in crossing off a chore, except his list had grown that much longer. With every passing minute he was falling further behind.

In his office he flipped the calendar to March. There, on the twenty-first, next to ROOT-X, was a check mark. It was no consolation.

All afternoon they waited in suspense. The lunch dishes sat in the sink.

They could use the toilet, they just couldn't flush. The basement stank. The waste of time discouraged him. When the guy finally called at half past four, it was too late to salvage the day.

Henry let him in through the hatch and stood by like a supervisor, training a flashlight on the drain as the man opened the cleanout and paid the flexible auger through a racketing machine that sent it spinning into the line. As the auger burrowed, the water in the drain rose and dipped as if it were breathing. Every so often the plumber stopped to attach another fifteen-foot segment. With all five, he could reach the street. By now Henry had seen the process so many times he could do it himself. He bent over the hole, focused on a blob of light that changed shape with the rising level. Beneath the surface, sediment boiled, and suddenly the water dropped a foot and stayed there.

"You got it," Henry called over the motor.

The plumber reeled in the auger segment by segment. The end bristled with hairy roots.

"I've been using Root-X," Henry said.

"It's this old pipe. Once they get in, there's not much you can do."

The bill was a hundred and thirty. Henry gave the man a check and shook his hand for saving them again.

Emily had held off starting dinner, so they ate late. She put in a load of sheets as he was rinsing the dishes, the water pressure cutting out on him. Once he got the dishwasher going, he went downstairs and squeegeed the puddle into the drain, then mopped it with a bucket of bleach and hot water. He set up a pair of fans to create a cross breeze, shooting air freshener through them to cover the stench. Every twenty minutes he checked on their progress, and by the end of the eleven o'clock news the floor was dry. He could still detect a faint note of sewage, but that would fade. He unplugged the fans and put everything back in its place. Surveying his work, hands on hips, he thought he'd earned a hard-fought draw—expensive and temporary, but a victory still, holding off the forces of chaos until the next time.

Add It to the List

MEMORIAL DAY THEY OPENED THE COTTAGE. HISTORICALLY, in a nod to democracy, the entire Maxwell clan gathered for the long weekend to tackle the list of chores passed down through the generations. Chautauqua, being a retreat from the grind of city life, was supposed to be rustic, and over the years, unlike their neighbors, whose places had grown apace with the stock market, they'd made few improvements. Henry took a special pleasure in knowing Justin and Sarah were washing the same windows he and Arlene had as children, even if the job they did was less than perfect. More than the cottage itself, this sense of belonging and continuity was their inheritance, and if they didn't appreciate it now, they would in time.

With the children living so far away, and the grandchildren busy with activities, every year it grew harder for all of them to get together. Lisa had to help her parents move into a new condo and couldn't come. "No great loss," Emily said, except with Sarah's rehearsal schedule, now there was some doubt about Margaret being able to make it as well. Emily worried that without help Henry would try to do everything himself, and lobbied Kenny to talk to her. Henry, who thought Emily was overreacting, wasn't privy to their discussions and resented being the subject of them, as if they were plotting against him. He might have slowed down some, but he wasn't an invalid.

After much back-and-forth, everyone was coming except Lisa and Sarah and Jeff.

"That should be more than enough," Henry said.

"I feel bad for Ella," Emily said. "She'll have no one to hang out with."

"I'm sure you two will find something to do."

"I'll put her in charge of the boys."

"They'll love that."

"I'm not surprised about Jeff."

"I'm not either."

Friday morning they left right after breakfast so they'd arrive around lunchtime. Arlene, who liked her sleep, was driving herself and would be up later. The kids both had to work and wouldn't pull in till after midnight, blearily unloading in the dark. The forecast called for scattered showers— a crapshoot, as his father would say, typical Chautauqua weather. Traffic would be bad either way—79 was constantly under construction. As they ate up the miles, dense forest and rolling farmland scrolling by on both sides, hawks perching on fenceposts, Henry kept expecting to see sprinkles on the windshield, a line of stopped cars ahead. There was nothing. He didn't re-mark on their luck, afraid he'd jinx them.

Heavy, with a mammoth engine, the Olds was at its best on the interstate. They rode in insulated quiet, Emily knitting beside him, counting to herself, leaning over every so often to peek at the speedometer while he watched the turnarounds for cops. In back, nestled against the cooler, Rufus slept. He was prone to a volcanic, prostrating carsickness and for that reason hadn't eaten. Henry didn't want to wake him, but since finishing his second coffee had been suppressing the urge to pee, and in a concession to age pulled into a rest area, taking the closest possible spot.

As he levered himself out and stood, his lower back spasmed, an electric twinge, as if he'd been jabbed with a cattle prod. He grabbed for it, gritting his teeth.

"Jesus please us."

"Are you okay?" Emily asked.

"I'm fine. Just creaky."

He thought he was stiff from sitting and from mopping the floor last night, the torsion doing a job on his spine. He'd be fine once he got moving, and he was, crossing the walk to the windowless building and back with no problem, but he'd never felt that kind of pain before. Now he worried it could happen at any time. He said nothing to Emily, knowing she'd seize on it.

At Erie they caught I-90, which was a mess, a double line of trucks crawling along, before jumping onto the new, unnecessary, completely empty 86. An old freight line shadowed the road, its raised right-of-way cutting through pastures, riveted iron bridges spanning creeks. He remembered when he and Arlene used to take the train to Jamestown, their grandmother Maxwell waiting for them at the station. From a safety island out front they boarded the trolley that ran to the Institute, the conductor making a special stop at Prendergast Point to let them off. The fall after the war, he'd come up by himself to do some fishing and was shocked to find the trolley gone, the tracks already overgrown, as if he'd been away for twenty years instead of two. One starry night, drunk, he walked them back from a bar in Ashville, expecting any second the rails to sing, a headlight looming out of the dark, a bell clanging a warning. All gone, like Sloan and Embree and his dreams of being a saint. He wasn't a boy anymore. He wasn't anything. Then he'd found Emily.

They got off at Sherman, cutting north on the county road, patched blacktop breaking up at the edges, beer cans in the ditches. For ages it had been dairy country, the hillsides dotted with cows the children used to count for one of their games. Now the barns had fallen, the stony fields reclaimed by nature, full of jagger bushes and spindly weed trees. Only the old farm-houses remained, pillared Greek revivals hidden in windbreaks.

"Imagine the winters," he said, not for the first time.

"I'm almost at the end of this row," Emily said, holding him off. "Okay, what?"

"I said imagine winter up here."

"No thank you. Was that it?"

"Yes."

"Sorry. I was supposed to have this done for Justin's birthday."

"I understand." Because he did. Once they got there, she'd be too busy to knit. He knew the impatience of suddenly being rushed after the slack weeks and months. Since retiring, he was so accustomed to his time being his own that even the smallest obligation—a ball game or a doctor's appointment on the calendar—felt like an imposition.

They passed the ramshackle bait shop and its abandoned school bus that let them know they were close, dipped across a shady creek and crested the last hill and the lake came into view, whitecapped, a sailboat heeling out in the middle.

"Looks breezy," he said.

Emily nodded, concentrating on her stitches.

In the corner of a cornfield, a billboard for Webb's Resort presided over the intersection with 394. He slowed for the stop sign. In back, Rufus sat up.

"He knows," Henry said.

"He ought to by now."

He took the back way, past the fish hatchery, craning to see if the ponds were full. After dinner they'd have to bring Rufus over and let him chase the geese.

The speed limit on Manor Drive, set by the homeowners' association to slow down the locals towing their boats to the launch, was a once-comic fourteen and a half miles an hour. He let up on the gas and the Olds floated. Rufus was standing, antsy, and Henry lowered the window for him. They were early. The Loudermilks' turnaround was empty, but Len Wiseman's white Caddy was parked by their garage. In the meadow across from the Nevilles' compound, a fleet of golf carts waited for the horde to descend.

The first thing he noticed about the cottage was the grass. The mowers must have just come. He was pleased, as if he'd cut it himself.

"It hasn't burned down," he said.

"That's good."

Closer, he could see there was moss on the roof and weeds growing out of the gutters. For years he'd been meaning to get rid of their old TV antenna, a winged aluminum monstrosity banded to the chimney, and added it to the list. The window frames, the screen porch, the whole place could use a fresh coat of paint, but that would have to wait till next year, if he could find the money. He was just glad it had survived the snows.

"Why do they do that?" Emily asked, aggrieved, because the mouth of the mailbox was stuffed with junk mail.

He pulled in, bumping over the grass, their tires snapping dead branches shed by the chestnut, stopping beside the kitchen door so it would be easier to unload. "Lafayette, we are here."

"Thank you for not driving like a maniac."

His back was fine, his knees no stiffer than normal.

Released, Rufus squatted in the middle of the yard and peed and peed.

"You know there's a whole field over there."

"Stop," Emily said. "We're not doing that again."

"We should have brought his rock."

As he was digging for his keys, he noticed a dead sparrow on the ground beneath the kitchen window, its wings spread, its neck bent. A common accident, mistaking the glass for air. He shielded Emily from it, letting her in first. "Here we go," he said, holding the door for Rufus, who came galloping after her. Henry separated a blue plastic bag from the organizer on the back of the door and wrapped his hand as if he were picking up Rufus's poop. The bird was surprisingly light, dried flat as a shingle. He tossed it in the trash and slipped back out, grabbed the sopping mail from the mailbox and threw that on top of it, as if hiding the body, then started bringing the bags in.

Closed since Labor Day, the place smelled of must and mold, the air dank, as in a cave or basement, unpleasant yet familiar. Overlapping plastic tarps wrapped the screen porch, casting the living room in dimness. On the mantel above the fireplace, among the matchbooks and flashlights and candles, mouse turds lay scattered like caraway seeds. The bait station he'd set out last fall was empty, whatever that meant. Upstairs Emily was opening windows. He went through the rear bedrooms doing the same, trying to get some circulation going.

The dresser in their room had been his as a boy, the ceramic knobs cracked, the burl veneer chipped at the edges. He stopped and patted the top as if it were an old horse. In a beaten tin change tray Kenny had made at camp sat a golf ball, a long-expired Putt-Putt coupon and a tortoiseshell barrette. Remnants of summers past, they held him for a moment, mysterious and obsolete, till Rufus came bounding down the stairs and poked his head in, breaking the spell.

"What do you smell? I bet you smell critters."

He and Emily teamed up to do the cooler, packed to the brim and heavy as a treasure chest. Once, he could have lifted it himself. Now, walking backward with his end, he was glad for the help. Rufus watched from the doorway. There was no room in the kitchen, and Emily banished him.

"Are you hungry at all?" she asked, meaning she wasn't.

"No, do what you need to do. I'll go turn on the water."

Last year the plumbers had left the pumphouse unlocked all winter and he'd had to give them a call. Now it was buttoned up tight, a spiderweb festooned with gnats strung from the knob. He turned on the pump and hot water heater and moved on to the garage.

Here, as on Grafton Street, was his true domain. Shaded by the chestnut, its rear windows overlooking the lake, the garage was half boathouse and half attic, a repository for kayaks and extension ladders and wicker rockers, gas cans and water skis and fishing rods, wheelbarrows and Adirondack chairs, bikes and trikes and life jackets and the grandchildren's many fancy inner tubes with their tangles of nylon line, all shoved in willy-nilly by various hands at the season's end. Through the years, behind this barrier of junk, like Br'er Rabbit in his briar patch, he'd cobbled together a serviceable workbench, hanging their rusty old kitchen cabinets for storage. Vacation, for him, meant the freedom to putter all day long. On the windowsill his transistor radio waited, tuned to the Pirates station from Erie. In the corner, Kenny's dorm fridge gaped, ready to be refilled with Iron Citys. Lazy summer afternoons, as heat and the scent of baking tarpaper gathered in the rafters, Henry would look up from the day's project to watch the grandchildren swimming off the dock or the *Chautauqua Belle* steaming past or a majestic procession of clouds and savor the rightness of life, nodding to himself as if it were a secret. Somehow it was. At home he never felt this way, only here. Emily would agree, and Arlene. Of the children and grandchildren he was less certain. These doubts, as much as the taxes and upkeep on the place, made him worry about the future. He wanted all of them to feel the way he did about Chautauqua.

The last thing in was the gas grill, a cast-iron behemoth from the sixties. He rolled it rattling over the grass to its place under the chestnut, giving him access to the folding tables and Adirondack chairs, which he set up facing the lake. The wheelbarrow with the life jackets and gas cans came next, then the flat-tired bikes and a dented steel garbage can full of kindling, all of which he set off to the side. Every year the pile grew more disorganized, yet he knew from experience that trying to fight it was useless. There was just too much stuff. Like the rain and the mice, it had become, against his will, a tradition.

He was unearthing the croquet set when she called him in for lunch— ham sandwiches and potato salad from the deli on paper plates. As always, anticipating his wishes, she'd made his with no tomato, when in fact he didn't mind. At the same time, he didn't like them enough to ask for them special, and let it pass.

"It's so nice out," she said. "I was thinking we could eat on the dock."

"Let me get a hat."

Rufus led them across the yard, already thinking of scraps, looking back over his shoulder as if they might ditch him.

In the old days, installing the dock had been the hardest job of the weekend, all of the men and male teenagers of Manor Drive pitching in, standing in the shallows in their swim trunks and holey sneakers, building it out piece by piece while Henry directed them, checking each new section with a level. Now the homeowners' association paid a crew to do it. They never anchored the sections correctly, so that they settled unevenly, leaving inch-high lips between them on which, all summer, the unsuspecting stubbed their toes.

As Emily and Henry made their way past the Klipspringers' Fireball and the Van de Meers' Chris-Craft, the dock shook beneath their feet like a funhouse floor. Afraid of dropping her sandwich, she stopped.

He gave her his arm.

"Oh, it's awful," she said.

"And guess who's paying for it."

"You should say something at the meeting."

"I do. It doesn't do any good."

The pilings at the end of the dock were capped with white plastic cones and strung with fishing line to discourage the gulls, and still the bench was spotted with droppings like slopped whitewash. Rufus waited for Emily to take a seat and planted himself in front of her, his nose inches from her plate.

"Go," she said. "Stop begging."

The wind was up, and as they ate they watched a lone powerboat far out smack through the whitecaps, the sound reaching them delayed—*whap, whap, whap*. Tomorrow the lake would be a speedway, buzzing with Jet Skis, but for now it was idyllic. The sun glimmering off the water made him squint. He chewed, luxuriating in the view of the far shore, a few high, bright clouds drifting south. His sandwich didn't need tomato. The pickles were salty and sweet. Even the store-bought potato salad was good. He hadn't known he was so hungry.

"This was a good idea."

"I have them every once in a while."

He held out a last morsel of crust to Rufus, who sniffed it before taking it gently.

"No wonder he begs."

"He's a good boy," Henry said. "It would be nice if it stayed like this."

"You know it won't. What time did Arlene say she'd be here?"

"She didn't."

"She's consistent, I'll give her that."

"She is."

Emily finished her pickles and Rufus padded over to the edge and lay down facing the water. On the Cartwrights' dock the wings of the wooden duck that served as a wind gauge twirled like propellers, creaking. The powerboat was gone, replaced by a catamaran tacking back and forth in front of the Institute. Wavelets lapped at the pilings. As if giving up, Rufus rolled on his side. They sat, basking, faces tipped to the sun. The bell tower chimed the half hour, the carillon's song thinned by distance.

"All right," Emily said. "Back to work."

"Yep," Henry said. "Here we go."

But neither of them budged.

Memento Mori

Every Decoration Day his mother took them to Allegheny Cemetery, where her brother was buried. There, dressed as if for a wake, among dozens of other families remembering loved ones taken too young, Henry and Arlene laid a black wreath with a gold ribbon at his grave, a polished marble obelisk pointing toward heaven. The stone bore his full name, yet was still troubling to Henry. They bowed their heads while his mother silently prayed, and he pictured his uncle lying in state in his grandparents' parlor. They carried out this ceremony regardless of the weather. When it rained, he stood dry beneath his umbrella, imagining water trickling through the soil and seeping in, leaving dark spots on his uncle's uniform, wetting his medals.

Henry dreaded going. Facing the grave with his mother's hand on his shoulder, he thought he should feel more. Though he'd never met him, relatives said he had his uncle's chin, and sometimes, by himself, looking at the picture on his mother's dresser or the sketch of Paris on the mantel, he sensed a secret connection between them, but not here. As with the Saturday afternoon funerals at Calvary, he wanted it to be over so he could go home and change into his play clothes.

During these visits, his father was strangely absent, as if he objected to the ritual, though in retrospect Henry could recall no evidence of this, his father being eminently reasonable and overly solicitous of his mother. Most likely he was working, since back then the holiday wasn't fixed, and by chance might fall in the middle of the week. Henry sympathized, being loath himself to waste a vacation day better spent at Chautauqua.

Every spring the three of them stood tribute, until Arlene decamped for college, leaving Henry to accompany his mother and place the wreath himself. When he came home from the war, he went with her out of habit. By then he had his own dead, and the restful, well-tended cemetery seemed a lie. At the same time, he couldn't deny her that meager comfort, and so he bowed his head and thought of Sloan and the night awaiting him like the promise of oblivion. Only after he married Emily was he absolved of the task, as if his responsibility was to her now, and the children, yet instead of relief, he thought of his mother buying the wreath, dressing and driving herself to spend those quiet moments alone with Henry Chase. The rest of the year he might lie forgotten, but Memorial Day, rain or shine, as sure as a new crop of miniature flags, she would be there to remember him.

She'd died in 1979. It was hard to believe she'd been gone almost twenty years now. He could still conjure her voice and all her silly sayings. *Lead on, MacDuff.* *"I see," said the blind man. Ready, Hesy, mi' lad?* He thought that when they got home he should really go visit both of them, his father too.

For Henry, grief, like love, was a private matter. He had no use for parades or speeches or moments of silence. He didn't need a special occasion to recall the dead. They came to him unbidden—Embree, Jansen and Davis, shot right next to him in the woods outside of Pforzheim. The gunner of the drowned tank, his bloated face wavering inches below the surface like a curious fish. The bodies on the road like so many piles of laundry. As much as he sometimes wished he could, he would never forget any of it. He'd tried.

Now, as then, being at Chautauqua helped, the cottage a retreat from the greater motion of the world. He celebrated the holiday anonymously, like any homeowner, by flying the flag.

Theirs had come from the old Ames on the way to Mayville, closed for decades. Topped with a bronze eagle, propped in a corner of the garage, it wore the manufacturer's original plastic sheath, fogged with dust and age. As he unfurled it, the sun-faded nylon released the fungal reek of mildew—a chronic problem, with the humidity. He let it air while he hefted the stepladder over to the screen porch and tested the legs for stability. Christmas, as he was stringing the outside lights, the extension ladder had slipped, dumping him in the bushes. He hadn't been hurt, just some scratches, but ever since then Emily had been nervous about him and heights. In this case he would be all of four feet off the ground, and rather than ask permission, he mounted the ladder and fit the pole in the holder.

The wind lifted the flag, the nylon swishing. He stood back and admired it, identical to their neighbors' on both sides, remembering his mother and Embree and Henry Chase, fending off the urge to salute, then folded the ladder closed and went to get started on the mailbox.

True Value

THE IDEA WAS THAT TONIGHT, WHEN KENNY PULLED IN, THE first thing he'd see would be the mailbox he and Lisa had given them for Christmas. Henry thought he could salvage the old post, but it was rotten from the constant dampness, soft as wet bread and crawling with carpenter ants, so he put together a list and headed off to Mayville. As he was backing out, Emily asked if he could stop at Haff Acres and pick up some strawberries for dessert—"but only if they're nice." He played it safe, getting them first, inspecting the stained paper cartons like a head chef.

Mayville hadn't changed in decades. A backwater county seat, it perched atop a hill presiding over the northern end of the lake. Great oaks lined its wide main street, shading turreted Victorian mansions in varying stages of decay. The ornate porch railings were missing spindles and everything was for sale—motorboats and pickup trucks parked in front yards, knobby-tired dirt bikes leaning against trees. The block-long brick downtown was a mix of empty storefronts and darkened law offices that served the courthouse, the only sign of life the Golden Dawn, its lot busy with weekenders stocking up for the holiday. Henry checked for cops before executing a slow U-turn in the middle of the street and took a spot in front of the hardware.

Like the town itself, Baker's True Value was a holdout, its narrow aisles crammed floor to ceiling like a general store, the garden and paint and automotive sections running into one another, the shelves a jumble of buckets and flowerpots and gas cans. It sold housewares to the summer people, and water skis and fishing tackle, and charcoal and propane and criminally overpriced bundles of firewood. Against the rear wall, by the bins of PVC piping, as if to entice customers to linger, a popcorn machine broadcast the movie theater scent of hot oil. Downstairs there were rolls of screening and panes of replacement glass, and out back a small lumber yard. To a newcomer, it might seem disorganized, but Henry was a regular. Three or four times a week during the summer he found himself here, ditching the crowded cottage for the momentary peace and air-conditioning of the Olds. Like the golf course, Baker's True Value was an island. Normally he wandered the aisles, inspired by the profusion of useful products, seeing in every spray can and tool a new project, but today he didn't have time.

Instead of Ted Baker, a girl in a blood-red apron and white nametag manned the register. She was reading a fat paperback and seemed content to ignore Henry, then when he set the Raid and the mouse baits on the counter, slipped the book into her apron pocket. Bailey, her name was. She had a ring through one corner of her lower lip, a teenaged affectation he would never understand. He didn't see any family resemblance, though he couldn't be certain. She scanned his purchases without a word.

"I'm also going to need a pressure-treated post for a mailbox and a bag of Sakrete."

"They're out back." She pointed.

"I know. I'll pay for them now and pull around, if that's all right."

"How big a bag you want?"

"What's the smallest you've got?"

She had to look on her computer, her nails clacking. "Forty pounds."

"That'll do."

Done paying, he asked her to give Mr. Baker his best.

"Yeah no, they don't own the store anymore."

"When did they sell?"

"I don't know, sometime last fall. It's been awhile."

"I'm sorry to hear that."

"Just pull around and Danny will take care of you."

"Thanks," Henry said, retreating.

He wasn't wrong. The sign was the same as it had always been. They were smart to keep the name.

The boy confirmed her story. At the end of last summer, the Bakers sold it to someone from Buffalo and moved to South Carolina.

"Tired of the snow," Henry guessed.

"Couldn't tell you."

Driving home, he thought it was another loss, and then he could barely lift the bag of Sakrete out of the trunk.

When he told Emily, she said she thought she remembered hearing that. "I'm sure they made a mint. Good for them."

"I suppose," Henry said.

He gathered everything he would need at the foot of the drive. The breeze had died, and the blacktop gave off waves of heat. Before he dug up the old post, he blasted it with Raid, sending the ants scrambling. The chemical smell was deadly. He donned a crusty pair of gloves to work the post loose, yanking it back and forth, finally toppling it and levering out the rusty coffee can that served as its base—Chock full o'Nuts, his parents' brand. He could see the cans lined up on his father's workbench, each labeled in his draftsman's hand. Did they even make it anymore? After Baker's, he was resigned to losing the whole world.

The broken bucket he was hoping to use as an anchor was bigger, the better to withstand the snowplows. The ground here was dense clay, and as he widened the hole, his shoulders and lower back protesting, his face reddened, his pulse beating behind one eye. Sweat soaked through his Pirates cap, dripping from the bill. He blew drops off the tip of his nose.

"Can't this wait till tomorrow?" Emily asked, bringing him a cold lemonade. "You're going to give yourself a heart attack."

"This is the hard part."

"I see that."

"The rest is easy."

"Have you heard from Arlene at all? It would be nice to know when to get dinner going."

"Shoot for six-thirty. If she's not here by then, tough."

"I was thinking we could do the asparagus on the grill and maybe some baby potatoes. I still have some of that Indian bread you like. What do you think of doing that on the grill?"

He agreed to everything, barely listening, thinking of how he could use two Adirondack chairs to hold the post upright, and then when she'd taken the glass back inside, felt ungrateful.

The hole wasn't deep enough. Twice he set the bucket in it and pulled it out again. An ant ran zigzagging up the handle of the shovel. He brushed it away with a glove. How long had the colony been there? He'd have to cut it up and bag the pieces, another chore.

When the hole was finally ready, he arranged the chairs on either side and brought the hose over. His hands ached from digging and the bag of Sakrete was heavy as a cannonball. When he dropped it in the grass, it split, spilling gray powder.

The ratio was supposed to be three to one. He knelt beside the bucket, adding water, gradually folding in more Sakrete, turning the slurry with a sawed-off broomstick too small for the job. He reached deep, stirring harder, trying to get rid of the dry streaks. It seemed thick, but he was already using too much water. He emptied the bag, tossed it away and changed position, getting down on all fours over the hole, grunting as he whipped the mixture. Still it resisted, a stiff mud. He took the broomstick in both hands and attacked, churning it clockwise, then changing direction, and back again, wild, straining, light-headed from the effort. Dark spots intruded on his vision, bloomed and massed like smoke. The world blurred and pitched sick-eningly. Too late, as in a dream, he realized he was going to faint. He was already falling, the hole rising up to swallow him. At the last second he dropped the stick and threw his hands out to save himself, plunging them wrist-deep in the muck.

Once, in basic training, at the height of the Louisiana summer, he'd passed out on a march through the dusty hills, coming to by the roadside, still wearing his pack. "Mornin', sunshine," Gunny Raybern said, pinching his cheeks. Now, as then, Henry was more embarrassed than scared, as if he were somehow at fault for his body's refusal to continue.

He glanced at the bedroom windows—empty. Emily hadn't seen him, and quickly he regained himself, rinsing his hands under the hose and splashing water on his face. He drenched his cap and mopped the back of his neck, hoping that would lower his temperature. He could rest after he sank the post. The Sakrete was as good as it was going to get. He felt better and used the broad arm of an Adirondack chair to stand. He was fine, he'd just overexerted himself. He'd learned his lesson: He should have rented a mixer.

He took his time centering the post, adjusting the chairs so the mailbox was level. Now all he had to do was let it set.

"What happened to you?" Emily asked when he came in for a drink.

"It's a little warm out, if you haven't noticed."

"I told you you should have waited."

"It's going to look nice."

"Good. Now go take a shower and cool off. It's almost five."

"I still have to get rid of the old one. It's full of ants."

"Do what you want," she said. "I'm having a glass of wine."

He was bagging the poisoned pieces when Arlene's Taurus pulled in. She'd taken the scenic route through Allegheny National Forest, meaning she'd stopped at the Seneca reservation to stock up on cheap cigarettes. She'd also bought strawberries.

"Great minds," she said, making Emily roll her eyes at him.

They ate on the lawn, retiring inside when the bugs got too bad. Emily, wise as Solomon, had cut all the strawberries, pairing them with freshly whipped cream for dessert.

After finishing the dishes and scraping the grill, he walked around front. The sun was down and bats wheeled squeaking above the trees. It had been two hours. The Sakrete would take a day to fully cure, but it was solid enough for now. He dragged the chairs clear and stood back in the middle of the road, arms crossed, a critic appraising a work of art. The mailbox was twice the size of their old one, able to handle packages. The black anodized coating was supposedly rustproof, guaranteed for life, which in his case was a bad joke. On the left side, in reflective white paint, he'd stenciled their name and street number. They glowed in the dusk, gratifying after the struggle, and he returned to the kitchen victorious, claiming for his reward a finger of Dewar's.

With the screen porch buttoned up, the cottage was too warm for a fire. Rufus stretched out on the hearth to keep cool, just like Duchess, his lips twitching in his sleep. While Emily knitted and Arlene read Agatha Christie, Henry went over the list with a pencil, assigning tomorrow's chores. So many that had once been his he now relied on the children to perform. Mucking the gutters, turning the garden, putting up the weathervane. The antenna would be a project. As much as he wanted Emily to be wrong, after his spell today he didn't trust himself, and he was grateful they were coming.

Even with the windows open to catch a breeze, the room was quiet, only the shrilling of insects and the chimes of the bell tower occasionally breaking the silence. He sipped, smacking his lips. Emily's needles clicked. Arlene turned another page. In the midst of this calm, the phone rang, startling as a gunshot. Rufus barked, thinking it was the doorbell at home.

"Shush," Emily said.

It was Margaret, calling from the road. There was major construction outside Toledo. They wouldn't arrive till after midnight.

"You'll still probably beat your brother," Emily said, "so please leave the outside light on. All right, dear. Drive safely."

"When did they leave?" Henry asked.

"I didn't ask."

"It was good of her to call," Arlene said. "That's a long way to drive by yourself."

"She'll be fine," Emily said. "She's had lots of practice."

A few years ago he would have waited up for them, but the scotch on top of the long day made it impossible. Emily said she'd be in in a little; she wanted to finish the sock she was working on. His knee ached (there was rain on the way), and before he brushed his teeth he remembered to take some aspirin. At first the sheets were cool against his skin. When they grew too warm he threw them off and lay on his back, splayed, welcoming sleep, picturing Kenny and Margaret driving through the night, imagining everything they'd get done tomorrow.

Hours later, he snapped awake as if shaken. For an instant he didn't know where he was, Grafton Street or some hotel in England left over from a dream. Beside him, Emily slept. The curtains held a glow from the outside light. Though he didn't feel the need to pee, he padded to the bathroom and tried. The living room was dark, and the kitchen. The microwave said it was 2:17, the number of his homeroom in third grade, his tired mind completing the meaningless connection. Behind Arlene's Taurus sat Margaret's minivan, the front wheel missing its hubcap. Kenny's wasn't there, and before heading back to bed, he made sure the door was unlocked. As he lay there listening for him, he kept hearing the swish of tires in the rustling trees, and then he was in the park, in the woods behind their clubhouse, digging with Davis and Embree and the rest of his company as the rain came down, all of them sopping, covered in mud.

In the morning, Kenny's minivan was parked behind Margaret's, leaving Henry room to get out. They'd pulled in around three, yet, predictably,

Kenny was up before she was. When Henry asked him how he liked the mailbox, he said it had been a long drive. He really hadn't noticed.

He made a show of going out to the road to admire it.

"It looks good, Dad. Merry Christmas."

"Thank you," Henry said.

The Duty Rooster

He didn't think Margaret was drinking, if only because she looked so good. He'd come in for a Ziploc bag to hold the screws from the screen porch tie-downs and found her in the kitchen, microwaving a cup of coffee. Since Christmas she'd lost weight, her face noticeably thinner, an achievement that, knowing her history, must have cost her a great effort. He was shocked by her resemblance to Emily at that age, the same high cheekbones and generous lips. He always knew she could be beautiful. He wasn't sure if she'd ever be happy, and wondered if it was too late.

In a T-shirt, camp shorts and sneakers, she was dressed for work. When she gave him a hug, her hair smelled of cigarettes, another addiction she'd supposedly quit.

"Hi, Dad."

"Thanks for coming. You look good."

"Ew, I'm all scuzzy, but thank you. I'm sorry Sarah couldn't make it. She really wanted to."

"I'm sure she's having more fun there."

"She is. She loves it. We never see her. I think Justin's a little jealous, so this is a nice break for him."

He thought she might volunteer something about Jeff, but she didn't, so he didn't ask. It was past ten. He and Kenny were almost finished with the porch, Ella and the boys busy washing the screens, Emily and Arlene off food shopping.

The duty roster was posted on the fridge.

"I've got you turning the garden, if that's all right."

"I'm glad I didn't take a shower."

"You can muck the gutters if you'd rather do that."

"I'm good," she said. "I'll be there in a minute. First I've got to have my coffee."

Outside, Kenny had the last tarp off and was folding it on the lawn. He stopped to dig the screws out of his pocket, dropping them in the bag Henry held open. He'd marked all the tie-downs with a Sharpie so they'd know where they went next year—a bonus.

"What's next?"

After they put everything away, Henry had him scrape the spongy tufts of moss off the roof with a putty knife and spot-clean the shingles with a bleach solution, a tedious job made harder by the steep slope. While the sun was out now, there was a good chance of a thunderstorm later. The goal was to be done with the gutters before it hit so the rain would finish the job. The antenna could wait.

Alongside the garage, Ella and the boys were scrubbing the screens.

"Whatever you do," he said, bending over to inspect their work, "do not get your old grandfather wet," and lingered, giving her time to squirt him and Rufus, to the boys' delight. As they grew older, they would turn sullen and superior, tending some secret inner drama. For now he could still charm them with silliness.

"All right," he said, "enough lollygagging. Back to work."

When he looped around to the garden to check on Margaret, she was nowhere to be found. The shovel lay in the dirt where she'd stopped, maybe a tenth of the way done. She wasn't in the kitchen or the living room. He called up the stairs, but there was no answer. As a teenager, she'd been a notorious shirker, hiding in the bathroom after dinner, leaving Kenny to do the dishes solo. The Duty Rooster owed its existence to her as much as to Henry's days pulling KP. They created it to make sure she did her fair share. Kenny had drawn up the very first one, misspelling the fateful word, cementing its place in their family history.

Henry was cutting through the screen porch when he saw her at the far end of the dock, pacing with her phone to her ear, jabbing the air with a cigarette to reinforce a point. Justin was watching her too. They were leaning the screens against the Adirondack chairs to dry in the sun. He set his down and paused a second, looking her way, and Henry wondered how much he knew. He was a quiet, sometimes fearful boy, and while Henry tried to give Margaret the benefit of the doubt in her marriage, he blamed her for his skittishness. Her anger was a mystery to him, its source impossible to fathom, well beyond the simple disappointments of childhood. Unlike Emily, he would never believe it was their fault.

Ella and the boys started another set of three, dipping their scrub brushes in the bucket of suds.

"Good job, you guys," Henry called, loud enough, he hoped, for Margaret to overhear, though she didn't seem to notice. For a long minute he stood on the lawn, his arms crossed like a foreman, watching her pace. At one point she stopped and looked directly up at the sky, her other hand covering her forehead as if in pain or disbelief, then kept walking, gesticulating, making her case. When he realized she was going to be a while, he left her to it and moved on to the woodpile, choosing only the best logs to bring inside. It was going to be a cool night after the storm came through, and they'd want a fire.

A 100% Chance

THE GREATEST PLEASURE OF BAD WEATHER, LIKE SO MANY THINGS in life, was the anticipation. Knowing the storm was coming, Henry, like the project manager he was, built it into the schedule. At noon the Jamestown station said the rain would arrive sometime around four. By three-thirty, though the sky above the far shore was a bright, unbroken blue, a legion of dark clouds had begun to encroach from the north, the contrast ominous. Kenny, done with the gutters, was helping Ella and the boys replace the downstairs screens. Margaret, having finally turned the garden, was in the kitchen with Emily and Arlene, relining the cupboards. Satisfied, Henry went out and rescued the cushions of the porch furniture, piling them on the glider. The wind had picked up. The flag was tangled, wrapped around itself. He took it down and leaned it in a corner of the porch, then thought better and put it in the garage.

He was at his workbench, unpacking a shoebox of screws, trying to find a nice pair for the spice rack, half listening to the Jammers game, when a cold gust reached in the window, chilling him. The sky was dark and low, ragged wisps of clouds hanging down, rotating slowly. Overhead, thunder rolled, a chain reaction like boxcars coupling in a switchyard. The chestnut thrashed, scattering leaves across the dock. Far out in the middle, a last fisherman motored for home.

"Too late," Henry said, worried for his safety. Hadn't he checked the weather?

On the radio, static crashed, obliterating the game, followed by a blinding flash that seemed to pass inches in front of his nose. The thunder cracked. Heavy drops lashed the roof and plopped in the water—not rain at all but hail, bits of ice like mothballs floating in the shallows. They plinked off the cars, gathered in the grass. The hail changed to rain and accelerated to a gallop, pounding the roof, blowing in through the screen so he had to close the window. The world melted and ran. He could see the Van de Meers' Chris-Craft pitching in its slip, but the end of the dock was lost in fog.

In the cottage, the lights were on. One of the boys stood at the door leading to the screen porch—Sam, probably, being the more adventurous. He waved and Henry waved back. The downspouts gushed. The lawn was a pond, the Adirondack chairs swamped. With no umbrella, he was trapped, but pleasantly so, safe and dry with the rain tapping in the rafters and the ball game playing, enveloped by the familiar smell of gas and hot tarpaper, and leaned in the doorway, admiring the fury of the storm, nodding at each blast of thunder as if he'd predicted it.

Puzzles

ON THE TOP SHELF BEHIND THE TV, REACHABLE ONLY BY STAND-
ing on a ladder-back chair carried in from the kitchen, above the ranks of
bargain bin VHS tapes and books swollen with humidity, decks of cards
worn soft and long-ignored board games (Flinch, Aggravation, Master-
mind), as if a last resort, resided the puzzles. Here, haphazardly piled to the
ceiling, in boxes reinforced at the corners with browning cellophane tape,
one might find Van Gogh's *Sunflowers* or a map of the ancient world or Old
Ironsides decked out for the Bicentennial. The subject barely mattered, only
the degree of difficulty. There were hundred-piece puzzles of puppies and
the Steelers logo and Snow White and the Seven Dwarfs, and an inlaid
wooden tray of the United States with stars for the capitals and cartoon cot-
ton bolls, crossed pickaxes and sawtooth-roofed factories representing
each state's major industry, but these occupied the children at most a few
hours, while the rain might last for days. When Margaret and Kenny were
kids, five hundred pieces was the maximum. Now, with the sharpness of
digital imaging, a thousand was common. There was even a three-thousand-
piece monster of the Great Hall at Versailles that had taken them most of a

housebound August, a feat never repeated, though Arlene, a puzzle nut like their mother, regularly lobbied for it.

The collection had gradually amassed over the years. Some, like the clumsily hand-tinted photo of the old mill pond in autumn, Henry remembered from childhood. Others, like the panoramic shot of Niagara Falls with its misty rainbow, Arlene could vouch for, but in most cases the provenance was shaky, lost to the ages. Whether gleaned from yard sales or the flea market at Dart Airport, or Christmas presents to the whole family from Santa, bought expressly for the cottage, the best puzzles were loved for their ability to tease them once again. When Emily said, "Oh, I hate that one," it was the deepest compliment.

There was no list of which puzzles they'd done last summer. Ella, typically, had taken a picture of each completed masterpiece, but had deleted them when she was low on memory, leaving Henry to guess.

"How about the Taj Mahal?" he asked, gripping the shelf with his fingertips like a man hanging from a ledge.

"We always do the Taj Mahal," Arlene said.

"Biplanes."

"Pass," Emily said.

"Westminster Cathedral." They'd been there on vacation, and he knew she couldn't resist it.

"Let's save that for later. We're only here till Monday."

"Something we haven't done in a while," Arlene said.

"The Grand Canyon."

"I know for a fact we did that last year," Emily said. "Ella, why don't you pick?"

"Yes," Arlene said. "Your grandfather's not making this easy."

"I'm just telling you what we have."

"We know what we have," Emily said. "What we want is a recommendation—and not the Taj Mahal."

"Windmills and tulips. Carlsbad Caverns. Winter in Vermont. The Fox and the Hounds. Stop me when hear one you like. Maine lighthouses. The clipper ship."

"The clipper ship," Ella said.

"The clipper ship it is," Emily said.

"Good choice," Arlene said. "The water."

"The water's hard," Margaret, who'd abstained so far, agreed.

Painted by some imitator of Winslow Homer, the three-master was breasting heavy seas in a gale, scuppers streaming. Henry remembered working on the sails and rigging, but whether that had been last year or ten years ago, he had no clue. He excused this lapse as trivial, reflecting that he'd been paying attention to more important things.

Naturally it was at the very top. On the dusty lid, mice had left tracks like footprints in the snow. He wiped it off with a tissue before handing the box to Ella.

Traditionally the card table went against the front windows, beside the loveseat, to take advantage of the good reading lamp and its three-way bulb. In her later years, before she fell ill, every Thursday his mother hosted her bridge club, her church friends gossiping over finger sandwiches and Prantl's almond torte as they doubled and redoubled one another. The table and padded folding chairs hailed from that era, a matching set in dark avocado Naugahyde. Shoulder to shoulder, Ella, Emily, Arlene and Margaret huddled around the light like a team of surgeons, turning the pieces right side up, culling the straight edges that formed the border.

"Are we using the picture?" Ella asked.

"No," the other three answered in chorus, and Margaret tossed the box on the floor, where Rufus sniffed it before settling again. Though the worst of the storm had passed, he was sticking close to Emily.

Henry stood behind her, watching them sort through the pile. Outside, the lake was gray, the rain falling in long streaks through the black background of the garage roof. It might have been evening. The room was silent, only the peeping of the boys' video games sifting down from upstairs. For dinner they were having his favorite, chicken à la king, and any minute Kenny, whose sweet tooth rivaled his own, would be back from Haff Acres with hot pies.

"We can squeeze in if you want," Emily said.

"I'd just slow you down."

No one denied it, the silence prompting laughter. He didn't mind.

"Ta-da," Arlene said, fitting two edge pieces together.

"It's a little early for a ta-da," Emily said.

"Ta-da," Margaret said.

"All right," Emily said, "if that's how we're going to play it. Ta-da."

"Ta-da," Ella said.

"You guys are sharks."

"You know what you could do for me," Emily said, and for an instant he feared she was going to ask him for a glass of wine in front of Margaret. "You could build us a fire."

"Yes," Arlene said as if she'd been thinking the same thing. "I'm freezing."

"Your wish is my command." It was a saying of his father's, lifted from some movie about a genie, and as he knelt and shoved crumpled newspaper under the grate, he thought it was true, he would do anything to make them happy.

It took quickly, roaring, warming his cheeks. "Ta-da."

"Thank you," Emily said, and turned back to the table.

Rufus waddled over to lie on the hearth, using Henry's foot as a pillow.

"You are one spoiled dog."

Outside, the rain came down. He stood at the mantel, ignoring his craving for a scotch, transfixed by the sight of the four of them working side by side. If they could just stay this way, but the spell was delicate, and their happiness, like all happiness, temporary. He thought he should take a picture.

Kiss the Cook

IN THE KITCHEN, EMILY TOOK HIM ASIDE LIKE A SPY. "MARGA-ret wants to make dinner for everyone tomorrow night."

He was immediately annoyed, as if his plans had been ruined.

"I thought we were doing burgers and dogs on the grill."

"We can do them for lunch. She wants to contribute."

"I understand that she wants to contribute. She doesn't have any money."

Emily looked over her shoulder as if he was being too loud. "She's not going to spend a lot of money. She's going to make that pasta with the pine nuts you said you liked."

"I do like it, I just don't want her spending money she needs for other things."

"I think it's good she wants to do this, so that's what we're doing. I'm just letting you know."

"I guess I don't get a vote."

"No," she said, "you don't. And you'll like it."

"I'm sure I will," he said.

The Evening's Entertainment

THOUGH AT HOME HENRY WATCHED THE PIRATES EVERY NIGHT, here, by design, they didn't have cable. The antenna, being obsolete, could pick up only a couple of snowy channels from Buffalo and Toronto, limiting their choices to old VHS tapes or DVDs rented from the Blockbuster in Lakewood. Kenny and Margaret were members, and once or twice a week, depending on the weather, they'd take the children down to choose the latest releases from Disney and Pixar, animated fables Emily found irritating and juvenile. As the girls grew older, she tried to interest them in black-and-white classics like *Wuthering Heights* and *Pride and Prejudice* that she and Arlene would end up watching together. Despite their differences, their taste in movies was surprisingly similar, both of them preferring the costume dramas and romantic comedies of their adolescence to anything modern. Kenny tended to go for low-budget horror flicks from the fifties that were supposed to be scary and fun, but which seemed to everyone else—the boys included—ludicrous and unwatchable. Margaret liked science fiction that addressed social issues, since her politics and Hollywood's generally agreed. Henry enjoyed westerns, a genre that operated by an older code. It was a rare film that kept everyone's attention, partly because the set was small and all the way across the room, and partly because they had books to read and games to play and puzzles to finish. They could watch TV anytime, and yet every night, after the dishes were put away and they'd settled in, inevitably someone asked, "Who wants to watch a movie?"

Because they'd been too busy during the day to make the extra effort, tonight's film came from the permanent collection—*Raiders of the Lost Ark*, selected by Kenny with the boys in mind, since the girls were hostages to the puzzle. Henry, who'd watched the original swashbucklers at the Regent in East Liberty, riding the trolley by himself and blowing his route money on licorice whips, took the recliner in the corner and followed the plot at a remove, reading an old *Smithsonian* article about Lewis and Clark, glancing up and getting lost in the action so that the two stories blended. Eventually he set the magazine aside to stoke the fire. He had to reach over Rufus, who lifted his head but didn't move.

"Don't mind me," Henry said.

They were making progress on the clipper ship. The border was done, and a dark corner of sky streaked with lightning. They'd segregated the pieces by color—a small island for the ship, a massive raft for the sea.

"Ratsafrats," Arlene said when one didn't fit.

"That's a lot of water," Henry said.

"We've done it before," Emily said, nodding encouragement at Ella.

Behind him the tape stopped, making them all look.

"Who," Kenny asked, "is ready for pie?"

"Oh, I'm so full," Emily said. "Maybe just a sliver."

"A sliver of which? We have cherry and we have peach."

She put her hands over her mouth like one of the three monkeys, as if afraid to speak. "Both?"

It was a popular choice. Besides the pies, he'd stopped and gotten ice cream. He took their orders, enlisting the boys to serve.

As Justin was coming through the doorway, he dropped a fork, leaving a dribble of vanilla on the carpet, and stood there paralyzed, as if he might cry.

"It's okay," Margaret said, taking the plate from him and turning him around by the shoulder. "Go get a clean one."

Of all the children, he would have the hardest life, Henry thought, with Margaret for a mother and Sarah for a sister. He didn't include Jeff in his calculations, and realized that after discussing it with Emily so long, he'd accepted the divorce as a fait accompli. He was tired, otherwise he would have dismissed the idea as the passing notion it was (the boy was five, no clumsier than any child, and exhausted). Instead, unguarded, he followed it to its conclusion. He hoped he was wrong. He'd been sensitive too, a hermit and a worrier, and he'd done all right.

They ate, watching Harrison Ford drop through a trapdoor into a pit of snakes. Rufus faced the boys, intent, making Henry shoo him. The cherry pie was tart. When Emily couldn't finish hers, Henry polished it off, knowing it would give him heartburn later.

"Oof," Arlene said. "Too much."

"I'll do the dishes," Margaret said.

"Thank you, dear," Emily said.

Usurped, Henry picked up Lewis and Clark again, doing his best to ignore the blaring music and Keystone Kop Nazis. The movie went on and on, one cockamamie escape after another. His legs were jumpy, and he shifted in his chair. It had to be past the boys' bedtime. They'd worked hard today. He thought of tomorrow and the antenna, how to get it down without damaging the gutter. The town landfill wouldn't be open Sunday or Monday. When he'd read the same sentence three times, he set the magazine aside and stood. His hips were stiff. In the ring of lamplight, like competing teams, Arlene and Margaret concentrated on the bowsprit, Emily and Ella the sails. It was too late to put another log on the fire, and he consolidated the remaining pieces with the tongs, gathering the brittle embers beneath them. Rufus sat up and yawned, his long tongue curling.

"Does he need to go out?" Emily asked.

It was still sprinkling, the air damp. Rufus crisscrossed the lawn, sniffing the grass while Henry stood at the door of the screen porch, looking beyond him at the blurry lights on the far shore. The wind rose, and fat drops spattered in the trees. "Quick quick. Quick like a bunny."

Normally it would be too late for a treat, but Henry relented. Emily, busy coaching Ella, paid them no attention.

The house felt stuffy after being outside. His gut was sour and he chewed some Tums. The movie refused to end. He took his seat again and tried to read, but the article was dull and the room was warm, and soon, though he fought it, lolling, blinking to stay awake, his eyes closed and he dozed off. He sat slumped over the magazine with his head bowed and his mouth open like someone dead, his thick breathing making the boys giggle and the girls turn around.

"Henry!" Emily said. "Go to bed."

Night Owls

HE WOKE, AS HE SO OFTEN DID NOW, AT AN ABSURD HOUR, A slave to his prostate. The curtains were dark and the time on the clock was demoralizing. Beside him, Emily slept with one arm flung above her head as if passed out, Rufus curled on the rag rug next to her instead of his bed. Henry pulled his robe on over his pajamas, tottered down the hall and peed by the glow of the nightlight, his jowly twin watching him in the mirror. The volume, as always, was underwhelming, a weak stream, despite the pills he took every day.

He wondered how Dr. Runco was doing. He hadn't thought of him in weeks, which seemed wrong. They ought to send a card, though instantly he realized how ridiculous that sounded. Flowers. Something. Emily would know what.

He trusted Kenny had banked the fire, but decided to check anyway, since he was awake. Beneath the grate, pillowed in ashes, a few embers still burned. He'd just picked up the shovel when he heard, distinctly, right outside, the murmur of a woman's voice—unmistakably Margaret's.

He stopped as if caught, his head cocked. It was past three. Who was she talking to? He strained to make out the conversation, listening to the rhythm of her words, as if that might provide a clue.

Arlene was her confidante. A fellow black sheep, she thought she understood Margaret better than any of them, but it was too late for her to be up.

Maybe she was on her phone, because she seemed to be explaining something at length. Michigan was an hour behind them. He pictured Jeff on the other end, raised from a sound sleep, lying in bed with his arm over his face, patiently enduring her accusations.

Eavesdropping like this reminded Henry of all the nights he stayed up waiting for her to come home as a teenager, his anger turning to guilty concern as the hours passed, only to have her stumble in at four in the morning reeking of dope and Southern Comfort, her lipstick smeared like a bar girl. Once, in the middle of winter, her so-called friends dumped her on the front lawn, covered in vomit. In the morning, heading off to the bus stop, he found a pair of her underwear in the snow. At dinner, she argued with both of them, as if there were a world in which this was acceptable, and then to punish them, ran away.

He crept toward the door, shovel in hand, ready, if challenged, to say he'd heard a noise. He sidled closer, keeping to the shadows, and peeked through the window.

Margaret occupied one half of the glider, still talking, but not on her phone, and not to Arlene. Beside her, facing the lake, absorbing her spiel without a word, sat Kenny, the two of them gently rocking in the dark.

She went on, holding out her empty hands as if carrying an imaginary platter, then letting them drop. With the house buttoned up, Henry couldn't hear what she was saying, only her tone, raised in protest one minute, quietly resigned the next. Aware that he looked like someone from a cartoon, he leaned in, turning his head, and pressed an ear against the cold window.

As if she'd heard him, she abruptly stopped, and he shrank back into the shadows.

She flicked a lighter, the flame illuminating her face, bent and touched the tip to a skinny hand-rolled cigarette. She blew out a cloud and passed the joint to Kenny, who took a hit.

Though he'd hoped they'd outgrown it, he wasn't entirely surprised. He supposed it was better than smoking it in the cottage. Though Emily complained, sometimes after the children were in bed, when it was too buggy outside or raining, Arlene had a last cigarette on the porch, so there was precedent.

Margaret started in again, softly, spinning her tale as if they had all the time in the world. What kind of shape would they be in tomorrow? When they were younger, Henry would have thought nothing of interrupting, making them hide the weed, reminding them to lock up before they went to bed, an unsubtle hint. Now that they were adults it was harder to play the stern father, and rather than embarrass all three of them, he retreated.

As he was returning the shovel, careful not to ring the blade against the brass stand, from the porch came a great blast of laughter. It was a shock, and after what he'd seen, baffling. Though he couldn't say why, for an instant, with the habitual self-doubt of the outsider, he suspected they were laughing at him.

Safely back in bed, he decided he was just being paranoid, and maybe jealous. There were nights after the war he and Arlene stayed up long after everyone else was asleep, stargazing on the end of the dock or taking a canoe out and letting it drift in the middle, lying back, the only sound the water sloshing against the hull. As if his voice belonged to the darkness, his words rose, hung for a moment and sank into the lake. In his own way he'd been as lost as Margaret, and while he'd spared Arlene the worst (he would never tell anyone about the boatman they killed by mistake, or the bombed monastery, or the gypsy girl they found crucified upside down), he would always be grateful to her for listening. His deepest fear (also unspoken, being unspeakable) was that in the despair and confusion he knew so well, Margaret would kill herself. Discovering that she and Kenny shared the same bond as he and Arlene heartened him, and in the vague, floating reaches before sleep, he was reassured, knowing they could at least talk to each other.

The Five Warning Signs

IN THE MORNING HIS FINGERTIPS WERE NUMB, TINGLING AS IF still asleep. While Emily went to put on coffee and water Rufus, he opened and closed his hands like a transplant patient, shook them like a swimmer on the starting block, trying to get some circulation going.

Though it regularly happened at home, he blamed the bed, a double, much narrower than their king, with a groove worn down the middle that pushed them together. It was hard to get comfortable, a problem made worse by his hips hurting, and his back, and his bad knee. All night he shifted, trying to find the right position, finally settling on his left side, spooning Emily with his left arm stretched high over her head, behind her pillows, and then in the morning his shoulder hurt and his fingers were numb. It wasn't anything new or surprising, just another annoying reminder of the body's inevitable decline.

The first few times it happened, he'd told Emily.

"That's not good," she said, and the following Sunday passed him a *Parade* magazine with an article listing "The Five Warning Signs of a Heart Attack." Yes, his cholesterol numbers were terrible, but even Dr. Runco agreed, as a symptom, indigestion was too broad. Emily didn't care. For months she had Henry taking baby aspirin until another study refuted the claim.

He heard her in the bathroom. The toilet flushed, followed by the squeak of the faucet and water running, then the squeak again. He kneaded his fingers, wringing them until the feeling returned. When she opened the door to let Rufus in, he was able to pull the covers aside and invite her back to bed. Morning had been their time, a bar of pure light from the east window warming her skin.

"It's eight-thirty," she said. "I'm going to go take my shower."

"You sure?"

"I'm sure."

To assuage his disappointment, she leaned across her pillows and gave him a kiss, automatically fending off his hand.

"And take that dog with you."

"I will," she said, collecting her towels.

When she was gone, he stretched out, sprawled across the bed, wide awake, flexing his fingers. His arthritis was worse than the numbness, being permanent. Every day they hurt, but he would never say that. She worried enough. There was no point upsetting her by telling her something she already knew.

The Last Antenna
on Manor Drive

WHAT HE SHOULD HAVE DONE WAS HAVE KENNY CUT THE TOP off with the Sawzall. A wide herringbone array, it was made of aluminum tubing, a softer grade than the lawn chairs, a piece of cake for a titanium blade. They'd have to break it down for the recycling anyway. But Henry came up with this solution only afterward. Just as Emily didn't trust him on the roof, Henry didn't trust Kenny on the roof with the Sawzall. Despite his bloodline, as Emily once noted, he didn't have the engineering gene. The idea was to keep it as simple for him as possible. Just balancing with the bolt cutters would be tricky enough.

Henry could have had him tie a line to the antenna first, tethering it to the chimney, but then lowering it down would be an extra step, subject to its own problems. Again, that was later. He was trying to avoid getting it hung up on the gutter, as if that was their worst case.

From years of field experience, he knew the best solution usually had the fewest moving parts. The pole of the antenna was attached to the chimney by a pair of rusty brackets and held in place by three metal straps. From the base of the pole, two wires ran through a patch of tar just above the flashing. Once Kenny cut the wires and the straps, he could lift the pole out of the brackets and toss the whole awkward assembly onto the lawn. Altogether it couldn't weigh more than ten pounds. With the pitch of the roof, he'd have to chuck it about fifteen feet to clear the gutter.

"Can you do that?" Henry asked.

"I can do that," Kenny said, and he believed him.

When it was time, everyone came outside to watch, standing a safe distance away in the shade of the chestnut. Henry held the ladder for Kenny and then handed up the bolt cutters. Years ago, when they'd redone the roof, Henry had crisscrossed the slope shouldering rolls of tarpaper and tall bundles of shingles. Now Kenny scaled it on all fours like a rock climber, almost crawling. When he got to the top, he sat straddling the peak and waved, holding the pose so Ella could take a picture.

"Go Dad!" Sam called.

"Be careful," Emily said, then to Henry, "The power's off, right?"

That had been Kenny's first question. Henry didn't go into how an antenna worked.

"There's no power," he said. "Snip away."

Kenny raised the bolt cutters, shying back as if the wires were live, and cut them. He leaned in close to inspect his work. "Okay."

"Now do the straps."

"Does it matter in what order?"

"Nope. Just be careful. There might be some tension on them."

"Good to know."

These took longer. The straps were cinched tight, and he had to slip the jaws in behind them and chew at the metal till they sprang free. One by one he threw them down and Henry folded them and shoved them in a garbage bag, avoiding the sharp edges.

"All right," Kenny said.

"If you're done with the bolt cutters, toss them down."

"Watch out. I don't want to hit you."

"You won't," Henry said.

He flung them harder than he needed to, sending them cartwheeling across the lawn. Henry retrieved them and stood back, instinctively placing himself between the chestnut and where the antenna was going to land, as if to protect the women and children.

Tentatively, using the chimney for support, Kenny stood. He clung to the lip, hunched over, trying to lift the pole with one hand.

"It's stuck."

"It's probably just rusted. Try twisting it."

Again, he used one hand. "It's not moving."

"Hang on," Henry said, and backtracked to the garage for a can of WD-40 and a hammer. Standing at his workbench in the cool gloom, he said to no one, "Nothing's easy."

When he returned, Margaret was gone.

He waited at the top of the ladder while Kenny descended. He'd been up there maybe five minutes and his face was dripping with sweat.

"Give it a couple squirts and let it work for a minute."

"Okay." He didn't seem convinced, but shoved the can in his jeans pocket and went back up. He was game, yet Henry wished he could take his place.

There were no pictures this time. Kenny stood again, bracing himself against the chimney. He sprayed, and while he was waiting, tossed down the can.

Emily and Arlene watched with arms crossed. The boys were bored, spinning each other on the tree swing.

"Okay," Henry said. "That should do it."

Hanging on to the lip with one hand, Kenny banged away at the brackets, bringing Margaret out of the house. He set the hammer on the chimney and tested the pole. As if sensing a signal, the whole antenna turned.

"It should lift right out," Henry said.

For this Kenny had to use both hands. He relinquished his hold on the lip and reached over to grasp the pole, hugging the chimney with his front.

"Be careful," Emily said.

"It's loose," Kenny said.

"Lift it out if you can."

It seemed to come easily, but he didn't trust himself. As he straightened up and the pole cleared the top bracket and swung free, to compensate he hunched forward, nudging the hammer, which tipped and disappeared down the chimney, clanking against the damper.

"Fuck."

Behind Henry, the rest of them were silent. "It's okay. We can get it later."

"It's slippery."

"Take your time. Get a better grip if you need to."

He wiped one hand on his jeans, then the other.

"Whenever you're ready," Henry said.

Deliberately, as if measuring a putt, Kenny looked from the antenna to the empty lawn twice, then bent his knees and with a grunt heaved the whole thing skyward. The motion was awkward, abruptly cut off. Even before he completely let go, out of self-preservation one hand was groping for the chimney.

In Ligonier, at the Highland Games, they'd seen red-bearded musclemen in kilts squat and toss the caber, sending it flying end over end. In the case of the antenna, the pole was solid steel, heavier than the array. Instead of turning over in midair, the assembly fell pole-first as if weighted, straight down.

Even with no follow-through, his throw looked like it might be far enough. It was going to be close. For a second, watching the antenna drop, Henry willed it.

No.

"Oh dear," Emily said.

"Look out!" Margaret called.

With a thump, the base of the pole struck the roof a good foot short of the gutter. The whole thing teetered, upright, then toppled forward, tumbling over the edge, its momentum swinging it back into the house, ripping the flag out of its holder and knocking over the ladder, the bones of the array punching through the screen porch like the tines of a fork before coming to rest.

"Oh my," Emily said.

"It's all right," Henry said, as if it wasn't a disaster. "I was going to go to Baker's anyway."

His first concern wasn't the damage but getting Kenny down, as if he were stuck up there.

The flag and the ladder were fine, and the gutter. It was just the one screen.

"Sorry, Dad," Kenny said.

"It's all right. We got it down, that's what counts."

And while that was true, for the rest of the day—for weeks and months, and every time they told the story at family gatherings—he second-guessed his decision, coming up with new plans for a job they'd never have to do again, when the real solution was the simplest, the one he'd known instinctively all along. He should have just done it himself.

Pillow Talk

AT DINNER HE HAD SECONDS OF MARGARET'S PASTA, COMPLI-
menting her on the toasted pine nuts. Later, after pie and ice cream and an
overblown sci-fi movie, while they were reading in bed, Emily thanked him
as if he'd done her a favor. Though it was quiet, she spoke softly, conscious
of Arlene in the next room, the need for secrecy lending her words extra
meaning.

He shrugged. "It was good."

"I know she appreciated it."

"Good."

Rufus grumped from his rug as if they were interrupting his sleep.

"Shush, you."

She was grateful, and yet by singling him out, it felt like blame. With her,
everything was personal, bound up in history. There was always some ulte-
rior motive in play. He couldn't just like pine nuts.

"I gave her money."

He lowered his book. "How much?"

"Forty dollars. She gave me back the change."

Why this made a difference, he couldn't say. She knew giving Margaret money would bother him. That's why she was telling him now instead of this afternoon.

"Does she have enough to get home?"

"I'm sure she could use some cash." When he didn't reply, she added, "I'm glad she could come. I think she needed to get away."

He thought of her talking on the porch with Kenny the night before. "She seems all right."

"She thinks Jeff's having an affair at work."

"When did she tell you this?"

"When you and Kenny were off doing your thing. It's bad. They're not sleeping together. They haven't been for a while."

"What's a while?"

"Since January."

"But she looks so good."

"She's not eating. Did you see her at dinner? I'm afraid it's just a matter of time. What I worry about is what's going to happen after he leaves."

Henry murmured agreement, battling dire, half-formed thoughts, and thanked her. "I wouldn't have known."

"I know," she said, and apologized, acknowledging how overwhelming the topic was, especially so late.

"No," he said. "It's good that she's talking to you."

As if nothing had happened, they went back to reading. He'd contemplated Margaret's situation before, so he had no reason to be surprised, and yet the idea of her and Jeff sleeping in separate beds disturbed him. She'd been a lonely child, most at home in her room with the door closed, where she could read her fantasy novels about faraway kingdoms and listen to records promising endless love and sneak candy bars from a poorly hidden shoebox in her closet. Later, after she dropped out of college, she smoked dope and drank away whole days in her apartment, seeing no one. Before she met Jeff, Henry had worried that she would always live an ingrown, solitary life. Their new arrangement seemed to confirm it.

Who slept where? Did Jeff move to the guest room as a concession, or did she leave their bed in protest? In the mornings, did they avoid each other, or did they pretend everything was fine for the children? Did they both still use the master bathroom, only in shifts, and who would go first?

Outside, a car cruised by, a stripe of light sliding across the ceiling. Tomorrow morning she and Kenny were leaving. He wondered how late they'd stay up. He imagined her making the long, flat drive across Ohio with Justin, knowing what she was going back to. At least she had Sarah.

They read, cocooned, Rufus moving from the rug to his bed and settling with a huff. Propped on her pillows, Emily whistled, asleep with her book open. He nudged her. Muttering something, she closed it, gave him a bleary kiss and rolled over. He was spoiled, having her beside him every night, and again he felt sorry for Margaret, whether it was her fault or not. As a father, he wanted her to feel loved. Once, long ago, that had been his job. He supposed it still was. Outside, another car crawled by, or the same one, casing the place—probably just local kids partying at the boat launch. It was past midnight. He tried to read, but couldn't concentrate. When he leafed ahead to see where the chapter ended, it was at least ten pages away, and he gave up, replacing his bookmark, and turned out the light. Even then he couldn't stop thinking about her.

Too Quiet

KENNY, HAVING FARTHER TO DRIVE, GOT UP EARLY AND LEFT right after breakfast. Emily told Henry to leave the dishes and come say goodbye.

"Please give Lisa our best," she said, an unnecessary dig. "We'll see you on the Fourth."

"Thanks for all your help," Henry said, holding him.

"No problem. Sorry about the screen."

"Forget it."

Ella and Sam hugged everyone, including Rufus. As they backed out, waving, Emily took Henry's hand. They watched them tool away—"Love you," Arlene called—then filed inside, subdued.

Margaret took longer, though she had only Justin's stuff to wrangle. Henry helped bring their bags down. The floor of her minivan was strewn with empty water bottles and straws, fast-food wrappers and a flattened roll of paper towels, as if they'd been living in it. Scattered about among gummy-looking stains were smashed French fries and M&M's and pennies. He collected the larger trash with both hands and took it into the kitchen.

"I was going to get that," Margaret said, "I just haven't had time."

"It's okay," he said, though her car—like her old room—was always a mess. She didn't need to be so defensive. He was only trying to help.

As they were leaving, Emily teared up, clinging to Margaret as if she might never see her again. "I'm sorry, I'm an old moosh. It's been so nice having both of you here, it's hard to let go."

Though her open display embarrassed him, Henry agreed with the sentiment, if only after the fact. Saying goodbye, he felt an enervating impatience to be finished with it, like any difficult task, but once Margaret had driven off, after the first bloom of relief, as the stillness returned to their rooms and the fact of the children's absence sank in, he felt let down.

The waste seemed plain. It was a sunny day, the lake glinting, a brace of sunfish racing by the bell tower. Bees zigzagged low across the lawn, crawling over clover blossoms. It was a mystery to him, as a boy, when they left at the end of the summer, how Chautauqua would go on without them. Nothing had changed. Home, he would think of the banjo clock in the kitchen ticking off the hours, the sailboat weathervane turning with the wind. While he closed up the garage, Emily scoured the house for things they'd forgotten—Justin's swimsuit and towel on the back line, Sam's toothbrush, Margaret's phone charger. The collection depressed him, and the prospect of going to the post office tomorrow. They could stay, stock the fridge and skip the traffic, except Emily was having her hair done, and he was signed up to help with the rummage sale at church.

"What time do you want to get going?" she asked.

"I don't know, one?"

Arlene said she'd get lunch on the road. She was taking the back way, making a day of it. She had a guide Margaret had given her for Christmas that recommended the best drive-ins and diners in the state. There was an ice-cream stand in Oil City that was supposed to make their own Eskimo Pies.

"You know she's out of her gourd," Emily said, watching her Taurus glide by the Nevilles' golf carts.

"She has fun."

"And we don't?"

"We do," he said. "Just a different kind."

They had sandwiches again, finishing off the lunchmeat and potato salad. The burgers and dogs Emily stuck in the freezer for next time.

It didn't take them long to pack. By design they were leaving most of their clothes. Once he got the air going and Rufus settled on his bed in the backseat, Henry went in and strategically placed the new mouse baits. The last thing he did was put out the garbage, rolling the can bumping over the grass and parking it next to the mailbox. While the windows could still use a coat of paint, the cottage looked better without the antenna (his Grandmother Chase had always hated it), and he was pleased.

"And we're off," he said.

"Did you close the trapdoor?" To the attic fan, vulnerable to squirrels.

"I did."

"What about the pumphouse?"

"It should be locked."

"Okay," she said, insinuating, as if he was taking a chance.

"It's locked," he said, definite, and swung the Olds onto the road.

"Goodbye," Emily said, waving at the dark windows. "Don't miss us too much."

The Poor Chair

As they were flying down 79, they spied on the right shoulder what looked from a distance like a pile of roadkill. Closer, it appeared to be some kind of construction debris—a sign flattened by a semi, or a tangle of bent pipe. It was only when they were on top of it that it resolved into a black-lacquered antique chair with a cane seat, smashed to pieces.

"The poor chair," Emily said.

Henry was picturing it sailing off the top of a pile bungeed in the back of someone's pickup when he saw the cop hidden in the median, his radar gun leveled at them.

"Very clever," he said, taking his foot off the gas, but by then it was too late.

Attic Treasures

EVERY JUNE, CALVARY HELD ITS ANNUAL RUMMAGE SALE, AND every June, as one of its many co-chairs, he tried to persuade Emily to get rid of some of the junk cluttering their basement. He wasn't so heartless as to suggest she part with the set of ruby-tinted Venetian goblets they'd never once used, a wedding gift from her beloved aunt June, or the chipped japanned tea service—yet to be unpacked from its nest of crumpled newspapers—left to her by her mother, but the flimsy metal shelves against the front wall were crowded with trendy Crock-Pots and blenders and breadmakers she was done with that might entice a bargain hunter.

He understood her reluctance. Having grown up, as she herself put it, with limited means, she was too aware of what these gadgets cost, even if, as he pointed out, she'd originally received them as gifts. Rather than seeing them as inert and worthless, she valued them as assets. Gifts or not, to relinquish them would be like throwing money away.

What else could go? Dusty old punch bowls and their cups and ladles, a grocery bag full of mismatched ice trays (the new fridge had its own ice-maker), two fondue sets with color-coded forks so no one stole yours, a retired waffle iron, an impossibly slow ice-cream maker, several cast-iron skillets bought at the Dart Airport flea market and then left to rust, a salad spinner, a poached-egg mold, an electric griddle with a melted cord, a manual juicer that clamped to the edge of the counter and worked like a hand pump, a Seal-a-Meal machine and a roll of special plastic bags, a mortar and pestle, a pizza stone for the grill still in its unopened box, a ceramic chip and dip bowl shaped like a sombrero, an old set of good German knives she'd been meaning to give Betty for years, a plastic lighthouse cookie jar that bellowed like a foghorn when you opened the top, a bagel toaster, a transparent Lucite ice bucket and tongs, a slate cheeseboard you could write on with chalk and its fragile glass bell jar, a giant sieve, a tan-and-red plaid thermos whose top doubled as a cup, complete with a handle, four identical but different-colored plastic pitchers that held orange and grape juice and lemonade made from frozen concentrate and the children's Kool-Aid and Emily's iced tea, a mahogany smoked salmon platter shaped like a salmon, a half dozen dented Christmas-themed cookie tins, a wok, a pressure cooker, her mother's old meat grinder she used to make ham salad, a whole box of Mason jars for canning, and on and on, a roll call of the unloved and obsolete.

She would not go through the shelves item by item with him. The one time they'd tried that, years ago, five minutes in, as he was trying to recall the last time she'd made her own pasta, she blew up and told him to just take it all. What did he care if these things were important to her? What about all of his precious tools? Why didn't he donate some of them? They could probably get good money for them, and look at all the space they'd save. She stomped up the stairs, slamming the door as if to seal him in.

The process now was almost formal. He reminded her gently that the deadline for the sale was coming up, mentioning as encouragement the list of things he was going to donate, and when he was out of the house, like a thief, she crept down to the basement, placed the few items she'd chosen in a box and left it on his workbench. There was no negotiating, and no recriminations. *You get what you get and you don't get upset,* his mother used to say at the table when serving something he or Arlene despised. Henry never liked the imperative high-handedness of it. He knew Emily to be generous in all other respects, and surely the flaw came from her parents struggling to pay their bills during the worst of the Depression (her mother, a school-teacher, had taken in laundry, a subject of gossip in their small town), just as his sense of charity derived from his family being comfortable, so it was hard for him to admit, though the truth, each June, was irrefutable, that she could be stingy.

To make up for her, he gave more. This year he'd culled his hand tools, going through his various toolboxes and gathering all the redundant screw-drivers and hammers and files and wrenches and pliers and hacksaws and vise-grips and chisels and squares he'd collected over the decades, turning up several socket sets he'd completely forgotten about, and a ten-pound maul he thought he'd lost. Though a few of the older pieces had likely come from his father or even his grandfathers, and a few of the newer ones from Kenny and Margaret, he prided himself on not being attached to any of them. Knowing the church would benefit and that someone else might get some use out of them was enough.

As the deadline for donations approached, he pointedly vacated the house, asking if she needed anything while he was out, casually slipping down to the basement on his return to find his workbench empty. The anticipation re-minded him of Christmas when he was a boy, their gifts magically appearing beneath the tree, waiting to be weighed and shaken. And then one day he came home from helping Ed McWhirter set up the tables in the parish hall and there was the box, a bright yellow wine carton from the state store.

Going through it was like opening a present. He was always surprised and enlightened by what she chose to get rid of, especially since she was under duress. From the wall of junk, she winnowed down her choices to a handful of things she cared absolutely nothing for, the final selection a test of her true feelings, so it was with a diagnostic curiosity that he parted the flaps and unpacked her castoffs.

The hand mixer he might have expected, since she'd recently bought a new one, but he'd thought the waffle iron, the star of so many breakfasts in the children's middle years, was untouchable. He'd just begun absorbing the loss when he discovered, at the bottom of the box, wrapped in flaking newspapers, his mother's grapes.

There were four bunches. The leaves and vines were made of fine green wire and the grapes clear glass the color of Chablis, with a green felt base. Purely decorative, they graced the table on holidays, extensions of his mother's prized centerpiece, an ornate blown glass cornucopia (a casualty of the move from Mellon Street). Arlene had assigned one to each member of the family by size, Henry's naturally being the smallest. How many endless meals had he wiled away, pretending his grapes were a race car, guiding them through a landscape of water glasses and salad plates? Later, when he was old enough to set the table, he fetched them from the sideboard, placing them in front of their customary chairs like talismans.

There were his father's, the largest. One of the grapes had been cracked. He unwrapped the others and was pleased to see his own were intact. On his bench they looked strange and fussy, an old lady's knickknacks. They had no practical use besides paperweights, but he'd thought Emily liked them. His mother had taken to her from the beginning, the scrappy small-town girl, hoping she might exorcise the ghost of Sloan. Among his family she was Emily's champion (Grandmother Chase would never be won over, thinking her a shameless social climber, coming, as she said, "from nothing"), and by example showed her how to dress and decorate and entertain. Henry could see his mother's influence in Emily's preference for pearls and silver jewelry rather than showy gold and diamonds, and every Thanksgiving, in an unconscious echo of their very first dinner together, Emily made her pea casserole with water chestnuts.

A whole wall of junk, and this was what she picked. Was it a protest, to show she could be as ruthless as him?

"Margaret doesn't want them," she said at dinner, "and the last time I offered something to Lisa she made fun of me, so I'm not doing that any-more. *I'm* not going to use them."

"What about Arlene, did you ask her?"

"If you want to keep them, that's fine."

"No," Henry said, "you made your choices, I made mine." He would abide by the rules. You get what you get.

And yet the next day, when it was time for him to load up the Olds and take everything in, he was tempted to stash the grapes somewhere in the basement Emily would never find them. No one was going to buy them anyway. In the end they'd be hauled off to the Salvation Army along with the other unsold junk.

His tools, her dishes—it was all going to go at some point. The idea was to get rid of it so the children wouldn't have to. He hauled the boxes out to the garage and shut the trunk, and when he dropped them off at church, he didn't linger.

The Saturday of the sale, he went in early to help Noni Haabestadt orga-nize the silent auction. Here were the big moneymakers—Steelers and Pen-guins tickets and Outer Banks time-shares, a round at Oakmont—all of which would bring a premium, yet for a decade Calvary had been operating at a deficit. His grandmother Chase, who'd left the bulk of her estate to the church, always said the rich were cheap. Henry, who was cheap, agreed.

When he and Noni were done, he browsed the aisles like the other volun-teers. There seemed to be more good china than normal, the pink-flowered, gold-rimmed Limoges and Haviland favored by his mother's generation. He marked the bargains, marveling, simultaneously, at the bad taste of his fel-low parishioners. It was hard to imagine anyone buying this two-foot-tall porcelain geisha or those leering, demonic Aztec masks, and he wondered how many donations had originally been gifts.

The grapes ended up not on the middle tables with the mixer and the waffle iron, but back in a far corner with some nut dishes and trivets and vases going for fifty cents a pop. He could buy them—volunteers were allowed five presale items—but resisted, strolling past as if they had no connection to him. Instead, as if to satisfy a different craving, he bought a paper plate of brownies from the women's club bake sale.

The weather was good, and the turnout, the high-ceilinged hall alive with babble. Like the congregation, the crowd was older and mostly female, along with a few antique dealers and college students from Shadyside. They shuffled through the maze of tables, stopping to examine a beaded purse or pewter teapot before replacing it. In an apron and nametag, Henry helped at the checkout, fetching banded packets of ones and rolls of quarters for the cashiers, wrapping and bagging and boxing, expecting, any second, someone to claim the grapes.

The mixer went early, and the waffle iron, snatched up by a young couple he recognized from coffee hour. He refrained from recounting its history, just double-bagged it, tucking in the cord, and thanked them. His tools came through in dribs and drabs, and while he felt a pang with each, he was glad someone wanted them. Outside, after lugging boxes to people's cars, he dawdled, imagining it would be easier if he missed the actual sale of the grapes. They might be gone already. He dwelt on the idea as he grabbed a sandwich and a bag of chips for lunch in the refectory, and heading back it was by sheer will that he didn't snake his way through the crowd to the far end and check.

The rest of the afternoon he spent in dread, as if expecting bad news, though he couldn't say which outcome would be worse. The only reason his mother hadn't left the grapes to Arlene was because he was married. By rights they should have been hers, along with the crystal. He could buy them and give them to her, but then Emily would know.

You get what you get. Weren't the brownies enough?

If he didn't look until the end of the day, the grapes would be gone.

If he didn't look, they'd still be there.

He didn't look. The last hour he kept busy, consulting his watch until he had to take it off and slip it in his pocket. As the crowd thinned, he could finally see clear across the hall. From this distance it was impossible to tell.

"Our silent auction will be ending in five minutes," Noni announced over the P.A., making the stragglers look up. "Five more minutes to get your bids in, people. Don't lose out at the last minute. I know yinz want them Stillers tickets. Remember, all bids are tax-deductible. Good luck, everyone."

Still, dozens of shoppers wandered the aisles, as if they planned to stay the night. They waited till the official announcement that the sale was over to get in line. As he bagged their purchases, he was seized by the idea that the very last customer—Lois Reardon, a former chair of the Altar Guild—would have the grapes.

She didn't, just a box of old teardrop Christmas ornaments for a quarter, which she plucked, after much searching, from her change purse.

"The new ones don't have any personality," she said. "These are actual glass, from Czechoslovakia. You can see the imperfections."

"Thanks for coming out," Henry said, bagging them. "We'll see you tomorrow."

"That's right," she said, surprised, as if he'd read her mind, and doddered off.

Once the doors were shut, he could relax. As he did every year, he helped gather the lockboxes and carry them upstairs to the church offices, where Sally Hilliard and Joan Follansbee counted out the bills in piles like numbers runners. Noni was going through the sheets from the silent auction. The Lovejoys had won the Steelers luxury box seats for three thousand dollars, a new record.

"God bless them," Father John said.

While they were occupied, rather than wait for the final tally, Henry stole downstairs. The hall was filled with the clashing of dishes. Like movers, the youth group was already boxing everything for the Salvation Army, Ed McWhirter rearranging the bake sale tables for coffee hour. Henry was relieved to see they hadn't reached the far corner.

All he had to do was take his plate of brownies and go home, but then he'd never know. It was silly. The tenderness he felt was for his mother, and possibly his younger self, the baby of the family, indulged and forgiven, not the grapes, which they hadn't used in decades. It was just nostalgia, a by-product of time.

He made no pretense, ignoring everyone, going straight to the corner.

They were gone. In disbelief he scanned the table as if they might have been misplaced, and there, half-hidden beneath a discarded cake stand, were all four.

He wrapped them separately, taking special care with his father's, and went upstairs to pay.

He hid them in the bottom of an old toolbox, locked away where Emily would never find them. For weeks on end he forgot about them, and then, sitting across the table from her, he would remember and feel guilty. At other times, alone at his workbench, he was tempted to pull them out and admire them, a miser and his secret hoard, yet he never did. Ultimately he didn't need to see them. It was enough just knowing they were there.

Visiting Nurse

AFTER PUTTING IT OFF TOO LONG, HOBBLING UP AND DOWN
Grafton on one of Doug's old canes, Louise Pickering was finally having
her knee fixed, and naturally, as her best friend, Emily promised to help
around the house until she got back on her feet. Months ago, when Emily
first announced her plan, Henry had gone along with it, suppressing his
reservations. The last two weeks of June they normally spent at Chautauqua, savoring the quiet before the hordes arrived, but Louise would need
her, and Emily wanted to. While he was against anything that upset their
routine, in this case he recognized he was being selfish. Nothing he might
say would stop her anyway.

It had cost him little to agree with her then. Now the day loomed like a
balloon payment, and he wished he hadn't capitulated so quickly.

"Are Tim and Dan coming?"

"Dan's coming for a few days. Tim couldn't get off."

Not a surprise. Dan was devoted, Tim aloof. They were estranged, their
childhood rivalry turned bitter. Henry never understood it.

"You said she's having a nurse come in."

"A visiting nurse. She'll look in on her, but she needs someone there all the time, just until she can fend for herself. With the new procedure recovery's supposed to go a lot faster. That's why she waited. The incision's only a half inch."

He knew, he just didn't believe it would be that easy. At their age, there were always complications.

Though Dan had rented a car, the morning of the surgery Emily enlisted Henry to drive them to the hospital. As a toddler, Dan had taken baths with Margaret in the Pickerings' claw-footed tub and given her her first kiss. Later he'd played quarterback for Shadyside, his blond hair fashionably long. At their block parties, Henry would see him breeze through, always with a new girl on his arm. Like Margaret, he was an indifferent student, kicked off the team his senior year for smoking dope. The Golden Boy, Doug called him ironically, a nickname that would prove apt. A ski bum and surfer well into his thirties, he was now a realtor in Hawaii. Deeply tanned and still fit, with a ponytail and sandals, he sat in back with Louise, watching the car lots of Bloomfield slide by, laughing as Emily recalled the wedding Margaret staged in their backyard.

"I remember we got in trouble for picking the flowers."

"My tea roses. Oh, I was so mad."

"It wasn't my idea. I was just doing what I was told."

"She had all you boys buffaloed," Louise said.

"She was bigger than we were."

How much he knew about Margaret's latest problems Henry wasn't sure. There were no secrets between Emily and Louise, an alarming breach of security that paradoxically made him more rather than less guarded around her. He and Doug had been friends for forty years, based partly on a mutual respect for each other's privacy. Henry would never think of questioning Doug's handling of Tim and Dan's feud or confessing his money troubles to him, and trusted Doug to return the courtesy. When Henry visited him in Presby, there was no need to talk about his prognosis. "Thanks for doing the leaves," Doug said, and Henry said he could do theirs next year. "Fair enough." Now, ridiculously, he was afraid Louise would never come home either, and what that would do to Emily.

He dropped them off in front like a cabbie, convinced it was the last he'd see of her, but when he'd found the visitors' lot around back and followed the purple line on the floor to Orthopedics, she was still waiting to give her information. The chairs were filled, everyone from teens to men Dan's age to Louise. He'd heard of surgeons doing operations all day, like an assembly line.

Dan knew a woman in Vail, an Olympic racer, who had both hips and both knees replaced.

"Not all at once," Emily said.

"First the hips, then the knees. Now she's skiing black diamonds."

"I just want to go up and down the stairs," Louise said.

When the nurse with the clipboard finally called her name, Dan went with her. Henry leafed through a beat-up *Motor Trend,* unsure how they were helping. Emily was busy making a shopping list. All week she'd been fretting over her menu as if the children were coming to visit, trying to divine what Louise would feel like eating, if anything.

A few minutes later Dan came back carrying her purse like a football.

"You guys don't have to stay. I'll let you know when she's out."

"Don't be silly," Emily said, ignoring his offer, patting the chair beside her. "What would you rather have with your chicken—orzo or couscous? Will you eat Brussels sprouts? How about artichokes? Kenneth won't touch either of them, so I always ask."

In her enthusiasm she spoke so the whole room could hear, which oppressed Henry, who sat mute and useless, relinquishing any hope he may have harbored for the day.

From the moment Louise proposed her surgery, like a hungry understudy, Emily had been waiting to take charge, and would not be deterred. They stayed until the nurse rolled Louise out in a wheelchair, and once she was installed in her bed at home, an ice pack Velcroed over one leg of her pajama bottoms, Emily assumed control of the household, acting as both nurse and housekeeper, leaving Dan nothing to do.

"He's gotten weirder," she said in bed. "I think smoking all that pot did something to him."

"At least he came."

"He watches cartoons."

"What kind of cartoons?"

"Weird ones. I heard him laughing at them."

What he thought of her, Henry couldn't imagine.

She set her alarm a half hour early so she could walk down Grafton and make breakfast for them, taking her knitting, and returned after dinner with an update and a new list. She was glad she was able to help, she said. The visiting nurse was there for fifteen minutes tops. All she did was check the dressing and make sure the stitches weren't infected. "It's a rip-off. Imagine what the insurance companies are paying them."

"Any cartoons today?"

"Today he was on his phone. Supposedly he's closing some big deal."

"You don't sound convinced."

"It's hard to take him seriously when he's wearing a tie-dyed shirt. I don't know, maybe Hawaii's different."

"The whole world's different."

"I suppose," she said, as if there was nothing to be done about it.

Thick, humid days, haze hanging like fog over Morningside. The city had opened cooling centers for the poor, and the news was full of warnings for pet owners. The zoo was closed. This was why they escaped to Chautauqua, the swampy, near-southern Pittsburgh summer recalling Camp Claiborne, washing down his salt pills with musty canteen water. He kept the house buttoned up, the compressor of their central air droning in the yard. It was too hot to work in the garden, too hot to wash the car. When Rufus came in from peeing, his coat held the heat of the sun. With Emily gone, he followed Henry from room to room.

"I know," Henry said. "It's no fun without Mama."

He didn't mind making his own sandwich, setting a place for one at the breakfast table and watching the noon news, but microwaving the Saran-wrapped plate she'd left for him and eating dinner alone seemed a punishment. As he was doing the dishes, the phone rang in his office. He picked it up with wet hands and then was angry when it was a recording trying to sell him life insurance. Was this how she felt when he had to work late? At least she could call. He went upstairs and watched their shows, answering the questions on *Jeopardy!,* noting the answers she would have gotten, listening for the front door like Rufus and following him down when she finally returned.

Rufus clamored around their knees while Henry kissed her.

"I think someone missed me."

"Two someones. How's Louise?"

"Fine. Bored. Their second floor is hot as blazes. I'm ready for a glass of wine."

According to the visiting nurse, everything was healing nicely, right on schedule. Dan was leaving tomorrow, meaning for the next few days Emily would be staying overnight.

As if to register his displeasure, Henry said nothing.

"I told you this," she said. "Someone needs to be there in case there's an emergency. It's only for three nights."

"I can't help it. I'm used to having you all to myself."

"Don't be jealous."

He shrugged it off like the joke she intended, but he was. Though they'd spent months apart when he was at Jackass Flats, that was different. The last time he'd slept alone in their bed was when she'd flown out to watch Sarah and Justin while Margaret was in rehab, another mission she'd volunteered for with no hesitation. She was needed, he wasn't, and now, like then, he felt snubbed.

The first night, as if to apologize for abandoning him, she cooked dinner, but after kissing her goodbye he was glum and annoyed with himself, leaving the lights off as dusk fell, pacing the gray rooms with a refill of scotch as if he'd been jilted, and turned in early. She'd taken her pillow, which made their king seem even emptier. As if to be closer to her, he slept on her side, setting his water on her nightstand, and when he woke at three to use the bathroom, for a moment he was confused. He had to step over Rufus, but when he came back, he'd moved. Spread-eagled in the middle of the now-strange bed, adrift, still muddled from the scotch, Henry fell prey to his imagination. The single dinner plate, the silent house, the tumbler in the sink—this was how it would be if he lost her. His mother had gone quickly, from liver cancer, the mass discovered too late. He thought of his father alone in his condo, crossing off days on the calendar like a prisoner. He'd survived her by thirteen years, yet every time Henry saw him, he quoted her as if they'd just spoken. Henry could picture himself doing the same to the children. He already lived too much in his memory.

Overnight it rained, and in the morning his vision of the future evaporated like the haze. He expected Emily to come back after breakfast, then lunch. By the time the phone rang, a little before three, he'd given up, and was surprised to hear her voice. He tried to sound blasé.

Could he pick up some DVDs Louise had ordered at the library?

"Anything else you need while I'm out?"

She had to check with Louise. "No, we're pretty well stocked. How's bachelor life?"

"Very exciting. Rufus chased a bunny."

"That is exciting."

"He misses you."

"It's just one more day."

And two nights, technically, but he knew better than to press her. He was just glad for the excuse to visit.

Waiting for him at the library were *Jane Eyre* and *Emma*, sentimental favorites from Emily's bookish girlhood. Like so many women her age, she and Louise were rabid Anglophiles, lovers of the repressed, well-bred universe of gala balls and shooting parties as if it were their inheritance. For years they'd dedicated Monday nights to *Masterpiece Theatre*, making an occasion of it with claret and chocolates, leaving Henry to watch football by himself, which he honestly didn't mind. Being married, he could stand only so much romance.

When he walked down to drop them off, Emily took him upstairs to see Louise, propped in bed with a fan blowing on her, her knee wrapped in an Ace bandage. Her toenails were painted the same pearly pink as Emily's, and he recalled the sleepovers Arlene and her friends used to have in the attic, chattering away till all hours. The TV was paused in the middle of something that might have been *Titanic*. On her nightstand, along with a bottle of Advil, was an open Hershey bar broken into pips.

"Thank you," she said. "And thank you for letting me borrow Emily."

It hadn't been his decision, but she knew that, and he asked how she was feeling.

"Fat and lazy. I haven't moved in the last week except to go to the bathroom. Your lovely wife's been making me gourmet meals."

"Yes," Emily said, "gourmet meatloaf."

"Chicken cordon bleu." One of his favorites.

"That's easy," Emily protested, giving him a look that said she'd make it up to him.

Downstairs, seeing him out, she said, "One more day."

"I know."

"Hey," she said at the door, the word pregnant, as if she had something important to say.

"What?"

"Would you mind doing the garbage? No one did it last week."

"Of course." It was Thursday.

After an overcooked burger on the grill, he did their own, emptying Rufus's poop bucket and rolling the cans to the curb. At least the night was nice. He sat on the back porch, drinking a beer and listening to the Pirate game as fireflies rose from the garden and dusk filled the trees. At Chautauqua it would be a good ten degrees cooler. They'd linger on the screen porch in jeans and sweatshirts, watching the last stragglers tooling for the launch, running lights bright as jewels gliding across the water. When it was dark they'd stroll to the end of the dock for a look at the stars, then go inside and have a fire. They'd be there next week, just the two of them, if everything went well with Louise.

He was patient. He could wait. They'd been married almost fifty years. There was no point moping about like a lovesick teenager.

Then why, not an hour later, rather than finishing the game, was he standing on the sidewalk in front of the Pickerings' with Rufus, gazing up at the flickering blue glow like a spurned suitor, hoping to catch a glimpse of her? The conversation coming from the open window sounded urgent, a man and a woman in trouble, but though he strained, he couldn't make out the words. A piano played a ponderous largo, Beethoven, maybe Schubert, and he remembered when they were first courting, as he crossed the lawn of her sorority with a bouquet of daisies, overhearing her practicing and feeling a vaulting joy, knowing it was for him. The glow wavered. A train whistled. The voices returned, insistent yet meaningless, beyond reach. If he were young and ardent, a hero in a movie, he might have thrown a pebble to get her attention, or burst into song, but knew she'd disapprove. He stood there an extra minute, giving Rufus time to mark the garbage can, then headed home.

Funny

HE THOUGHT HE'D SLEEP BETTER AFTER SHE CAME HOME, YET their first night he was wide awake. His hips hurt, and his shoulder. He'd grown used to having the whole bed to himself and felt crowded. He was shifting to find the right position when she murmured with pleasure and said clearly, gaily, as if responding to a remark at a party, "That's funny."

He waited, alert, hoping for a clue to the context. She mumbled something and rolled over, and soon she was under again.

That's funny. That's remarkable, or odd, ironic. With only the one line to go on, he had no idea what it might mean. She'd seemed amused and interested, and the throaty, almost carnal murmur, as if she were flirting, fawning. It was probably nothing, part of a harmless dream, except, knowing her voice so well, he had the distinct impression that she wasn't speaking to him.

Wish List

THE SUNDAY BEFORE FATHER'S DAY, IN HIS PRESENCE, EMILY reminded Margaret to call him next week, as if she might forget. School was out, Sarah was headed off to cheerleader camp that Saturday, and from what he could deduce, Margaret was dreading being home with only Justin as a buffer. Emily commiserated with her at length, shaking her head at Henry to relay how bad things were there, and then she and Margaret were trying to recall which cookbook had Aunt June's corn chowder. "Would you like to talk to your father?" Emily asked, and, after a final digression concerning the proper brand of chowder crackers (Westminster), handed him the phone.

"So, what do you want for Father's Day?" Margaret was on her cell, and he had to decode what she was saying through the static, the delay making their conversation even more awkward.

"Nothing. I just got through telling your brother I have everything I need."

"It's not about what you need, it's about what you want."

"There's nothing I really want. Corn chowder."

"If you don't ask for anything, you can't complain about what you get." It was an old saw of Emily's, probably from her mother.

"Have I ever complained?" He couldn't remember what they'd gotten him last year (Margaret a solar-powered emergency radio/flashlight for Chautauqua, Kenny a work light with flexible legs Henry had used when he squeegeed the basement, actually very handy).

"You're not making this easy."

"If I think of something, I'll let you know."

He'd asked for nothing partly because he didn't want her spending money on him, but also because it was true. He wasn't being selfless, just honest, but as the week passed, the question nagged at him. At his age, materially, what was left to desire? He could buy himself anything he wanted within reason, yet even at the Home Depot there was nothing he coveted. The sweets he liked were bad for him, and he had more scotch than he could possibly drink. Something for the house, something for the car. His mind emptied, seized.

"Your happiness," he might say, but that could set her off.

When the children were little, they made him presents—popsicle stick and glitter picture frames with magnets for the fridge, plastic bead necklaces he still kept in a cigar box in his dresser. Drawings and paintings and clever origami. On his desk sat a bumpy banana-yellow pencil holder Margaret had turned at day camp crammed with pens and markers and scissors, its glaze crazed like a vase from the Ming dynasty, her initials gouged into the chalky bottom. He'd made something similar for his mother, an innocent token of his love, and remembered the pride he felt seeing its place of honor on her vanity, but also, years later, the shame, because it was clumsy, unworthy of her.

He was wary when it came to gifts—giving and receiving—as if the idea embarrassed him. It was like trying to read someone's mind, a skill he lacked (unlike Arlene, who tied her own bows and always chose the perfect card). As the children grew, from year to year he never knew what to get them, which made him feel old and out of touch. Emily did their Christmas shopping, leaving him to choose the hardest gift of all, hers. She dropped hints, and when that failed left dog-eared catalogs on the coffee table, circling the sizes and colors for him, and then Christmas morning, opening her presents, joked, "How did you know?"

Receiving was just as problematic. A gift was what another person thought of you, and over the years he'd come to understand, by consensus, that his children saw him as someone who wore a tie to work, used power tools, played golf and drank scotch, which, while all true, seemed a superficial view of him. And yet when asked directly, he couldn't say what he wanted. Nothing.

Friday a box arrived via UPS and was promptly confiscated by Emily, who whisked it upstairs for safekeeping. Saturday he expected a second package, but there was just a flyer from the Giant Eagle, and he assumed that Margaret's would show up next week.

Normally they would be at Chautauqua by now, with its own Sunday-morning rituals, and were forced to improvise. Getting ready for church, Emily asked if he wanted to do anything special afterward, like go to the club. No, he said, he'd rather relax and read the paper. When they came back, he couldn't stop her from making him eggs Benedict, and knew better than to argue.

When she called him to the table, a present was waiting at his place—a book, from the look of it, wrapped in navy blue paper with a squashed gold bow. Accompanying it was a miniature envelope. In the past Kenny had given him fat biographies of presidents and Revolutionary War histories, the same stolid bestsellers he'd bought his own father. This was thinner. Maybe a mystery, the latest spy thriller.

"Wait," Emily said, and brought him a mimosa. They clinked glasses. "Happy Father's Day."

"Thank you. I take it these two go together."

"Open the card and find out."

HAPPY FATHER'S DAY, it read, in a charmless font, LOVE MARGARET AND KENNY.

"Interesting." He looked to her as if she were in on it. Of course she was.

The book was light because it wasn't a book at all but a transistor radio, a slim, digital Grundig that fit in the palm of his hand, the design a triumph of German engineering. The rubberized case was waterproof. Supposedly it floated.

"In case you drop it overboard," Emily said. "Or throw it, knowing the Pirates."

"It must have been expensive. Grundig's top of the line."

"Do you like it?"

"I love it. Thank you."

"I had nothing to do with it." She held up one hand as if taking an oath. "They came up with it all by themselves."

Astonishing as it was, he believed her. Kenny was a big Red Sox fan, always complaining about the Yankees. Henry just wished they hadn't spent so much money on him.

He was in the backyard, listening to the game, when Margaret called.

"I thought you'd like it," she said.

"It was your idea?" He tried not to sound surprised.

"Sarah has her earphones on all the time, and I thought, what do you listen to?"

"Thank you," he said. "It's perfect."

And it was. Besides AM and FM, it picked up shortwave and world band signals, reminding him of his parents' old Philco, pulling cryptic voices out of the air. The reception was crisp, and there was a hold button so he could lock in stations. He took his new toy, as Emily called it, everywhere, slipping it in his pocket, listening in the backyard and the garage, or walking Rufus around the block. At night he left it on his dresser with his wallet, in the basement made a place for it on his workbench. Even when it wasn't on, each time it caught his eye, the sheer style and ingenuity of it exhilarated him, and he was grateful, marveling at how quickly it had become one of his favorite things, this extravagant gift he hadn't known he'd needed.

GetGo

FINALLY, THE VERY LAST WEEK OF JUNE, LOUISE WAS AGILE enough on her crutches so that Emily felt comfortable leaving her by herself. Henry said it was fine, there was no rush. He didn't have to say they'd already missed his favorite part of vacation, because it was hers too. She appreciated how patient he'd been, and she was ready. Raised in a backwoods mountain town, she hated summer in the city. The Edgewood Club's pool was a zoo and it was too hot to sleep at night. They needed to be at Chautauqua.

They chose Wednesday, to beat the weekend traffic. He turned off the mail and the paper and called Arlene, asked Jim Cole to look after their garbage cans.

The day before they left, he drove over to the GetGo on the edge of Wilkinsburg to fill up the Olds so they wouldn't have to stop on their way out of town. He had a plastic loyalty card on his key ring, along with one for AutoZone and CVS and Staples. For every ten dollars they spent at the Giant Eagle, they received three cents off per gallon, making the trip well worth it. If the neighborhood was iffy, it was no worse than East Liberty, and the next closest GetGo was all the way across the bridge in Fox Chapel. He'd been to this station dozens of times. In the middle of a weekday, right on the main drag of Penn Avenue, he didn't anticipate any problems, but out of habit, as he pulled up, choosing a front pump so he couldn't be blocked in, he noted the other cars, and was reassured to see his two fellow customers were both women.

A flat canopy shaded the plaza, teenybopper pop jangling from hidden speakers. His discount was seventy-two cents a gallon, and the Olds had a massive tank. He did the math automatically, the numbers irresistible— he'd be saving over thirteen dollars. He pressed YES to accept, fit the nozzle in and started pumping. The mini-mart at the far end was hopping, as always, people stopping for sodas and chips and cigarettes. He'd had panhandlers accost him before, and was glancing around, nonchalant, checking the sidewalk and the lot of the Rite Aid across the street, when, through the music, he heard a siren approaching.

The women looked up, turning like Henry toward Penn, where a line of cars waited at the light. The siren rose and fell, growing louder, closing on them. Though he scanned the road, he couldn't locate the source. A block down, across from the Wendy's, there was a hospital. It was probably just an ambulance dropping off, and then another siren joined in, urgent, filling the air with a whooping like a car alarm, and another, wailing high and sustained in the distance as if to signal an air raid, all three speeding to the rescue, the noise soaring, reverberating all around. Behind the sirens, growling like a pack of motorcycles, came a roaring of engines, mounting, racing straight for them.

Henry saw the lead car, a black SUV chased by two cruisers. They flew down the middle of Penn Avenue, traffic parting on both sides as the sound radiated ahead of them like a shock wave, overtaking the GetGo, drowning out the music. Drivers trapped at the light jumped the curb. Still holding the nozzle, he watched as the SUV and the cops blew through the intersection, a McDonald's cup tumbling in their wake. Caught in the slipstream, it spun like a top, wobbled and rolled to rest against the curb, the sirens receding, the street returning to normal.

The women shook their heads at each other, united in disapproval, as if they were tired of this kind of foolishness. Henry would have shaken his head in sympathy, but was afraid it wasn't his place, and concentrated on the pump until he was done.

"You're lucky you didn't get shot," Emily said when he told her, and while she was being melodramatic, he thought she was at least partly right. As the SUV was flying by him, he didn't duck behind the Olds as he should have, using its tanklike bulk for cover, just stood there transfixed, watching it all like a TV show, his soldier's instincts deserting him. In basic, before anything, they'd learned to hit the dirt. The hedgerows were full of snipers, and more than once that simple training had saved his life. On patrol he was alert for the smallest sound—a cough, a rustling of grass—prepared to be shot anywhere, at any time. Embree laughed at him, sneaking up behind him in camp and clapping his hands to see him drop. Once, after he was back, a professor snapped a piece of chalk at the blackboard and Henry found himself crouching in the aisle beside his chair. He'd been embarrassed then, the brave G.I. betrayed by his reflexes. Now their degradation bothered him, as if he were defenseless, an easy target.

"From now on," Emily said, "you're going to Fox Chapel."

"There's nothing wrong with Wilkinsburg."

"Maybe *I* should shoot you."

"Maybe you should," he said.

At five they turned on the news, but there was no mention of it, and in the morning they were gone.

The Last Time

RUFUS KNEW. WHEN HE SAW THEIR SUITCASES, HE HUNG HIS
head as if he was being punished. He followed Emily around the house as
she packed, whimpering at the back door as she took a box of food out to
the car.

"Stop it," she said. "Now."

"He's worried."

"He should be."

It was only half a joke. She'd been short with both of them all morning,
muttering under her breath as she stalked from room to room. She was the
same way when the children were little, overwhelmed, accusing him of not
helping enough, as if she were solely responsible for the whole family. He
knew not to take it personally. Any vacation, the last frantic minutes before
leaving flustered her, even that brief chaos too much for her nerves. Her
anger was the fuel she used to keep going. Once they were on the road she'd
be fine.

He drew the curtains in the living room.

"I'm not done in there," she said, hauling herself upstairs, and he opened
them.

"What can I do?" he called after her.

"Nothing."

He wandered through the dining room and peered outside. The grill was covered, the gas turned off, the hatch locked. He'd meant to tie back the few renegade raspberry canes reaching into the yard, but it was too late.

Rufus came bounding down the stairs ahead of Emily. She stopped by her chair to gather her knitting into a bag. "Now I'm done."

They started off right on time, slipping out of town in the lull after rush hour. The day was cloudless, a train crossing the river with them, the trestle mirrored in the water. In Sharpsburg, a painter in a bosun's chair was giving the great onion dome of the Russian church a new coat of gold. Emily, fully recovered, took the time to look up, then went on counting stitches. Beyond the cliffs of Millvale, downtown rose like a postcard, his father's buildings conspicuous, the fountain at the point spouting its trademark white arc. They swung north, climbing the long bypass up Observatory Hill, shooting through the suburbs as if released, free of the city's gravity. Outside of Wexford the road split. In minutes they were surrounded by forest, every curve and hillside familiar. He'd paid the bills, taken back her library books and DVDs. If the grass burned, it burned. Finally they were leaving, summer beginning again, life returning to its true rhythm.

Emily didn't have to warn him about going too fast. After his ticket he was gun-shy and kept to the right lane. In the backseat Rufus lay curled on his blanket as if he were freezing. Instead of three weeks to themselves, they would have three days. He wanted to take her golfing, and out on the boat, and to dinner at Andriaccio's, just the two of them. He'd checked the weather: It was supposed to be perfect.

"So," Emily said, "what did we forget?"

"Nothing. This time we remembered everything."

"That would be a first."

"Nothing we can't live without."

They were clipping along through farmland—gray, peeling barns and new blue silos, neatly spaced rolls of hay. The light on the fields was golden, mist rising from ponds.

"I talked to Margaret yesterday. She said Jeff's coming."

"Just for the weekend," he guessed.

"No, the whole week."

"Are they getting along any better?"

"I think it's well beyond that at this point."

"Really." He wasn't surprised, and yet, having been with Emily so long, he couldn't imagine just giving up. He was sorry for Margaret. At the same time he couldn't completely blame Jeff.

"I don't know what I was hoping," Emily said. "I don't think they ever recovered from the last time."

"You might be right."

"Not that that's any excuse for him to go running around on her, if what she's telling me is true, and I think it is."

"So why is he coming?"

"Why doesn't he just stay there and shack up with his little chickie? I'm sure it's for the children. Which is not always for the best."

"Now I wish he wasn't coming."

"You're not to say a word of this to anyone," she said, threatening him with her needles.

He zipped his lips and tossed the key over his shoulder, but as they spun along through the empty middle of the drive, the idea of Jeff being there all week bothered him. For years he'd thought they'd been on the same side when it came to Margaret. How had that changed, and what should he say to him?

"Look out for the deer," Emily said, pointing with her knitting at a doe grazing on the grassy slope to the right. "Where there's one . . ."

He slowed, though they were already past any danger. "It's not the time of day for deer."

"It is for this one."

Farther on, as if to prove how unforgiving the world could be, the left lane held a massive bloodstain, tire tracks spreading dotted lines across the concrete like wet paint. Emily shivered.

"Oh deer," Henry said.

She shook her head, still counting.

He wouldn't let Jeff ruin the few days they had. Golf, a romantic dinner, a fire every night. He might take her out in the canoe like they used to, drifting in the middle, watching the dark spaces between the constellations for meteors, except he wasn't sure he could get in and out of it anymore. They could take a blanket and stargaze from the end of the dock.

"Shoot," Emily said.

"What?"

"My slippers."

"Darn it," he said. "So close."

"No," she said. "Not close at all."

Miles later, outside of Erie, he remembered the radio in the basement, sitting on his workbench, but said nothing.

Fly Me to the Moon

IT WAS THE BUSY SEASON, EVERYONE MAKING IMPROVEMENTS and taking care of repairs before the big holiday weekend. Up and down Manor Drive, their neighbors' turnarounds were full of plumbers' vans and contractors' pickups, and from sunrise well into cocktail hour the shearing squeal of power saws and the rhythmic thunk of nail guns vied with the buzz of Jet Skis, drawing sighs from Emily, trying to read her book in peace. The mowers arrived, driving her inside. Henry, having been on the board of the homeowners' association, was reassured by the noise as if it were a sign of progress. He had no major projects scheduled, but, inspired by all the activity, grabbed a sanding block and started prepping the window frames.

"The children can do that," Emily said.

"They can paint them."

"You don't trust them."

"They can paint them."

After lunch, as he'd promised, he took her out on the lake, cruising through the no-wake zone by the Institute, past the marina and the beach and the bell tower, then goosing the throttle and running all the way up to Mayville, the bow bucking over the waves. Emily basked behind her sunglasses, a hand clamped to her hat. She pointed to oncoming traffic as if he were unaware.

"Thank you," he said. "I see him."

When they were younger, she loved to drive the old boat. Those first years, before the children, they spent the whole summer on the water, dropping anchor in a cove and swimming off the side, taking turns skiing, the towrope yanking him upright, pulling him jolting across the surface. Bright, pagan days. He remembered her in her white suit, lean and deeply tan, standing with one knee on the seat to see over the windshield, her hair snapping straight back like a flag. Now she was content to let him pilot her around, and though he couldn't say why, he thought it was a loss, and felt vaguely unfaithful, as if her younger self were another woman. Though she might disagree, he liked to think he hadn't changed that much.

He grilled steaks for dinner, and garlic bread. The red he'd bought wasn't available in Pennsylvania, and he was pleased when she said they should bring some home. Afterward, to make room for pie, they took Rufus for a walk around the ponds of the fish hatchery, where he chased the geese until his tongue hung out the side of his mouth. He drank two bowls of water before flopping down on the hearth. Henry built a fire and they had peach pie, her favorite, hot from the microwave, topped with vanilla ice cream. When he came back from doing the dishes, she'd taken the corner of the loveseat under the lamp and was working on her knitting, and he knew better than to disturb her.

Tomorrow was their last full day alone together. It would go fast. They had a nine o'clock tee time at Chautauqua Shores and reservations at Andriaccio's. In between he was hoping to get a coat of primer on the window frames. He read his biography of Shackleton half-heartedly, fretting about Jeff and Margaret. On the hearth, Rufus galloped in his sleep, paws twitching. Henry pointed, and Emily nodded over her bifocals. Shackleton's ship was icebound, his men starving. The clock in the kitchen ticked.

Finally she set her knitting aside and massaged her hands. "Did you want to take a walk down to the dock?"

"So you *were* listening."

"You only said it about ten times."

"Let me get a blanket." Rufus was up now, not wanting to miss out.

"We're not staying if it's buggy."

"Fair enough." Victorious, he was willing to grant any condition.

When he opened the door of the screen porch, Rufus shot across the lawn as if he were after something, then circled back, sniffing the grass like a bloodhound. The air had cooled, and there was a ring around the moon, softening it. The night was still, the flags limp. In the chestnut, cicadas chirred. Knowing where they were headed, Rufus led them on. The dock shook beneath their feet and Henry gave her his arm. A night like tonight, when they were dating, they'd take the canoe out to the middle of the lake and lie side by side, kissing for hours, the stars turning above them. Even now he could recall the moonlight on her skin, the dark hollows of her throat.

The bench was empty, and the Cartwrights' dock. Across the water, the lights of the amusement park twinkled, making him think of the old casino at Bemus Point where they used to dance. He set down the blanket and rested his hand on her hip, pulling her closer.

"What are we doing?"

"Dancing." Rufus watched them, unsure.

"Shouldn't there be music?"

"*Fly me to the moon,*" he sang in her ear, "*and let me play among the stars.*"

"Are those the only ones you know?"

"*Something something something, on Ju-piter and Mars.*"

"Where did all this come from?"

"We only have one more night together."

"Please," she said. "We're always together."

"Not like this."

She sighed as if he was being difficult.

"You know I'm crazy about you."

"You're just crazy," she said. "I thought you wanted to look at the stars."

"I do. With you."

They sat on the bench, the blanket spread over their laps, faces tipped to the heavens. The sky was the same, unchanging as the lake, and summer— both Dippers, the Pleiades, the line of Orion's Belt. High up, a plane glided between the stars, a light blinking on a wingtip. When he squeezed her hand, she snuggled into him. He wrapped his arms around her, nuzzling her neck, smelling her familiar perfume. It was all he wanted, this closeness. If he missed those early years before desire gave way to a more lasting affection, his love for her was still extravagant. He could have happily sat like this forever, listening to the waves slapping the pilings, but it was chilly and the mosquitoes were bad, and after a few minutes she patted his arm for him to release her and stood, cueing Rufus, and he folded the blanket and followed them back inside.

Sleeping Arrangements

EMILY AND LISA HAD NEVER GOTTEN ALONG. THE REASONS WERE legion, the foremost, according to Emily, being that Lisa was spoiled. From the beginning the two of them had fought bitterly, and now, twenty years later, had reached an uneasy peace. They barely spoke, leaving Henry and Kenny to act as go-betweens, every visit a diplomatic mission.

Jeff Emily liked. A former offensive lineman raised Methodist by his ex-missionary grandmother in the hinterlands of Michigan (the tip of the mitten, as he said, holding up a massive hand), he was even-tempered and polite. He worked as an administrator in a retirement community, and if Emily wished he were more ambitious, she would always be grateful to him for helping Margaret.

"It's a shame," Emily said in bed. "We're losing the wrong one."

"You'd never know it to look at them."

"Oh, I can."

They had to whisper because of Arlene, plus Margaret was still up, ensconced on the screen porch, waiting for Kenny and Lisa to pull in, maybe right now getting high. Henry could hear Jeff running water directly overhead, and imagined how strange it must be for him. He and Margaret would have to sleep together. There was only the one bed.

For years, calling on an inner censor he'd adopted when she was a teenager, Henry had actively suppressed any vision of them making love. Now he couldn't summon one to save them.

Who knew what happened in a marriage, what bargains and compromises people struck? He and Emily were opposites in many respects, yet well matched, both of them practical at heart. Jeff had wanted to rescue Margaret, an impulse Henry distrusted. He thought he should be grateful they'd stayed together this long, though that only made it harder for everyone involved. He wanted, above all, to suspend judgment. There was fault on both sides, he was sure, and then felt disloyal to her. Jeff was the one who was leaving.

"Are you reading or are you sleeping?" Emily asked. "Because I'm done."

"I'm thinking."

"That's dangerous."

"It is."

"There's nothing you can do about it tonight."

"I don't think there's anything we can do at all."

"Probably not, so turn the light out."

He did.

She rolled his way and gave him a good-night kiss. "Stop fretting, you'll never get to sleep. I'll talk to her tomorrow and find out what's going on."

She was right. In minutes she was snoring, releasing a subtle whistle with each breath. As so often with Margaret, he felt helpless. He needed to know what he should hope for.

At three, when he padded to the bathroom, Kenny and Lisa's SUV was sitting in the drive, and in the morning, as he was putting water on for coffee, Sam and Justin were already outside playing croquet, the balls tracing paths in the dew. The day was bright, the shadow of the chestnut swallowing part of the garage. Henry left his cup on the screen porch to give Sam a bear hug, lifting him off his feet.

"All right," he said, choosing a mallet, "who's ready to lose?"

"You are," they said.

He was. He wanted Justin to win, as if to provide him some small consolation. He tried not to make it obvious, but Justin overshot the middle wicket and Sam beat him anyway. From the porch, Emily and Kenny cheered.

By ten everyone was up. Though it was the Fourth, there were still chores to do and errands to run. While Emily and Arlene got started on the potato salad, Lisa and Margaret headed off to Wegmans with a list, leaving Kenny and Jeff and the children to decorate the place. Ella and Sarah paired off, wrapping the tree trunks in patriotic crepe paper while Sam and Justin planted a border of miniature flags along the road. Jeff held the stepladder for Kenny to hang swags of bunting around the screen porch. Watching from the garage, Henry wondered how much Kenny knew, and whether he and Jeff talked. He doubted it.

The woman he was seeing was supposed to be younger, as if that were her whole appeal. A nurse, the two of them working with the same patients, eating in the cafeteria, passing in the halls all day. Where did they go? What did they say to each other? Henry thought of Sloan, their stolen hours, though that had been different. It was hard to picture beefy, red-faced Jeff with his gold-rimmed glasses and thinning hair in the throes of that kind of madness. He'd always been so sensible.

Last night, when Margaret and Jeff had arrived, Henry had shaken hands with him and received the same firm grip as always, as if nothing had changed. "I like the new mailbox," he said. "Much easier to see." As they unloaded the car and got the children settled, Henry listened for any extra tension between them but could detect none, just the normal exhaustion after a long drive. Jeff went to bed before she did, not unusual, since he had to wake up at five-thirty every morning. Henry didn't expect them to fight outright or punish each other with silence, as he and Emily sometimes did, but remained alert for evidence of how they were really feeling. Was it all an act, or had they accepted the inevitable, gone beyond anger?

Lisa and Margaret returned with an enormous load of groceries and horror stories about the crowd at the checkout. Like everyone else, Jeff helped bring in the bags, then disappeared upstairs after Margaret. Henry lingered before the open door as if he was waiting for the bathroom, hoping to catch at least the tone of their conversation, but all he could hear was the drone of the attic fan, and he busied himself putting away the Kleenex and toilet paper. When they came down, Margaret had changed into her bathing suit and jean shorts and they were both laughing at something.

"Maybe next time," she said.

"Maybe."

The joke was private, clipped off as they rejoined the group, confusing him further.

It was lunchtime. Following tradition, he manned the grill, doling out hot dogs and burgers, toasting the buns on the top rack. There wasn't room for everyone in the screen porch, and the children sat in the shade of the chestnut, paper plates in their laps, shooing Rufus until Emily had Kenny take him in the house. Margaret ate only half of her burger and left the top bun. Arlene noticed it too.

"She's too thin," she said in the kitchen. "I don't think she looks good."

"Don't tell her that," Emily said. "She's worked so hard."

"It can't be healthy."

"I think she looks fine," Henry said in her defense.

"I thought she looked fine at Christmas," Arlene said.

"Little pitchers," Emily warned as the boys thundered down the stairs in their swim trunks and water shoes, Jeff following them out with an armload of towels. She waited till they could see him crossing the lawn. "He looks like he's lost a few pounds."

"I think so."

It was possible. Henry couldn't tell. At Christmas he'd missed signs that seemed obvious to both Emily and Arlene, and again he felt slow, as if he hadn't been paying close enough attention.

Their chores done, the young people were going out on the boat. He'd

188

filled it with gas and blown up the big triangular inner tube, untangled the towrope. He helped Kenny get the engine started and everyone piled in. The girls were leggy in their life jackets, the boys' foreheads smeared with sunscreen. They barely all fit, Kenny and Jeff taking the captain's chairs, Lisa and Margaret in back with the boys on their laps. Emily wanted a picture, and as they waited, holding their smiles for her, their eyes hidden behind their sunglasses, Henry thought that no matter how nicely it turned out, they'd remember it as the last summer they were all together.

"I'm going to take another just to be safe."

They groaned.

"Shush," she said. "Thank you. All right, be careful."

"Have fun," he said like an idiot.

Without them the cottage was still as a painting, only a white butterfly fluttering around the lilacs. In the lull, he gave the window frames a coat of primer, taking his time, using two brushes that were different widths. Later, he knew, Emily would ask him why he couldn't wait and let the children do them, as if he were impatient, when it wasn't the case. He just needed something to concentrate on. He stood at his workbench, cleaning his brushes with turpentine, the scent intoxicating. The day was heating up, cicadas shrilling in the trees. Distorted by imperfections in the glass, powerboats roared up and down the lake. Normally this was his favorite part of Chautauqua, everyone off enjoying themselves, taking advantage of the place. Emily and Arlene were busy in the kitchen, and, guiltily, knowing he shouldn't succumb to the urge, he glanced back at the door to make sure no one was coming, opened Kenny's old mini-fridge and grabbed a can of Iron City.

He cracked it and guzzled a long first draw, as if he were parched. It was fizzy and cold in his throat, and he let out a foamy burp, wiping his lips with the back of his hand. He could see himself and stopped as if caught. There was no need for secrecy. When Margaret was sober, she encouraged them to drink around her, as if welcoming the test. He would have a beer at cocktail hour and another with dinner, but right now only this breach, illicit and private, could quench his craving, and like a pledge being initiated, he emptied the can in three gulps, crushed it in his fist and buried it deep in the trash so no one would know.

He wanted another but held off until they'd docked and showered and Emily sent Ella out to the porch to take drink orders. Lisa and Arlene were having wine, Kenny a beer. Jeff abstained as always, asking for ice water as if in solidarity with Margaret. Why was he even there? Beer in hand, Henry wondered if his girlfriend drank, and thought of Sloan sitting up in bed with a cigarette and a jelly glass of scotch, telling him shocking stories about the girls at her boarding school. After she moved to New York, they never spoke again, a limbo that still puzzled him. If nothing else, Jeff and Margaret would always have Sarah and Justin to connect them. In some way, it seemed unfair.

"How's the home?" Henry asked innocently.

Jeff seemed surprised by the question, looking to Margaret as if it were a trap. "Good. Busy."

"There's no shortage of us old folks."

"No, that's right. We're actually expanding. I've got a lot of new hires I'm training."

"I'm surprised they let you take a week off."

"I've been there long enough. They know this is our vacation time."

The phrase was self-incriminating. Henry left it alone.

"The problem is," Margaret said, rescuing him, "he's built up too many vacation days. They want him to take them."

"Well," Arlene said, "we're glad you could make it."

When Margaret had first announced that they were getting married, Jeff had come to him like a supplicant, needing his blessing. Now Henry thought he should have to formally ask permission to leave her. An apology—was that what he wanted? Some explanation. The porch was no good. He'd have to get him alone. Maybe golfing.

After dinner, when dusk had fallen and bats flitted between the trees, Kenny lit sparklers for the children, who ran about the lawn, swinging them in wild circles, drawing arcs that lingered on the eye. Later they all gathered on the dock to watch the fireworks across the lake at Midway. Each year the display grew gaudier, prompting Arlene, inevitably, to wonder how much the park had spent. The night was cool, the stars sharp. On the bench, in their sweatshirts, Henry and Emily huddled for warmth. As the first volley bloomed, an orange chrysanthemum bronzing the water, she took his hand. Kenny and Lisa were snuggling under a blanket, the boys and girls paired off as they had been since arriving, while Margaret and Jeff sat side by side. Jeff had his arm around her, his hand cupping her waist. When he turned to whisper something, she leaned in, bowing her head. With a thump like a mortar, another shell went up.

"Did you see them?" Emily said in bed.

"I saw them."

"I don't know what's going on. I was so busy today I didn't have a chance to talk to her. Who knows. I don't think she does."

"I certainly don't," Henry said.

Fairness

IN THE CHILDREN'S WIFFLE BALL GAMES HE WAS BOTH OFFI-
cial pitcher and umpire, a position requiring endless discretion. While Sam
smacked shots back up the box that made him duck, Justin struggled to
make contact. Henry wanted everyone to have fun, and pitched to each
according to their abilities, wearing his Pirates cap cocked sideways, keeping up a joking commentary gleaned from a lifetime of radio. The Eephus
pitch, the slurve, the fadeaway. He threw between his legs and behind his
back, routines he'd used on Kenny and his friends thirty years ago. The
idea was for them not to take the game so seriously. Now that the girls
were older, they didn't care, ignoring his corny patter, barely paying attention when they were in the field. The boys, being younger, were desperate to win, a hunger he recognized from his own childhood, pitted
against Arlene, who at twelve was not only smarter than he was but a good
foot taller.

Checkers, hearts, badminton—he could never beat her, though he came
close, the rare narrow defeats followed by tears, accusations of cheating and

banishment to his room, where, like one condemned, he would await a visit from his father, who sat beside him on his bed, explaining the values of sportsmanship with an engineer's maddening calm. His father, being omnipotent, didn't understand. Just once Henry wanted to win.

"You will," his father said. "Until then, you will lose like a gentleman. Is that understood?"

They shook on it, but the bargain was impossible for Henry to keep, and soon when anyone suggested a game, his mother would tell him he couldn't play if he was just going to get upset. He promised, under duress, thinking maybe this time would be different, only to be overwhelmed in the end, fleeing hot-faced and seething with shame, blinking back tears as he climbed the stairs to his room, vowing vengeance on them all.

"Why do you have to be such a baby?" Queen Arlene asked.

He didn't want to be. He tried not to, but couldn't stop. It was a weakness, something wrong with him. When it happened, no one was more disappointed than he was. He tried to soften the blow, telling himself in advance that he was going to lose, but knowing only made him hate it more, until the mere idea of playing a game filled him with dread.

When he finally won—beating her at dominoes one afternoon on the Oriental rug in the sunny back parlor—the feeling didn't suddenly lift like a broken curse. It took him years to accept defeat. He was clever and athletic, a dutiful student, and though he received straight As and won more than his fair share of spelling bees and forty-yard dashes, what he remembered was the disgrace of coming in second. While a necessary lesson, it was always a disappointment to discover he wasn't the fastest or smartest or best at everything. In basic he was a passable marksman, but didn't kid himself, like Embree, that he had a sniper's eye. He was no hero, as Emily liked to think, just an average soldier, and while some of the work his team did on the Odyssey was groundbreaking for its time, no genius.

Now, inning by inning, as he called his own balls and strikes, he knew how

Justin felt, expecting Sam to beat him once again, and at the end, how Sam felt when he lost because Ella muffed a pop fly and then threw the ball away.

"Good game, everyone," Henry said.

Scowling, Sam stormed around the side of the house.

They were using paper plates for bases. Before going after him, Henry had Justin and the girls collect them.

He found Sam on the far side of the garden, sitting behind a tree with his arms wrapped around his knees. He hid his face, sniffling, and Henry remembered his own inconsolable anger and shame. He put a hand on his shoulder.

Sam shrugged it off. "Go away."

"Come on, let's get some lemonade."

"She missed it on purpose."

"Sam. She did not miss it on purpose. Come on."

"She sucks."

"Stop. That's not how you talk about your sister."

"All she had to do was catch the stupid ball."

"You've never dropped a fly ball."

"Not one that easy. Then she can't even throw it."

"It was a terrible throw," Henry conceded, getting his attention. "She did hit a home run, you've got to give her credit for that."

"I guess."

"Do you want to know a secret? I don't like losing either. When I was your age, every time I lost I felt just like you do right now. No one likes to lose, but someone has to, it's part of the game. If you won every time it wouldn't be any fun. Do you think Justin likes losing?"

"No."

"No," he agreed, letting it sink in. "You hit the ball really hard. You almost took my head off with that liner."

Sam picked up a buckeye and winged it at the nearest tree, missing. He did it again. The third time he hit the trunk.

"You want to go get some lemonade or do you want to sit here? I'm hot. I'm going to get some lemonade." He offered him his hand.

Sam took it. Henry pulled him up, and together they walked around front to rejoin the others. After all the nonsense with Jeff and Margaret, he counted it as a win.

Waste Not

IN THE DOWNSTAIRS SHOWER THEY SHARED WITH ARLENE, IN a fake-chrome, recessed niche in the stall, in a ridged dish that kept the bottom from going soft and scummy, sat a smooth gold bar of Dial soap with a green sliver of Irish Spring grafted to it like a scab. Henry was used to these two-toned mutants, products of Emily's humble upbringing. In her parents' house in Kersey there was no shower, only an old claw-footed tub with a spray attachment you waved blindly over your head as you sat. They weren't poor or backward. They lived right in town. Her father was a building inspector and would-be architect. It was as if he saw the shower as a fad that might not catch on, a mistake that made selling the house after her mother died a trial.

Each time Henry noticed the soap, he thought of the girl Emily had been, and that lost world of which she'd never be completely free. No one used soap anymore. Even Arlene used the same expensive bodywash as the children. There was no need to hang on to these worthless slivers, just as there was no longer a need to save their bacon fat for explosives or the tinfoil from their chewing gum for the riveted skins of dive bombers, yet whenever he saw someone flick a half-smoked cigarette into the street, like the soldier he'd been, his first instinct was to dash into traffic and pluck it up so he could add the loose tobacco to his stash.

Like memories, the exigencies of the past still compelled them. Just the other night he'd had a dream in which he looted a bakery, liberating a whole sack of baguettes for his buddies, a bounty so great he felt cheated when he woke up and discovered it wasn't real. There was a value in learning what it meant to be hungry that their children would never know. He wasn't embarrassed when they made fun of his love of leftovers. "Don't throw that out," they imitated him, a grouchy old bear. "I'll have it for lunch." Then why, this morning, stepping into the shower, did he despair at the sight of Emily's homely soap, as if their lives were outmoded?

Frowning, he took the bar from the dish, turning it over so the green side was exposed. He lathered his chest and arms vigorously, his armpits and crotch, his bottom and his legs, front and back. The water was hot, and the steam smelled minty. The bar still held a faint smudge of blue. He scrubbed hard, raising suds, trying to use it up.

The Brabenders

The Brabenders' was for sale. He noticed the Re/Max sign while he was taking Rufus for his morning walk. The windows were dark and there was a lockbox on the doorknob. It was a shame, Henry had always liked them.

"We knew that," Emily said.

"I didn't."

"Yes you did. I told you, they want a fortune."

"The Brabenders?"

"The Brabenders. Mal had that bad stroke, so they don't come up enough."

Funny. He couldn't recall any of it, and though he suspected she'd told someone else—maybe Kenny or Margaret or the porch at large while he was doing the dishes—he didn't ask her how much. And then when he found it online he remembered.

Luck

THOUGH THERE WAS NO REAL SCHEDULE, THEIR DAYS ASSUMED the same shape—chores in the morning, swimming in the afternoon. Lunch was sandwiches and leftovers on paper plates, dinner something on the grill. It was why they came year after year, the comfort of the familiar, why they told the old stories as they sat on the screen porch while the sun set, recalling long-gone great-aunts and -uncles and their crazy dogs. Even the errands they ran were to favorites like the Lighthouse or the Cheese Barn, destinations tinged with nostalgia. They had to have fresh corn and peaches and tomatoes from the one farm stand in Maple Springs, and pies from Haff Acres, fetched home still molten. They had to take the Stowe ferry over to Bemus Point and back and get ice-cream cones at Hogan's Hut. They had to go to Johnny's Texas Hots. They had to catch a Jammers game. And they would. The only thing that could stop them was the weather.

It wouldn't be Chautauqua if one night they didn't take the children to the Putt-Putt across from the Institute. Wednesday was two-for-one from six till closing. As always, Emily and Arlene begged off, preferring the quiet, leaving Henry to represent their generation.

The place hadn't changed in decades, worn indoor-outdoor carpeting for greens, the boards and fences and obligatory windmill painted a candy-corn orange, the bottoms of the bowl-like water hazards swimming-pool blue. The night was mild, the course so crowded they had to wait. Rock music bombarded them from all sides, making it impossible to talk. Mayflies swarmed the lights, coating the poles, dropping exhausted to the concrete walks. Sam nudged one with the blade of his putter and Lisa pulled him away, just as the P.A. called their number.

"Here we go," Kenny said.

On top of the shack that served as a clubhouse sat a bank of colored floodlights corresponding to the different balls—red, blue, green and yellow. If you made a hole-in-one while your color was lit, you won a free game. Kenny, who'd played there all day as a boy, made sure each foursome had all the colors. The trick was to let whoever had the right ball go first.

The girls were already bored, more interested in the packs of boys and older teenagers out on dates. The crowd was mostly families, and Henry spied middle-aged husbands in polo shirts and Bermuda shorts eyeing Sarah. Tall and tan, with Margaret's strong chin, she drew attention wherever she went, even wearing a ratty sweatshirt and warm-ups. If he hadn't known, he wouldn't have believed she and Ella were the same age. It was unfair, he thought, but they were as devoted to each other as sisters. Paired with Margaret and Jeff, they went first.

Number one was plain, straight uphill. Ella, whose yellow was lit, bounced her tee shot directly over the hole, making them holler. She laughed as if it were an accident.

"Almost," Henry said.

No one else came close. While they were taking turns putting, a cheer went up from a far corner and a boy wearing an Indians cap dashed for the shack, holding his ball out in front of him like a prize.

"We have a winner," the P.A. said. "Red is next. Red is your lucky color."

Kenny had it.

Sam huffed as if he'd been cheated.

"Stop," Lisa said. "You'll get your turn. All right, Tiger. No pressure."

The rubber mat had three holes. Henry would have picked the middle by default, but Kenny chose the one on the right. He settled his feet, looked from his ball to the cup like a pro, drew back his putter and swung.

"Nope," he said, before the ball topped the rise. It was wide to the right by several inches, kicking off the rear wall and stopping.

Lisa's didn't reach the top, rolling back past her so that Kenny had to make a kick save. Justin missed badly, and Sam, his whole body slumping in disappointment.

Henry set his green ball in the center of the mat.

"All right, Dad," Kenny said. "Show us how it's done."

Technically, fivesomes weren't allowed. He could feel the people milling around behind them waiting for him. He hated being rushed. The putter was light, a variable he factored into his calculations, along with the incline. He didn't bother taking a practice swing, just stepped up and hit it.

From the moment it left the blade, he knew it had a chance. He had the right line, the right speed. As it crested the hill, it bent slightly to the left and crossed the flat, still on track.

"Get there!" Kenny said.

"Get right," Henry said.

It was hard enough but broke left as it slowed, and then, just before it reached the hole, it hit something—a pebble, a piece of a leaf—gave a hop and straightened out so that it caught the side of the cup, swung around the lip and dropped in.

He had to laugh.

"Nice one, Dad."

"I should quit now." He accepted high fives all around.

"It's not the right color," Sam said.

"That's okay, I'll take it."

Number one was a tease. As they went, the holes grew more complicated, featuring ramps and mounds, concrete ponds and obstacles they had to bank the ball off or avoid. The windmill, the clown's mouth, the barn. The layout was the same Kenny had played thirty years ago. It was his domain, the rest of them were just visitors. Like a coach, he showed them the exact spot on the rail they needed to hit. Justin came close on four, leaving his ball an inch short of the hole. After hitting his tee shot on six into the water, Sam raised his putter over his head like an ax, and Lisa pulled him aside for a time-out. The next hole, she couldn't stop her ball on top of a rise, crisscrossing it several times before picking up. Kenny, who was scoring, didn't ask what she had.

All the while, people around them were winning free games, the lucky color changing from blue to red to yellow. Henry finally had his chance on eight, but couldn't sneak by the triangular island guarding the hole.

"Not even close," he said.

At the turn, for dessert, the children were allowed to choose from a display of candy bars. Though there was cherry pie waiting at home, Henry indulged in a Milky Way.

The lucky color was blue—Justin's.

"All right," Kenny said, "let's get lucky," but the hole was a loop-the-loop, and Justin's shot was too soft, dropping out of the chute with a clang and bouncing across the walk.

Kenny went last. From endless rounds of practice, he knew how hard to hit the ball. It curled ringing through the loop, ran past the hole, knocked off the back wall and drained straight in.

"That's what I'm talking about!" He flourished his putter like Zorro.

"We're not too competitive," Lisa said.

"Hey, Dad's still beating me."

"Is that right?" Henry asked, though he had an idea.

"Go Grampa!" Sam said.

"It's still early," Henry said.

Now after every hole the boys wanted to know the score, Justin racing ahead to inform Margaret and Jeff and the girls. Henry tried to downplay it, but found it impossible not to count Kenny's strokes against his own. He was up one with three holes to go when the green light came on.

Sixteen was two-tiered, and simple. The upper level was a dead end with three holes. Hit the one in the middle and the ball would drop through a pipe to the lower level with a good shot at going in. Put it in the hole on either side and it dumped you in a corner behind a triangle.

Stepping up to the tee, he discovered he had an audience. Margaret and Jeff and the girls had stopped to watch.

"Go Grampa!"

"It's like Arnie's Army."

"Grampa's Army," Margaret said.

"Quiet in the gallery," Kenny said, holding up both hands like a marshal.

Henry settled his feet and stuck it in the middle hole.

"That should do it," Kenny said, as Sam and Justin scampered around to see the ball come out.

Sam squatted on the green, facing the pipe, his feet spread wide so he wouldn't interfere.

"Get out of there," Kenny said, but it was too late.

The ball shot out of the pipe, rolling between Sam's feet, headed directly, inevitably for the hole, drawn on by invisible forces. It had the line and more than enough speed. Henry was already raising his arms when it struck the cup dead center, catching the back lip, and popped straight in the air. It hung a split second as if it might fall in, then landed just beyond the hole, its momentum carrying it to the far wall, where it came to rest.

"How did that not go in?" he asked, looking around for witnesses.

"It should have," Ella said.

"It's not always automatic," Kenny said.

As if to prove it, he put his ball in the middle hole. His went in.

"It's all skill," he said.

The boys booed him like a villain.

Henry needed to make his putt to stay even. He was allowed to move his ball away from the wall the length of the blade, but the boards limited his backswing, and he left it short.

"*Hit* the ball, Henry," he said.

No one had claimed the free game, so he led off again on seventeen. He had to jump his ball across a pond swimming with mayflies. The ramp had a shallow slope to it, and remembering his last shot, he swung too hard, launching the ball over the back wall, hitting Jeff in the calf. With the penalty, there was no way to catch Kenny unless he blew up.

The eighteenth was like a giant Skee-Ball machine that collected the balls. Kenny landed his in the center ring for another hole-in-one.

"Are you happy now?" Lisa asked. "You crushed us."

"Yes," he said, offering Henry his hand. "Good game, Dad."

"Not good enough, obviously."

After the noise, the ride home was quiet. He sat in back with the boys, the three of them subdued, poor sports. The course across from the Institute was dark, only a chore light burning above a barn door. Gulls dotted the fairways, bedded down for the night. They had a tee time Friday. Losing made him impatient to get out again and redeem himself.

"How'd we do?" Emily asked as they filed in. "Who's the big wiener?"

"Who do you think?" Lisa said, and Kenny gave a sheepish wave, adding the scorecard and little pencil to the collection on the mantel.

"It was close," Henry said. "I really thought I had him this time."

"You always say that," Emily said, and though he wanted to argue, he had to admit it was true. Because this, too, was a tradition.

The Lost Art
of Conversation

MORNINGS, BEFORE ARLENE AND MARGARET AND THE GIRLS
were up, while Emily made the boys their favorite soft-boiled eggs and toast,
Kenny, Lisa and Jeff tugged on their running shoes, zeroed their sports
watches and walked. Rain or shine, they got eight laps in—down to the marina, up past the fish hatchery, through the woods by the tennis courts and
down Manor Drive again, chattering all the while. The mailbox was their
finish line, and as Henry sat on the screen porch enjoying his coffee and the
Jamestown paper, the lake flat as glass beyond the dock, he heard them count
off the laps as they passed, their laughter and the slapping of their soles pro-
voking a throaty warning from Rufus.

"You're fine," Henry said. "We know them."

As to what they were laughing at, Henry could only guess. Lisa could be
cutting, and had an opinion about everything, where Kenny was irreverent,
eager to play the clown. They seemed a strange trio to him, Jeff even more
of a third wheel now. It had to be awkward, Henry thought, though if Jeff
was looking for a sympathetic ear, Kenny and Lisa knew Margaret's problems better than anyone.

By the time they finished, the boys were done eating and Arlene and

Margaret were up. Neither of them ate breakfast. They took their coffee out on the dock where their cigarettes wouldn't bother people, using a tuna can as an ashtray. Henry watched them hail a fisherman drifting past, trolling the shallows. The light was golden, mist lifting from the water like steam. They sat like an old couple, smoking and gazing across the lake, bowing their heads to sip, every so often leaning toward each other to confer. In the stillness he could almost hear them over the plinking of the boys' video games. These were the exchanges he wished he were privy to, the gist of which he hoped Arlene would share with them.

Emily, having made a second batch of eggs for the girls, joined him on the porch, wordlessly noting Arlene and Margaret before taking up the paper. He knew she resented Arlene usurping her role as confidante, and that she blamed them both. He sympathized, having been shut out of Margaret's life for so long, yet secretly he thought this proxy arrangement was better. If it kept them in suspense, it was also less volatile. The goal, in the end, was peace, and he trusted Arlene with these delicate negotiations, her temper being closer to his own. In his helplessness, he was grateful. He wouldn't know the first thing to say to Margaret, never had.

The bell tower sounded the quarter hour. Upstairs, the walkers were showering, emptying the hot water heater, a relic from the sixties he'd been meaning to replace. Kenny and Lisa came down together and occupied the glider, and Jeff, wet-haired, ducking out the side door to get a charger from their car. When Arlene returned from the dock with her mug, Henry watched him as if he might go to Margaret, but he was lost in his laptop. A few minutes later she came straggling across the lawn in a baggy sweatshirt and flip-flops, her hair in pigtails like Sarah's. On her way inside, she touched Jeff's shoulder, making him look up, but whether his expression was engaging or impatient, Henry couldn't say.

Once Ella was done with the breakfast dishes, they reconvened for morning chores, the girls watering the garden, the boys helping him restock the firebox. The weather had been surprisingly good so far, and they'd taken care of most of the larger items on the list, and praising their efforts like a coach, he set them free. While Emily and Arlene headed off to Wegmans, everyone walked up the road to play tennis, leaving him alone again.

At his workbench, mending the ripped screen, he imagined Emily and Arlene in the car. The drive down to Lakewood took twenty minutes, and then twenty minutes back, time enough to cover a range of subjects, and he wished he'd gone with them, eavesdropping from the backseat. He wondered if they ever discussed him.

"Of course they do." He frowned, embarrassed he'd said it out loud.

Rufus, flopped on the cool concrete, eyed him warily.

What did Margaret and Kenny say about him, or Jeff and Lisa? That he could be rigid and judgmental, that he held a grudge, that he cared too much what other people thought—faults he was well aware of. He liked to think he knew himself. Unfairly accused or not, he couldn't worry about it.

"Too late now. Isn't that right?"

Rufus stretched, spreading his paws.

"Exactly," Henry said.

He needed to be patient. He'd have to wait till they were in bed to hear what Arlene said, and then it would be Emily's drastically edited version. It was like playing an endless game of telephone, a satellite relaying a degraded signal. He wished he could sit down with Margaret and ask her directly, but that wasn't a possibility, and rather than revisit their failures, he focused on the work at hand, cutting a patch with the tin snips and bending the edges, the wire pricking his fingertips as he fixed it to the mesh. She was her own woman. What did they say in Al-Anon—don't make their problem your problem. "That's right." Worrying like this was pointless, and probably bad for his heart, yet he couldn't stop, and all morning he knocked around the garage, talking to himself, waiting for them to return.

Double Exposure

He'd seen Lisa's breasts before. In their first apartment in Brookline, before she and Kenny were married, they hung over the fireplace, inescapable. Disembodied, in gauzy black and white, they were supposed to be art. Kenny had shot them as part of his master's thesis using a box with a pinhole, the long exposure giving them a ghostly quality.

Emily admired Kenny's effort. It was the public display she questioned. "She's obviously trying to shock people. Exactly who, I'm not sure. I'm sorry, but I'm not shocked. We all have them. It's not a secret."

Henry thought she had no reason to be jealous, but agreed. His ideal of womanly beauty included modesty. He preferred busty, wholesome girls like the pinups that helped them win the war, their ripeness all coy promise. Lisa was a tomboy, slim-hipped, with the toned arms of a long-distance runner. The picture wasn't supposed to be sexy, just a life study, a blurry one at that. What struck Henry was how narrow-chested she was, slight as a bird.

After Ella and Sam were born, the picture moved to Kenny and Lisa's bedroom, where Henry glimpsed it in passing, though over the years, as their visits to New England dwindled, his recollection of it dimmed. Most likely he wouldn't have thought of it again if he hadn't been coming through the back hall just as Sam barreled past with a squirt gun and shouldered open the bathroom door to reveal Lisa sitting on the john.

They'd been swimming, and her one-piece was bunched around her knees. She hunched and covered herself, yelling at Sam to get out and shut the door, which he did, too late to erase the vision of her tanned arms and lard-white front from Henry's mind, and the shocking pink of her nipples, so much bigger than in the picture—so much more present—that he couldn't reconcile the two. Her breasts were larger as well, full and womanly, belonging to someone else entirely.

His first instinct was to pretend he'd seen nothing.

"Sorry," he called, retreating, like Sam, before the closed door, and would have been happy to forget it ever happened, an idea he realized was wishful.

By cocktails it had become a story, Lisa mimicking the shock on his face, making them all laugh. It wasn't true—his eyes didn't pop like some cartoon character, his mouth didn't drop open—but he didn't mind being the butt of the joke. A husband, he had practice.

Now that the secret was out, he felt free to tell Emily the truth. Later, as they were reading in bed, he brought up the picture, wondering if at some point Lisa had had a boob job.

"That's what happens when you have kids," Emily said, as if he were being dim. "Or don't you remember?"

The comparison embarrassed him, and honestly he didn't. She had always seemed lush to him. Nearly fifty years, yet in his arms she seemed the same girl he'd courted, kissing her good night on the porch of her sorority, the house mother lurking behind the door, enforcing curfew. After Sloan, he coveted her innocence as much as her flesh. In many ways he still did. "I remember."

The joke played for a few days, along with his reminder to lock the door, which the children latched on to as a tagline, shouting it out in chorus. What troubled him more was the fact that he couldn't stop seeing Lisa in that split second before she could cover herself, her damp suit a hammock between her knees, her tan lines and the surprising pink. Again and again the vision returned, unbidden, as if he were purposely rewinding it for his own gratification. Not so, he protested. He thought she actually looked better in Kenny's shot, the unblemished symmetry classical, but now, against his will, whenever he saw her—on the glider or at the dinner table, watching a movie or leaning over the puzzle with the light behind her—he pictured her new breasts inside her shirt and scourged himself like someone caught in a lie.

No-Show

"WHAT'S THE BIG PLAN FOR TODAY?" EMILY ASKED.

"No plan. I might make a dump run later. We've got the Jammers game tonight."

"Do you mind if I don't go? I'm so close to being finished with this shawl, I just want to be done with it."

"That's fine," he said, but then, doing the dishes, brooded. They were together all the time, as she'd reminded him the other day, yet he was always disappointed when she chose not to be with him. Without her, the game wouldn't be the same. Now, though it had been his idea, he didn't want to go either.

A Debacle

HE'D MEANT TO CALL WHEN THEY FIRST ARRIVED. HE'D PUT IT off, busy futzing with the windows, and then, as with anything not written down, he'd forgotten, and between the summer people and the women's league, the only tee time he could get was two o'clock, in the heat of the day. It also meant they'd eat late. Emily said that was fine. It was just chicken on the grill. If they went long, Arlene and the girls could feed the children.

He didn't expect any objections. The offer to reschedule was more of an apology, a mea culpa for his dereliction. They had only two days left, and both Kenny and Jeff had brought their clubs. They were going to play.

The question, as always at Chautauqua, was the weather. The forecast called for scattered showers in Mayville and late-day thunderstorms in Jamestown. By lunchtime the cloud cover was solid, the air thick with humidity. Just past one, from the tolling of the tower bell, the wind turned, riffling the chestnut, its leaves baring their pale undersides. The temperature had dropped. On the dock, the boats rocked in their slips.

"I don't know," Emily said, as if he could do something about it.

"Wait five minutes," he said, but in five minutes it was so dark that Arlene turned on the lights.

In the garage he prepared his bag as if he were summiting Everest. Rufus knew he wasn't invited and watched him glumly. Besides his trusty Westinghouse umbrella, he had an olive-drab poncho and rain pants stuffed in its own matching drawstring bag, a birthday present from Kenny he'd resorted to a few times over the years, ignoring Emily's warnings that he'd be struck by lightning. He fished through the zippered compartments, grabbing her an extra towel. This was the first time she'd been out all year, and her clubs were dusty. He wiped them down and hefted them into the trunk of the Olds. Drops stippled the rear window, gathering steadily. Kenny and Jeff stood ready, good soldiers, though he noticed that Kenny had snapped his rain hood onto his bag.

"You really think we're going to get it in," Emily asked.

"We're going to try."

"Okay," she said, as if the decision was all his.

She let Jeff sit in front with his long legs, happy to be in back with Kenny. One round a year they were a team again, as they had been before Lisa, mother and son ganging up on Dad. Henry liked to think the matchup was even, or as even as it could be. Jeff, for all his size and strength, was a duffer, a latecomer to the game, forever apologizing for his mistakes. Secretly Henry enjoyed carrying him, the pressure making their inevitable victory that much sweeter. He'd downplay it afterward, saying he was the only one who played regularly, but when he stuck a nine-iron inches from the pin or sank a putt, he pumped his fist like a pro. Without Jeff, what would they do? Again, as they backed out, leaving the cottage behind, Henry wondered what his and Margaret's situation was, and how much he should say to him. There was mystery at the heart of any marriage, secrets even people close to it would never know. Unlike Emily, he wasn't sure it was their business.

Under the trees the road was dry. He held off using his wipers, as if that had some magical effect.

The drive was less than a mile, the fourteenth running alongside them, directly across from the Institute. A few carts dotted the fairways.

"There are some real golfers," he said.

"They're some real somethings," Emily said.

The lot was half empty, a bad sign. As if required by law, the guy who rang them up in the pro shop said there were no rainchecks. Henry was tempted to ask for a discount, but knew it was pointless. The foursome ahead of them had canceled. They could jump on whenever they liked.

Outside, parked nose to tail, the carts waited in ranks.

"Find us a dry one," Emily told Kenny.

Following tradition, he and Henry drove, Emily and Jeff strapping their bags in behind the passenger seats. Henry dropped the see-through awning to cover their clubs. Puddles were forming on the asphalt. Normally there was a crowd on the putting green and a starter with a clipboard who enforced tee times like a drill sergeant. It seemed strange to waltz right on.

It was sprinkling as they spread out and swung their drivers to warm up. His knee didn't like the dampness. He wished he'd thought to bring his brace.

"I believe you have honors from last year," Kenny said.

"Go ahead if you're ready. I'm going to be awhile."

The first was a boring par-four, straightaway, with traps flanking the green. Kenny plucked up some grass and tossed it in the air to test the wind—blowing left to right. His drive was dead center, rolling to a stop beside the 150-yard marker.

"That's where you want to be," Emily said.

"Okay," Henry told Jeff. "Put a charge into it."

Jeff wound up slowly but overswung, peeking at the last second, and skulled a grounder that died in the wet grass. Already he was downcast, shaking his head.

"Take a mulligan," Henry said.

"No, it'll play."

Using his driver like a cane, Henry bent down and teed his ball high. When he glanced at the fairway to align his feet, a fat drop struck his cheek. He wiped it away like a tear. The pines behind the green were swaying,

Kenny's windbreaker whipping like a loose jib. Henry took his practice swings and addressed the ball. Shoulder in, head down, follow through.

Even before he made contact he could feel the club turning in his hands, the face opening, producing a slicing line drive, a satellite spiraling out of orbit. "Come back."

"I didn't see it," Emily said.

"It's not bad," Kenny said. "It's in the light rough by that second tree."

"I cut it," Henry said.

By the time Emily was settled on the ladies' tee, a steady drizzle was falling.

"Should I bother?"

"You might as well," Henry said. "We're already wet."

"That is true."

When they were newly married, before the children, she'd taken lessons so she could play with him. Her swing was textbook, short and compact, sacrificing distance for control. Kenny would outdrive her by a hundred yards all day only to give those strokes back around the green. The last few years she'd lost some of her strength, but her irons were still deadly.

She didn't waste time. A single practice swing and she stepped up and punched one down the middle.

"Nicely done," Henry said.

"Thank you," she said, pleased with herself, and they parted, heading to their respective carts. To keep from churning the fairways to muck, the 90-degree rule was in effect.

They didn't have far to go for Jeff's ball. As if to make up for it, he clobbered a three-wood that almost reached the green.

"There you go," Henry said.

"Should have done that the first time."

"Shoulda woulda coulda." It was a saying of Emily's, a schoolyard taunt from her backwater girlhood. He was aware, even before the words were out of his mouth, that it applied to more than Jeff's second shot.

His own faded late, bounding across the apron and running for the left bunker.

"Sugar."

"It might have gotten hung up."

"I think I'm in."

In the cart, zipping along with Jeff right beside him, Henry saw his chance, but it was too early. All week he'd planned this ambush. Now that he was there, it seemed wrong. How was he supposed to broach the subject, and really, what could he say? Golf was supposed to be an escape. He hated to ruin it, and as they tacked down the fairway, waiting for Emily and then Kenny to hit, he decided to hold off until later, the evasion nagging at him as much as the unpleasant task. When they got back, as soon as they were alone, Emily would interrogate him. No matter how detailed his answers were, they wouldn't be good enough, as if he'd done a bad job, or didn't care, when in truth he needed to know as keenly as she did—more, if that was possible, because he knew so little.

As he'd thought, he was in the trap. His ball sat in a coffee-colored puddle, rain dimpling its surface. He grabbed his sand wedge and putter and let Jeff take the cart. The water was a casual hazard. He fished his ball out, moved it to a damp patch of sand no closer to the hole, dug in his feet and blasted it on.

"Nice out," Emily said.

"It's like concrete."

The green was a sponge, the cup filled with muddy water. Jeff must have fluffed his chip, because he was in the other bunker. They waited, marking their balls as he took a couple tries to get it out, and then it sped past the hole and down a slope, coming to a stop on the far fringe. He was away, and rushed his putt. The ball didn't make the hill, stalling and rolling back. His second was just short.

"That's good," Emily said, and no one objected.

"What'd everybody have?" asked Kenny, entrusted, as he had been since childhood, with keeping score.

"I had a five," Emily said.

"Five."

Jeff had to count his strokes. "Eight."

"It's early," Henry said.

As much as he wished, the rain didn't let up, pattering in the trees as they slogged along, the wind knocking down their short irons, pushing their errant drives out of bounds. Even with the cover in place, his grips were wet, and he was glad he'd given Emily the towel. No one was scoring. The fourth tee crowned a knoll that commanded a view of the Institute and the lake beyond, gray and pitching beneath the clouds. There was only one other cart on the course, a twosome finishing eighteen. A raft of gulls had already gathered on the fairway behind them.

"I think that might be a sign," Kenny said.

Inwardly, Henry agreed. It was a day to sit by the fire and read.

"Come on," Emily said, "we're not quitting now."

He couldn't tell if she was being sarcastic or just practical, and as they rolled on, he decided they could honorably retire after nine, have a drink in the clubhouse and be back in time for dinner.

Jeff's struggles continued. Normally quiet, rather than bitch about the conditions, he was content to ride along in silence. It was a trait Henry appreciated in a partner, sharing it, but in this case left him no opening. He didn't want to be obvious. He felt like the stuffy father in one of Emily's costume dramas. What, sir, are your intentions toward my daughter? As if he had any say. How did you preface a question like that? We're all worried about Margaret. So, how are things between you two? His interest was honest, yet the bluntness of it discouraged him, and again he deferred, trusting the right time to present itself.

They were on six when the rain picked up, tapping at the roof of the cart.

Like a doorman, Kenny held Emily's umbrella for her while she selected an iron, then stood back to let her hit. Across the fairway, Henry and Jeff waited. As they watched her shot kick onto the apron, the sky let loose a sheeting rain. Caught by surprise, he hesitated a second before grabbing his ball and dashing for the cart. The rain pounded down, drumming his umbrella, the sheer volume inundating the already sopping turf. After nursing hope for so long, like that their day was over. Splashing with every step, he had to laugh.

There was a shelter in the trees between the green and the next tee. Henry ditched the 90-degree rule and aimed straight for it, cutting cross-country, jolting over roots. He beat Kenny easily, and ventured out with his umbrella to meet Emily.

The shelter had no walls, just a roof and a rude bench like a bus stop.

They sat, digging clumps of mud from their spikes, watching the rain come down. A rumble of thunder broke and rolled in the distance.

"Whose dumb idea was this?" Emily asked.

"That would be me," Henry said.

A Present

IN THE MORNING, HE AND EMILY SHARED THE DOWNSTAIRS BATH with Arlene, but once the day began and people were outside working, by sheer proximity it became the restroom for the whole household, and though Emily encouraged the children to use their own, often for Sam and Justin the call of nature was too strong. At some point during their stay, after finding the seat defiled yet again, Emily would choose a lull in dinner conversation to gently remind the boys, for all of their sakes, to please aim, and for days they stuck to the one upstairs. Henry knew she included him and Kenny in her complaint, and took care hitting the bull's-eye, wiping the rim whenever he splattered. He'd regularly policed the head in his barracks at Camp Claiborne and later the Schenley Grill, and if he didn't agree that all men were slobs and less considerate than women (he'd fished too many scummy clumps of hair from clogged drains to let that one pass), he had sympathy for her. No one liked cleaning up someone else's mess.

He was also sensitive to the issue because he spent more time in the bathroom now, thanks to his pills. The beer didn't help. He'd have one at lunch with his sandwich, and a second in the baking garage while everyone was out on the water, and maybe another listening to the Pirate game, so that it seemed he was making the trek to the house and back all afternoon.

Friday, their last day together, he was cobbling a new A-frame for Emily's snap peas out of dowel rods and fishing line when he couldn't ignore the urge any longer and emerged from his lair into the blinding sunlight. Emily and Arlene were reading on the dock, waiting for the children to return. They were going to Webb's later, so there was no dinner to prepare. He wove through the croquet set abandoned on the lawn to the screen porch. The house seemed dim after having been outside, and as he closed the bathroom door he flipped on the light and lifted the lid, and there, steeping in the bottom of the bowl, dark as chocolate and long as a cigar, the water adjacent tinted like tea, lay a single, perfect turd.

He gaped at it a second, shaking his head faintly, a stunned double take, before pressing the handle. The turd shot down the hole like a torpedo, the water sucking away with a glug, the bowl refilling, leaving no trace, but as Henry unzipped and did his business, his Flomax-induced stream bubbling to the edges, he frowned, seizing on the insult as if it were one of Emily's whodunits.

Like her, he automatically wanted to blame the boys, but they'd set out hours ago. Could it have sat that long? It was too late to do any forensic tests. He'd flushed the only evidence. His two most likely suspects were sitting on the dock, yet he couldn't imagine either of them forgetting.

There had been no toilet paper, so maybe it was a leftover, a simple hiccup of plumbing rather than a mystery. When Kenny was little he'd been famous for holding it for days and then delivering potato-sized marvels that sometimes refused to go down. Emily would call Henry in before she flushed so he could stand ready with the plunger, the two of them watching the whirlpool swirl like bettors at a roulette wheel.

This was different. There'd been no smell that he could recall, and he sniffed the air like Rufus.

There were too few clues to reach a solution, yet his mind kept trying to make sense of it. As an engineer he was part detective, used to working backward from disaster, and as he washed his hands, his face in the mirror knotted in consternation, another, more horrifying possibility came to him: Maybe they hadn't wiped.

Except there was a whole roll of toilet paper.

The sole witness, he thought of letting it drop, but even outside in the light of day the strangeness of it—the affront—bothered him.

"Someone left me a present," he told Emily and Arlene, as if it were a joke.

"Don't look at me," Arlene said. "I haven't gone in two days."

"Thank you for sharing," Emily said. "I'm sure it was one of the boys."

"How would you tell?" Henry asked.

"Probably Sam." Emily thought Lisa babied him. Now Henry was sorry he'd mentioned it.

There was nothing to prove it was anything but an accident, just bad luck on his part. He'd never know. When the children finally returned, it was time to get ready for dinner, and they disappeared upstairs to take their showers. They'd all brought one set of good clothes for tonight, Webb's a kind of banquet celebrating the end of their week together. In their polo shirts and khakis, their wet hair neatly parted, the boys were miniature versions of their fathers. The girls seemed grown up in their pearls and lipstick, while Margaret and Lisa both wore sundresses that showed off their tans. Kenny set the timer on his camera and took a shot of the whole family with the cottage behind them Emily would use as their Christmas card. Everyone looked so presentable that Henry regretted his suspicions, though, logically, as in a game of Clue, one of them had to have done it. After dinner, when they came home and changed and put on a movie, every time someone used the bathroom, he waited until they'd settled again, letting a discreet interval pass before sneaking down the hall to check.

Useful

THEY LEFT IN A FLURRY, SKIPPING BREAKFAST, THE WAYBACK
of Margaret's minivan piled so high with bags there was zero visibility. Lisa
said she was sorry for not washing their sheets and towels, an apology Emily
brushed off as if it had never been a point of contention. Though no one had
asked, she'd fixed them sandwiches to eat on the road, using up all of the
cold cuts. She made sure the hot sauce Kenny had bought at Wegmans found
its way into their cooler, and tried several times to give him the pies. When
they filed outside, Lisa had already started the car.

"You're fine," Henry told Rufus, who hadn't touched his breakfast either.
"You're not going anywhere."

They said goodbye to Sam and Ella first, letting them get buckled in. As
Emily hugged Kenny, Lisa thanked Henry for everything.

"Of course," he said. "We wish you could stay longer."

"Have fun at the Cape," Emily said, embracing her.

"Let us know when you get home," he told Kenny.

"I will."

Sarah and Justin waited by the minivan, Walkmans in hand.

Emily held on to Margaret, leaving Jeff to Henry.

"Sorry we didn't have a chance to talk more," Henry said.

"It always goes too fast."

Feeling false himself, Henry couldn't tell if he was being sincere.

They backed out, snapping branches in the grass, honking as they pulled away like a caravan, coasting past the Wisemans' and Brabenders' and the Nevilles' marshaled golf carts, leaving Henry and Emily and Arlene waving beneath the chestnut until Emily folded her arms as if holding herself and turned for the kitchen door, Rufus loping ahead like an escort.

It was Saturday and sunny. The lake would be busy. He had things to do, but in the wake of their leaving he felt aimless, as if the day were over. Emily and Arlene attacked the upstairs, stripping the beds and vacuuming as if preparing for new guests. Reprieved, Rufus crunched his kibble. In an attempt to make himself useful, Henry volunteered to take the sheets and towels to the laundromat.

Emily was skeptical. He'd never offered before.

"It's my job," she said. "If I need help, I'll ask, don't worry."

She took her book, a baggie of quarters and a jug of detergent. She wouldn't be back until lunch, and while Arlene smoked on the screen porch and Rufus dozed in a square of sun, Henry busied himself at his bench, finishing the A-frame, listening to the brothers on *Car Talk*, stopping everything to hear the brainteaser, which he could occasionally get, though not this week's. Like the basement at home, the garage held a residual chill from the night before that dissipated as the fishermen trying the shadows under the docks gave way to powerboaters gunning up and down the lake. The chimes from the Institute and the BBC News were pleasingly synchronized. Right on time, the *Chautauqua Belle* chuffed by, blowing its throaty steam whistle. The sky was blue, the clouds bright white, a breeze making the wings of the Cartwrights' duck pinwheel. Normally this would have been his favorite time of day, but as he strung the nylon line, pulling it taut, he frowned as if he'd missed an opportunity. They were gone. It hadn't been three hours, and already he was thinking of Thanksgiving. He couldn't recall whose turn it was, not that it mattered.

"It's so quiet," Arlene said when he came in from the garden.

"I know. I don't like it."

Emily said the same thing at lunch, and, laughing meagerly, they agreed. Without the children the house felt empty. It happened every time they visited, and still it was a surprise.

The afternoon dragged, even with the game on. He'd been meaning to give the window frames another coat, but couldn't motivate himself to begin. Instead he had a beer, taking it out on the dock now that Margaret was gone. Kenny could never quite get the cover on the boat right, a quirk that made Henry smile like a running joke. While he was there, since no one else was going to use them, he brought in the extra life jackets and the big triangular inner tube, hanging the coiled towrope in its designated spot. The boys had put away the croquet set without cleaning it. Using a hooked dental pick he'd bought at the flea market, he dug the dried mud out of the grooved mallet heads, which killed some time. Finally he was reduced to going through his many sets of drill bits, culling the rusted and dull ones, sizing the orphans with a plastic gauge until the bells let him know he could quit and head up to the house for cocktail hour.

He was just relaxing on the porch with a gin-and-tonic when the phone went off like an alarm, the ring jarring. Emily picked up in the living room. Through the window, he could hear her thank Margaret. They must have made it home.

"It was a real treat to have him for the whole week," Emily said, before taking the phone into the kitchen.

Henry thought there was no need to overstate the case. Though he had nothing new to say to her, he was prepared to talk to Margaret, so he was both relieved and disappointed when Emily came back and hung it up.

She noticed he was watching. "Sorry. Did you want to talk to her?"

"I take it they got home okay."

"They did." She shrugged as if stumped. "She seemed good."

"She did," Henry agreed.

"It's always hard to know with her."

They both looked to Arlene as if she might add something. "She seemed upbeat to me."

It was the answer they wanted, and if she seemed noncommittal, they understood. With Margaret, everything was temporary.

With just the three of them for dinner, the dishes went quickly. Later, as dusk was falling, he took Rufus for a walk down to the marina. The driveways were full of cars. It was the season, everyone was up. The Loudermilks were throwing a birthday party, a bunch of pink balloons marking the mailbox, teenagers wandering the yard, talking on their phones. Henry didn't miss those days, yet as he passed he was drawn to the lit windows and the music playing inside.

Spooked by all the noise, Rufus barked.

"Stop. You're not helping."

They strolled down the middle of the road. The bats were out, fluttering above the trees on their nightly mission. A diesel pickup with giant side mirrors chugged up, towing a boat, making them step off into the grass. Manor Drive was private, but people routinely ignored the signs. Blinded, Henry waved, neighborly, but couldn't tell if the driver waved back.

In the parking lot of the marina, a truck with an empty trailer waited. The garbage can by the Porta-potty was overflowing, a feast for the raccoons. He steered Rufus wide of it. They followed the circle to the launch and out onto a concrete pier lined with old tires, at the end of which stood a bench facing the lake. From habit Rufus sat, sniffing at the goose poop. Any other evening Henry would linger, looking out at the lights on the far shore, listening to the frogs peeping in the reeds and the slopping of the water, remembering summers before the war, when there was nothing here but a meadow that flooded when it rained. Tonight, rather than dwell on the past, he thought it better to keep moving.

"Here we go," he said, jingling the leash.

Kenny had called while they were out. Everyone had gotten home safely, Emily said, as if that were an accomplishment. Henry supposed it was. He couldn't say why it grated on him, and cut himself a good-sized piece of pie.

While he ate, Rufus attended him, lying at his feet like the Sphinx, ready to pounce on the smallest crumb, but once Henry was done he moved to the hearth, flopping on the cool stone. It was too warm for a fire. The Pirates had already played so there was no game to listen to, and Henry settled in between Emily and Arlene with his book. He'd barely made a dent in it. For weeks now, Shackleton and his men had been stuck in the ice with no food. Henry, who used to chew the laces of his mitt waiting for the next pitch, imagined having to eat his old Army boots. Was it too early for a scotch? The only sound was Emily keeping count under her breath, which she apologized for, stopping herself, her lips moving as her needles worked. After the boys' video games, he thought he should appreciate the quiet more.

As if by mutual agreement, the three of them had achieved an almost total silence, when, from above, like the pattering of rain, came the scampering of tiny feet across the ceiling.

"What in the world," Emily said, looking up.

She knew. Like the squirrels invading their attic on Grafton Street, the mice were part of Chautauqua.

They all followed the noise. Rufus raised his head, confused.

There was more than one. It sounded like they were chasing each other. It was funny, Henry thought. He hadn't seen one all summer.

"I guess I know what I'm doing tomorrow."

"I guess you do," Emily said.

The problem, being intractable, interested him more than Shackleton. He stopped reading to make a list. The next morning he was off to the True Value, and spent the day happily at war.

Thin-Skinned

"YOU'RE BLEEDING," EMILY SAID, POINTING TO HIS HAND, AND with mild surprise he discovered she was right. He'd been working on the outboard and come inside for a glass of lemonade. Somehow, replacing the fuel filter, he'd managed to split open a knuckle and smear blood on his pants. She had him hold still, like a child, and dabbed at the spots with cold water.

"You should put something on it so it doesn't get infected. If it isn't already."

His hands were dirty, the whorls of his fingers filled with grease. He used the sink in the bathroom, where they kept a rusty tin of Band-Aids. The soap and hot water stung.

If she hadn't told him, he wouldn't have known. He hadn't felt it at all, but his hands were calloused. He was used to nicks and scratches from working around the house. He thought of his father. At the end, his skin was thin as paper. He accidentally scratched off scabs, blotting the beads of blood with wadded Kleenex Henry found all over his condo.

"Do you need help putting it on?" she called.

"No," he said, as if she were being absurd, and then struggled to apply it one-handed, one wing limply folding over, sticking to itself. He swore and tore open another, the counter littered with trash. A hundred years of packaging and they couldn't come up with anything better.

The next night, as he was getting ready for bed, Emily stopped him, lifting his pajama top and turning down his waistband to inspect his hip. "Where did you get this bruise?"

He had to think. "Maybe getting in and out of the cart the other day."

"It looks bad. Does it hurt?"

"Not if you don't poke at it like that."

Later that week, looping around the foot of the bed to raise the blinds, he banged his shin on the metal frame and had to lean against the wall to stay upright. "Jiminy Christmas." At first he worried that his leg was broken, but there was just a lump, at the livid center a white shred of skin he pinched off. He limped into the kitchen, where Emily was making him some eggs.

"What is going on with you? You're falling apart."

"I am," he said, shaking his head as if it were a joke.

Dog Days

WITH AUGUST CAME THE LONG, BREATHLESS AFTERNOONS, THE chestnut becalmed, waves shimmering mirage-like off the roofs of the cars. They were breaking records, according to the Jamestown station. Stalled, an inversion sat atop the Great Lakes like an overturned bowl. In Chicago five people had died, including a toddler forgotten in her car seat. Each morning the radio issued another heat alert for seniors and small children. They were to stay indoors and avoid exerting themselves, a pointless warning. It was too hot to golf, too hot to be out on the water. The lake was flat, the shallows choked with weeds. Henry wedged a racketing old box fan in the garage window, and still the sweat soaked through his Pirates hat. To keep busy he was replacing Emily's rotted window boxes one by one, getting a head start on next year's projects. She brought him glasses of ice water as if he might forget to hydrate, forcing him to stop work every so often and make the trek to the bathroom. Rufus didn't move, panting where he lay, tongue lolling, leaving wet marks on the concrete. It was too hot to grill, too hot to drink scotch. For dinner they ate salads and rotisserie chicken from the Lighthouse. They turned in early, sleeping with their doors open and the attic fan barreling away, the whole house thrumming like the belly of a bomber.

The days were the same, the air thick, cicadas simmering in the trees. Arlene had a gel pack she froze and hung around her neck. She and Emily went shopping at Wegmans and came back raving about the air-conditioning. At dusk he watered the garden. Their tomatoes were monsters.

The irony was that it was cooler in Pittsburgh. Without the children, there was no reason to stay, but the idea of leaving was unthinkable.

When he was working at the lab, he saved his two weeks of vacation for Chautauqua. Even then, by the end he was itching to get back to the city. Now they spent the entire summer, and while he loved the cottage, he missed his workbench and his office at home, and their big bed. It happened every year. He could relax only so much without feeling lazy and aimless, and as the days passed, as predictable as the moon cycling through its phases, he found himself adrift in the muggy doldrums. He was sick of making the same window boxes over and over, sick of fighting the mice to a draw. He was paying for their important mail to be forwarded, and though Jim and Marcia Cole were looking after the house, and Dave Ferguson's guys taking care of the grass, the idea that by his absence he was somehow falling behind haunted him, like Arlene feeling the need to prepare her lesson plans for the coming school year long after she'd retired.

When he couldn't shake the thought, he sighed, taking in a deep breath and slowly releasing it as if he were deflating, a bad habit he'd picked up from Emily.

His impatience would fade, he knew, yet from time to time he caught himself gazing out the window, unfocused, his mind wiped clean. It took him longer than it should have to recall what he was doing, and why. He'd spent most of his life managing schedules and deadlines, it was only natural he should feel slack, lacking a tangible goal. He wanted to believe he was just daydreaming, but there was something unnerving about the blankness that descended on him. He worried Emily might walk in and think he was having a stroke. He hated this muzziness. Recovered, he attacked his work with total concentration, precisely measuring and marking his cuts with his father's T-square, overcompensating for the momentary lapse as if it had never happened.

The heat wave broke, as the radio predicted, overnight, a thunderstorm waking him from a dream of skiing to the South Pole, making him go through the house room by room, closing the windows against the downpour. The next night it was cold enough for a fire. He shoved crumpled newspaper under the grate and sat back with his scotch, watching the first fluttering rush of flames.

"That's nice," Emily said.

"I've had a lot of practice."

"You're hired."

A high moved in and stayed. The days were blue and fall-like, the nights cool and cozy with a fire going. It was their reward, Arlene reckoned, after how horrible it had been.

He thought his mood would change with the weather too, but he was still distracted. Rather than finish the window boxes, deliberately, at half-speed, he began to organize and put away what he could so the Tuesday after Labor Day, he had nothing to do but run the boat down to the Smith Boys and set out an array of sonic gadgets designed to repel the mice. He left the baits, just in case.

In the back of the Olds, Rufus curled up on a faded beach towel with his head down, already slobbering.

"You're fine," Emily said. "Go night-night."

"Next stop Pittsburgh," Henry said.

The day was bright, the gatehouse at the Institute busy. As they climbed the hills to the interstate, the lake spreading blue and glittering behind them, he agreed with her that it was a shame they had to leave.

Incompetence

THE PAPER WASN'T SUPPOSED TO START UNTIL TOMORROW, BUT
there it was on the front walk as they pulled in.

"I hope that's today's," he said.

"Marcia wouldn't let anything sit out too long."

"I hope not."

"She wouldn't."

Then why is it there? he wanted to say.

The garden had survived, and the grass, if they hadn't edged it quite the
way he'd asked. He'd forgotten, he needed to tie back those raspberry canes.

Rufus darted to the middle of the yard and squatted, releasing a killing
stream.

"That's not where you go," Henry scolded.

"He's been in the car all morning," Emily said, as if that were a defense.

Once Henry had lugged in all the bags and put away their clubs, he went
out front and picked up the paper. It was today's. The two suspects in the
Euclid Avenue shootings were finally being arraigned. Mary the carrier
must have gotten the restart date wrong. He laid it on the coffee table, thinking he'd read it later.

The house was stuffy, having been buttoned up for so long. It was just lunchtime, but after the drive he felt scattered, and had to force himself to keep going. His knee clicked as he climbed the stairs. Emily already had laundry started and was making a grocery list. He went around the second floor, opening windows. In Kenny's room, behind the blinds, a fat fly buzzed against the pane, evading his jabs until he trapped it in a corner with a wadded tissue, pinching it to make sure. There were more in Margaret's room, the hatchlings too fast for him to catch, and with a grim face he tromped down to the pantry for the swatter.

Rufus was helping Emily empty the cooler.

"Are you hungry?" she asked. "Do you want a sandwich?"

"Give me three minutes."

He didn't really want egg salad, but she'd brought them all the way from Chautauqua and they wouldn't keep. He waited, poised, letting the flies settle on the glass, then attacked, slapping at them after they dropped to the sill, still kicking. He had to wipe a few off the swatter, their blood staining the tissue like wine.

"Thank you," Emily said, as if he'd saved her the trouble.

"Thank *you*," he said, though they'd had the same coleslaw and potato chips all weekend.

They ate off paper plates as if they were still on vacation. Instead of the lake, their view was of the lawn and the garage. He recalled as a child how gloomy the house on Mellon Street felt after the cottage, the sense of letdown and ending. He remembered looking out the attic window at the empty street. Summer was over, school would be starting again soon. He was eight, nine. Even then he'd known Time was an enemy.

"Anything you want or desire from the Jyggle?"

Cookies. Pie. "Nothing I can think of."

She flipped the laundry and headed out, leaving him alone. Though the day was barely half over, it felt too late to start a new project, and he holed up in his office, answering emails and deleting the trove of spam that had accumulated. His main job today was dealing with the mail. Last year the electric bill had arrived at Manor Drive after they left, hibernating inside the box all winter with the Mayville *Pennysaver,* causing Duquesne Light to threaten to shut off their power. This year, as a precaution, he'd had their forwarded mail stopped a week early.

Rufus lay like a speed bump across the threshold of the office, where he could keep an eye on the hall. The mail normally came around three, announced by his barking and charging for the door, a habit Emily had tried to break him of using a pop can filled with pennies. As the hour neared, Henry watched him like a clock. He was reading a ticket offer from the Pirates when Rufus perked up his ears and huffed a warning. Next door, the Yablonskys' lid clanked shut.

"Stop it," Henry said, pointing at him. "No. You stay."

Rufus whined as if he were being poisoned.

"I know. I can hear him. We want him to come here."

He made Rufus wait, one palm out like a crossing guard, listening for the clank of their mailbox. When, after a stretch, it didn't come, Henry released him and they both went to investigate.

The box was empty. The mailman in his silly pith helmet and shorts was already past the Buchanans' and headed down the hill.

Rufus growled low in his throat.

"I agree," Henry said.

Aries and Virgo

MORNINGS THEY WOKE TO HIS CLOCK RADIO, AS THEY HAD WHEN he was still working, though the alarm didn't go off until seven now and occasionally Emily showered first, depending on her schedule, calling for him when she'd finished washing her hair. Their order varied, but not their routine. They got dressed and then took their pills. Whoever made it downstairs first let Rufus out and filled his dish, turned up the thermostat, opened the curtains and retrieved the paper from the front walk. Whoever was second made the bed and let the sun in around the upstairs.

They reconvened in the breakfast nook, eating with the local news on the little TV for the weather, trading sections of the paper and going over their plans. Since the demise of the *Press*, the *Post-Gazette* had noticeably shrunk, and while Emily made fun of its skimpiness, preferring the encyclopedic *Times*, Henry relied on the *P-G* to keep him informed of happenings around town. The day couldn't start until he'd pored over each and every page, weighing the conflicting letters to the editor and skimming the obituaries for familiar names and faces, catching up on the box scores and his favorite comics just as he'd done when he had his own route. That it took only fifteen minutes was a bonus.

Another daily pleasure the paper afforded him was the horoscopes, tucked back among the classifieds. Though, like most people in the space program, he didn't believe the stars capable of prophecy, it had become a ritual of his to check theirs—hers first—and when they fit his mood, like today's, to read them aloud for her benefit.

"'Aries: Get going while the going is good. There's no obstacle that you can't conquer or problem you can't solve as your energy and enthusiasm will be in high gear this week.'"

"I'm afraid this *is* my high gear," Emily said.

"'Offering help to a friend in need will be effortless.'"

"I would hope that's always true."

"'Virgo: Tighten your shoelaces and take big strides. Powerful minds can find ways to turn a problem into an asset.'"

"It sounds like we're going to have a lot of problems."

"'Rather than blaming someone else for a mistake or error, find a way to turn it to your advantage.'"

"Using your powerful mind, no doubt."

She had a second cup of coffee while he did the dishes, handing him her empty mug when she was done, and then, together, with Rufus leading the way, they went upstairs to brush their teeth, taking turns at the sink before splitting to start on their separate lists.

That afternoon, at the packed Home Depot, he was standing in line with a bouquet of wire stakes for the garden when he realized he'd forgotten to bring their empty propane tank. Instead of going home and grabbing it, he paid for another one and stood outside by the cages with the receipt, annoyed at himself, waiting for an orange-aproned associate, and then in the car thought it was a good move—overdue, really. This way when they ran out they'd have a backup. He'd turned his mistake into something positive, exactly as foretold by his horoscope, and would have been tickled, except by that time, like every day, he'd forgotten what it was.

Side Effects

Now that they were home again, he made the trek to the Giant Eagle's pharmacy department to refill their prescriptions. It was cheaper than the CVS in East Liberty, and if he sometimes had to wait, he could use the ATM or pick up items Emily had forgotten. All of their information was in their system, yet he still brought the scribbled slip from the doctor, as if they might question him. The co-pays were always changing, the prices outrageous. Despite its claims, Medicare didn't cover everything, and like most Americans their age, they took a lot of pills. The size of the crosshatched plastic reminders he and Emily relied on—organized by the days of the week, further divided into slots for morning, noon and night like a tackle box—had become a morbid joke among the children. When Emily turned her ankle, the nurse in the emergency room asked if she was taking any medications. Between the two of them, they couldn't remember all the names. From then on, tempting fate, Henry kept a list of his in his wallet.

Lipitor he took for his cholesterol, like all of the Fearsome Foursome.

Prilosec let him eat stuffed banana peppers and marinara sauce and drink his scotch.

Warfarin was a blood thinner he took at bedtime to reduce the chance of a stroke, though he noticed now he bled more easily.

Lisinopril replaced metoprolol for his blood pressure, still so high that Emily had stopped salting their food, substituting Mrs. Dash and lemon juice.

Lasix processed excess water and helped with his blood pressure, but, according to the fine print, might have caused his light-headedness at Chautauqua, a question he meant to ask Dr. Prasad.

Klor-Con, a potassium supplement, he couldn't take on an empty stomach, knocking it back it after breakfast, before he brushed his teeth.

Dulcolax, which Emily had recommended, kept him regular enough.

Flomax, in the commercials, was supposed to turn his weak stream into a Niagara, but only made him go more often.

Glucophage treated his blood sugar, which hovered on the borderline of prediabetes.

Neurontin, which he took three times a day, tasted like banana and didn't completely stop the needle-like pains in the soles of his feet.

Lumigan was an eye drop for glaucoma he took at night that stung and left his vision too blurry to read.

Ambien he'd quit taking because it didn't always work, and when it did, made him groggy in the morning.

Centrum Silver was the multivitamin Jeff's place gave its older patients.

Vicodin he had left over from his knee. Margaret said it was dangerous, but when a storm was coming and Advil wasn't enough, he was glad he had it.

Aleve, Bufferin, NyQuil, DayQuil, Sudafed, Benadryl—the medicine cabinet was full of antihistamines and analgesics for colds and bug bites and minor aches and pains like his back after weeding. Emily had read somewhere that aspirin was bad for the kidneys and Tylenol mixed with alcohol did liver damage, so he was more likely after golfing or mowing the lawn to ask her to rub some Ben-Gay into his shoulders, but not often. He tried to stay active, walking Rufus three times a day, twice when it rained, and while she complained about her hands every night at bedtime, showing him her swollen knuckles—just a blur, after his drops—he was grateful, at his age, that there was nothing seriously wrong with him. Most of the time he felt fine.

FOD

WHEN HE FIRST RETIRED, FEELING THE NEED TO DO HIS SHARE around the house, he'd tried to apply his skills as a project manager to their habitual chores, only to be rebuffed.

"No," Emily said. "Go. You're driving me crazy."

Haphazard as her methods seemed, she had a system so intricate that any assistance on his part would knock it off kilter. She made no concessions to his new role, and now, a decade later, he knew to stay out of her way. Their domains were separate and sharply demarcated. The basement and attic were his, and his office, as they'd always been, along with the lawn and the garage. The rest was hers.

He'd learned to ask before cleaning anything, but, being compulsive, sometimes he couldn't wait. The living room carpet was the color of champagne. What the Tabriz didn't cover showed every speck of dirt, and the Tabriz, like Rufus, shed heavily. Henry couldn't cross the room without stopping to bend over as if touching his toes and pluck up dark bits of lint and clumps of dog hair.

"Just leave it," Emily said, knitting. "I'm vacuuming tomorrow."

He spied a crumb of a dog treat, a dot from a three-hole punch.

"Stop."

At Jackass Flats they called any scrap of metal that might get sucked into the engines FOD, short for foreign object debris. At the lab they had dedicated FOD control techs, but in the desert, whenever they ran a test, everyone spread across the runway, design engineers and mechanics hunched over like prospectors, combing the baking tarmac for lost cotter pins and sheared rivets. More than once Henry's discriminating eye had staved off catastrophe, yet he was just as vigilant at his workbench, or in the yard, offended by a cigarette butt on the sidewalk or a candy wrapper on the lawn.

He'd always been fastidious, unlike Arlene (unlike Margaret), and looking back, maybe that neatness sprang from a need to please. His mother kept her kitchen spotless. Henry remembered her inspecting the silver he helped polish when Grandmother Chase came for dinner, stopping him to point out the pink Tarn-X caked in the border of a knife handle and asking him to do it again. His father's livelihood hinged on compliance, the glass-faced bookcases in his office ranked with uniform editions of the county building code, his drafting table shrouded like an altar. An eager student, Henry had learned early to pay attention and be precise. In basic his rack was the standard Gunny Raybern used to shame the rest of the barracks, his footlocker squared away, and if after the war his apartment was a mess, courting Emily restored his sense of order. Like him, she was tidy, a stickler for rules.

Picking up the lint did nothing, yet, trained to spot the smallest defect, he couldn't stop. He was an engineer. When he saw a problem, his instinct was to fix it. In the last few years, with boundless time and nothing larger to concentrate on, that tendency had become exaggerated. Now when Emily caught him perseverating over the carpet, he worried he was becoming a fussy old woman.

"If you really want to help," she said, "you can vacuum."

They both knew this was a bluff, and would only upset her. Instead, he pretended to ignore the FOD, all the while spying more. He waited until she'd left the room to police the area by his chair, slipping the pinch into his pocket before sitting again.

Seeing Things

THE DAYS WERE GROWING SHORTER, THE NIGHTS COLD. HIS THIN windbreaker was no longer enough for Rufus's after-dinner walk around the block. Late one overcast afternoon he was in Kenny's room, digging a sweater out of the cedar chest, when a flurry in his peripheral vision made him turn his head. As he did, an instant too late, a dark shape the size of a cat flitted around the corner of the doorway as if fleeing him.

Its presence was so unexpected, for a moment Henry only stared after it as if it were a trick. A mouse or even a squirrel that had found its way down from the attic he might have understood, but this was bigger. The windows were closed, so where would it have come from?

Sweater in hand, he scanned the den and the hall beyond, gray in the muted light. In Margaret's room he got down on all fours and looked under the bed. Just dust.

There'd been a raccoon in the alley, shredding garbage bags left overnight.

Cat or raccoon, it made no sense, unless one had chewed through the drywall.

He whistled for Rufus, who came bounding up the stairs, bright-eyed, his tongue hanging out.

"Where's the kittycat? Get the kittycat."

Rufus closed his mouth and cocked his head, intent.

"Cat? Squirrel? Bunny?" Henry tousled his ears. "I know you know squirrel."

Together they checked the other rooms, Rufus tagging after him. Henry left the lights off, creeping through the gloom, listening for any movement. He wasn't surprised to find nothing.

"You think it was a haint?" Emily asked.

"I saw *something*. I could have sworn it was an animal."

"Not a mouse." She was squeamish when it came to them.

"Definitely not a mouse."

"Did it make a noise?"

"I don't remember any."

"It was probably just a shadow from the window. A bird flying by."

"It was big."

"Maybe a cloud."

"Maybe."

As a boy, if he'd never seen his uncle's ghost, he'd felt his presence. A lifelong Christian, he accepted the earthly intervention of angels as part of his faith, yet if questioned, he would have denied any belief in the spirit world. While Emily claimed to have some vestige of the Sight passed down from her homespun grandmother, he'd never had visions, only normal dreams that unspooled like movies and evaporated come morning. What happened in Kenny's room had been the very definition of an optical illusion: He'd seen something that wasn't there. Whether his eyes were tired, or his mind, he trusted there was a physiological explanation, most likely related to age, and was tempted to view the cat as yet another symptom of his decline. He kept the outside possibility of a brain tumor to himself.

At the same time the strangeness of the encounter fascinated him, and when his mind was unoccupied—too often now—he found himself replaying the moment, breaking it down in slow motion, the blurry stirring off to his left, then swiveling his head with the sweater still in his hands, the shadow already slipping around the door frame before he could tell what it was—all silently, elusive and disquieting as a nightmare. He stayed on guard if it should happen again. When he entered a room, or even the garage, he checked the floor and the corners to make sure he was alone, and every so often glanced up from what he was doing and peered around as if something might be sneaking up on him.

He was prepared for another phantom animal or fleeting apparition, so he was surprised late one night, as he padded back from the bathroom, to look outside and find a man standing on the Millers' walk. Stock-still, in silhouette, he hid behind a brick pillar of their gate like a mugger about to pounce. Henry's phone slept on his dresser, charging. He was trying to remember what number the Millers' was when, from another angle, he realized the man was just a flat shadow cast by the streetlight, and shook his head at how easily he was fooled.

Later he came awake and in the meager light of his clock radio his bathrobe slung over the closet door was one of the big tiki heads from Easter Island.

He didn't tell Emily about these little slips, or flashing on the headline PHILLY MAYOR ACCURSED, when on second glance it was clearly ACCUSED. While curious, they weren't uncommon, like seeing shapes or faces in clouds, yet privately he counted them against himself.

The cat was enough of a novelty.

"Your father's finally lost it," Emily told Kenny when he called after church, and though Henry resented her teasing, he played the straight man.

"It was fast. Even if it was real, there was no way I was going to catch it."

"What about Rufus?"

"Please, he doesn't have a clue."

Margaret, veteran of a dozen twelve-step programs, wanted it to mean something. "What's eluding you in life right now? What are you missing?"

Sleep, he could have said, but didn't want to broach the subject. "Nothing. I've got everything I need and then some."

"You said it was dark. Was it a black cat?"

"I couldn't tell you what color it was."

"Cats can be good luck too."

"That's what I'm hoping. How's everything there?"

"Good," she said, and then it was her turn to change the subject.

He was more interested in the cat as a natural phenomenon than an omen, though once she'd suggested it, he couldn't get the idea out of his head. Symptom or omen, it begged investigation. There wasn't much to be concluded from a singularity. To prove anything, he needed the behavior to be repeatable, and while he prided himself on treating it logically, he had to admit he was intrigued. If he interrogated his brush with the uncanny like a scientist, it was because it was a wonder. Having glimpsed the unknown, he wanted a closer look, and so he kept watch, trying to duplicate the conditions under which he'd first observed it, wandering the upstairs on cloudy days, haunting the empty rooms, the subject of his own experiment.

The Company of Heaven

DR. RUNCO HAD DIED, FINALLY. THE NEWS CAME VIA A MASS email, which Emily considered tacky. Henry, ever practical, could see both sides. To call all of his patients would take days, and he was sure the office was pure chaos. The funeral was Saturday at St. Paul's Cathedral, with a viewing Friday night at McCabe's in Shadyside.

"I didn't know he was Catholic," Emily said. "Why did I think he was Greek Orthodox?"

"I'm pretty sure Runco's Polish. I know he grew up in East Liberty because he went to Peabody."

"Runco, Runco," she said, testing, as if for her crossword. "I wonder if they shortened it."

Dr. Runco dead. Though not unexpected, it was still hard to accept. Both Class of '49, they'd grown old together. Henry—muddled and out of shape, with terrible cholesterol—thought it was wrong that he'd outlived him. But that was a tribute to him, wasn't it? He'd kept Henry alive this long. From now on, he assumed, he would see Dr. Prasad, with whom he shared nothing.

"I'm sorry," she said, as if they were close.

"The last time I saw him he seemed fine."

"He probably knew. I'm not sure if that's better or worse."

"I don't know." His father had gone quickly, pneumonia, the old man's friend, hurrying him along. He didn't want to think about it.

"Does it say anything about flowers?"

"No. Wait, yes."

Before he'd finished with the rest of his email, she'd ordered an arrangement.

"The big question," she said, leaning in the doorway with the calendar, "is whether we need to go to both things or just one."

"What's your feeling?"

"What's *your* feeling? He was *your* friend. I'm willing to go either way."

"I think just one is enough."

"Which do you prefer? We've got nothing going on this weekend."

"Let me see what time the funeral is."

"Eleven," she said, and she was right. Where disaster sharpened her, he felt dull. He'd already forgotten the time, if he'd noticed at all.

"It'll be longer," he warned.

"If it's at the cathedral I'm sure it'll be full-blown mass. That's fine. I'd rather sit through mass than stand around McCabe's making small talk."

"Let's do that then," he said, as if it were his decision.

His day, otherwise, was the same. He fed Rufus and picked up his poop. He replaced a bulb in the upstairs hall. He paid their estimated taxes for the third quarter, taping the envelopes closed, and dropped them in the drive-up mailbox at the post office, an unhappy task that, once complete, provided a grudging satisfaction. He kept crossing chores off his list, but every so often he'd remember Dr. Runco and go blank, biting the inside of his cheek as if lost in contemplation.

It was dumb. Despite Emily's insistence, they weren't what Henry would call friends. Beyond his tanned and sturdy family and their condo at Okemo, Henry knew little about him. Their relationship was strictly professional.

The only place they saw each other was at the doctor's office, in a window-less, fluorescent-lit examination room, for at most fifteen minutes, followed, weeks later, by a computerized bill. All those months Dr. Runco had been in St. Margaret's, Henry had hardly thought of him, partly, he could admit, because he was afraid of confronting his own fate, but mostly because, un-less he had an appointment coming up, he didn't think of him.

The next morning at breakfast he looked for him in the obituaries. There were three full pages plus a gerrymandered arm encroaching on the classi-fieds, a reminder of how old the city had grown. Normally he skimmed the columns with the same gimlet eye he trained on the stock quotes, checking the ages of the newly deceased against his own. He would be seventy-five in a few weeks, which seemed around average for the dead. Having outlived his uncle by fifty years, he was both very aware of and grateful for the time granted him. Without gloating, he pitied those in their fifties and sixties as if they'd been cheated, just as he envied those in their eighties and nineties. What attracted his eye now were the young, victims of accidents and over-doses and the occasional murder. They died not *peacefully, at home, sur-rounded by family,* but *suddenly, unexpectedly,* their pictures innocent, clipped from yearbooks. He read their stories as if they might explain more. They never did, despite some going on and on, which Emily thought in poor taste.

Dr. Runco's was appropriately medium-sized, topped with a dated shot of him smiling like Gatsby in a tux and bow tie, his hair slicked back, maybe at his wedding. Used to his lab coat and shiny dome, Henry tried to reconcile the man he knew with this toothy imposter.

75, of East Liberty, after a courageous battle with brain cancer.

"Jesus." Though Henry only dimly understood the mechanism, brain cancer seemed worse than the other cancers, more painful, and for a pan-icked second, remembering the cat, wondered if that's what he had.

"What?" Emily asked.

"It was brain cancer."

"That's awful."

Like Henry, he'd enlisted right out of high school, then come back, graduated from Pitt, set up shop and never left again. He was survived by his wife, three sons and a long list of grandchildren. Like so many obituaries now in the *Post-Gazette*, it let readers know he was a fan of the Pirates, Steelers and Penguins, another tic Emily lamented. Besides the three sons, Henry realized, it might have been his, and before he could cut off the thought, he wondered what picture Emily would use. Not their wedding photo, he hoped.

She'd chosen his father's. Henry had spent the final days at his bedside, sleeping on a rollaway cot behind the array of monitors that told them there was no hope. He and Arlene were supposed to trade shifts, but he'd been flying back from the desert when his mother died and vowed that would never happen again. His father was comatose, there was nothing they could do for him but hold his hand, squeezing it, willing him to sense their presence. His chin was bristly, his skin a mushroom gray, and every night before Henry took off his shoes and lay down on the narrow cot, he kissed his forehead as if he were a child. When he coded—crashing as the orderlies were serving dinner—Henry and Arlene were both there, mercifully, along with Emily, who made sure the nurses gave them some time alone with him after cleaning up all the IVs and wires. Leaving, she remembered his father's glasses, in the top drawer of the nightstand, and his bathrobe, hanging in the closet. She was the one who took charge, planning his service with Father John and Donald Wilkins, helping Henry choose the casket and the vault. She paid his father's last bills and returned his cable box. Having lost her mother a few years before, she knew what to do. He and Arlene were so overwhelmed sorting through his father's condo, they welcomed the help, marveling at her energy.

Where grief paralyzed him, she was ruthlessly efficient. Often now, projecting his own death, he imagined her helpless without him, when the opposite was true. She would busy herself with the arrangements, making menus and readying the house for the children. Without her, he wouldn't survive long. He'd end up like his father, eating TV dinners and drinking away the evenings, falling asleep in his chair to the news.

Rufus ducked his head under Henry's hand to be petted, rescuing him from his thoughts.

"Here," he said, and slid the page across the table.

"Who's the mobster?"

"He's a little younger there."

She'd just begun reading when she let out a puff of dismay. "Why do they have to say 'courageous'?"

"Probably because it took so long."

"I don't know why, it bothers me."

"I don't think it's supposed to be a comparison."

"It comes off that way."

"Don't you want to be courageous?"

"I'll take peacefully, thank you. Or quickly."

"Instantaneously."

"Wouldn't that be nice," she said, as if it had no chance of happening.

Despite her quibbles with the obituary, she fetched her scissors and neatly excised it. Later she'd slip it between the pages of her mother's Bible for safekeeping, as if commending him to heaven with their parents and her beloved aunt June and the roll call of old friends and neighbors they'd buried over the years, and who was Henry to say he didn't belong?

Friday night he watched the Pirates, whose season was effectively over, all the while recalling the last time they'd been at McCabe's, for Margo Schoonmaker's, the candles and piped-in music and thoughtfully placed boxes of tissues. The rooms always seemed too warm, the radiators ticking even in summer. The carpeting was thick, as if to absorb noise, the sofas and chairs overstuffed, the velveteen drapes from another era. Around the periphery, ranked on easels, propped on mantels and sideboards, would be baby pictures of Dr. Runco, school portraits and snapshots of him in uniform, or the whole family grinning in their ski togs, and on the many coffee tables, fat photo albums visitors were encouraged to leaf through. The Pirates were getting killed, and Henry was sorry they hadn't gone. Though no one would notice their absence, he felt cowardly, letting their flower arrangement stand in for them. He hoped there was a good crowd.

Happily, there was at the cathedral the next morning. When they arrived, a solid half hour early, a sea of people mobbed the front steps as if expecting a bride and groom to burst from the doors. At the curb, instead of a limo, sat a hearse, a gleaming new-model Cadillac he'd never seen before. With Pitt in session, parking was ridiculous. Only on his second pass did he realize the valet stand was for them. He assumed it was free, an extra amenity provided by McCabe's. He'd still have to tip, and hoped he had a couple of ones.

"I wonder how much that cost," he said.

"Too much," Emily said.

It would take them forever to get out of there, but he had no choice. Inching forward, he couldn't turn the car off to lock the glovebox, where he kept a Sucrets tin full of quarters. Rather than ask her to bury it under his insurance and registration, he resigned himself to fate. It always felt wrong, handing over control. He left the engine running, setting the parking brake before climbing out. The stringy dude who gave him the chit had a ponytail and gray teeth. "All right, boss," he said. Henry watched him swing the Olds into a gap in traffic and around the corner as if he were never coming back.

The cathedral had three sets of massive fortified doors worthy of a castle keep, but everyone was funneling into the center one. Emily took his arm and they joined the line, moving up a step at a time. He steered her to the iron handrail, shielding her with his bulk.

"Look at all these people," she said.

"I'm sure a lot of them were his patients."

"This was not well thought out."

"No," he agreed. "I wonder what the holdup is."

Secretly he was intimidated by the size of the crowd, comparing it to his own future service. His mother's had been well attended, partly because she'd died young. His father's was sparse. Not proud, Henry thought he'd take that trade.

An ambulance wailed by, making heads turn. A man behind them laughed—a raucous bark. For a solemn occasion, there was a lot of chatter. Though the day was warm, he was surprised to see several women ahead of them with bare shoulders, and others in bright colors, as if it were Easter. He expected Emily to comment, but she was more concerned with staying upright.

Finally they reached the top of the steps and crossed the threshold, moving from lucent sunlight into a cool gloom redolent of dust and tallow, recalling all those Saturdays at Calvary. The delay turned out to be at the guestbook, where Linda and Carmen from the office were holding an impromptu receiving line. Inwardly he balked, knowing he'd be obligated to say something. *He was a good man. He'll be missed.* Both true yet insufficient. How did you sum up a life in one line?

He let Emily sign for both of them in her perfect cursive before greeting the girls. While they weren't strangers, he feared embracing them would be too familiar, and offered his hand.

"Linda, I'm so sorry."

"Thank you."

"This is my wife Emily."

"It's so good to finally meet you," Emily said, brightening. "I've talked to you a thousand times on the phone. I was just telling Henry how nice it is to see so many people here. From what he's told me, I'm not surprised. He was obviously well loved."

"Thank you."

Why had he worried? In matters of etiquette, Emily was always proper and always prepared. He should have known he could rely on her.

"I don't know what they're thinking," she said once they were out of earshot. "They can do that after."

"I don't know either." Why did he feel the need to apologize?

They left the entryway and stepped into the soaring nave. Softly, as if to calm them, the organ played something low and droning she identified as Duruflé. "A safe choice."

It was hard to grasp the sheer size of the cathedral from the outside, surrounded by high-rise apartment blocks and the Doric-columned halls of the university. Used to Calvary, itself a bulky monument, Henry appraised the monstrous granite pillars and airy vault above with a surveyor's eye. Like Chartres or Westminster Abbey, the scale seemed designed to remind the faithful of their insignificance. The stained-glass tableaux of saints comprising the east wall blazed forth in the morning light, isolated rays slanting operatically over the now-subdued crowd. The middle pews were packed except the last few rows. Emily thought they'd have better luck in the wings, and led him up the right aisle. After a pantomime exchange to make sure seats weren't being saved, they slid in beside a young couple whose toddler was defacing a program with a box of crayons. Henry popped his eyes and received a smile.

While Emily noted the musical selections, he settled in, admiring a shadowy niche to the side where tiered rows of votives flickered at the feet of a beatific Mary. On their trip to England, they'd hopscotched from cathedral to cathedral through the drizzly Midlands, dropping the shilling in the National Trust box to light a candle at each, figuring it couldn't hurt. Smoke and soot and damp stone. They'd walked the Stations of the Cross and viewed the shinbone of Saint Ambrose. The rituals were at once familiar and mysterious, predating the Dark Ages, robed monks intoning the Latin mass. Emily often said if she weren't Episcopalian, she could imagine converting, a claim he never took seriously, though he could see the allure.

She patted his leg and pointed to her program, leaned in and whispered, "It's the bish."

The bishop of Pittsburgh, she meant.

Henry nodded, mildly impressed. He'd seen him on the news dozens of times, often at St. Paul's, his home base, but was surprised he'd preside over the funeral of a simple parishioner. Henry wondered what connection he had to Dr. Runco.

Directly behind the family, as if next in the line of succession, sat the immaculately groomed Dr. Prasad. Henry craned to see who he was with just as a burly man in the front pew twisted around to shake his hand. Henry's eyes weren't perfect at that distance, but they didn't need to be. The city had so little true royalty, there was no mistaking it. From the man's huge shoulders and the same neatly trimmed beard he'd worn during his heyday with the Steelers, Henry recognized him instantly as Franco Harris.

He poked Emily, trying to hide his excitement.

"What's *he* doing here?" she asked.

"I have no idea."

"Maybe he *was* part of the mob. I don't think he was Polish." She showed him the list of pallbearers. Joining the doctor's sons were Nicholas Framiglio, Paul Sodini and Frank Santoro. "All they're missing is a Costa and a Zappala."

"I'm sure they're here somewhere."

"Probably up front."

The answers to these diverting questions would have to wait. The organ abruptly stopped, leaving a scattered coughing, then lit into the processional. All stood, looking back and crossing themselves as a whole retinue moved up the aisle, the bishop with his impressive headdress and shepherd's crook at the center, behind him the pallbearers not carrying the bronze-colored casket but rolling it on a skirted gurney—a cheat, Henry thought. They halted short of the sanctuary steps, taking their places, waiting for the hymn to end.

Shaking the rattle-like aspergillum, the bishop sprinkled holy water on the casket. A priest assisting him draped a white pall over it. If the significance of the ritual eluded Henry, he appreciated the ceremony, practiced as a magic act.

Often, those Saturdays at Calvary in the midst of the Depression, it was just Father McNulty and himself and a handful of family. No music, no flowers. Those austere hours were the worst. He had to be perfect. Any slip would be remembered forever, and in the silence there was no disguising the survivors' grief. More than once, adults he knew from Sunday school and the summer picnic flung themselves sobbing on the bare casket. Mothers, husbands. Without a pause, Father McNulty patted them on the back and pulled them off, restoring them to their families. Henry stood by with the good news of the Gospel, as if that might help. Deep in the woods of the park, his friends would be lounging around the clubhouse, reading comic books and smoking, and he imagined himself there, free of the sadness of others. It was still true. Nothing had changed, really. He was the same selfish boy he'd been, evasive, wishful, quick to absent himself from anything unpleasant, a problem when it came to Margaret, even if there was nothing to be done.

The first reading was by the eldest son. From his crisp enunciation, it was clear that he'd practiced. "Let not your hearts be troubled," he projected so the back rows could hear.

No, Henry thought. He wanted his heart to be troubled. Death was the purest test of faith. What was a funeral for if not to contemplate one's mortality and how best to spend the time one had left?

Beside him, the child was kneeling on a hassock, facing backward so he could use the pew as a table. On the program, with great concentration, he was scrawling a red whirlwind of circles. He looked up at Henry solemnly, then kept drawing.

With so many visitors in attendance, when the middle son finished the second reading, the bishop motioned with both hands for the congregation to stand, as if exhorting them to do the wave.

"I guess we were too slow," Emily whispered.

The Gospel was an old chestnut. "In my father's house are many mansions." The generosity of this promise agreed with Henry's conception of heaven. He took comfort knowing there was a room prepared not just for himself, but all of them.

They sat for the homily, delivered by the bishop, who called Dr. Runco a warm and giving soul, a sentiment echoed in the remembrances offered by his youngest son, by an older brother Henry had never heard of, and finally by Linda, who had to stop and dab her eyes, confessing that she knew she'd cry but didn't care. At the office she and Carmen had been bawling all week. One of them would start and get the other going so there was no one to answer the phone. It was good to cry. It was right. Dr. Runco was a good man and a good boss. They would miss him and always remember how he made them laugh.

Emily tapped his arm. "Why do they have *her* doing this and not Dr. Prasad?"

Henry shrugged, though he saw no problem with it. "She's known him longer."

Who would remember him at the appointed hour? Kenny? Arlene? What would they say, that he was a warm and giving soul? A good father? He could have done better with Margaret, obviously, but that was not all his fault. Part of the problem was the times, the shift in generations. His own family, like most of their social set, had been proper, not demonstrative, abjuring emotion in favor of manners, and then, necessarily, Emily had been closer to the children when they were little. His work at the lab was exciting (was, in retrospect, historic, a privilege bestowed on very few), and he'd pursued it with a focus he would never know again, staying late despite not making overtime, shutting himself in his office after dinner to sketch out fixes. He might read the children their bedtime story and see them at breakfast, but his days were spent traveling at light speed away from Earth. He was aware that he could be self-absorbed and distant, like his father, whose formality now seemed an affectation. Time stole everything. In his final years his father swore at the news and hid dishes under the bed, melted ice cream drying like glue. In his eulogy, Henry had called him a gentleman, which he'd thought the highest compliment. What, truthfully, could he say of himself?

He was hardworking. He was reliable, and honest, and good with his hands. That was the best he could hope for, he supposed.

He didn't want to ponder the prospect too deeply, and checked his watch—past noon. Beside him, the child had covered one program and begun another. Henry admired his quiet industry. He was tempted to ask if he could borrow a crayon, but instead searched the stained-glass windows for saints he knew.

As the bishop was consecrating the Eucharist, a bell rang, as if someone were at the door. It reminded him of those cozy pubs they'd closed, that rainy vacation, jet-lagged and trying to trick their bodies to sleep. *Hurry up, please, it's time!*

They couldn't take Communion but were welcome to receive a blessing.

"I'll pass," Emily said, "but please, feel free."

"No," Henry said, "it'll be a zoo."

"They certainly have enough servers."

"Maybe it'll go quicker."

The couple took the child with them, the husband carrying him, leaving behind an unfinished page.

The hymn the choir sang was new, the melody eluding him, full of slurred notes.

Our lives are bu-ut a si-i-ngle breath, we flower and we fa-ade.

Yet all our da-ays are in your hands, so we retur-urn in love what lo-ove has made.

"It's very modern," Emily said.

"I'm not sure how people are supposed to sing along with it."

"I'm not sure we're supposed to."

They stepped out into the aisle to let those returning by. While the parents bowed their heads in contemplation, the child filled the page with a green tornado. The windows blazed. It was warm, and Henry tugged at his collar. The line at the rail dwindled, finally, the last of the faithful filing back to their seats as the bishop and his assistants tidied the altar.

The music stopped, leaving dead air, a baby complaining. Emily checked her watch. Henry understood. He was ready to go too. If this were a regular service, all that would be left was the dismissal. *Walk in love, as Christ has taught us. Thanks be to God.*

Everyone waited as the bishop descended the chancel steps, his footfalls picked up by the microphone like a killer's in a movie. When he reached his mark, he paused, looking out over the congregation for several long seconds before he nodded and an altar boy stepped forward and presented him with a censer. He paced around the casket, the smoke rising into the lights. Its heavy perfume reminded Henry of Margaret burning incense in her room to mask the telltale smell of pot, and as the bishop commended Dr. Runco to heaven, Henry gazed up at the saints and hoped, for all their sakes, that there truly was a place for everyone.

The recessional blared, the brass triumphant, proclaiming Christ's victory over death as the crucifer led the whole entourage back down the aisle, the pallbearers rolling the casket, followed by the family and, mysteriously, Franco. Pew by pew, the cathedral fell in behind the cortege. Dr. Prasad passed without glimpsing Henry, and by the time he and Emily joined the throng, there was no sign of him. They shuffled toward the entryway, where Mrs. Runco and her three sons and their wives were receiving condolences.

"Have you ever met her?" Emily asked.

"I met one of the boys once, years ago."

"You remember which one?"

"I knew you'd ask me that."

They were strangers, the link between them broken, and yet it seemed important to acknowledge the past.

Mrs. Runco was tall as a model, her hair dyed white. She laughed at some memory, squeezing a woman's shoulder before passing her to her sons. Henry imagined she must be tired, but, like a good hostess, she showed no outward sign. Again, he let Emily lead, though this time he thought he knew what to say.

"Henry Maxwell. I was a patient of his."

"Of course," Mrs. Runco said, taking his hand.

"We were in the same class at Pitt. He kept me alive. I'll always be grateful to him."

"Thank you," she said, patting his arm, and let him go. Though he sensed no recognition on her part, what he told her was true, and she seemed to appreciate it. He was satisfied with that.

Outside, the sun was blinding, as if they'd been in a cave. As they waited for the valet, he was tempted to shed his jacket, but hung on until the same man who'd taken the Olds was holding the door for him.

"How much did you tip him?" Emily asked.

"Five."

"That's more than I would have given him."

"It was free. You're going to pay more for two hours down here."

"I suppose."

They circled the Cathedral of Learning, where they'd first met—it seemed impossible—over fifty years ago.

"Well," she said, "that was long."

"You knew it would be."

"I'm surprised it was such a mob scene, pardon the pun. And what was with Franco? Next time you're in you'll have to ask Linda what the story is."

Henry would have preferred to leave his presence, like the bishop's, a mystery. Though his own funeral would be modest, and the testimonials less glowing, he wasn't jealous, not really. He was happy for Dr. Runco and his family, as if they'd achieved a noble feat. The grandeur of the service was humbling, making his own earthly worries seem petty. There was a lesson in it, he suspected, a higher way of living he should aspire to during the time he had left.

He tried to hold on to the feeling as he drove, forgiving a gold minivan for cutting him off without signaling and then slowing so he missed the light. Emily was going over the program, comparing Purcell's and Handel's ceremonial music, on the windshield there was a splotch of bird droppings dotted with seeds he hadn't noticed before, and gradually the world and all of its demands and distractions returned.

Dr. Runco was gone, he reminded himself, as if he might forget. He was glad they went, but he'd be glad to get out of these clothes. It was Saturday, and already past lunchtime. At some point this afternoon he had to cut the grass, front and back. What else? There was no traffic going home, and still he felt late, a list of chores waiting for him. Once they pulled into the garage and turned off the car, he couldn't resist unlocking the glovebox and checking his Sucrets tin, heavy with quarters. Though he couldn't say for sure, he didn't think anything was missing.

Depósito

AS A NATIVE PITTSBURGHER, HENRY TOOK PRIDE IN OWNING stock in local companies. Like his father, he was a buy-and-hold man, and if his father had stood by Jones & Laughlin, the Penn Central and U.S. Steel too long, squandering, by his loyalty, a small fortune, Henry still believed it his duty to invest in the city, especially after it had lost so much. Among his portfolio he counted his employers, Westinghouse, as well as traditional Dow blue chips Alcoa, Koppers, Kennametal, Bethlehem Steel and Gulf Oil, all, like him, past their prime, or perhaps that was just the market now. He'd procrastinated on the NASDAQ, and his picks lagged badly behind the drivers of the current tech boom, Microsoft and Intel. The one consistent winner he owned was Heinz, whose flashy annual report he paged through like a supermarket flyer. While the American steel industry had contracted in the face of state-subsidized Japanese and Korean dumping, Heinz had gone global, acquiring dozens of companies worldwide, stripping them of their more lucrative brands, then spinning them off again. Del Monte was one of these culls, the number of shares he received in the split so meager the stock wasn't worth watching. Each quarter he received a dividend check for sixteen cents, less than half what it cost to mail the thing, and for that reason—as if to teach them a fiscal lesson—he didn't bother switching to direct deposit.

The check arrived Friday afternoon, along with a birthday card from Arlene that Emily promptly garnisheed, propping the Hallmark envelope against a pewter candlestick on the mantel to wait for Sunday. He'd already been to the Home Depot and hadn't planned on going out again. To have any chance of beating the school buses, he needed to leave now, and though the check was worthless, he endorsed it, adding the tax information to the folder in his desk drawer, and set off for the Waterworks.

Rush hour started early on Fridays, but the bridge hadn't backed up yet, and as he sped across the river for Aspinwall, he felt pursued by the entire city. Freeport Road was stop and go. Ideally, he'd make his deposit and come back on 28 before traffic got too bad. Rather than wait for the light at the mall entrance, he snuck through the Eat'n Park. The bank branch was new, an atoll in a corner of the lot. When he swung the Olds around the side, there were two fancy SUVs in line.

He dug out his card and flattened the check on the dash.

"Okay," he said. "Here we go."

A lot of people got paid on Friday, but these appeared to be what Emily called Fox Chapel ladies of leisure. Rather than ride the brake, he put the car in park. As he sat, watching one and then a second minute slip by, a contractor's broken-down pickup pulled in behind him, and a low-slung Honda with tinted windows. He could see the woman leaning out, pushing buttons, still not done.

"What in the world."

He was thinking of just taking a spot and using the ATM in the lobby when her taillights flared and the car ahead of him moved up.

The second woman deposited a check, then another, then another.

"Unbelievable."

By the time she was done, the line stretched around the building.

Two yellow posts guarded the machine. He eased the Olds in close as if he were docking a boat, careful of his side mirror, and still he had to lean out to reach it. Keeping the car in drive for a quick getaway, he fed the slot his card, his finger at the ready. Before he could enter his code, a screen appeared, asking whether he wanted English or Spanish. In his haste to get rid of it, he jabbed the wrong button.

The screen that followed was mostly gibberish. During the war, like everyone, he'd picked up enough French and German to get by. The little Spanish he knew came from eating breakfast with his flight crew at the Mexican restaurant outside the gates at Jackass Flats, and that had been twenty years ago. "Ay, Papi," the techs said when a hydraulic hose blew. El Jefe, they called him, El Presidente.

The words were foreign, but the menu had the exact same format. If he took off his glasses, he wouldn't know the difference.

Desca un recibo con su transacción?

With your transaction. Did he want a receipt?

Behind him, someone honked.

"Sí," he said, and rather than hit cancel and start all over again, he forged on, decoding prompts he'd followed for years without thinking. After he'd successfully deposited the check, he nodded, impressed with his resourcefulness, and was disappointed the receipt was in English.

Did he want *una otra* transaction?

No was still no. The machine spit out his card, and he pulled up before fitting it back into his wallet.

Traffic on the bridge wasn't bad. As he cut through the zoo, he realized that Del Monte was Spanish as well, a funny coincidence. He wondered what it meant. Of the Mountain? He'd have to look it up.

"Hola," he said, home, fending off Rufus at the back door, and told Emily what had happened. She was only half listening, battling an involved recipe. The cutting board was bloody, the sink full of bowls and measuring cups powdered with flour.

"Oh, I know," she said. "It's maddening. I don't know why they do that.

I understand the rest of the country, but really, when's the last time you saw a Hispanic person at the Waterworks?"

"It was no problema for Enrique."

"Well, you have more patience than I do," she said, searching the crowded spice cabinet for something elusive, and rather than explain how he'd figured it out, he took the receipt into his office and added it to his bank folder, dismayed, as always now, at the implacable balance of their account. Though his computer was right there, he didn't bother looking up Del Monte, and while the name returned to him several times over the next few days, teasing, easily within reach, he never did.

The Birthday Boy

As HE DID EVERY YEAR, HENRY ASKED EMILY NOT TO MAKE A fuss over his birthday.

"Don't worry," she said, "I won't," though they both knew it was for comic effect. He'd seen the box of cake mix when he was bringing in the groceries, and that was fine. He wouldn't take that pleasure away from her, but he didn't want the children spending money on him. If Emily didn't quite enforce this, she did mention it.

"I'm going to get you something anyway," Margaret said over the phone, "so it might as well be something you want."

"I don't want anything. Really."

"You are no fun."

"I am so fun. I'm just old."

He was going to be seventy-five—a big one, as they never tired of reminding him. He wasn't embarrassed by his age, but, like living longer than his mother, neither did he see it as an accomplishment. Birthdays were for children. When he was small, his mother would wake him up by buttering his nose, touching a dollop like sunblock to the tip, an old Cornwall tradition they'd tried to pass on, with mixed success. For breakfast she made him his favorite,

Belgian waffles, and for dinner, chicken à la king with no mushrooms, suspending the household rule of ladies before gentlemen to serve him first. Prince Henry, his father joked, as if this royal treatment might spoil him. Once he started kindergarten, his mother threw elaborate parties, mailing fancy invitations to his friends and classmates, who filled the front parlor, spilling punch and cake crumbs on Grandmother Chase's good rug, playing post office and blindman's bluff. As a child, he loved how with a string of lights she transformed the backyard into a carnival, but as he grew older he came to dread the tortuous preparations leading to the day itself, and the awful, drawn-out ceremony of opening presents in front of everyone, until, beginning high school, he finally asked her to stop. She was hurt but honored his request. His first birthday away from home, waking up in his soaking cold bivvy outside St.-Lô, he wished he'd been kinder to her. Even now the memory had the power to chasten him. Like a funeral, a birthday wasn't yours but for the people who loved you. Why resist the inevitable? Better to acquiesce, and yet the prospect depressed him, he couldn't say why. Seventy-five years was a long time.

Late Saturday afternoon he was in the garage when a FedEx truck rumbled up out front—a gift from one of the children, most likely, yet what leapt to mind was the expense. He and Emily would never spend that much for shipping.

Rather than intercept the package, he gave her time to hide it, and then at dinner couldn't help kidding her, wondering what had come.

"Never you mind, Mr. Nebbynose."

"I hope they didn't send it overnight."

"What do you care? You're not paying for it."

"That is true," he said, though technically, in Margaret's case, he was, since every month they sent a check to help cover her bills. His great fear was that after he was gone, she would bleed Emily dry—another reason he needed to fix his will, a job he'd been putting off for months, not because he couldn't face his own mortality but the shortfall he'd leave her. It seemed unfair. All his life he'd been careful with money.

"I just hope you like it."

"Do you know what it is?"

"I do."

"Are you going to give me a clue?"

"No." She seemed pleased that he was interested, and he happily played along, but then, after he did the dishes, reading a fat biography of George Washington Father John had recommended, the gloom settled on him again, inescapable. Death and taxes, the joke went. He'd been lucky to outrun both so far.

In bed, kissing him good night, Emily threatened to butter his nose, and while she'd never follow through, Henry was grateful she remembered.

He'd been born just past two in the morning, so when he woke up to use the bathroom, he was a year older. He preferred to think he didn't feel any different, but then in the morning his hand was asleep, his fingers tingling. He kneaded them under the hot shower, trying to recall if he'd mentioned it to Dr. Prasad. Dr. Runco would know.

Dr. Runco was seventy-five.

At breakfast, Emily hijacked his horoscope, reading aloud: "'If September twenty-second is your birthday: Your gregarious nature will be in full bloom during the upcoming two to three weeks. This is a good time to join an organization or to circulate within a new social group. Watch your credit card statements and carefully scrutinize contracts in December and June, when you could easily be fooled by surface appearances.'"

"My gregarious nature."

"You do go over your credit card statements. I don't see you joining any groups, though."

"Maybe they mean the Building Committee."

"I wouldn't call that new."

"What's the regular one say?"

"Nothing interesting."

"Let's hear it."

"Okay, but it's not specifically yours, so keep that in mind."

"Uh-oh," he said.

"Stop. Now I'm sorry I said anything. 'Virgo: Logic may fail you. A practical approach won't be much help when a problem stems from a completely irrational situation. You may need to put your creative juices into overdrive to find a solution or avoid the matter altogether.'"

Margaret, he thought. Avoid the matter altogether. "That's not so bad. What's yours say?"

"Mine's boring. 'Aries: Smiles can be contagious. A positive and upbeat attitude will light up your surroundings and make you a pleasure to be around this week. Competitions will be about enjoying the game rather than who wins or loses.'"

"That *is* boring, but true. You're always a pleasure to be around."

"Now who's buttering whom?"

At church, during the Prayers for the People, in the silence left for the congregation to remember their dead, he thought of Dr. Runco and his father, though he couldn't see an immediate connection, and shrugged it off as maudlin—another reason he disliked birthdays, the temptation to look back and take stock. He did that enough at his age without prompting. The past was rich, a vast storehouse of memory. Behind one door, Sloan waited for him, behind another, the war. This time of year, especially, it was harder to find something to look forward to, like the children visiting. Thanksgiving was two months away, Christmas three. Maybe they could take a vacation, go to England again (no, the flight was far too long, too expensive), revisiting the places they'd stayed the last time, winding through the rainy Lake District on the wrong side of the road, stopping at every lichened churchyard and wayside inn to fill up on shepherd's pie and stout. The urge was perverse. He loved fall, the park turning colors, reading by the fire at night with a scotch and Rufus sprawled on the hearth, and yet he saw the months ahead as an empty plod. It was just the day making him restless, as if his age were an intractable problem to be solved. Tomorrow he would be free of it, and glancing up at the transept, the stained-glass tableaux fired by the morning sun to a jewel-like brightness—ruby, sapphire, emerald—he found the haloed Saint Michael with his sword, as he had as a child, and prayed for courage, wisdom, and above all, patience.

Home, he hung up his suit and put on his work clothes. Dinner would be a production, so lunch was last night's leftovers. For one day he wasn't allowed to do dishes, Emily shooing him out of the kitchen to make his cake. He was surprised to see a can of Duncan Hines frosting. Even before she put her pans in the oven, she apologized.

"I hate a box mix, but you said you wanted a plain yellow cake with white icing, so that's what you're getting." He wasn't fool enough to ask why she didn't make it from scratch, like his mother. She hated his taste, not the box. He was just happy they were having cake, and breathed in deep as the house filled with the warm scent of vanilla.

He was giving their old martin house a new coat of paint at his workbench when, directly above him, he heard her curse, the word freezing him in midstroke, followed by the crash of the silverware drawer. While her tantrum was at least partly for his benefit, he debated whether he should investigate. There was no hiding. She'd seen him go down to the basement. Deliberately, with the concentration of a watchmaker, he finished the trim of the chimney, set the wet brush on the can's edge and went up.

On his mother's cut-glass stand sat the bottom layer of his cake, bisected by a ragged fault line Emily was trying to plaster over with icing. Rufus, wisely, was nowhere in sight.

"Stupid thing fell apart when I took it out."

"It doesn't look so bad."

"It looks terrible. I should have made the cake I wanted to make."

"I'm sure it will be delicious."

"Stop." She slathered on more frosting, evenly covering the top, and then, her attempt at disguising the crack failing, jammed the spatula in the can and turned her attention to the second layer. "Go away."

"I'm going, I'm going," Henry said.

Back in the basement, craning close to do the eaves, without thinking, he said, deadpan, "Happy birthday."

Later, she'd recovered, and they didn't speak of it. Kenny called, and Margaret. Over the speakerphone, Justin asked how old Henry was.

"Older than I ever thought I'd be," he joked, which, once true, was no longer.

Arlene came for dinner, bringing what was obviously a bottle wrapped in Little Mermaid paper.

"You know me well."

"I do," she said, as if it were a simple fact. "I've known you your whole life."

They were having steak. Once Emily had the baked potatoes going, they opened presents in the living room. There were more cards on the mantel, most of them hand-drawn by the grandchildren, including one from Rufus, signed with his paw print. He'd also gotten Henry a thirty-foot retractable leash. Arlene's bottle was a Glenfarclas 25 ("I couldn't afford the 75," she said), and Emily confessed that for months now, like a spy, she'd been secretly knitting him a lobsterman's sweater for their walks around the reservoir. The FedEx package was from both children, the photo of the whole family at Chautauqua this past summer in an antique oak leaf frame Margaret had found at the flea market, perfect for the cottage. Again, he was touched by how thoughtful all of their gifts were, and in retrospect felt ungrateful for saying he didn't want any. It happened every year, a kind of miracle, so why was he surprised?

The steaks were rare, the wine dry. The cake—good-looking, despite Emily's vigorous disclaimer—had only two candles, a 7 and a 5, the flames wavering as Emily and Arlene sang a duet to him, a gift in itself.

"Make a wish," they said.

He gathered his breath, thinking what a strange birthday it had been, closed his eyes and wished for another.

Good News

TUESDAY, IN THE STILL MIDDLE OF THE AFTERNOON, AS HE WAS paying the bills, the phone rang in the living room, making him look up from his blotter. Emily, who'd been knitting, needed a second ring to answer. From her tone he knew it was Margaret.

"Oh honey," she said, soothing. "I'm sorry."

He assumed it was bad news, but what form that might take and to what degree was a mystery. Margaret seemed to be doing all the talking. Emily had gotten up with the cordless and was pacing around the dinner table, her end of the conversation waxing and waning as she passed the door of his office, and rather than eavesdrop and torture himself with scraps, he gently closed it, sealing himself in.

He tried not to speculate, but, bent over the ledger of his checkbook, he expected it had to do with money. He didn't mean to be cynical, but usually when she called out of the blue like this, she needed help. It was the end of the month, everything coming due at once. She couldn't rightly petition him on his birthday. Emily would lecture her about living within her means before giving in and asking how much, then write the check herself, since he refused to anymore, a pointless moral stance that engendered some bitterness between them. At dinner she would divulge the amount grudg-ingly, as if it were his fault, and the rest of the evening he would dote on her, overly solicitous, offering her a glass of port or warming a cookie for her in the microwave, so that by bedtime they would be made up, a team again.

Jeff was the other possibility, the whole nursing home soap opera blow-ing up. Whatever had happened had been sudden. They'd just talked with them the other day, and while Jeff hadn't said much, he never did. Henry remembered his foghorn bass when they were singing, so he'd been there. At his most faithless, Henry believed he would leave her, not because of another woman but because she was such a mess. That Jeff was more patient than either he or Emily, he didn't doubt, but even a saint's patience had an end. Then what would she do, middle-aged with two children and no mar-ketable skills?

Why wasn't she at work? It was the middle of the day. Among her catas-trophes over the years she'd lost so many jobs that he couldn't keep track of them all, though she seemed to like this new one, at a dentist's office, even if it paid little. The children had their teeth fixed for free. He didn't think she'd risk that by drinking, but by nature she was habitually late and quick to take offense. Once she'd been fired from a dollar store for going five minutes over on break, cursing out the manager as she tore off her vest, a story she told as if it were a joke—as if she were still a teenager.

It wasn't something with the children, an accident or broken bone. Emily would have let him know immediately if that was the case.

A relapse, perhaps, though Margaret talked about her addiction only when she was clean, framing her behavior in the psychobabble of rehab, her poor decision-making miraculously relegated to the past. Clean slate. Atti-tude of gratitude. Let go, let God. Most likely it was another setback anyone who knew her could have predicted but that she would chalk up to her chronic bad luck. A bounced check. A towed car. A lost phone. She was forty-seven and still thought the world was against her, as if the world cared. Whatever the news was, it would be expensive, and ultimately he'd foot the bill.

He shouldn't let her distract him. He stuck a leftover snowman stamp from last Christmas and a free address label from the SPCA featuring a beagle on the water bill, paid it and logged the check in the ledger before sealing the envelope and adding it to the stack. The gas, the electric, the phone and internet and cable—each had its own color-coded folder with this year's records in the right-hand pocket and last year's in the left for comparison. He took a miser's pleasure in his bookkeeping, alert for the smallest overcharge. His system seemed so self-evident to him that while he'd never explained it to Emily (she wasn't interested, didn't want to know), he was comforted by the idea that she'd be able to pick up right where he'd left off.

As he was vetting their American Express statement, from the living room came the stately *bong bong bong* of the grandfather clock. In its wake, he strained to hear Emily, thinking with relief that maybe they were done, and then seconds later she passed his door, still commiserating. She ran the tap in the kitchen until he recognized the burble of her filling the brass watering can. It stopped, and he pictured her going around the downstairs, the phone to one ear, topping off her plants. Her disinterest reassured him. The news couldn't be that serious if she was only half listening. Like Arlene, Margaret could ramble.

He didn't pay all the bills. The cable wasn't due till the twentieth, and Duquesne Light gave him till the fifteenth before they charged a late fee. Otherwise he was done, and though he wanted to put the stack out with a clothespin for the mailman to take, he stalled, winnowing his email, deleting a bunch of old junk, aware of Emily orbiting beyond his door. Normally he liked the quiet of his office, an orderly hiding place from the chaos of the world, yet now he felt trapped, barricaded against impending disaster, hoping that by ignoring it, it might magically go away.

Holding his breath, he tracked Emily's footsteps, and wasn't surprised when they finally stopped outside his office.

She knocked as if she needed permission to enter.

"It's open."

She didn't come in, just poked her head through the crack.

"That was Margaret on the phone."

"How's she doing?"

"She's got some kind of bug. She can't keep anything down. She sounds miserable."

"It's too early for the flu," he said, daring to hope that was the extent of it. "How's everyone else?"

"Good, so far. Of course she's convinced they're all going to get it. I guess Jeff is doing the cooking."

"Can Jeff cook?"

"I think he cooks like you cook. Anyway, she sounded pretty down. I'm going to send her some flowers."

"I think that's a good idea." They'd be expensive, but in a larger sense, he figured they'd gotten off easy.

She looked at him as if there were something else, both of them uncertain, waiting for the other to speak, and for a moment all the awful possibilities he'd conjured for Margaret rose up like ghosts.

"That's all," she said, cheery, as if she didn't mean to intrude, and backed out, closing the door so he wouldn't be disturbed.

Singleton

ONCE AGAIN, WELL BEFORE THE FINAL WEEKEND OF THE SEA-
son, the Pirates were assured of finishing in the cellar. Henry watched the
last game anyway, a loss to the hated Reds, rooting to the end as Jason Ken-
dall stranded the tying run on third. While he might look in on the playoffs,
there would be no more Buccos baseball this year. Summer was over, fall
already started. The feeling didn't hit him till the next day walking Rufus
up to the park after dinner. Twilight had fallen. The evening star was out,
the gables of Highland stark against the clear sky. The leaves were turning, acorns crunching underfoot, and as he passed a picture window where
a couple was watching the news, he realized there would be no game on TV
later. The prospect left him strangely bereft.

It was too early for football, though by now the Steelers were 2–1 and a
shoo-in to win the Super Bowl, if you believed the *Post-Gazette*. That Sunday after church, he settled in before the TV like the rest of Pittsburgh to
watch them whip the Seahawks, the outcome foregone, only mildly satisfying. He watched the late game half-heartedly as the sky darkened and the
smell of pot roast rose from downstairs, warming the house, and once it was
over, he was marooned again.

Tuesday the Fearsome Foursome played their last round of the year before Fred decamped for Florida. The air was damp, carrying a tinge of woodsmoke, and leaves dotted the fairways, making it harder to spot their balls. "Winter rules," Cy joked, moving his from a drift. Normally being out on the course was an escape, the pastoral setting and leisurely pace creating an illusion of timelessness, but as they crisscrossed the fairways after their errant drives, trading the lead, Henry found himself counting down the holes they had left, and, distracted, dunked his tee shot in the pond on sixteen and ended up having to stand lunch. Following tradition, they toasted the season past and pledged to return again next spring, God willing. They said goodbye in the parking lot, envying Fred's extra months of sun but not the bugs and humidity and geriatric traffic. Inching light to light through the commercial strip of Murrysville, Henry thought it was another loss.

The next day, as if to taunt him, the weather was perfect. He thought of calling Cy and Jack, but they'd never played as a threesome. By some brotherly logic it seemed a betrayal of Fred. Henry doubted they could make it on such short notice anyway. Emily had her bridge club at one, otherwise he would have asked her.

There was nothing stopping him from going alone. His Grandfather Chase was famous in his later years for rising before dawn at Chautauqua and walking the lake course with just a five-iron, his beagle Ollie hunting down his ball. Driving a cart wasn't nearly as dashing, and maybe it was that Keystone Kops image of himself hopping out, hitting and hopping back in again that kept Henry from throwing his clubs in the Olds. A tee time for one, please. No, it would be embarrassing. His grandfather aside, solitary golfers struck him as a squirrelly, self-involved breed, like hermits or fly fishermen. A lot of places didn't take singletons, he wasn't sure about Buckhorn. They'd probably make him play with strangers. The last thing he wanted to do was fill out someone else's foursome.

He dithered, intimidated by the idea as much as the energy required (he'd have to explain to Emily afterward, a confession he'd rather skip altogether), and by the time he made up his mind, it was too late. Rather than moon about the house, he took Rufus for a walk around the reservoir with his new leash. The sun off the water warmed his face, and he wished he'd gone. What did he care what people thought? He was seventy-five, he could do what he pleased.

When Emily came home—victorious, splitting the kitty with Louise—he asked if she had anything going on tomorrow.

"Besides my book club, which you knew about."

"Right, sorry. I thought if it was nice out we might shoot a round."

"It's that time of year, isn't it? Poor Henry, no one left to play with."

"What are you doing Friday?"

"What *am* I doing Friday?" she asked him, as if he should know this too. "Friday I'm making the dad-blammed cookies for the bake sale. Do I need to put it on the calendar?"

"No."

"It's supposed to rain all day anyway."

"Is it?"

"I'm sorry, Henry, I'd love to play with you, but you need to give me more warning."

While it sounded like a valid excuse, she didn't really mean it. They hadn't played anywhere but their one round at Chautauqua for years now, and stung by this hypocrisy, he decided, with the righteousness of the jilted, to go by himself.

The guy on the phone said he didn't need a tee time, which Henry refused to believe. The forecast was cool and overcast, but not cold enough to stop real golfers. The pro shop opened at eight. He left early, gunning the Olds up the long hills of the Parkway East, hoping to beat the rush, and pulled in to Buckhorn to find four cars in the lot, all parked at the far end: employees'. He threw on his shoes, paid and grabbed a cart. Clamping a scorecard to the steering wheel, he realized he'd already won.

The grass was still dewy, soaking his shoes and socks. Even with his windbreaker on over his sweater, he was chilly, but it would warm up soon enough. The course was his except for the greenskeepers, who seemed to be right where he wanted to hit. They buzzed in slow circles on their mowers, deafened by earphones, paying him no attention. On four, a par-three, he waited for one to finish and trundle off, then plugged his tee shot in a bunker.

"Come on, Henry."

It was different playing by himself. He was playing badly, maybe because he was going too fast. He wasn't taking the time to size up his next shot the way he would in a foursome. There was no one to consult on club selection, no one to read off a yardage marker, no one to show him how the greens were breaking, but mostly there was no one to talk to. When he almost holed out a chip, clanking it off the pin, he spun around, arms wide, as if appealing to an invisible audience. He didn't see how his grandfather did it. Maybe if he took Rufus with him.

He was coming back toward the clubhouse on seven when he spied in the distance, walking down the middle of the fairway opposite, a fellow singleton. As Henry drew closer, he saw it was an older woman, bandy-legged and deeply tan, pulling an antique rolling bag behind her like a ghost from another era. She waved at him as if they were members of the same club, and Henry waved back.

"Peas in a pod," he said, quoting Emily.

Discouraged, his feet freezing, he was ready to retire after nine, but he'd paid for eighteen. He stuck it out as the course filled up, shooting a hard-earned 93. The card was his, tempted as he was to pitch it. He skipped their usual sandwich and beer, just returned the cart and peeled off his wet socks in the parking lot.

Home, he brought his clubs straight inside, making Rufus back up.

Emily was getting a head start on her cookies. "Did you have fun?"

"I had golf."

"That bad."

"Ninety-three."

She whistled in sympathy. "I'm sorry."

"How was your book club?"

"Better than ninety-three. You can put mine away while you're at it."

"That's what I was going to do next." When in truth he hadn't thought of them at all.

As penance, he did hers first. In the basement, beneath the warm light of his workbench, he cleaned each club, scrubbing away the dried mud and grass stains, tugging the plush covers over the woods. He snapped on the hood to protect them from the dust and shrouded the top half in a white garbage bag before stowing it on the far side of the furnace, beside their luggage, the matching suitcases taking him back to England and the possibility of escape—futile, he knew, and yet he imagined surprising her with plane tickets and romantic plans to revisit all the places they'd stayed. Putting away his own clubs, he wondered why England, why not somewhere else? Was it too late to make new memories, easier to simply recall the old ones, happy or otherwise? They'd never been to Spain or Egypt or Thailand, and now they never would. He leaned his bag against hers, the pair hooded and bound like captives in the dim corner, and, frowning, squared away his workbench and turned out the light.

"Thank you," she said when he came upstairs.

"You're quite welcome," he said, as if it were nothing.

Friday, as Emily had forecast, it poured, and she baked cookies, her apron powdered with flour, holding ghostly handprints. A mound of dishes filled the sink, but he knew better than to intervene. He kept to the living room, Rufus at his feet, the two of them exiled, occasionally padding to the front window to watch the rain, gray and relentless. Rufus curled up on his bed and sighed.

"I know, buddy," Henry said. "It's no fun."

After lunch, she ran out of cream of tartar and sent him to the East Liberty Jyggle for more. He was glad for the distraction until he walked through the sliding doors and found himself surrounded. The floor managers and cashiers, the older fellow restocking the produce section, the young mother pushing a cart with her toddler—everyone was wearing their Steelers jerseys.

He'd been so focused on his mission that he'd forgotten it was Football Friday, Pittsburgh's one great civic show of faith, and would be every Friday all the way through the playoffs. While he was a lifelong Steelers fan, being nine years older than the team, he felt separate and left out in his Pirates hat, as if he'd shown up to the wrong party.

"Isn't it a little early for that?" Emily asked, but she was skeptical about the city's obsession with football in general, and more concerned just this minute with her snickerdoodles.

"They should win the division."

"They always win the division."

He shrugged. "People love a winner."

"Not like your Pirates"

"It's only week four."

"Who are they playing?"

It was the Bills—the hapless Bills, who'd gone to the Super Bowl four times in four years and lost them all and hadn't done a thing since. Sunday was no different. The game was a mismatch. The Steelers ran inside at will while the defense knocked out their quarterback, piling up a big lead, yet Henry wasn't particularly interested. He tried watching the baseball playoffs instead, but didn't care for either team and felt dislocated, between seasons, finally turning the TV off altogether.

He wandered downstairs, where Emily was absorbed in the *Times* crossword.

"Aren't you watching the game?"

"I don't feel like it."

She squinted, suspicious, and beckoned him closer, tested his forehead with her hand. "You're not hot."

"I'm going to take Mr. Joyboy here for a walk."

"Take a coat, it looks a little breezy."

He'd hoped she might come with him, but once they were out in the sun he was grateful for the solitude. There was no traffic on Highland—everyone was at home watching the game. On their circuit of the reservoir they met a solo jogger, a tall girl in black tights, winter gloves and a headband. Henry had seen her before and was ready to raise a hand in greeting, but she was wearing headphones and veered wide of them as if Rufus might bite her. Leaves fell and drifted on the water. He imagined they were a problem, catching in the filters, clogging the mains. Strange. All around him the leaves were dead—dry and shriveled, drifted against the fences—while the trees were still alive. He wondered if Dr. Runco's death had anything to do with his mood, or turning seventy-five. Usually he liked this time of year.

Margaret had called while he was gone—secretly a relief. Emily said she'd seemed fine, whatever that meant.

He had a couple of Iron Cities with the late game and surrendered to the crowd noise and balky rhythm of the play clock, talking back to the set, poking fun at the smarmy commentators and their cherry-picked statistics.

"That's why they call them the Bungles."

"What?" Emily yelled from downstairs.

"Nothing!"

Kenny, who'd grown up during the heyday of the Steel Curtain, waited till the game was over to call. He'd had a few beers too. "*Here* we go, *Steelers*," he chanted, the speaker making him break up.

"Yes," Henry said. "Here we go, Steelers."

Mr. and Mrs. Henry Maxwell

EVERY FALL THEY HAD THEIR PICTURE TAKEN FOR THE CHURCH directory, a slim, no-frills compilation kept with the latest White and Yellow Pages in the front hall table, and especially handy now that so many of their contemporaries were moving to condos and retirement homes. Though Henry disliked having his picture taken, and everyone at Calvary knew who they were, as a member of the vestry he felt compelled to lead by example, and so, the day of their appointment, he shaved and put on the same suit and tie he'd worn the year before.

"I think it's time for a new suit," Emily said.

"I like this suit."

"It's old and it doesn't fit you anymore."

"It fits fine." He showed her the sleeves, perfectly even with his wrists.

"It's too tight through the shoulders." Which was true, it did bind him. "We should go look at Nordstrom this weekend. They'll have something nice. You're going to need one for Sarah's confirmation."

"That's not till February."

"February's going to be here sooner than you think."

"I still like the suit."

"Do you remember when you bought it?"

"I don't know. When I was still working."

"So at least ten years ago. How much did you pay for it?"

"No idea."

"Whatever it was, you've gotten your money's worth out of it. Time for a new one."

"What about the tie?" Navy with diagonal gold stripes—Pitt's colors—which she'd given him ages ago.

"The tie's fine."

Driving over, his checkbook in his jacket pocket, he was still ruffled. Whether she was right or wrong, he would never think of criticizing her clothes. Not because he had no fashion sense (as a designer and a craftsman, he liked to believe he had a good eye), but because he respected her. He wasn't a ten-year-old getting ready for church. The suit was fine, just a little tight, but, as with most of their minor disagreements, he knew he'd eventually give in, if only because she cared more.

During the shoot, he was afraid the camera would capture his displeasure and tried to disguise it with his best vestryman's smile, beaming into the bright lights. The photographer, a beanpole of a young man with brilliantined hair and a bow tie, was a one-man band, constantly adjusting his reflective screens, checking an open laptop and fiddling with his lenses, keeping up a nonstop barrage of questions, sometimes laughing before they answered, at others outright ignoring them. He was flirty and theatrical, dropping in and out of a not-quite-British accent. He brought over a stool for Henry to sit on and had Emily stand behind him, a pose Henry thought odd but went along with.

"Now if the gentleman could turn to his left, like so. Left, left, right there, yes. Knees together. And if the lady could put her right hand on his shoulder. Head straight, chin up. Lovely. And if the gentleman could look up here. And a smile. Wonderful. And again. Very nice. You've done this before, I can tell. Are both of you right-handed?"

The basic package—not cheap—included a single four-by-six print of the shot they used for the directory. Normally, as they previewed their choices on the laptop, the photographer used the opportunity to upsell them, pushing eight-by-tens and wallet strips to share with family members, forcing Henry to politely decline, but this one didn't bother.

"I'm surprised," Emily said on the drive home. "Isn't that his job?"

"I'm assuming they work on commission. Is it my imagination, or was he wearing makeup?"

"He had on more eyeliner than I do. And he smelled like cloves."

"'The lady.'"

"'The gentleman.'"

"He was interesting."

"I'm sure it's not an easy job."

"No," he said, and thought of Kenny with his degree, developing other people's pictures. Henry had done his best to counsel him but feared none of his advice applied.

Reconciled, they rode in silence.

"We can go look for a suit tomorrow, if you want," he said. "Traffic won't be as bad."

"Well! What got into you?"

"The power of suggestion."

"I guess so. I'd say that was almost too easy if it hadn't taken ten years."

The next day she held him to it, helping him choose a suit he couldn't live long enough to get his money's worth out of, but which, because it was roomy and made her happy, became his favorite. Yet the real legacy of the shoot belonged to the photographer, who they gleefully imitated around the house, exaggerating his tics, turning him into a goofy cartoon. "The lady," Henry would say, finding her on the john. "If the gentleman could move his lazy carcass out of the lady's way." "If the canine could pee and poop today. Yes, wonderful." They weren't being cruel, or didn't mean to be. Theirs was a private language, not shared with the rest of the world, and so exempt from censure, sheer burlesque. One reason they fell back on it so often, Henry thought, was because they liked playing him. Their impressions were as much a tribute as a spoof. He was a character, free to do or say anything, and when the directory arrived, they had to admit, after everything, he took a pretty good picture.

Nature Boy

FALL, LIKE SPRING, MEANT YARDWORK—LEAVES, ENDLESSLY, AND pruning the raspberry canes, taking down the birdhouses and hanging the feeders, restocking seed and suet. They awaited the first frost like Druids, reading the sky at night. The weather was warm, forcing him to pull out the mower and do the front and back a last time, and then one morning the grass was rimed stiff and brittle-looking, crackling underfoot. While a squirrel taunted Rufus from the peak of the garage, they prepared the garden for winter, tearing out the withered annuals, planting pricey mail-order bulbs and wrapping the more delicate shrubs in burlap. Emily knew what to cut back and what to let rot. Henry did the grunt work, rolling the wheelbarrow to the compost pile, lugging bags of lime and peat moss from the trunk of the Olds. There was something satisfying yet also melancholy about burying the flower beds under a fresh blanket of mulch, like putting away his clubs or closing up the cottage. It was just the time of year.

Thanks to Emily's plastic rock, his grass had filled in nicely, besides a few bare spots. His plan was to overseed the whole yard and let the snow-melt soak in come spring, a technique he'd seen online but never tried. As with any unproven solution, he worried that he might be throwing his money away.

To give the grass a fighting chance, he needed to keep after the leaves. The sycamore had dropped its load early, only seedballs dangling from the branches, but the pin oak that belonged to the Coles was still holding on, every breeze floating a few wayward leaves over their fence. Watching from the French doors with Rufus, Henry had to stop himself from breaking out and grabbing a rake. Until the tree was bare, there was no point, yet several times a day he checked and was stung to find they'd multiplied.

The front was worse. The houses on Grafton were staggered so their yard faced a gap between the Bowdens' and the Millers' through which the prevailing wind drove any untended leaves, sending them tumbling across the street to pile up in the gutter and at the bottom of their steps and on the lawn and in the hedges and on the porch, where, first thing in the morning, he saw them when he ducked outside to retrieve the paper. The supply was infinite, the wind tireless. He could rake the night before and the next day they'd be back. In the past Emily had discounted this claim as an exaggeration until he made a point, one blustery afternoon, of showing her the stampede in progress, as if it were a wonder of nature.

She just shrugged.

"They're not even our leaves," he said.

"The wind never blows the other way."

"Not often enough, obviously."

"You're never going to get all of them," she said, as if he were being unreasonable, advice he found especially deflating, since that was precisely his goal.

By now the leaves were down, only a few holdouts like the Coles' oak among the bare maples and sycamores. While some of the new people on the block gathered them the old-fashioned way, dedicating the better part of a Saturday or Sunday afternoon to it, making piles for the children to play in, stuffing oversized bags printed like jack-o'-lanterns, most paid scruffy mercenaries who came during the week with gas-powered blowers and protective headphones, made a racket for a couple hours and then hauled everything away. Henry didn't care how they did it. He just wanted them gone.

Part of being a good neighbor, he believed, was taking care of your property. The yards along Grafton were perfectly neat, like theirs, with three exceptions. A glance from the bedroom window made it clear who the shirkers were: the Collucci-Browns, a new couple with two toddlers up by the corner of Sheridan who Emily had welcomed to the neighborhood with cookies but with whom, besides the wife returning their plate, they hadn't spoken since; the Hennings, another young couple with small children, but they were all the way down by Farragut; and the prime culprits, being right across the street, the Millers, now just Kay, alone in their huge house, and who, according to Emily, was having serious eye problems.

"Do you think she'd mind if I offered to rake their yard?"

"I don't want you raking their yard. It's too big. She must have someone who does it."

"It's getting a little late for that."

"I can ask her. Is that what you want?"

"No," he said, without force.

"I'll ask her."

It was a gift of hers, being direct. He wondered if she'd let slip that it was his idea.

She went over after lunch. Through the sheer curtains he watched her unlatch the gate, climb the porch stairs and ring the bell. She stood back and waited, then pressed it again. Finally she turned around and came back.

She tried calling but got their machine.

"I don't know, maybe she's visiting Peter and Tammy. She didn't say anything about it."

"That's all right," he said. "Thank you for trying."

Friday it was supposed to rain. Thursday he raked, despite the Coles' oak, setting a heavy bag beside the trash. With the rain came the wind, and in the morning the front yard was covered again. It was already sprinkling when he put Rufus out and grabbed a rake from the garage.

"Are you out of your mind?" Emily called.

"It'll take me five minutes."

He was being wishful. It took him half an hour in a steady rain, rushing the entire time, the leaves soggy and hard to rake. When he came in he was out of breath and sweating, his nails packed with mud.

Emily was reading the paper and wouldn't look at him. "You shouldn't be doing that. You're going to give yourself a heart attack."

"I'm not dying, I'm just out of shape."

"That's how it happens—to men a lot younger than you."

"If I don't get them up, they'll kill the grass."

"I don't care about the grass, I care about you."

He'd miscalculated, he saw, and though he was still glad he'd gotten it done in time, he apologized. When, later that day, a downspout plugged and the gutters overflowed, against every instinct he agreed to pay someone rather than climb the ladder in the rain and do it himself. The concession placated her, as he'd hoped, but at the cost of more than just his pride. The two-man crew who showed up the next morning parked their van facing the wrong way, and while they did clear the gutters, after writing them a check and watching them pull off, Henry discovered they'd done a half-assed job of cleaning up, leaving several piles of muck where they'd landed. He circled the house with a shovel and a trash bag, feeling abused on all sides. In the driveway, as he stooped to scoop another wad of decomposed leaves and maple seeds, he bent at the waist and his breath pressed out of him. Before he could slip the shovel under the mess, a tightness in his chest like heartburn made him wince and stand up straight. The feeling passed, dissipated like a bad case of gas. It was just a coincidence, the power of suggestion, yet he slowed down and took his time now, moving at half-speed, resting a moment to catch his breath before lowering himself creakily to one knee, like an old man.

Temptation

INSTEAD OF DRIVING THE WHOLE FAMILY OUT TO A RUSTIC FARM-stand in Butler County and riding a jolting haywagon over the sere and stubbled fields, now they bought their pumpkins from the parking lot of Shadyside Presbyterian—one for each of them, including a baby for Rufus that Emily accessorized with fuzzy pipe-cleaner whiskers. They were expecting close to three hundred trick-or-treaters, most from the other side of Highland, a trend that made Emily apprehensive but that Henry saw, like the changes in the neighborhood, as the inevitable product of lax zoning, the conversion of grand old one-family homes to apartments exploding the population density. Halloween was a free-for-all. High schoolers with no costumes showed up, young mothers with neck tattoos holding babies dressed as superheroes. Last year they ran out of candy, so Emily took advantage of some twofer coupons and bought extra, sticking the bags in the downstairs fridge, where he encountered them each time he opened the door for an Iron City. He didn't care for Payday or Nestle's Crunch, but she knew he couldn't resist Reese's Cups, so why did she buy them?

"You can have one or two, just don't eat the whole bag."

While it was true—once they were open, he couldn't help himself, would sneak a couple into a pocket and gobble them in secret like Margaret, bury-ing the wrappers in the trash—he resented the assumption, and resolved not to have any. It helped that Emily waited till the Monday before Halloween to stock up, and still, all week they preyed on his mind. He allowed himself a syrupy splash of Drambuie at night, counting down the days, and by a su-preme effort managed to deny himself, earning the even more delicious re-ward of proving her wrong.

"I'm impressed," she said, emptying a bag into the big salad bowl on the front hall table.

"Why?"

"I guess I shouldn't be. You're the stubbornest man I've ever met."

"Thank you."

"It's not a compliment."

"Maybe a little."

She pinned him with a look. "No."

They ate at five-thirty so they'd be ready for the early birds. Henry lit their jack-o'-lanterns with the butane wand and, like every year, Emily took a picture to send the children. The sun was down, the streetlights just warm-ing up. The weather was mild and dry, promising a heavy turnout. In the dining room the extra bags waited, ranked on the table like evidence from a drug bust.

"Now I'm wondering if this is going to be enough."

"It'll be enough," he said. "If not, we'll lock the door and turn out the lights."

Officially, trick-or-treating started at six and ran till eight. Once the fire siren blew, she couldn't sit still, stirring the candy as if to mix it, going to the front window and pulling back the curtain to peek at the street.

"Here they come."

"Good," Henry said, as if they were overdue.

When she opened the door, Rufus, exiled to their bedroom with the radio on to soothe him, barked as if they were being robbed. Their first customers were two toddlers who had to be prompted to say "Trick or treat." Emily fawned over their scarecrow and fairy princess getups, bending low so they could grope in the bowl. By chance, a fair number of Reese's Cups had migrated to the top. They each took one.

"Good choice," Henry said.

"What do you say?" the mother asked.

"Thank you."

"You're welcome," Emily said. "Happy Halloween."

The parents were new people he didn't recognize. Emily, with her network of spies, tried to recall the last name. "They're around the corner on Sheridan. They have those little yappy dogs they leave out on the porch all the time."

"I know where you mean."

The first hour was all new people, the young families who'd replaced their friends. Emily knew a few, and while Henry had passed them while walking Rufus, they'd never shared more than a neighborly greeting. Once he'd known every child who came to their door, could guess by the size and shape and eyes who was peering out from under the bedsheet or behind the mask with uncanny accuracy so that it was a triumph when one of them fooled Mr. Maxwell. Now he was a stranger, the old guy with the dog, relegated to a bit part, his only lines throwaways.

Once night fell and the moon rose, the crowd changed, both sides of Grafton swarming with roving packs of pirates and witches and linebackers in eyeblack and shoulder pads and actual Peabody jerseys. They came charging up the walk with their pillowcases, trampling the grass, cutting each other off to reach Emily first, the mob shoving in, grabbing fistfuls.

"Whoa, whoa." She pulled the bowl away. "Let's be ladies and gentlemen. Just take one, please. Leave some for everyone else."

In back someone made a joke, and a gaggle of girls laughed. These were Arlene's students, sharp-tongued and quick to take offense, serving their time in the city's dying schools before graduating, if they were lucky, to jobs as fast-food cashiers and nursing home aides and postal workers or no job at all. Arlene kept a folder of browned press clippings chronicling their rare successes, along with a surprisingly thick clutch of obituaries.

"Okay," Emily said, offering the bowl again. "Just one now."

Henry stood beside her like a bodyguard, ready to enforce the rule.

There was no need. They were still children, trained to obey their mothers. They waited politely to choose their favorites, thanked her and filed away into the night. He wondered if any of them were from Mellon Street, if, by wild coincidence, one might be living in his old room, sneaking down the box stairwell at night, haunting the alleys and backyards of his childhood.

Dracula, Batman, Catwoman. Zombie cheerleaders, bloody surgeons, evil clowns. He wanted to go sit down, but the onslaught was constant, the bowl quickly dwindling to just a few Clark bars. When she sent him to fetch more, he checked the grandfather clock. It was only seven-twenty.

He brought back some 5th Avenues he didn't care for, some Baby Ruths and the next-to-last bag of Reese's Cups. "I don't know. It's going to be close."

"How many bags do we have left?"

"Three."

The Reese's went first, and, quickly, the Baby Ruths. One cornrowed Batgirl looked at the 5th Avenues and turned around. With ten minutes to go, there was another rush. They had to replenish a final time, and then, as if the siren had blown, the sidewalks emptied. Next door, the Coles' porch went dark. In the lull, they could hear the swish of traffic on Highland. At some point Rufus had stopped barking.

"I'm sure he needs to go out," Emily said.

"He's probably sleeping."

"I think we're going to have just enough."

"We shall see."

The last wave was even stranger—a pair of minivans that stopped at the top of the hill to let the children off and followed them down, a joyless if efficient strategy. What neighborhood they came from was a mystery—Stanton Heights, maybe, or Morningside—yet every year they arrived as if on a set schedule, maximizing their haul, then disappearing. Henry watched them paw through the bowl and noted with a miser's glee that there were still some Reese's Cups.

"Happy Halloween," he called after them, giving the drivers a wave.

"I think that's it," Emily said.

"I think you're right."

As they waited for the siren, watching the invaders hit the Buchanans' and pile back into the vans, a police car silently cruised through with its red-and-blue lightbar wheeling, as if to clear the street. Inside, the grandfather clock chimed. Before it could count off the hour, the wail normally reserved for fires wound up, its long, soaring note filling the night sky.

"We made it," he said, kissing her cheek.

"Barely." She showed him the bowl. "That's sixteen bags. Next year it wouldn't hurt to have a couple extra."

In the shadows thrown by the porch light, it was hard to see exactly what was left. It was only after they retired inside and he freed Rufus that he could properly assess the spoils. There were just two Reese's Cups, a disappointment. The rest were boring 5th Avenues and Nestle's Crunches. Following tradition, she set the bowl in the middle of the dining room table like a dare, where it remained until, one by one, in three short, headachy days, he ate them all.

Whole Life

HE WAS WORTH MORE DEAD THAN ALIVE. SO WAS SHE. WHILE the stock market rose and fell, death was a sure bet. The problem, as always, was timing.

By design, since he'd retired, he used their Social Security to cover their premiums, a happy trade-off initially, secure in the knowledge that one of them (Emily, most certainly) would receive the full lump-sum benefit, except now with their carrier's hefty annual increases, and since men didn't live as long, his payments had ballooned so that with each month he continued to breathe he was losing money. So many of their investments were failing. True or not, it was especially galling to think that, as an asset, he was depreciating.

With all of their sunk costs, it was too late to get out, though occasionally their agent pitched him on converting to whole life. The idea was tempting—having access to the equity they'd built up over the decades—but if they switched they'd lose a good bit of it, and at their age borrowing money, even from themselves, was dangerous. The premiums for whole life were also higher, the original source of his discontent.

The prudent move, he knew, was to stay the course, yet every month he felt like a fool, mailing off a hefty check for himself and Emily, receiving nothing in return but another bill. As with any investment, he needed to take the long view, which, in this case—as in no other—was guaranteed. Overall, he thought, it was a small price to pay for a little peace of mind.

A Tough Cookie

THOUGH HE MIGHT JOKE, THERE WAS NO DENYING THAT HIS memory, like his strength, was going. More and more often he caught himself breaking off in midsentence, unable to find the right word, or, halfway across a room, turning on his heel to retrieve a tool or piece of paper he needed. For torturously long seconds he forgot what simple household items were called, or struggled to put names to faces. Sharp as the day they met, Emily had a store of knowledge he relied on when he couldn't recall something—in this case, an actress from the past.

"I have no idea who you're talking about."

"She was a big star right after the war. I can see her face."

"Blonde, brunette?"

"Dark-haired. Big eyes."

"Bette Davis."

"Taller."

"Greta Garbo."

"American. A dame."

"Lauren Bacall."

"No."

"What kind of character did she play?"

"A tough cookie."

"Joan Crawford."

"Like Joan Crawford but not as classy. More of a broad, always snapping her gum."

"A big star who snapped her gum. Now I really have no idea. Sorry."

"That's all right. It'll come to me."

The next day, when it did, he held on to it like a prize to tell her. "Joan Bennett."

"What about her?"

"Nothing. I just couldn't think of her name."

Emily shook her head. "You're lucky that I love you."

"I know," he said.

The Borrowers

THE COLD DROVE THE MICE INSIDE. IT DIDN'T MATTER HOW well he sealed the hatch and weatherstripped the basement windows, they could squeeze through the smallest cracks. He never saw them when he was working. They came out at night, when it was quiet, leaving their droppings on the shelves among Emily's Mason jars and kitchen gadgets, gnawing holes in boxes of laundry detergent and SOS pads. Years ago he'd made the mistake of keeping the birdseed at the bottom of the stairs, the inevitable spillage providing them an accidental feast. Now he kept it in a raccoon-proof bin on the back porch. The warmth of the furnace drew them anyway. They were foragers, stealing dryer lint from the wastebasket to line their nests, as if they were settling in for the long winter. While Henry couldn't stop their cousins from colonizing Chautauqua, he refused to let them take over his one haven.

"Our little friends are back."

"Oh good," Emily said. "Let me know when they're gone."

Poison was too dangerous, with Rufus. Glue trays were cruel. Having tried all the high-tech options, Henry bowed to tradition, using the same spring-loaded traps his father had on Mellon Street, the classic design never bettered by later generations of inventors. He baited each trigger with a gooey dollop of peanut butter, gently set them along the walls and waited. Long after nightfall, when he'd watered Rufus a last time and chained the back door and they'd gone up, the mice would come out, scooting across the open floor like wind-up toys, climbing the shelves in search of easy plunder. In bed, he pictured one crawling over his workbench, beady-eyed in the red glow of his battery charger, whiskers twitching, sniffing at the leather holster of the nifty multi-tool Kenny had given him for Christmas. They chewed wires and carried fleas and shat everywhere. He would do what he had to do.

From experience he knew he needed to be patient, yet the next morning, before breakfast, like a lobsterman checking his pots, he crept down to the basement to see if he'd caught anything.

The trap under the stairs was sprung, tipped on its side, the force of the bar snapping closed flipping it. With a toe Henry nudged it over. It was empty, the peanut butter missing.

"Tricky tricky," he said, and knelt like a detective, careful not to disturb the crime scene.

It had tripped, no question, yet the trigger was clean. The bar had dented the soft wood, but there was no blood or fur, no pink string of a tail left behind.

The rest, strangely, were untouched. He stood in the middle of the floor, rubbing the back of his neck with one hand like a farmer, trying to figure out why, and then, hearing Emily above him, retreated upstairs.

"Any luck?" she asked.

"We got a nibble."

"Is that good or bad?"

"This early," he said, "it's promising."

After breakfast he reset the trap, and though the mice never ventured out during the day, every time he went down to the basement, he checked all eight, walking the perimeter with a flashlight like a security guard.

The next morning the same trap was sprung again, the others ignored. He tested it on his workbench, first a dry run, poking it with a pencil, then baited. Emily, hearing the trap clack shut, asked if he was all right.

"I'm doing an experiment."

"Here's an experiment: Call the exterminator."

"Thank you."

"You're welcome."

The problem, he hypothesized after several trials, was how easily the peanut butter slipped off the trigger, too viscous. He needed something more rigid so the slightest nibble would trip it. The solution he hit on was genius: cheese.

"How long did it take you to figure that out?" Emily asked.

"Longer than I'd like to admit."

She had some prepackaged squares of American left over from Chautauqua that she let him use. He rolled the cheese into a ball he squished around the trigger, cocked the bar and set the spoon in the catch. He just touched the cheese with the tip of the pencil and the bar snapped down, breaking the lead.

"You really think that's going to make a difference?" she asked.

"I think it's an improvement."

Whether it would work was another matter. After being shut out twice, he didn't expect to succeed immediately, so he was surprised the next day to find the trap at the bottom of the stairs occupied.

The mouse was on its side, pinned by the neck, a dribble of blood from its nose staining the wood. Felled, it was small and harmless-looking, its mouth open, its pink feet curled like hands. Instead of celebrating, Henry remembered taking Duchess to the vet to be put down. She lay on the gurney the same way, an ear flopping in her face, her foreleg shaved where they'd taped the IVs. It was supposed to be like going to sleep. Her eyes were fixed, her breathing shallow, slowing, but as he and Emily were petting her, saying it was going to be all right, a bright rill of blood seeped out of her nose, pooling on the metal like spilled paint. No one had told them this might happen, and while he wasn't angry with the vet like Emily, he knew it wasn't right. Duchess had trusted him to take care of her, and in those last moments he'd failed her. Now, looking at the mouse, he felt a similar guilt. Killing something so small and powerless was no accomplishment, just an unhappy task that had to be done. In the bedtime stories he read Kenny and Margaret, the mice were always the heroes, which, in this case, made him the villain.

The trap was useless now. The others would smell the blood. Before he threw it away, he levered the bar up with a screwdriver and tipped the mouse into the trash as if freeing it.

The other traps were empty. He had more under his workbench, and he unwrapped one and trudged upstairs for some cheese.

"Success?" Emily asked.

He nodded. "One."

"You don't sound pleased."

"It's not a pleasant job."

"I told you to call the exterminator."

"You did."

"They can't be that expensive."

"They can."

"It might be worth it."

"It's early," he said, taking the whole package.

"That's what I'm afraid of."

As he was setting the new trap, wondering why she was second-guessing him now, the spoon slipped—the bare metal lacking the friction to keep it in place—and before he could pull his hand back, the bar snapped, catching his fingers.

"Goddamn son of a bitch!" He yanked the trap off and flung it away, cradling his hand, already throbbing.

Emily ran to the top of the stairs. "Are you all right?"

"I'm fine! Just dumb."

She couldn't resist playing nurse. She came down and held his hand under his work lamp. The bar had smashed the tip of his index finger, leaving a plum-colored blood blister under the nail.

"You're probably going to lose it," she said.

"Wouldn't be the first time."

His carelessness embarrassed him. Even worse, with just one hand he couldn't set his traps. Against every instinct he called an exterminator, who scattered a half dozen black plastic boxes he assured Henry were pet-friendly and said he'd be back next week.

"How much was it?" Emily asked.

"You don't want to know."

"Actually, I do," she said, then whistled at the figure.

"I told you."

"You did."

Before the exterminator could return, her prediction proved true. The blood blister grew, an insistent pressure, the dead nail fading a translucent gray before sloughing off. The skin beneath was swollen and sore, pink as ham, and each time he forgot and tried to button his shirt or use his phone or turn a page of the morning paper, the pain reminded him of the money he was wasting, and he cursed the mice, as if it were all their fault.

The Gold-Plated Anniversary

BECAUSE THEIR ANNIVERSARY HAPPENED TO FALL ON A MONday, the possibilities were limited. Everything on Mount Washington was closed, along with most of the nicer places in Shadyside. Taking her to the club was a last resort, sure to be held against him, though if asked, she would say it was fine. He needed to be creative. He'd heard good things about La Lune Bleu in Aspinwall, except that meant they'd have to cross the bridge at rush hour. The Landing in Verona was supposed to be fancy. Café Sam in Oakland. Henry hedged, checking their menus, scrolling through their reviews, dissuaded by complaints of bland food and bad service. It seemed risky, on such an occasion, to go somewhere new.

It was their forty-ninth, one shy of the big one, as if fifty was the finish line. Emily and Arlene and the children had already started planning for next year. Lisa wanted to be part of it, which annoyed Emily. Trying to find a venue was a production, and then there were the food and drink packages, and whether to hire a band or a DJ and putting together the guest list and invitations. Henry eavesdropped on their progress, alarmed at the cost, but kept his misgivings to himself, as if paying for everything excused him from participating. It was not his responsibility.

This anniversary was. Last year they'd gone to The Point, an old favorite, and while the food wasn't memorable, there was a jazz combo they stayed to hear, moving to the bar for a nightcap. It was too much, on top of the wine, and she'd kissed him on the way to the car, her hot mouth shocking him, and at home, after a glass of sherry, thanked him for the nice evening. Now he scoured the listings in *Pittsburgh Magazine,* certain no one would be playing on a Monday night.

They used to go to Minutello's with the Pickerings and the Millers, taking home straw-jacketed Chianti bottles to make candleholders for the back porch, but it wasn't what Emily would consider fine dining. The same for Poli's and Tambellini's, and anything in Bloomfield. Sushi he ruled out, as well as Chinese, Thai, Indian and Mexican—all too hard on the stomach. Of the few remaining choices, none was wonderful, and knowing it could be a mistake, rather than book something he wasn't thrilled with, he called The Landing.

The woman who answered was British and chipper, which immediately reassured him. He asked for a quiet table with a river view.

"And would this be a special occasion?"

"It's our anniversary."

"I'll make a note of it. Congratulations, by the way."

"Thank you."

He was glad he'd called. He felt better having reservations, as if the rest would be easy.

If the fiftieth was golden, he and Emily joked, the forty-ninth was gold-plated. He had no gift for her besides roses, an old standby, and again he was tempted as the weekend passed to book them two tickets to London. Waiting for dessert, he'd slide the envelope across the table and watch her face change. A third honeymoon, just the two of them, wending their way north through Yorkshire, driving on the wrong side of the road, stopping at pull-offs to walk the windswept moors like characters out of the Brontës. They'd stay in castles and take the train up the coast to Glasgow, eat kippers and eggs for breakfast and spend the day visiting distilleries. If it all seemed a pipe dream, it was because they'd been happy there, free, for a short time, of their normal lives. They were alone, no cell phones or email to break the spell, plus it had been twenty years, the hassles of travel softened by time, leaving only the highlights—long, inimitable dinners and late-night taxi rides. He recalled standing naked at the window of their inn one morning after having made love to her and looking down on the tourists posing before the statue of Shakespeare and feeling a strange exultation, as if he'd discovered the secret to life. It would be different if they went back now— that animal happiness no longer possible—and yet the idea returned again and again, tantalizing. Next year he'd be expected to come up with something big, so maybe then. He'd have to do a little legwork, put together a folder. The prospect pleased him, and he felt lighter, as if he'd already surprised her.

He wrote the time on the calendar, but not the name of the restaurant.

"So we *are* eating dinner," Emily noted. "We just don't know where."

"I know where."

"Not the club."

"Not the club."

"Have we eaten here before?"

"We have not eaten here before."

"The plot thickens."

"I hope you like it."

"Why wouldn't I?"

"I don't know. It's a pig in a poke. It could be wonderful, it could be terrible."

"Where did you hear about it?"

"If I told you, it would ruin the surprise."

"I hate surprises."

"I know," he said.

He kept her guessing to the end. As they were dressing to go out, she asked him to help her with her necklace. She sat at her vanity, bowing her head as he battled the tiny clasp.

"You're really not going to tell me."

He fastened the catch, took her by the shoulders and kissed her neck. "You look lovely."

"Thank you, so do you. That doesn't answer my question."

All afternoon a steady rain had fallen, and traffic was bad. He'd left extra time, and still, crawling along Washington Boulevard with everyone heading home, he was afraid they were going to be late.

"That new Spanish place in Aspinwall," Emily said, thinking they were taking the bridge.

He shrugged, mum.

"You are a stinker."

At the light, when they peeled off and headed upriver, she shook her head as if it couldn't be right. "What's in Oakmont?"

"A very nice golf course, I hear."

"I'm serious."

"So am I."

Though it was only two lanes, and narrow, Allegheny River Boulevard was fast, an overtaxed commuter route. He expected traffic would get better as they went, but instead of thinning out and picking up speed, it stopped altogether. They sat at a standstill, wipers shuttling, taillights spangling the windshield.

"We're not moving," Emily said. "There must be an accident."

Ahead of them, cars were turning around.

"That's not a good sign," she said.

"I don't know where they think they're going."

"There must be a back way."

"Not that I'm aware of."

"Maybe if you cross the river and come back."

"That's all the way past Oakmont."

They inched up and waited. The clock on the dash changed. He thought he'd left enough time, but obviously not. He hated being late, and had to quell a rising panic. It was Monday, they wouldn't give away their table.

"I'm feeling a bit peckish," she said.

"Me too."

They were under a tunnel of trees. When the wind blew, rain knocked on the roof. More cars were pulling three-pointers, pickup trucks four-wheeling over the weedy shoulder and gunning past the other way. The Olds was too big to swing around, another reason to wait it out. He tried KDKA but the news told them nothing.

"This is ridiculous," Emily said.

"It is."

"I take it we're late."

"I don't think it'll be a problem."

"I can call them."

"I don't have the number with me."

"That's convenient."

"I'm sure this will clear up. It's not that far."

Sitting there watching the clock tick off the minutes, he blamed himself. He knew he shouldn't have picked a new place. They should have just gone to the club. After all this time, why did he still feel the need to impress her?

Behind them a siren wailed, growing louder. A police car raced up the oncoming lane, its Klaxon blasting a warning.

"They're just getting here now?" she said.

He shook his head, as stumped as she was, and then when they finally got going again and caught up to the police car, it wasn't an accident at all. The stoplights by a strip mall were out. In a reflective yellow vest, a policeman stood in the middle of the intersection, directing traffic with a flashlight. The state store was dark, and the Giant Eagle.

"I hope wherever we're going has power," Emily said. "Otherwise we're not eating tonight."

"Don't jinx us," Henry said, too late.

All of Verona was out, from the train tracks down to the river. When they pulled up to The Landing, it was dark and the lot was empty.

"I've heard about this place," Emily said. "It's supposed to be very good."

"I guess we'll never know," Henry said.

There was a handwritten sign on the door too small to read. He got out, braving the cold, and climbed the steps to investigate. SORRY! it said, CLOSED DUE TO POWER FAILURE. As he was returning to deliver the news to Emily, the door swished open behind him, and a bright voice called, "Are you the Maxwells?"

"We are."

It was the woman he'd spoken to on the phone, not a pasty Brit, as he'd imagined, but deeply black, long-limbed and pretty, confusing him. "I'm terribly sorry. I know this is a special occasion. What I can do is call around and try to find a table for you somewhere else, if that's all right. I know Oakmont has power. How do you feel about Moody's? It's got a view, and their food is excellent."

Henry balked, still wanting some say in their fate.

"I think you'll like it. Let me give my friend Christian there a call." She was dialing before he could disagree, and turned away, a hand clamped to her ear.

Emily lowered her window and beckoned him over. "What are we doing?"

"She's going to try to get us in somewhere in Oakmont."

"It's nice of her to do that."

"I'm sure she feels responsible."

"It's not her fault the power went out."

The woman descended the steps. "You're all set. Just ask for Christian. He'll take care of you."

Her name was Alison, and she was right, Moody's was easy to find, and cozy. Christian had champagne waiting for them, a thoughtful touch, refilling their glasses until Henry declined, saying he needed to drive. Emily kept going through dessert, a white chocolate espresso torte she polished off, scraping the plate with the edge of her fork.

"Thank you," she said in the car. "It was definitely a surprise."

"To me too. Happy Anniversary."

"Happy Anniversary. I hope you don't mind if I close my eyes. I think I've had too much to drink."

"Probably a good idea," he said, and as they drove home along the empty road, the streetlights shining down all around them, he understood how lucky he'd been.

Highway Robbery

THE OLDS' STATE INSPECTION STICKER WAS UP AT THE END OF the month, and he wondered, as if he'd just noticed, where the year had gone. He made an appointment with Marty at the Sunoco, dropping it off first thing in the morning, asking them to change the oil while they were at it. They were cheaper than the dealer and he trusted them, so he was surprised when Marty called later that day and said he needed new tires.

"I swear I just bought those," he said, though he couldn't recall when.

"I don't know how old they are, but there's definitely some cupping going on. The rear you can probably get away with, but the front ones won't pass. I can swap them so you can drive it, if you want to look somewhere else. Or if you just want to get it through, we can slap some retreads on it."

"No." He believed him, and still it seemed wrong. "Can you hang on a second?"

In his desk, along with their finances, he kept a folder on the Olds. For this express reason, his receipts were in reverse chronological order. He expected the tires to be near the front, maybe the year before last, three at the most, but as he flipped through the pink and yellow carbons, not seeing it, his certainty evaporated. According to the printout he ultimately discovered, he'd bought them six years ago, which, for the amount he drove the car, seemed about right.

"Okay," he said. "No sense messing around. Let's do it."

"We don't actually have those in stock. They don't actually make them anymore."

Of course they didn't.

With mounting and balancing, the set Marty recommended cost over seven hundred dollars. The number shocked Henry, but the alternative was taking it to someone he didn't know, and he gave him the okay.

"Retreads," he said after he'd hung up. He supposed people did that. He couldn't believe it was legal.

Emily, who'd been eavesdropping, caught him in the kitchen, sneaking a couple of Thin Mints from the freezer. "So, are we buying a new car?"

"Not quite," Henry said. "But close."

Standby

IT WAS KENNY AND LISA'S TURN FOR THANKSGIVING. THEIR
previous visit, Lisa had backed out at the last minute, Kenny flying down
with the children by himself, and Emily was skeptical.

"How much you want to bet?"

"Nothing." He thought she was teasing, or maybe just being wishful.
"They already have their tickets."

"You watch, she'll find an excuse."

"I thought you two were getting along at Chautauqua."

"She didn't say boo to me."

"That's what I mean."

"It's rude. She's rude. Remember what she said about the pea casserole
last time?"

He did, but only because she brought it up every few months. He refrained from saying he wasn't wild about pea casserole either.

These tests of loyalty were never ending, and this was just the beginning.
As Emily readied the children's old bedrooms, she commiserated with Betty,
whose former daughter-in-law enjoyed sole custody of her two grandsons
despite the house being filthy. The unfairness of it nettled Emily. Over

dinner she wondered what they would do if Lisa ever tried something like that, when, realistically, it was more apt to happen to Margaret.

"I don't think we have to worry," Henry said. "Anyway, we're too old."

"You think I'm too hard on her."

"I don't think anything."

"I don't know what I'm supposed to do. I've tried being nice, she's just not interested. I feel bad for Kenny and the children."

He agreed, though secretly, as with Margaret, he thought she was at least partly at fault. His own contribution was harder to quantify. In their feud, as in any needless unpleasantness, he aspired to a blameless neutrality, seeing both sides, calling for peace and restraint. In practice, instead of a referee, his impartiality left him a bystander, a witness to ugly scenes and an apologist after the fact. He remembered feeling the same way when they visited her mother in Kersey, the grudges of the past waiting in the old place like ghosts. He liked to believe he didn't have any enemies, that if not pure of heart, he tried to treat everyone equally. That kind of passionate hatred baffled him. Most frustrating was how little had changed over the decades, and as Wednesday approached, instead of looking forward to their arrival, as he had all fall, he began to dread it like a punishment.

Tuesday they were in the middle of dinner when the phone rang.

"Honestly," Emily said. With the election, they'd been plagued by robocalls, and he hesitated, fork in hand, chewing a bite of smothered pork chop, waiting for the machine to reveal who was intruding on their privacy.

The beep gave way to a staticky backdrop, a radio between stations. The voice that broke through warbled as if underwater, cutting in and out. "Henry, Emily, this is Jeff. I'm calling from the hospital. I just wanted to let you know Meg's been in an accident. She's pretty banged up but she's going to be okay."

Emily, being closer to the living room, beat him to the phone. "We're here. What's going on?"

"Put him on speaker," Henry said, and then had to help her find the right button. They stood by, Emily clutching her napkin like a handkerchief. Drawn by the commotion, Rufus leaned against his knee.

She'd been driving home in the snow when another woman hit her. They both went off the road. It was no one's fault—meaning, Henry understood, that Margaret hadn't been drinking. The car was totaled.

"She's got a broken leg and a couple of broken ribs. The doctor said her head's okay, it just looks bad. The police said she was lucky she was wearing her seatbelt. I guess the other driver's not doing so well."

Henry wanted to ask if her "head" meant her face.

"What hospital are you at?" Emily asked, pen poised over a notepad. "Does she have a room number?"

"Not yet. Right now she's having her leg set."

"I'll be there as soon as I can."

"You don't have to come out."

"I want to. You're going to need someone to take care of things, and I'd like to see her. Is she awake?"

"They have her on painkillers, so she's not all there."

"That's not good," Emily said.

"They didn't know."

"You told them though."

"I will. I only just got here."

"Who's with the children?" she asked.

As the shock wore off, Henry didn't understand how it could have happened, and why now? Kenny and the children were coming tomorrow. Bitterly, as Emily went on about finding flights and renting a car, he imagined the whole Rube Goldberg chain of events that led to the accident—the cold front spawning snow, changing the flow of traffic, Margaret's shift ending, the line out of the lot and then the random sequence of traffic lights putting her minivan in the wrong lane at the wrong time. A momentary carelessness, one or both of them traveling too fast for conditions. It was just more of her bad luck, and yet he was angry, as if someone more alert might have avoided it—and the drugs, another problem.

"This is the last thing I need right now," Emily said after they'd hung up.

She held out her arms for him to hold her. Only then, in his embrace, did she let a muffled sob escape.

After a minute she sighed. "I have to go."

"I know. It's not the best night for it."

"I'll go standby. There have to be a dozen flights to Detroit. I'll go tomorrow morning if I have to."

"You can use our miles and go first class if it's easier."

"We'll see." She released him and headed for the stairs.

"Aren't you going to finish your dinner?" he asked.

"I don't think I can eat right now."

"Should I save your pork chop?"

"I don't care. Yes, save it. You can have it for lunch tomorrow."

He tried a bite but the onions had gone cold, and he took his plate into the kitchen, Rufus following him, wagging his tail as if Henry might toss him a scrap.

"Go lie down."

He needed to call Kenny and Arlene and let them know, though there was nothing they could do.

He fit the pork chops into a Tupperware sandwich holder like puzzle pieces, noting the marrow. One of his stranger points of pride was that despite playing football and going to war and once rolling a car in the desert, he'd never broken a bone. So much of life was chance. Embree died, he lived. It would never make sense to him.

The stove was a mess, the controls spattered with grease, the handle of the cast-iron skillet still warm.

"Leave it," Emily said, hauling her coat on. He'd never seen her pack so fast, but knew better than to mention it.

On the way she gave him instructions on how to cook the turkey. "All you have to do is remember to put it in early and keep checking it when it gets close. It's not that hard. Arlene can help you."

He could read a meat thermometer. He was more worried about the mashed potatoes, his favorite. He had only the vaguest idea of how to make gravy.

"You'll be fine. Just follow the recipe. It's like putting together a bookcase."

"I doubt that."

"I wish I could stay and help. You're just going to have to fend for a while."

"I will."

"I know you can."

Beyond Carnegie it was dark, taxis whipping past, a black Town Car, not signaling. There were deer out here. The season started next week, the schools taking the day off. There'd been no reason to discuss the possibility, no time, but now, as he slowed for the exit, ridiculously, he wanted to go with her.

"You'll have a good time with them," Emily said. "Kenny will help, and Ella. I'm sure Lisa will be thrilled I'm not there."

"That's not true."

"It is too true. Don't let her bully you. She'll take over if you let her."

Even as he pledged to resist her, he thought it would be so much easier if she cooked.

Despite a police car stationed with its lightbar flashing and a cop in a reflective vest waving people on, the curb at departures was double-parked, the crowd at the counter mobbing the sidewalk. Henry had to wait for an opening to angle the Olds in closer. He stopped and popped the trunk. Before he could get out, a skycap had Emily's bag.

She shrugged and gave Henry a kiss. "I'll call you when I know what flight I'm on."

"Good luck."

"Are you going to be all right?"

"I'll be fine. Give everyone my love."

"I'm sorry."

"Do you need money?"

"I stole two twenties from your dresser."

They couldn't part without saying "I love you," a ritual by now almost precautionary, as if they might never see each other again. She turned to mount the curb and beckoned the skycap to follow, waving a last time before the sliding doors swallowed her.

A massive Escalade had blocked him in. Rather than wait, he shifted into reverse and swung his nose out. The speed limit was fifteen miles an hour, like at Chautauqua, keeping him from gunning it. He nodded to the cop guarding the crosswalk and headed for the exit, thinking he'd be back again tomorrow. As he piloted the Olds along the swooping ramp, a plane was taking off, its lights slicing through the clouds. He should have parked and gone in with her, made sure she could get something tonight, but she'd rushed him. He wanted to circle back and fly standby himself, surprise her in Detroit. She was a terrible driver, and even worse at night. He could imagine the police calling, saying she'd been in an accident, the irony foreseeable. He should have gone, she should have stayed home, but with Margaret involved the notion was inconceivable. Emily would always be the one who rescued her. He would always be the one who didn't understand, the one who didn't love her enough. He wanted to say it wasn't true, admitting, finally, that there wasn't time for them to start over.

On the highway the new tires sounded funny, louder, droning as if they were snows. It was cold enough. Beyond his headlights the darkness was solid, herds of deer moving invisible through the woods. By tomorrow the front would be here, making an even bigger mess of the holiday traffic. Their flight arrived midafternoon. The tunnel would be backed up for miles. He had to get gas. He had to heat up the lasagna and the garlic bread and throw together a salad. They were staying four days. Already he felt overwhelmed, and kept to the left lane, racing for the city as if he were late.

11 at 11

WHILE HE WAS DRIVING HOME, EMILY HAD CALLED KENNY TO let him know.

"Are you sure you still want us to come? We're worried it might be too much, on top of everything."

As dearly as Henry wanted to accept his offer, he resented the implication that he was helpless. Primed by Emily, he could also recognize the hand of Lisa behind it, another front in their endless proxy war.

"It'll be better if you're here, honestly. Arlene will help. We'll all pitch in. Plus I want to see you guys."

"Okay," Kenny said, hesitant, as if he were making a mistake. "Just let us know what we can do."

"Don't worry, I will."

She hadn't called Arlene, who, after overcoming the shock, volunteered that it might be easier if they went to the club.

He admired her practicality, but there was no guarantee they could get a reservation, and he'd already steeled himself for the challenge. "That's not Thanksgiving."

His argument was unfair, being sentimental. Like their mother, she loved the holidays, decorating her classroom through the seasons. Even now her door would be festooned with Indian corn.

"I did buy pie makings."

"It's one dinner. The rest of the weekend we'll eat leftovers."

"Turkey soup."

"Hot turkey sandwiches."

She was game, though once they'd spoken he wondered how much help she'd be. Living alone, she relied on her microwave, stocking her freezer with Lean Cuisine, occasionally baking a batch of cookies to feed her sweet tooth.

Lisa watched the Food Network, printing out recipes from their website to test on Kenny. For Christmas she ordered fancy vinegars and infused olive oils from catalogs Emily thought were a rip-off. The temptation was to surrender and let her take over. He fretted, hedging, afraid that giving her the potatoes would be seen as a betrayal. Better to take a stab at them himself and fail. He could hear them telling the story years from now, passing it around the table like an old favorite.

On the fridge Emily had posted the menu and a long shopping list. Focused solely on dinner, he'd forgotten the waves of appetizers she plied them with all afternoon while they watched football—spinach dip and stuffed mushrooms and chicken curry puffs in phyllo dough, shrimp cocktail and smoked salmon with dill sauce on party rye, a slate platter with Hillshire Farm salamis and three different cheeses from Penn Mac. It was too much. By dinnertime they were full, and yet it was a tradition, the parade of delicacies reflecting the overflowing bounty of their lives.

Smoked capers, fresh sage, 3 lemons, 1 qt half & half, 2 cans crabmeat, 4 oz. chopped walnuts. Her handwriting was a point of pride, rightfully, and he was glad of it. The Jyggle would be a madhouse tomorrow, but it was too late to go tonight. They could use some beer, probably a couple bottles of red wine, and he thought of Margaret spending the day in her hospital room, eating Thanksgiving dinner from a tray.

Rufus had followed him in and stood looking at the back door.

"All right," Henry said. "But make it quick."

He didn't go out on the porch in the cold but watched through the window, and when Rufus trotted back in, gave him a treat. The dishes were clean, so he put them away and hung the dishtowel on the handle of the oven to dry. He poured himself a scotch and went up and watched a magazine show about a murder in a small town.

Was she in flight? Was that why she hadn't called? Any minute he expected the phone to ring, for her to say she'd gotten on, that she'd talked with Jeff again, that Margaret was conscious, but there was nothing, and as the hours passed and the real-life mystery gave way to the news, he began to fear she was still sitting in the airport and that he'd have to go out and save her from spending the night there.

She had to be on. There wouldn't be anything going out this late, unless it was delayed.

They were going to get one to three inches of snow tomorrow.

"Great."

At the end of the news, cued by the music, Rufus got up and stretched, padded over and rested his head on Henry's knee.

"I know, pal. It's past mine too."

He tried her number and got her voicemail. "It's just me. I'm assuming you were able to get something. Let me know." When, after a few minutes, she didn't call back, he locked up downstairs and started getting ready for bed, brushing his teeth and washing his face deliberately, as if stalling.

Usually she was the one who remembered the electric blanket, so the sheets were cold. He read for a while with his phone beside him on the nightstand, imagining her turning the wrong way out of the rental lot, the darkness hiding patches of black ice. He didn't see the point of being here. She was the reason they were coming, not him.

It was past midnight when he turned out the light. He didn't think he'd sleep, but he must have, because when his phone woke him, it was almost two. The ringtone plinked and plinked, Rufus grumping and moving to the foot of the bed.

"I made it," she said. "I had to go through Chicago, but I made it."

"I was worried."

"I figured. I saw your call."

There was no news. Jeff seemed to be holding up. She hadn't spoken to the children. Visiting hours started at eight. She needed to get to bed if she was going to be in any shape.

"You've got a big day tomorrow too. I meant to tell you in the car, I ordered a centerpiece from the Jyggle."

"Hang on. Let me get a pen to write that down."

"Probably a good idea."

"It's quiet here," he said.

"Not for long."

"Rufus misses you."

"Give him a kick and a hug for me."

At this point, saying he wished he'd gone with her wouldn't be helpful, so he held off. "I should let you go. Let me know when you know anything."

"I will."

He shouldn't have worried. Despite her driving, she knew what to do, where he would be lost. He understood he was being childish, put out at having been left behind. While he was still anxious about tomorrow, just hearing her voice soothed him, and he was able to sleep, but in the morning the room was gray and gloomy and he didn't want to get out of bed.

Honeydew

SHE CALLED WHILE HE WAS IN THE JYGGLE, CRUISING THE HUGE, confusing archipelago of the produce section, trying to find the shallots. He could barely hear her, and pressed the phone against his ear, bent over the handle of his almost empty cart. She hadn't had time to do the bathrooms. The whole house needed to be vacuumed, with all the dog hair, and his grandmother's candlesticks could stand to be polished. Could he please ask Arlene to iron the good linen tablecloth? The one hanging in the front hall closet, still in the dry cleaning bag from Easter.

"I know this is going to sound silly, but can you have her do the napkins as well?"

"Not silly at all. Anything else?"

"I'm sure I'm forgetting something. Margaret's sleeping, so I've been sitting here fretting."

Around him, other shoppers pawed through yams and weighed tomatoes. He wasn't a fan of cell phones, and considered people who broadcast their private conversations in public rude. His instinct was to whisper and get off as quickly as possible. "How's she doing?"

"They've got her doped up to the eyeballs. I guess with her ribs it hurts to breathe."

"Did you talk to her?"

"I did. She says she doesn't remember anything. She's pretty out of it. The doctor says her knee's going to take some work."

"I didn't know it was her knee."

"Apparently it's common, because of where it is."

"Makes sense." He could almost see the diagram of where the kneecap made contact with the dash. He wanted to ask about her head, but figured Emily would have said something.

"At least she was wearing her seatbelt. I saw the other driver's family in the little lounge they have. It doesn't sound good."

Reflexively, though Jeff had said the accident was no one's fault, Henry wondered if Margaret had secretly been drinking, or stoned, and then was ashamed of his suspicions. Why did he always think the worst of her? She might never learn the lesson life had taught him—that even a momentary carelessness could have lasting consequences—but this was different. She was innocent, and hurt, and he remembered her cutting her foot on a clamshell as a little girl and him carrying her across the lawn to the cottage, where Emily would make everything better.

"I'm glad you're there."

"So am I. She's so helpless, it's awful. I guess she and Jeff haven't been doing well, and this doesn't help."

"No," he agreed.

"How does the centerpiece look?"

She wasn't asking. She was reminding him, thinking he might have forgotten it, which he had. "I don't know. I just got here."

"Hang on a sec. No," she told someone, "you're not interrupting anything."

She was sorry, she had to go. The day nurse had come in to do something with Margaret's IV, and Emily wanted to talk to her. She'd try him again later. "Good luck there," she said, and without waiting for a reply, she was gone.

CALL ENDED, the screen said.

"Okay then," he said.

The list was long and he still had no idea where the shallots were. He thought he should be relieved it was only Margaret's knee, but with all of his new tasks he felt he was losing ground, and knowing he'd forget the center-piece if he put it off, he abandoned his search and went to stand in line at the flower department counter like he should have in the first place. He waited a good five minutes while the people in front of him had their bouquets wrapped, and then when it was finally his turn, it wasn't ready.

The Host with the Most

ACCORDING TO THE AIRLINE'S WEBSITE, THEIR FLIGHT WAS ON-time. Arlene ironed, he vacuumed and picked up poop. The house was ready, there was nothing left to do, yet he felt he could have used a few more hours—and today was the easy day. The one to three inches was just a dusting, and traffic was surprisingly light, no backup by the mall in Robinson, making him early. He stood at the foot of the escalators that led to baggage claim, witness to a cavalcade of happy reunions, but after a while his knees hurt and he had to sit down. He wished he'd brought his book, and killed the minutes watching the constant stream of people. He strained to hear the P.A., the voice from the ceiling dissipating in the noisy atrium. Twice he thought he heard Boston called and checked the big board. The third time, it said their flight had arrived five minutes ago. They were probably already on the tram.

He was used to Emily taking the lead with the children. Now, without her, he was unprepared. There was no reason for his trepidation. It wasn't as if he was being asked to entertain strangers, so why did he fear he had nothing to say to them? He foresaw awkward stretches at the dinner table, Arlene gabbling on, trying to fill the silence. Just contemplating the energy required to make small talk tired him.

Finally they appeared on the right-hand escalator, Sam and Ella emerging first, waving as they descended. He crossed the floor and positioned himself to the side so they wouldn't block the other passengers getting off.

Sam abandoned his carry-on and tackled him around the waist, knocking him back a step.

"Easy there, bud," Henry said, tousling his hair.

Ella, in pigtails and smelling of strawberry bubble gum, rose on tiptoe to give him a kiss. "Hey, Grampa."

"Hey, yourself."

Kenny and Lisa straggled behind. To get the best fare they'd had to wake up at five and lay over in Philly, and they were dragging.

"How was your flight?"

"Long," Lisa said.

Kenny shrugged. "It's USAir."

"Can I take your bag?"

"That would be wonderful," she said. "Thank you."

"Is this everything? We're this way. I was early, so I was able to get a decent spot. We were supposed to get snow but we barely got anything. Emily's not here, but her lasagna is. I hope you're hungry." As if to compensate for their exhaustion, he played the chipper host, broadcasting a nonstop enthusiasm. He popped the trunk and helped Kenny with the bags. "There you go, perfect fit."

It wasn't until they were on the parkway that Lisa asked after Margaret. He wondered how much Emily had told Kenny. Per the Geneva Convention, if captured, all you were required to give the enemy was your name, rank and serial number.

"She's going to be fine," he said, glancing at her in the rearview mirror, "it's just going to take some time."

"That's good."

"The doctors said she was very lucky."

"It sounds like it could have been a lot worse," said Kenny, sitting beside him.

"A *lot* worse. It's a good thing she was wearing her seatbelt."

That was as much as he wanted to say for now. He expected they'd revisit it later, after the children had gone to bed.

"How is Emily?" Lisa asked with exaggerated gravity, as if she'd been injured as well.

"Good. She's sorry to miss you guys, but she's glad she's there. I am too."

"I bet Jeff's happy to have the help."

"Oh yeah," he said, though he and Emily hadn't delved into that, and was relieved when Lisa sat back. It wasn't quite the beginning of rush hour, and he was satisfied to concentrate on the road.

At home Arlene greeted them, and Rufus, wiggling and whining at the sight of the children, his tail whacking the front hall table. The timing was right. While they got settled, Henry put the lasagna in the oven and prepped the bread. Arlene was in charge of the salad, normally his job.

"What can I do?" Lisa asked.

"Nothing. You can have a glass of wine and relax."

"That would be wonderful. I feel like I'm still moving."

Kenny brought him a beer from downstairs, clinking it with his. "Thanks for having us. I know it's a lot of work."

"It's our pleasure," he said out of habit, belatedly nodding at Arlene. "At our age, we'll take any excuse."

If the logic of it wasn't precisely true, the sentiment was. With night fallen outside and a fire on the hearth and Rufus sprawled with his head in Ella's lap, the house felt full and warm, like a real holiday. When he put the bread in, the lasagna was bubbling, the smell drawing compliments from the living room. Arlene helped the children set the table while he opened a second bottle of red. The only thing he'd forgotten was to take out the grated parmesan so it wouldn't be cold.

Arlene sat in Emily's place at the head of the table.

"It looks really good," Kenny said, and Henry was as proud as if he'd made it himself.

They held hands while Ella said the blessing, finishing, "And please help Aunt Margaret get better."

"Very nice," Arlene said.

The pan was hot, so Henry served everyone.

"Just a half for Sam, please," Lisa said. He was finicky—he was spoiled, according to Emily—and regularly left his vegetables untouched. Rather than battle him at the table the way Emily or Henry's own mother would have, Lisa let him skip the dishes he disliked, with the result that sometimes he ate nothing but bread. His salad plate was empty. Lasagna wasn't a tough sell, Henry thought, but layer by layer, with the patience of a brain surgeon, Sam dissected his half piece, scraping off the sauce and ground beef and cheese, eating just the noodles.

"You're missing the best part," Henry said.

"It's his loss," Lisa said, a philosophy Henry disagreed with, but kept his objections to himself.

"Remember the time," Arlene asked, "with you and Grandmother Chase and the liver?"

It was a story they'd all heard before, illustrating how stubborn the two of them could be. He was seven or eight, their parents away for some forgotten reason. Long after Arlene had eaten her dessert and run off to listen to *Little Orphan Annie,* he sat with his napkin in his lap, frowning at the cold gray meat on his plate, Grandmother Chase sitting across from him like a prison guard. He'd managed several bites by wrapping them in pieces of biscuit and washing them down with milk, but now the biscuit and the milk were gone, and she wouldn't let him be excused until he'd finished everything. He still hated liver, as he hated the story. It had happened just the once, he might have said in his defense, but sat silent as if chastised, waiting for it to end with the final bites left untouched and him being sent to bed, the moral elusive, if there was any.

"And did it make you like liver?" Lisa asked.

"No. It's liver. Nobody likes it."

"Granny Chase was a tough nut," Arlene said.

"She was," he agreed. "I seem to remember someone else having a problem with lima beans."

"That was different," Arlene said.

"I remember having to eat aspic," Kenny said, willing to tell one on himself.

"What's aspic?" Sam asked, and then at Kenny's description made a face that made them laugh.

"See?" Henry said. "Lasagna's not so bad after all."

"It's delicious," Lisa said.

As if to prove it, Kenny asked for seconds, Ella as well.

Henry passed the bread basket, encouraging them to finish it. "The goal is no leftovers."

In the same spirit, they killed the second bottle and moved on to coffee with dessert, Arlene's take on their mother's Indian pudding with hard sauce, a favorite of the children, as it had been one of his as a child. As they sat around the table, sated, he recalled the house on Mellon Street, its ornate mantel and fireplace, and himself as a boy, dressed for company, waiting, like Sam, to be excused, and wondered how many times, in one form or another, he'd eaten this dinner. There was a mysterious continuity to life that was reassuring, if the true significance of it escaped him.

The children helped clear and disappeared upstairs with Rufus. Once Kenny finished the dishes, the adults retired to the living room, gathered around the fire, the lights dimmed for atmosphere. Henry raised his glass to admire the flames wavering in his scotch—the Glenfarclas Arlene had given him, nutty and then sherry-sweet. The talk, as expected, turned to Margaret.

"It's been a rough year for her," Lisa said.

"It's a shame," Arlene said, "because she's been working really hard on herself. I think she's figuring out what she needs to do."

"You mean with Jeff," Lisa said—fishing, Henry thought.

"With everything. It's all connected."

"I think it's hard for her," Kenny said, "because he's always been there. What happens if things don't go well and now there's nobody there?"

"Is she afraid she'll lose the kids?" Lisa asked.

"I'm sure that's it. If she relapses, there's no safety net."

"Jeff wouldn't do that," Arlene said.

On that question Henry kept his opinion to himself. It was all speculation anyway. People were going to do what they were going to do. After a certain age he'd ceased to believe he might influence their lives.

"He wouldn't have a choice," Kenny said. "If she's the way she was two years ago, he'd have to take them."

"That was the worst," Lisa said.

Had they come to Chautauqua? It was frustrating that he couldn't recall.

"She doesn't want to be by herself," Kenny said. "I can't blame her."

"Nothing against Jeff," Lisa said, "but she'll never get better if she stays with him. He does everything for her."

Wasn't that what married people were supposed to do? He was tempted to break in and say it was none of their business. At the same time, he didn't want to interrupt and risk missing something. As he did talking with Emily in the car, he felt privy to secrets he'd never find out otherwise, and sat sipping his scotch like a spy.

"How's it going there?" Emily asked later, once she'd filled him in on Margaret's progress. The knee surgery was routine. They'd asked the doctor to switch her to something non-narcotic.

"Okay," he said. "Tonight was the easy one."

"You'll do fine. Just follow the instructions and don't check on it every five seconds. You got the centerpiece."

"I did."

"I thought it looked festive."

"It is." It cost twenty-nine dollars and looked like a bunch of shellacked gourds left over from Halloween wired together so they spilled out of a miniature wicker cornucopia.

"The horn should face away from the host and toward the guests."

"I would not have known."

"I know you wouldn't, that's why I'm telling you. If it was up to you, we wouldn't have a centerpiece at all."

"No, it looks nice."

"What about Christmas? Did you ask Lisa about Ella's pearls?"

While he knew the necklace from Christmases past (Sarah had a matching one), he couldn't recall Emily mentioning it recently, and rather than be accused of not listening, he played along, adding it to his list.

"I miss you," he said.

"I miss you too. Now get some sleep. You've got a long day tomorrow."

"You too," he said, but when he'd finally hung up and turned out the light, he kept remembering details he knew he'd forget if he didn't write them down, like putting the canned cranberries in the fridge, and had to roll over and grope for the pen and pad on his nightstand. In protest, Rufus moved to the other side of the bed, settling with a huff.

"You're fine," Henry said.

He dreamed of Duchess launching herself off the dock after a tennis ball, and woke at five, surprised to find Emily's pillow empty. It was winter. She was in Michigan. Normally he was up at two or three to use the bathroom, and congratulated himself on getting in six unbroken hours, but then at eight, when his alarm went off, he smelled bacon—Lisa, he assumed, taking over the kitchen while he slept, except when he went down to check, it was Kenny making the children soft-boiled eggs.

Not an invasion but a tribute. A Grandma breakfast, they called it, yet another tradition that bound them together, like watching the Macy's parade or taking the children for a walk around the reservoir at halftime of the early game. How empty the house would be without them, with her gone, and he realized—astonished by his own Scrooge-like obtuseness—that they'd come not to test his skills as a host but to save him from being alone.

He wasn't making half the food Emily did, and still there was a fair amount of prep work. The plan was for Arlene to come over around eleven and help him get the appetizers going. He figured she'd be late, and she was. By the time she arrived, bringing pie, he had his chicken phyllo triangles and sausage pinwheels in and was chopping vegetables for the dip. Like the project manager he'd been, he'd built some fat into his schedule. Even before the first game started, it had evaporated, the clock becoming his enemy.

"How can I help?" Lisa asked from the doorway, Kenny right behind her.

"We're good for now, thanks."

"Let me know if you need another pair of hands."

"We will."

"Dad, beer?" Kenny asked.

"Sure, if you're going down."

"Arlene," Lisa asked, "would you like some wine?"

No, Henry thought. It was sabotage. After two glasses she'd be useless.

"I'd love some, thank you."

He couldn't protest. Drinking all afternoon while they watched the games was a tradition they couldn't indulge in when Margaret visited. By dinnertime they'd be tight, dropping their silverware and laughing at the silliest things. Like overeating, it was part of the holiday. He just hoped she didn't cut herself.

Heeding Emily's advice, he meant to get the turkey in early, but the stuffing took longer than expected. Rather than raise the temperature and risk drying the bird out, he pushed dinner back to six-thirty. They could wait. After the appetizers, no one would be hungry anyway.

There were too many dishes, too many ingredients, and the recipes Emily had left only distracted him. He needed to peel the potatoes and the yams, and get the pea casserole going, and the nippy onions no one liked. He swigged his beer and set to gutting a green pepper. As if he'd jinxed himself thinking of Arlene, he slipped and the blade caught his fingertip, leaving a flap.

"Mother," he said, and sucked it, tasting blood. It stung.

"Are you okay?" Arlene asked.

"I'll live."

It wouldn't stop bleeding, and he went downstairs and wrapped it with the Band-Aids he kept on his workbench. When he came back up, Lisa was crouched in front of the oven, peering in the window.

"How's it look?" he asked.

"It looks good. Smells good too. Let me know if you need help. I'm not doing anything."

"Want to peel some potatoes?" Arlene asked.

"I can do that," Lisa said.

If Emily was bleeding out, she would have told her they had things in hand and shooed her from the room. Henry couldn't, and deseeded his green pepper while she and Arlene worked side by side, whittling wet strips of skin into the sink.

"You're fast," Arlene said.

"Practice."

The potatoes, the yams, the onions, the separately wrapped neck and heart and liver for Rufus. The stove had four burners, more than enough normally. Now it was crowded, the pots boiling away, steaming up the window over the sink. He imagined Emily, an hour behind him, making the same dishes, and his mother, years ago on Mellon Street.

"Crud." He'd forgotten to take the bag of peas out to defrost.

"Use the microwave," Lisa said. "That's what it's for."

"Have you made this before?"

"Twice a year for twenty years."

"Would you mind putting it together?"

"Mine's a little different. Instead of onion rings, I make a crust like a pot pie. It takes the same amount of time and the kids like it better."

"That's fine," he conceded, recalling what Emily had said. Lisa wasn't insinuating herself, he was just being practical. A good manager knew how to use his talent.

The turkey was browning nicely, and he had a handle on the yams and mashed potatoes, but the cheese sauce for the onions was beyond him. Lisa took over, folding in handfuls of shredded white cheddar until it was the right consistency. Later, when everything else was ready, he needed her help with the gravy as well.

The turkey turned out perfect. The table was set, the wineglasses and water goblets filled. They joined hands and bowed their heads as Ella said grace.

"What is everyone thankful for?" Arlene asked, another tradition, and they went around the table, starting with the youngest.

Sam was thankful for the new *Star Wars* movie.

"As we all are, I'm sure," Arlene said.

"I'm thankful Aunt Margaret's going to be all right," Ella said, and they agreed, nodding solemnly.

"I'm thankful for this delicious meal we're about to eat," Kenny said, "but I don't see any cranberry sauce."

"Oh no!" Arlene said.

With everything they'd had to make, he'd forgotten it. "It's still in the fridge."

"I'll get it," Kenny said, but Henry fended him off.

Emily would have pulled it out ahead of time to warm up and remembered to put their ceramic turkey salt and pepper shakers on the table.

"Sorry," he said, "I'm new at this."

"The turkey's nice and juicy," Lisa said.

"Mm," Kenny seconded with his mouth full.

They didn't have to say the stuffing was dry.

"I don't know what happened. I followed the recipe."

"It tastes fine," Arlene said.

"That's kind of you to say."

"It's true."

Overall he'd acquitted himself well. The mashed potatoes were creamy, the yams sweet, and if everyone raved about Lisa's gravy, he was glad for her help. He made coffee to go with Arlene's pumpkin pie and lingered over his as the children cleared the table. The hard part was over. He and Kenny would have to hand-wash Grandmother Chase's good china, but for now he could relax and look back on the day with pride.

Later, when the children were upstairs watching *Home Alone*, Emily called. He took the phone into his office and closed the door.

"So," she asked, "how was your Thanksgiving there without me?"

While he'd missed her, it had been a good day. They'd all gotten along, but he couldn't say that. At the same time there was no point lying. In the end, she'd get the truth out of him.

"Busy," he said. "How was yours?"

The Old Lamplighter

PERHAPS IT WAS HIS BRAHMIN UPBRINGING, OR EMILY'S LACK of one, but he enjoyed the trappings of the season more than she did. On Mellon Street, his mother and Arlene cleared the mantel above the great fireplace, dressing it with sweet-smelling pine boughs and bayberry candles, while outside, bundled in a puffy one-piece snowsuit, he helped his father hang the wreaths and blinking lights. Later, when his parents moved to Fox Chapel, they purchased a herd of twiggy white deer, one of which roboti-cally dropped its head to the lawn every thirty seconds as if grazing. Along with their hand-blown ornaments and vintage train set, Henry had inher-ited their love of the holidays, for one month re-creating the past in a corner of the living room. Emily withstood this trespass on her domain with the largesse of an absolute ruler, waiting for Three Kings' Day to help box it away again. Left to himself, he would have kept it up all year.

Normally they bought their tree the Saturday after Thanksgiving. When the children were little, they'd pile in the station wagon and drive out to a farm in Butler County, tramping through the snowy rows with a borrowed saw to cut their own. Now he and Emily chose from a truckload from Que-bec grouped by species on the netless tennis courts of the School for the

Deaf—less romantic and more expensive, but, as he pointed out, for a good cause.

He told her he could wait till she got home.

"Don't," she said, "please. I may be here a while."

He made it their mission, glad to have a task they could share. He could count on Kenny and Arlene and Ella to lend a hand. Sam was absorbed in his Game Boy, but relented when Kenny said he could bring it. Lisa, reading by the fire, asked how cold it was. Outnumbered, she finally gave in to their cajoling.

Rufus wanted to go too, jumping up when Henry opened the front hall closet as if he might grab his leash. "Sorry, buddy." He put some carols on the stereo to keep him company, hitting repeat. Leaving, they waved to him, watching from the French doors as they crossed the yard.

The School for the Deaf, as Emily would say, was on that slickety slide. Though it was the first day, the selection was meager, the trees still bound in mesh netting, lined up against the fence as if they'd been captured. He didn't see any wreaths, and the one volunteer—a round man in a Steelers tassel hat—was busy cutting a trunk with a Sawzall for the one other customer. Sam ran ahead, picking trees for Kenny to hold upright. Beyond the fence, the grass was matted yellow and frozen, the oaks bare. Henry wished it were snowing.

"Know what kind you're looking for?" the volunteer asked. "We've got sharp needles and soft needles. Soft costs more."

Henry had never heard this pitch before, and was sure it was bogus.

The man took off a glove. "Feel this. This is a Scotch pine. That's a sharp needle. This is a Douglas fir."

To Henry's chagrin, he was right.

"That's nice," Arlene said.

Ella and Sam tried it.

"Easier on the tootsies too," the man said.

Even if it was true, Henry didn't like being sold. The tree cost fifty-six dollars, and after they lashed it to the roof of the Olds and were driving home—charity or no—he felt he'd been taken.

To make room, he moved his chair next to Emily's, exiling his lamp and end table to the basement, trading them for the platform his father had made, painted white to resemble snow, the train track permanently fixed to it. Once he and Kenny got the tree into the stand and onto its customary spot, they took a lunch break. The lights, the ornaments, the train, the crèches and pinecone wreaths and stuffed polar bears and themed throw pillows and stained-glass suncatchers—everything else was stacked in the attic and had to be handed down through the trapdoor, an ordeal Emily would be happy she missed.

The attic was unheated, and freezing. Last fall, when they'd had their squirrel problem, the floor had been littered with acorns. Now he was pleased to see it was clean, only a few windblown sycamore seeds, the wire screening on the gable vents stapled firmly in place. He pulled the plastic drop cloth off the wall of boxes and began handing them down to Kenny, perched on the ladder, who passed them down to Lisa and Arlene and Ella and Sam, who lugged them down to the living room. They had enough ornaments to do three trees. Cornhusk angels, pinecones spray-painted gold, the faded paper chains Margaret had made in kindergarten—Emily had kept everything. Once they found the star, it went quickly.

Among the decorations, filling a dozen boxes labeled in his mother's hand, was her Dickens Village, a collection of ceramic cottages and storefronts whose windows were eternally frosted, their chimney pots snowcapped. Each year his father gave her a new one, the town threatening to outgrow the platform, a running joke until her diagnosis. Henry didn't know why, but the Christmas after she died, he was surprised to see his father had set it up the way she always did, the train crossing by the bakery, the mill's waterwheel turning, the old lamplighter climbing his ladder in his battered stovepipe hat and scarf. How that false and fragile world had survived her was a mystery he felt even now, pulling the buildings from their squeaky Styrofoam sarcophagi. His father lived another dozen years. When he moved to his condo, he didn't have room to store the village and offered it to them, and how could Emily refuse?

Henry didn't have to do anything. Ella showed Sam how to lay out the streets, plastic mats printed to look like cobblestones. The accessories were expensive and elaborately detailed—denuded yew trees and wrought-iron fences, park benches and postal boxes, an octagonal bandstand, a flagpole with the Union Jack. Teams of horses drew carriages about town while strollers peered in store windows at the holiday displays, children skated on the millpond, dogs ran free, and if the train was out of scale and from another era, it didn't matter. Ella and Sam, who'd never known his mother, knew where it was all supposed to go.

The village, like the tree, was at its most magical after dark, each window shedding a cozy yellow glow, and when they'd finished dinner, Henry built a fire and they sat with their faces tinted by the lights, remembering when Margaret and Jeff tried to deep-fry a turkey on their back deck and almost burned down the house. Sam and Ella took turns running the train the way Henry had showed them, slowing for the tunnel, blowing the whistle at each crossing. The clock tower in the town hall shone, hands frozen on all four sides. Tomorrow their flight left around nine, time enough for him to make the late service.

"So," Arlene said, "now that Thanksgiving's over, what does everyone want for Christmas?"

"Oh God," Lisa said. "It's too early for that."

"It's in four weeks. I need to know what people want if I'm going to order it."

"What do *you* want?" Kenny asked.

Every year they had the same conversation. The wheel turned, the water purled. On the hearth, Rufus slept, Ella resting a hand on his belly. Warmed by the fire and a dash of scotch, Henry thought: This.

"It sounds like you had a nice time," Emily said.

"We did."

"Here I did laundry all day."

"I'm sorry."

"That's why I'm here."

"How's Margaret?"

"Crabby. They won't let her go home until she can walk on crutches."

"When's that going to be?"

"Soon, I hope. I think she's going a little stir crazy. I know I am."

He couldn't cheer her up, and finally let her go, downcast himself, as if the whole day had been ruined.

In the morning, the first thing he did was turn on the tree. It was waiting for him like a present when he came back from the airport, along with Bach's *Christmas Oratorio*, a favorite of hers, filling the house with joyful horns. He left the music on while he was at church, and all afternoon, the tracks changing while he watched the Jaguars beat the Bengals, Rufus using one of his slippers as a pillow. He needed to do their sheets and towels but didn't feel like moving. He lay down on the couch and pulled an afghan over his legs. The late game was in Buffalo, where it was snowing so hard they couldn't see the lines. As the day faded, the room grew dark, the TV reflected in the glass of his father's bookcase, the players running the wrong way. He was just dozing off when Rufus shoved his wet nose under his hand, asking for his dinner.

"I hear you," he said, though he still had ten minutes.

It was dusk out, a few stray flakes in the air. The hall was gray. Rather than break the spell, he kept the lights off, letting Rufus go down first, sliding his hand along the bannister. From below, a flourish of horns proclaimed the good news. He turned on the outside lights and the village and stood there a moment, mesmerized by the tree shimmering in the pond until Rufus circled back as if he'd forgotten him.

"Okay, okay, just cool your jewels."

He thought a walk might wake him up. It was night now, and cold out, snow swirling through the streetlights. On Sheridan, three porches in a row were edged with skirts of white and blue icicles blinking out of sync.

"Not a big fan of those," Henry said.

On a lawn, spotlit, sat an inflatable snowman tall as a dogwood. He'd seen some at Home Depot and wondered who in the world would buy them. Snowmen were supposed to be made of snow, by children staying home from school. Like the icicles, they seemed proof of a decline in public taste— if not outright common sense—he found demoralizing. As he was about to pass judgment on the next display, he could hear Emily calling him a grumpy old fart and stopped himself.

"All right," he told Rufus, "get some work done."

By the time they made it home he was hungry. He had to put on the kitchen light to microwave his plate of leftovers, and once he'd eaten, turned it out again. He sat by the fire with a scotch, admiring the tree and listening to the waterwheel like the night before, but it wasn't the same. All in all it had been a nice visit. He didn't know why he'd been so nervous. Now he was sorry they were gone. With Margaret laid up, there would be no one coming for Christmas. Usually the idea would have appealed to him, the two of them alone together, but in the wake of the children leaving, it seemed wrong, and the scotch only sharpened the thought. When he'd finished, he rocked himself out of his chair and took his glass into the kitchen, then went upstairs to strip the beds.

And Then There
Were None

HE WAS ROUNDING UP THE TOWELS WHEN HE NOTICED A SPOT like a drop of spilled coffee on the bathmat that hugged the front of the toilet. Beside it on the tiles, one end crusted in a dark blob like a match head, arced a swipe of dried blood. He froze and took a step back as if it were forensic evidence, set his armload of towels on the counter and crouched down, looking for more.

That was it. He dabbed at the mat with a fingertip. It came away dry. The swipe was no wider than a shoelace and already flaking, the blood soaked into the porous mortar between the tiles.

Mornings, since Emily had been gone, Rufus joined him in the bathroom, sprawled on the mat as he waited for him to finish showering and let him out. Henry's first thought was that he'd cut one of his paws.

He whistled, and Rufus rumbled up the stairs.

"Good boy. Sit."

He knelt to check his feet. His pads were rough and scratchy from the cold weather but Henry didn't see anything.

"Okay, take a break. No, you are not getting a treat for that."

The next most likely suspect was himself. Despite his pills, with all the rich food, he'd been having pain in his feet. It struck without warning, day or night, like a needle being pushed through his sole. He hadn't told Emily, since there was nothing to be done and it would only upset her. His toes were tender, his skin thin. He hadn't felt anything, but he was prone to mysterious nicks and bruises he had no recollection of, as if he'd fallen while sleepwalking.

Expecting to find a bloody mess, he sat on the edge of their bed and took off his shoes and socks. Besides a cracked big toenail, he was fine.

"Hmm."

Last night Arlene would have used the half bath downstairs. That left his guests. It was a mystery out of Agatha Christie or one of Emily's *Masterpiece Theatres*. He stood in the doorway, revisiting the scene of the crime, pondering, logically, why someone would be bleeding on the toilet, and embarrassed at having taken so long to put two and two together, realized, grappling with his own deeply rooted squeamishness and ignorance of female hygiene, that it was probably Lisa, Ella being too young.

He supposed he'd never know. It wasn't exactly something you could ask, and so he folded a generous portion of toilet paper and wet it at the sink and, kneeling, holding the wad at arm's length as if the blood might infect him, swabbed it up, tossed the wad in the toilet and flushed. The mat he washed by itself. When it finally dried, he replaced it, standing back and taking satisfaction at having restored order. Later, after another dinner of leftovers drenched in gravy, he reclaimed the space, attended by Rufus, and still he felt strange, as if she'd just been sitting there.

To kill the evening he watched TV, and at nine o'clock remembered to turn on the electric blanket, essential now, with Emily gone. Their controls were separate and preset, hidden under the edge of the bed so Rufus couldn't trip them. Henry steadied himself with the post of the headboard to toe the button. As he did his side, he noticed on his pillowcase an almost black stain the size of a dime.

"Funny," he said.

He must have had a nosebleed in his sleep and then at some point gone to the bathroom. Had other people seen the blood and wondered? He thought there would be traces on his pajamas, but they were clean. No spots on the carpet, no used tissues in the wastebasket. The stain was undeniable, even if he didn't remember a thing. Now his suspicion of Lisa seemed doubly shameful, as if he'd slandered her, and he felt foolish, the great detective tracking down clues, when all along it had been him.

Bon Appétit

HE WAS DONE WITH THE ONIONS AND DIDN'T CARE FOR THE YAMS, but there were enough mashed potatoes and stuffing and pea casserole to last a week, plus extra turkey and gravy in the basement, in case Emily was gone longer. She'd bought a twenty-pounder to feed seven people, two of whom were children. More than once, over the phone, she'd needlessly instructed him not to throw away the carcass so she could make soup, which she said she liked better than Thanksgiving dinner, a confession that struck him as blasphemous. It was his favorite. Lunch and dinner he prepared the same plate, making a crater in his potatoes for gravy, covering it with Saran wrap and fishing it from the microwave with oven mitts, giving the cranberry its own separate dish. He ate in the breakfast nook, watching the news, meaning he saw it three times, the stories repeating until he knew what the neighbor down the street from the fire or the drug bust or the home invasion was going to say. He quickly ran out of Lisa's cinnamon whipped cream, and while he blamed the pumpkin pie for his heartburn, he liked having it. At his side, Rufus waited, angling for a bite of crust.

He didn't mind eating alone so much, but as the week passed he was surprised to find he missed doing the dishes. Dinner, especially, seemed incomplete. With no mixing bowls or Cuisinart parts or pots and pans to clean, he could go days without running a load. Each time he rinsed his plate and added it to the rack, he saw it as a loss.

Emily worried that with her not there to feed him, he wasn't eating right. "What did you have for dinner?"

"L.O.'s."

"Uck. Aren't you sick of them yet?"

In Bastogne, surrounded, they'd eaten a horse they'd found frozen in a flattened barn. The horse was small, and the rats had been at it. The joke was that it was some kid's pony. They roasted it over a fire, the meat sizzling, and lined up with their kits like a regular mess call. As they ate, they laughed and licked the grease from their fingers. It was too rich for their empty stomachs and made them sick, half of the company throwing up in the snow. In his bedroll after lights-out, Embree made neighing sounds. That winter, how many times had Henry dreamed of his mother's Thanksgiving dinner?

"No," he said. "I like them."

"I thought you were supposed to be watching your salt."

"I'm supposed to be watching my everything."

"Enjoy it now, mister, 'cause come Sunday things are going to be different."

"Promises, promises."

"It's true. She's coming home tomorrow, ready or not, and I'm getting the heck out of here."

"Sounds good to me."

"I'm not so sure it is, but I'm done arguing with her."

He celebrated with a piece of pie—a mistake, he realized later, swallowing glass after glass of water to keep down the sour reflux. In Bastogne, he'd eaten his fill with no ill effects besides some wild dreams. Now a slice of pie kept him up half the night.

Knowing she was coming home, he didn't feel the need to change his diet—in fact, the opposite. Her first day back, she'd go shopping and make soup. His job now was to clean out the fridge, and he attacked it with purpose, each meal doing double duty as he chipped away at what remained—finishing the pie, then the cranberry sauce and mashed potatoes and stuffing, and lastly the pea casserole, running a load of Tupperware—trying to fix it so that by the time she arrived, it would be all gone.

'Tis the Season

HE THOUGHT THAT WHEN SHE RETURNED THEY'D FALL BACK INTO their routine, but her time at Margaret's had put her a good week behind. While she was away, she'd made lists. She was grateful he'd decorated, though she noticed right off—before he opened the back door—that they needed wreaths. She hoped the Altar Guild still had some poinsettias left. She hadn't even started her real shopping. She didn't have anything for Sam or Lisa, and everything needed to be shipped. "I don't see how I'm going to get it all done in two weeks."

Technically she had eighteen days, but he didn't say that. The holidays always set her off, and after Thanksgiving, he knew the feeling.

"Let me know what I can do," he said, an offer she deflected with a put-upon look, as if he were joking.

Her first big job was sending out Christmas cards, the shot of the whole family on the lawn at Chautauqua. Fortified by a cup of tea and some Handel, she set up shop at the dining room table, going through last year's pile, editing her address book as she went. How many times had he offered to type the master list into his computer so all she'd have to do was hit a key to print the envelopes, but she insisted on doing them by hand. Her penmanship was a source of pride, though with her arthritis she had to stop every so often and knead her fingers. It was a project, one she threatened to make his or stop altogether, yet every year she battled her way through the stack.

As if in sympathy, he spent the morning at his desk, organizing his tax receipts, listening to her mutter under her breath. He was muttering himself, adding up a long column of medical expenses, when she asked him a question he didn't quite catch.

"Hang on," he called, and came out. Rufus lay under the table, half in the sun. "How's it going?"

"Didn't the Beardsleys move? I swear they moved."

"Did we get a card from them last year?"

"I'm pretty sure that's their old address. Do we know a Gregory?" She pointed to a red envelope addressed in a curling, girlish script. "They're not from church. I checked the directory."

"No idea."

"How about this Knapp?"

"That's Fred." Henry had known him more than forty years, yet Emily never remembered his name.

She centered a new envelope in front of her and took up her pen again. He leaned in to steal a kiss. "Okay. Go away."

He left her alone, letting her get into a rhythm. When the clock struck one, she stopped for lunch.

Her back hurt, she complained, and her eyes. "I started too late. Usually I'm done with them by now."

"You'll be fine. Most of them are local. They'll only take a day or two to get there."

"That's not what I'm talking about. I can't do anything until I'm done with them. It's already the ninth. I still have to buy everyone presents and wrap them and box them up and ship them ten different places."

"I can help ship them."

"No, you can't, because I haven't bought them yet. I can't buy them until I'm done with these stupid cards."

"Fair enough."

"That's not helpful," she said. "You know what you can do, you can go buy me a hundred stamps. That would be helpful."

"Any particular kind?"

"I don't care. You make a decision for once."

In the car, he argued that he made decisions all the time. He understood that she was overwhelmed, but that was no excuse. He'd offered to help. He wasn't sure what else he could do.

The line was slow at the post office, his fellow customers balancing precarious armloads of packages, as if to prove her point. There were three positions but only one open. "Anyone just dropping off?" a clerk from the back in a Pirates hat asked, and several people behind Henry piled their boxes on the counter and took off. When it was finally his turn, his choice was between a simple green wreath or a gilded Renaissance Madonna and child Emily would like in a museum but might find too Catholic for their Christmas card. The wreaths were boring. To be safe, he bought a hundred and twenty of them.

She thanked him and apologized, not getting up from the table. "I just need to get these done, then I'll be fine."

"I understand," he said, but of course once she finished them she was in a panic at not being able to find Sarah the perfect gift, and about how they were running out of time to ship everything, and what she was going to make for Christmas dinner now that it was just the two of them. It was normal, and foolish of him to expect anything different. While she was away, he'd forgotten how powerfully she broadcast her feelings, filling the house like a kind of nerve gas. Now, as the days passed, he grew used to it again, its absence—that brief period of calm—harder and harder to recall. She could be cutting and abrupt, unthinking, and yet, for all her faults, working beside her in the kitchen, or after dinner, watching her go over her lists, or in bed, listening to her sleep, he was glad to have her home.

Charity

IT WAS THE SEASON OF GIVING, AND EVERYONE WANTED MONEY.
The Heart Association and the Community Food Bank, the Special Olym-
pics and Goodwill—all worthy causes he would have considered if they'd
asked him properly. Instead they sent junk mail, lazy computer-generated
letters, just hoping he'd take the bait. Emily was bombarded by Carnegie
Museum and the Heinz History Center, the symphony and the Frick, a
higher class of beggar. Every day more came, filling their mailbox. Habitat
for Humanity and the Little Sisters of the Poor. It was almost comic. They
must have gotten on someone's list, because he couldn't remember it ever
being this bad.

The holidays were expensive enough. Besides the eventual credit card
bills looming like icebergs, everyone expected a tip. He gave Mary the
paper carrier forty dollars, which he suspected was too much. Legally their
mailman wasn't allowed to accept gratuities, but Henry left another forty
for him in a festive envelope. Emily gave Betty her bonus closer to Christmas, as if it were a present—a hundred dollars in crisp twenties he made a
special trip to the bank for, along with twenties for the garbagemen and his
barber.

While Henry was careful with their money, he was happy to support organizations where there was a personal connection involved. Emily was always writing checks to the YWCA and the library and QED and Phipps Conservatory and the Oratorio Society, and rightfully so. As a parent and good neighbor, he'd bought his share of Little League raffle tickets and marching band candy bars and Girl Scout cookies. He understood fundraising as part of the social contract. Now, though he hadn't asked for them, he felt cheap keeping the Humane Society's self-sticking address labels and chucking the rest, but if he gave to every place that sent him some freebie, they'd go broke.

The one charity he contributed to every December was Calvary Camp, a summer retreat on Lake Erie where the children had taken tennis and archery lessons and advanced lifesaving. His mother had served on the board, and he gave in her memory, a legacy. Like their monthly pledge to the church, it was tax-deductible, yet Thursday, when their annual ask letter arrived, among several others, rather than feeling relief at the chance to support a cause close to his heart, he noted with dismay that the upper range of suggested donations had risen to ten thousand dollars.

As a former chair of the church's capital campaign, he recognized the message. If few families could tick off the last box, it put a subtle pressure on the rest of them to give more. In the past he'd given five hundred, even last year, after the market crashed. There was no doubt that by the end of the month he'd write the camp a check, the only question was how much. For now he stuffed the letter back in the envelope and tucked it behind their other bills so he wouldn't have to look at it.

During the vestry meeting the next week, Alan Humphries, in his most flamboyant tone, opened their new business with, "Behold, I bring you tidings of great joy." Sometime in the spring they hoped to receive a mid-six-figure gift from an angel who wished to remain anonymous, but who, Alan coyly made plain without saying, was Evvie Dunbar. Henry, who'd spent years trying to raise funds for a new heating system, was thrilled but also jealous, and comforted himself with the fact that the money was most likely her father's, a banker allied through marriage with the Mellons. The accountants for the diocese were still in discussions with her people over the best way to accept the gift, so there would be no public announcement, but it was practically a done deal.

Normally Henry couldn't wait to share news like this with Emily, but kept quiet. She'd find out soon enough, he figured, and what if it fell through? What did mid-six-figures mean? The possibilities staggered him. With half of that he could set up an irrevocable trust to pay taxes on the cottage in perpetuity. Evvie had no family to take care of. She could have just as easily left it to the church as part of her estate, so why now?

He knew he was being petty. It wasn't Evvie's fault. He liked to think he'd do the same in her position. If his reaction was any gauge, he thought it was smart of her to remain anonymous.

Throughout the holidays, on its front page, under a Hungerford cartoon of a roly-poly man wearing a fake beard and lugging a bulging sack of presents, the *Post-Gazette* ran a list of people and businesses who'd donated to buy gifts for the city's needy children. When he was a boy, socking away nickels and dimes from his paper route, Henry had wanted to be on the list, as if it were a kind of honor. He never understood why people would choose to be anonymous. Though he knew better now, nothing had changed.

The gas and electric bills were due on the fifteenth. When he'd finished with them, all that was left was the envelope with the camp logo, its rustic A-frame chapel facing the rays of a Lake Erie sunset. The inclination to clear the decks and be done with it was stronger than his desire to put the job off again, and with the same grimace he wore when he paid the gas and electric, he bent over his checkbook, thinking of Evvie's gift and his mother and their dwindling portfolio, and wrote down the same amount he gave them every year.

A few days later, Emily had to write a check for Betty and saw the record in the ledger.

"That was generous of you," she said, as if he'd been extravagant, and he remembered the girl who kept a log of her expenses to the penny and insisted on going Dutch. She, of all people, understood.

"It was," he said.

Clutter

EMILY DIDN'T APPRECIATE MAGNETS ON HER NEW REFRIGERA-
tor. They looked messy, she said, and were forever falling off. Summarily
banished, the Lucite-framed pictures of the grandchildren and the plastic
chip clips and the cartoon box trucks with the plumber's and furnace man's
numbers and the Pirates' and Steelers' and Penguins' schedules from the
beer distributor crowded the old avocado GE downstairs, since that was
Henry's domain, leaving her stainless steel prize unblemished. The one concession she made was on the side by the wall phone. Here, in case of emergency, kept in place with a simple black disk, was Dr. Runco's business card,
which Henry noticed one morning while he was pacing, on hold with the
cable company. *Joseph P. Runco, M.D.* He couldn't believe he hadn't seen it
in all the months that had passed, and felt bad, as if he'd forgotten him, and
though the office number hadn't changed, with his free hand he slid the card
from under the magnet and crumpled it up, stepped on the lever that popped
the trash can lid and dropped it in.

Do You Hear What I Hear?

THE CHRISTMAS PAGEANT DREW THE BIGGEST CROWD OF THE year at Calvary, bigger than Easter or the midnight service Christmas Eve, and for good reason. Directed by Susie Pennington from a script they themselves had written, the combined Sunday school classes acted out the story of the nativity, complete with topical jokes, mumbled dialogue and a menagerie of rented animals that bleated and peed and pooped without warning. Henry and Emily had front-row seats, in this case a mixed blessing. One year, as the three kings knelt in tribute to the baby doll playing Jesus, a camel blocking Emily's line of sight passed gas with the volume and duration of a foghorn, nearly asphyxiating her, and then there was the lamb that wriggled out of its pint-sized shepherd's arms and darted around like a greased pig until one of the handlers tackled it in the morning chapel. Like a traveling carnival, the pageant brought with it a playful air of anarchy. Anything could happen, and so as this edition's Mary and Joseph searched the alleys of Bethlehem for lodging, when a commotion broke out in the rear, Henry expected it to be animal-related, and was surprised to see Ed McWhirter and two paramedics hustling down the aisle, one of them lugging what looked like a tackle box.

Twenty rows back, the congregation had parted. Someone was lying flat on the pew, a silver-haired woman in pearls tending to them until the paramedics took over. The pageant didn't stop, which Henry thought was wrong.

"Can you see who it is?" Emily asked.

The paramedics wore blue latex gloves as if they expected blood. "No idea."

He thought it was probably a stroke or a heart attack—a reasonable fear now, the sudden, overwhelming blow. If that was his fate, he hoped it was quick. His father's final stroke had left him paralyzed on his right side, his mouth twisted, one eyelid drooping as if he were sleepy. In the hospital he was too weak to hold his own water glass, and dipped his head, his lips fishing for the straw.

"I think that was Sally Burgess trying to help," Emily said. "She's a nurse."

"They're lucky she was there."

He considered it in bad taste to stare, and faced forward. The pageant dragged on, a less urgent spectacle. Tinsel-haloed and ponytailed, the angel broadcast her glad tidings from the pulpit, the microphone cutting out, making her repeat her big line with naked impatience. "Seek ye him by the light of a star."

The organ pealed, startling the donkey, and they all rose. A gaggle of kindergarteners dressed like stars zigzagged down the aisle, followed by robed shepherds carrying lambs. On both sides, like paparazzi, parents leaned in to snap pictures, their cameras clicking.

Away in a manger, the congregation sang, *no crib for his bed,* as the paramedics worked over their patient.

Next came the wise men, leading this year's camel, its handler walking alongside, a palm on its shoulder. When the parade had passed, one of the paramedics headed for the rear of the church and returned in the middle of "We Three Kings" with a gurney. Ed McWhirter steadied the frame as they lifted the patient onto it—a woman, from her dark-stockinged feet. Once they had her strapped in, they raised the gurney and rolled her away, her family trailing, a daughter, Henry assumed, carrying her purse and shoes.

"Maybe one of the Dewhursts," Emily said. "The girl looked like Gerry."

No, they would have seen Brooks, but he didn't want to feed the speculation. "I'm sure we'll find out."

First they had to sing "Joy to the World" and give the cast their customary standing ovation, complete with a bouquet for Susie Pennington, then pass the peace, always a chaotic scene.

In the announcements, Father John said that obviously there'd been a medical emergency, and asked them to please keep the family in their thoughts and prayers. He thanked Susie and the cast for all of their hard work, and wanted to assure any guests or newcomers to Calvary that services weren't normally this eventful, getting a laugh from neither Henry nor Emily.

To make things even stranger, when they went up for Communion, as Henry bent his head to the chalice, there was a half-submerged wafer floating in the wine, as if someone had missed or spit it out. Back at the pew, Emily gave him a horrified look.

He shrugged. "It's the pageant."

"Brings out the riffraff."

At coffee hour they found out who the paramedics were there for—not one of the Dewhursts but Phyllis McGovern, who he knew from the rummage sale. Not a heart attack. According to Judy Reese, she'd fainted. She was speaking, and making sense. She said she was fine but they wanted to take her in for tests, just to be safe.

"You can understand why," Emily said.

"It's the law," Judy said, as if she knew from personal experience. "Any unexplained loss of consciousness."

"I imagine it's a liability issue for them," Henry said.

"It's frightening is what it is," Martha Burgwin said. "You don't expect something like that in church."

None of them could remember it ever happening before, as if that confirmed the event's momentousness, which led to the usual handwringing over Calvary's future, given the age of the congregation. He was glad it wasn't serious, yet well after they'd gotten home and changed their clothes and he'd settled into the Steelers game, the idea stayed with him. Of all the ways to go, dropping dead in church—kneeling in prayer, ideally after Communion—had its appeal. Maybe if the church were empty. He didn't want an audience. It was selfish of him, he was certain, but he didn't want the children to fly in and stand by his bedside, listening for his last breath. The only person he wanted there—the one he'd do anything to spare her having to see it—was Emily.

He was being silly, imagining his death as if he had any control over it, when he knew full well it wouldn't happen that way, and shook his head to dispel the daydream.

On third-and-goal, Kordell Stewart rolled out, fumbled, picked up the ball again and threw a duck for an interception.

"What a yutz, huh?" Henry said, scratching Rufus behind the ears. "What a numbnuts."

Have Yourself a
Merry Little Christmas

"IT DOESN'T FEEL LIKE CHRISTMAS," EMILY SAID, AND THOUGH he did his best to convince her otherwise, she was right. Without the children, the house felt empty, the tree a formality. Only three stockings hung from the mantel, the middle one Rufus's, stuffed to overflowing. There was no reason to get up early and go downstairs in their robes and slippers. They showered and dressed like it was any other day and gave him his new chew toys and peanut butter treats and a knotted rawhide bone he took into the dining room.

There was no big family breakfast, no champagne.

"Well, maybe a kir," Emily said.

"Merry Christmas," they toasted, clinking glasses by the fire.

"All right," she said, "let's get this over with."

Normally opening their presents took hours, Henry handing them out like Santa Claus, Kenny or Jeff holding open a garbage bag to catch the wadded balls of wrapping paper. All year long, even before they'd submitted lists, Emily stockpiled gifts for the children, then at the last minute, fearing she didn't have enough, bought more. If it was too much, as Lisa and Margaret protested, Emily made it a lesson, pointing out how blessed they were. Now the pile by her chair seemed meager repayment, and he wished he'd splurged on a third honeymoon rather than getting her exactly what she'd asked for.

"I bet I know what this is," she said, ripping the grinning snowman paper to expose the Eddie Bauer logo. "How did you know?"

"You told me."

She got up and gave him a kiss. "Thank you."

"I bet I know what this is," he said, hefting what he hoped was a Makita variable-speed orbital sander.

"Open it and find out."

It was a sander, but a DeWalt, the Home Depot's house brand, with just the one speed. "Very nice."

"They didn't have the one you wanted, but the man at the store said this was a good one. I kept the receipt so you can exchange it if you want."

"No, it's perfect," Henry said, and gave her a kiss.

Ella was taking a pottery class and had made them a glazed cobalt bowl Emily claimed for herself, leaving Henry the leather change purse Sam had laced together at camp. Sarah and Justin had gone in on a clever see-through birdfeeder that attached to a window with suction cups. Emily voted they put it over the kitchen sink.

From Kenny and Lisa he received a fancy Dremel kit he'd asked for last year.

"I'm surprised they remembered," he said.

"I'm sure she keeps lists."

Through some mix-up, they'd also bought Emily the Eddie Bauer sweater. Since he still had the box, it would be easier to send back his, meaning essentially that he'd gotten her nothing for Christmas.

"I could use another kir," she said.

"I could use a couple."

"We'll just drink all day."

Like every year, Margaret and Jeff had gotten him golf balls. They were Titleists, his favorite, but he still had last year's in the basement.

"Obviously you need to lose more balls," Emily said.

"That's my goal for next year."

Fittingly, the last gift was the biggest, a brass sundial for Chautauqua that Emily thought was too expensive. "When did she have time to shop?"

"I'm sure it was Jeff."

"I like it."

"I like it too," he said. "I just don't know where we're going to put it."

"Are we done?"

"We are done."

"Thanks be to God."

They killed the champagne. Later, watching the basketball games, he switched to beer. It was gray out, and felt like a Saturday. Arlene was coming for dinner, and Louise Pickering, a last-minute addition.

"I'm going to lie down for a bit," Emily said, "if that's all right."

"Do you want company?"

"I didn't sleep well last night. Someone was snoring."

While she napped, he took Rufus for a walk around the reservoir, passing no one. It was cold and the streets were deserted as if the city were under curfew, only birds sitting in the trees. Everyone was at home. As they left the park and started down Highland, faintly, a bell in East Liberty tolled the hour, and he remembered how on Mellon Street he'd lay awake Christmas Eve, listening to the chimes of the Theological Seminary strike midnight, calling the novitiates to worship. He imagined his uncle's ghost floating over the dark houses and trolley tracks, drawn by the sound, his death and faith a mystery Henry couldn't unravel, though at times he came close, meeting him in dreams, having conversations that answered all of his questions only to evaporate on waking. He hadn't dreamed of him in years, which seemed wrong, as if he'd abandoned him. These were the same houses, the same streets, maybe even the same church bells his uncle Henry had heard a century ago, and his mother and father, and Grandmother Chase with her Missionary cross, all of them gone, just as he would be, no trace left but a stone. As a child, he wondered why anyone would want eternal life. Now, out of necessity, the promise enticed him, if he still didn't understand how it worked.

Rufus had to poop, and settled in gingerly on the wet grass.

"There's a present," Henry said. "Here, let me wrap that for you."

At home, Emily was just getting dinner started. She was made up, in the black velvet dress she wore for their anniversary.

"You scared me," she said. "I woke up and you were both gone. I could have slept longer. I've got a splitting headache. I really don't feel like entertaining."

"I know."

"Margaret called."

"How's she doing?"

"Who knows. Sorry, that was rude. It was short—she was making dinner. She sounded good. She appreciated the check."

"I'm sorry I missed her." It was both true and a relief, to be honest. He was tired after their walk, and wished he'd had a nap. "Can I help set the table?"

"It's already set, but thank you. Are you going to shave today?"

"I am," he said, as if it were his plan all along, and headed upstairs.

He shaved and dressed and was back down in time to light the candles on the mantel and change the CD to Charlie Brown. The house smelled of ham and brown sugar, and when he put Rufus out, there were flakes in the air.

He called her. "Look, it's a white Christmas."

"I don't see anything sticking."

"It counts."

"Barely."

Louise was early, bringing a bottle of chardonnay and tales of Daniel's real estate dealings. Two boozy glasses of eggnog later, Arlene appeared with a cherry pie, a bottle of scotch for him, a fancy Italian pasta maker for Emily, and for the cottage, her traditional gift, comically fawned over but in fact quite useful, the new Chautauqua calendar. The glossy shot of the bell tower prompted Louise to tell the story of Daniel and Margaret taking the canoe out one night to get stoned and drifting away and Douglas and Henry having to track them down with the motorboat, which prompted Arlene to tell how Henry and Emily used to do the same thing but not to get stoned, which prompted Henry, in his defense, to tell how in college Arlene and her beau used to swing on the glider on the screen porch and how their father could tell when the two of them were necking because the glider stopped squeaking. The eggnog was in his mother's cut-glass punch bowl on the sideboard. By the time they sat down at the table, they'd polished it off. "Remember our grog parties?" Louise asked. "That stuff was lethal." The ham was salty and fatty and sweet, the scalloped potatoes creamy, and he opened a second bottle of merlot. At some point he changed the CD, because Nat King Cole was singing. They laughed at Douglas having to bail out Daniel on New Year's Eve, and Margaret taking down the Prentices' fence. Without the children, they could talk freely of disaster. Old friends, there were no secrets between them, and as the wine and the stories flowed, Henry was glad Louise had come.

"I am too," Emily said, when everyone was gone and they were closing up. She was drunk, and sorry for being a Gloomy Gus earlier.

"That's all right."

"Thank you, honey. It wasn't Christmas, but it was nice."

And though the snow was coming down steadily now, Grafton Street blanketed white outside, he agreed. He turned off the village and the tree, took her hand and helped her up the stairs.

In Memoriam

THE LAST WEEK OF THE YEAR, THE NEWS HAD NOTHING BET-
ter to do than remind them of all the celebrities who'd died——Sonny Bono
and Harry Caray and Dr. Spock and Gene Autry. Like Emily, Henry
thought it was morbid, but also wrong. The famous didn't need to be remembered again. The world had already noted their passing. What about
Dr. Runco and the rest of them; didn't they count? He told himself he wasn't
jealous, but each time a tribute to Henny Youngman or Roy Rogers or Frank
Sinatra ran, he had to fend off a surge of resentment, as if they'd taken his
rightful place.

Not Maureen O'Sullivan, though. He'd always liked her.

Signs and Wonders

AFTER THEIR BACCHANAL AT CHRISTMAS, NEW YEAR'S EVE THEY paced themselves, watching the ball drop, then heading straight to bed, and were up with the sun. The weather said it was going to snow overnight, but opening the blinds, it was still a surprise—four or five inches defining the wires and branches, softening the cars. The sky was cloudless, a summery blue. Like the boy he'd been, he wolfed his breakfast so he could go to the park.

Rufus heard the knob of the front hall closet and bounded around the couch.

"Did you want to come?" he asked Emily, but she was filling in their new calendar.

"Let Jim do the driveway." She wouldn't let him shovel anymore, terrified of finding him sprawled on the ground. In this case he didn't mind.

"I'll do the sidewalk later."

"We'll see about that."

"We will."

Rufus banged through the storm door and frolicked in the yard, rolling on his back and snapping at the snow, wild-eyed, popping up and barking for Henry to play with him.

"Yes, I know," Henry said. "It's very exciting."

The sun was deceptive, and he was glad he had his scarf. The air froze his nose hairs, the snow powdery, drifted against the front steps. No one had shoveled yet, everyone sleeping off last night. As they trudged up Highland, the smooth lawns sparkled like mica. Rufus plowed ahead, stopping to look back, his tongue hanging out the side of his mouth.

"I'm coming, I'm coming." He tossed a snowball at his butt and missed. "Doofus."

A day like today, they'd go sledding behind the reservoir, where the road curved down to the zoo. The hill had no name, just the sledding hill, the whole neighborhood gathering there. When Henry was little, their father had taken them, soaping the runners, letting him sit on his lap, and again he thought what a shame it was that Sarah and Justin couldn't come. Maybe next year.

Snow capped the twin statues guarding the entrance of the park, shrouded the flower beds around the drained fountain. A squirrel scrabbled up a tree and Rufus strained at the leash, pointing as if Henry were a hunter. The road was untouched, and the broad stairs leading to the reservoir. At the top he expected to find a line of cross-country skiers, but they were alone, the only tracks the tiny tridents of birds. On the water, a flock of geese sat like a fleet at anchor, turning with the wind. Out of breath from the climb, Henry leaned against the railing and tipped his face to the sun. With no cover, they were exposed, the sky a wide, unbroken blue. When he closed his eyes, he could hear a crow scolding, a second nearby echoing it. For once there was no traffic, only a boundless quiet that reminded him of church.

Rufus nudged his hand.

"Hang on, Mr. Impatient. I'll tell you what, you go ahead. I'll meet you here."

The circuit took a half hour when the ground was bare. With the snow, it was work. Soon he was sweating, his breath wetting his scarf. His knee was creaky. He thought of Dr. Prasad and resolved on the spot to lose weight. He was tired of waking up with his fingers tingling. Now that the holidays were over, he vowed to drink less and exercise more. It would make Emily happy, a goal worth any sacrifice.

He would try to be nicer to Margaret. They were coming for Easter, a makeup date. Spring wasn't so far off—days in the garden, baseball on the radio. Golf, the company of old friends.

He wanted to spend more time at Chautauqua. Maybe they could go up early. He'd have to check the calendar.

There was money, but he would always worry about money. A man could only change so much.

They were almost to the far end, where the spillway emptied into a rocky creek that ran past the remains of their old clubhouse, when Rufus stopped, stock-still, locked onto something. Henry followed his eyeline. In the hollow below, bedded down in the grass beneath an apple tree as if they'd sheltered there for the night, sat a ring of deer.

They were gray and sleek, arranged nose to tail around the trunk as in a medieval tapestry. He thought they might spook, seeing Rufus, but they didn't. Regal and heavy-chested, the one buck eyed Henry impassively.

Rufus whined.

"Shush," he said.

He wished he had a camera so he could show Emily. The light was precise, making them seem even closer. He could see their whiskers twitch, their breath curling like smoke as it rose through the low branches.

Rufus barked.

"Stop," Henry said, but it was too late, they were standing, turning away. Silently, as in a dream, he watched them file into the woods, holding off until they were all gone to finally move.

Later he would see this as a premonition, but unlike Emily, he didn't have the Sight. At the time, he had no reason to assign it a darker meaning. The light was pure, the park silent. Standing there with Rufus, entranced, he knew only that he was in the presence of something strange and sacred, like the visions given to saints, and he was grateful, overwhelmed by his good luck. Like a rainbow or a shooting star, it felt like a blessing on the year ahead. Tramping home through the bright, perfect world, he couldn't wait to tell her.

Acknowledgments

As always, thanks to my faithful early readers for their wisdom and generosity:

Paul Cody

Lamar Herrin

Michael Koryta

Trudy O'Nan

Alice Pentz

Mason Radkoff

Susan Straight

Luis Urrea

Sung J. Woo

And for their never-ending efforts to put my books into readers' hands, my ever-lasting gratitude to David Gernert, Rebecca Gardner, Ellen Goodson Coughtrey, Will Roberts, and Anna Worrall at the Gernert Company; to Sylvie Rabineau and Carolina Beltran at WME; and to Paul Slovak, Jess Fitzpatrick, Roland Ottewell, Chris Smith, Haley Swanson, Shannon Twomey, and Alan Walker at Viking. Without you, I'm just some guy in a room mumbling to himself, so thank you.